Bombay Time

Bombay Time

A NOVEL

THRITY
UMRIGAR

PICADOR
NEW YORK

www.picadorusa.com

Picador® is a U.S. registered trademark and is used by St. Martin's Press under license from Pan Books Limited.

For information on Picador Reading Group Guides, as well as ordering, please contact the Trade Marketing department at St. Martin's Press.
Phone: 1-800-221-7945 extension 763
Fax: 212-677-7456
E-mail: trademarketing@stmartins.com

Title-page image used courtesy of Photodisc

Library of Congress Cataloging-in-Publication Data

Umrigar, Thrity N.
Bombay time / Thrity Umrigar.
p. cm.
ISBN 0-312-27716-4 (hc)
ISBN 0-312-28623-6 (pbk)
1. Apartment houses—Fiction. 2. Bombay (India)—Fiction.
3. Businessmen—Fiction. 4. Paris—Fiction. I. Title.

PS3621.M75 B66 2001
813'.6—dc21 2001021933

First Picador Paperback Edition: July 2002

D10 9 8 7 6 5 4 3

For Noshir Umrigar,

The gentlest, most decent man I know,

Who, luckily for me,

Also happens to be my father

Acknowledgments

It takes a village to write a book.

I believe that. Although writing is an infinitely solitary and lonely way to spend one's days, the writer is never quite as alone as she imagines. She sits at her computer, wrapped in the warm blanket of memory, surrounded by family members and friends—alive and dead—who stand guard around her. It is they who urge her on through moments of despair, who cheer her when she wrestles with demons, who celebrate with her when the writing flows as easily and richly as mother's milk. When the book is done, it is the writer's name that appears on the jacket. But she knows how much help she had in writing the book, from the people who grace her life. Here are the people who helped make my book possible:

Colleen Mohyde, my "miracle" agent and good friend, and Carrie McGinnis, my extraordinary editor.

Bill Kovach, former curator at the Nieman Foundation at Harvard University, for giving me the fellowship that allowed me to write the novel.

Brad Watson and Patricia Powell, my creative writing professors at Harvard, and novelist Bapsi Sidhwa, for their wise suggestions and words of encouragement.

The *Beacon Journal,* for giving me the sabbatical for the Nieman Fellowship.

Hutokshi and Perveen Rustomfram, who came into my life at the right time and never left.

Cyndi and Nate Howard, Anne Reid, Ray Chathams, Jenny Wilson, Arvind and Pat D'Souza, Peggy Veasey, Regina Brett, Ruth Schwartz, Barb Guthrie, Cathy Mockus, and Wendy Langenderfer—friends who have expanded my definition of family.

Noshir and Freny Umrigar and their daughter Sharon, for the trip that changed the course of my life.

Ronnie, Caps, and Blue, for their lessons in love, dignity, and loyalty.

Eustathea Kavouras, a one-woman cheering squad, for her caring and support every step of the way, and Harriet Kavouras, for her prayers.

Above all, I thank my family—my father, Noshir, for his unconditional love and good example; my mother, Ketty, for her constant encouragement and her pride in me; my aunt Homai, for teaching me the meaning of grace; my cousins Gulshan and Rointon, for being a necessary and joyous part of my life; and lastly, my aunt and uncle, Jeroo and Jamshed, who, though deceased, remain alive in me.

Bombay Time

Prologue

Bombay is awake. All over the city, alarm clocks ring. Their ringing awakens the sun, so that it rolls out of bed and begins its slow, reluctant climb across the sky. Along the way, it leaves behind a drool of red, like the scarlet streaks of *paan* spit that color the city's walls and buildings. The men doing their daily exercises at Worli Sea Face barely notice the lightening sky and the sun's ascendancy. They grunt; they sweat; their muscled bodies gleam like dark branches in the morning light. Soon, they will be hurtled from the dark bosom of the predawn and its anonymous, elusive peace. But for this brief moment, they own the city, these shadowy men, an army of grunting, sweating silhouettes, as they do their sit-ups, practice their wrestling moves, perform their yoga exercises, breathe in the sweet morning air. For a short, precious moment, no boom box blares Hindi film music; no taxis speak in the harsh language of beeps. Just the sounds of their own breathing and of the sighing ocean as it tosses and turns in its sleep. So that it is easy for these men to believe that they own this dark city—its warm air, its palm trees, its hollow moon, its foaming waters.

But now, the city owns them. Bombay is awake to another day.

Across town, Wadia Baug on Bomanji Road is stirring with life. Whispers of, "Come on, it's late. *Ootho,* get up," compete with the clanging of alarm clocks. An occasional "Please, Mummy. Five more minutes to sleep" merges with threats of buckets of cold water being emptied on old sleepyhead if he doesn't get out of bed, *fatta-faat,* this very moment. The damp smell of yawns gives way to the sharp scent of toothpaste. Then comes the thudding noise of fists on the bathroom door: "Hurry up. You're not the only one living here. Minoo has to do potty urgently." In the first- and second-floor apartments, water flows freely out of the kitchen taps. But on the third and fourth floors, the tap chokes and gurgles like an old asthmatic woman and the women beat it with their open palms, trying to coax a trickle of water. "Greedy pigs," they mutter about their fortunate neighbors. "Using water as if Niagara Falls is flowing in their house." Still cursing, the women dip a plastic cup into the bucket of water they had filled up the night before. With this, they brush their teeth.

Soon, the first doorbell rings. Bhajan, the butcher, is delivering meat. The women stand at their doors in their duster coats, some with scarves on their heads. At every apartment where Bhajan drops off a slab of goat meat wrapped in butter paper, a woman opens the packet, inspects the contents, and asks for a meatier cut. "All *haadis,*" she says. "Who you saving the good parts for? We're paying for meat, not bones. And this piece looks gray, like it's ten days old." Each time, Bhajan protests, singing the praises of the meat he sells, swearing he shows no partiality among his customers. Then he gives them each a different package, containing another bony cut. Each woman takes the second packet and shuts the door with satisfaction. That *badmash* Bhajan. You have to watch him every time.

Wadia Baug is now ringing and lighting up like a telephone switchboard. First, it's the *pauwala,* dropping off fresh rolls of bread. Next, the *doodhwala* rings the bell. Another fellow you have to watch carefully. Just to keep him on his toes, the women accuse him daily of mixing water in the milk. Some mornings, the women on the same floor all gang up on him, accusing him of the same foul deed. Together, their chorus of complaints drown out his feeble protests. They laugh at him and grumble to one another about how expensive food has become in Bombay, about the latest sugar shortage or the absurd cost of butter and cheese, about how all the best and biggest prawns and pomfrets are being exported to the Gulf. Same with fruits and vegetables. The older ones remember vaguely the good old days of British rule. And now that the women have said good morning to one another, they hurry inside their apartments, feeling better.

While their wives are cooking breakfast, the men prepare for their bath. After a quick bath, they emerge smelling of Lifebuoy or Lux or Hamam soap. Those with relatives abroad smell of Camay or Dove or Yardley. The women suddenly feel self-conscious of their sour, sweaty bodies.

Now it's time for breakfast. The women serve the largest portion of the scrambled eggs to their men. Next, they serve their elderly relatives and their children. They keep the least amount for themselves. Usually, they eat directly from the frying pan, using the bread to wipe it clean of grease. One less plate to wash.

The men read the *Times of India* or *Indian Express* while they eat. The children fight over the comics page. There they are, their daily friends: Archie and Jughead. Ritchie Rich. Mandrake the Magician. Phantom, the Ghost Who Walks. Tarzan, King of the Apes. Lost in the comics, they barely hear their mothers' endless droning: "Drink your milk." "Do you have all your homework? Look at your shoes. Didn't I tell you to polish them last night? Your teacher will think I'm raising a beggar boy." "Here's money for *batatawadas* during snack break. Don't spend the money on film-star photos, okay? If you bring home one more photo of Sanjay Dutt, I'll tear it into little-little pieces, I swear to God."

Here come the school buses. Abandoning half-drunk glasses of milk and mothers in the middle of lectures, the few young children left in Wadia Baug race down the stairs. Despite their small numbers, they sound like a herd of cattle as they stampede down the wooden stairs. Their mothers race to the windows in time to see them turn and wave a hasty good-bye that the children hope their friends will not notice. Then they are gone, swallowed up by the old, sighing school bus. Swallowed up by a world of best friends and window seats and spitting contests and Chiclets and *Mad* magazines.

The men leave for work around the same time. The ones with no cars, who rely on the unreliable BEST bus system, leave first. The ones with the expense accounts that pay for cabs leave next. Finally, the ones with the cars are ready, too. Usually, their cars have been washed that morning by one of the homeless men who have adopted Bomanji Road. These men awake early each morning from the pavement, where they sleep in long rows of shivering bodies—men, women, children, and infants—and stretch the cold and soreness out of their limbs. Then they hurry up to the apartment buildings to pick up the washcloths and buckets of soapy water from the car owners. The smarter ones use the water to perform their toiletries secretly, out of the view of the car owners.

The older residents of Wadia Baug sit at their windows, watching the last of their neighbors leave for work. Some of the more feeble ones go back to sleep or turn on the television, flipping channels until Bill Clinton and Sanjay Dutt and Mel Gibson and Atul Bihari Vajpayee become one blurry image. Clintonduttgibsonvajpayee. Others make their beds, preparing for the usual trickle of visitors who come bearing news and gossip.

At some point today, all of Wadia Baug's residents will interrupt their routine for one additional task—preparing the envelope. According to their means, they will stuff a white envelope with crisp rupee notes of different denominations. Regardless of the total amount, they will add a one-rupee coin to the envelope before licking it shut. For good luck. With hands made steady by good health and youth or trembling with frailty and old age, they will each write on the envelope with a red pen. "All the best, Mehernosh," they will print. "Good wishes for a long and happy married life." Before the day is over, Mehernosh Kanga, a boy who grew up on their knees, will be a married man. This is a day of joy, an auspicious day.

Now the sun is wide awake, baring its teeth, making the sweat run down people's back. Before it will make its way across the sky and into the waiting arms of the Arabian Sea, so much will have happened: migrations into the city, births, marriages, dowry deaths, illicit love affairs, pay raises, first kisses, bankruptcy filings, traffic accidents, business deals, money changing hands, plant shutdowns, gallery openings, poetry readings, political discussions, evictions. Every event in human history will repeat itself today. Everything that ever happened will happen again today. All of life lived in a day.

A day, a day. A silver urn of promise and hope. Another chance. At reinvention, at resurrection, at reincarnation. A day. The least and most of all of our lives.

One

Rusi Bilimoria glanced at his watch for the fifth time. Damn that woman, he thought. It was 7:15 P.M. already and still she was not ready. After nearly thirty years, Coomi's inability to be ready on time still rankled him. For years, he had lied to her about the time they were to leave for an engagement, deliberately telling her they had to leave at least half an hour sooner. At first, it had worked. But over time, Coomi had either gotten wise to his little trick or had slowed down even more, so that even this didn't work anymore.

For instance, he'd told her earlier this morning that they had to leave the house that evening at 6:30 sharp. He didn't want to be the last to arrive at Mehernosh Kanga's wedding. The memory of a month ago, when old Kaizad had greeted them at the entrance of Cama Baug and boomed, "Well, if it isn't Mr. and Mrs. Latecomer! I was just wondering if you went to the wrong wedding or what. *Chalo,* you are at least in time for dinner" still made him hot with embarrassment when he thought about it. To make matters worse, Coomi had turned to Kaizad and said, "So sorry, Kaizu. But you know how bad traffic is these days. And poor Rusi works so hard at his business and gets home so late. And then he has to shower just to get all that paper dust off him." And Rusi had marveled at his wife's audacity, how she had neatly transferred the blame onto him, ignoring the fact that he had been home at five o'clock and had been pacing the apartment in his gray suit and dark blue tie for an hour while Coomi was still deciding what piece of jewelry to wear with her light pink chiffon sari.

Truth be told, he didn't even want to go to the wedding. It would be the same crowd, the women fixing their sharp gazes on Coomi and him, trying to figure out if they were on speaking terms that night, the men breathing on him with their hot, drunken breath. He dreaded the hunt for a taxi on the busy Bombay streets, the inevitable traffic jam near Grant Road, where the beggar children would swarm around the cab like locusts. He hated walking down the long, dark alley to the reception hall, past the lepers and the legless beggars on skateboards. The older he got, the less Rusi wanted to leave his home, except to go to his factory. The Bombay of his youth—or at least the Bombay of his memory—had given way to a fetid, crowded, overpowering city that insulted his senses. Stepping into the city was like stepping into a dirty sock, sour, sweaty, and putrid.

And more and more the city—its noise, violence, pollution, filth—was invading his home. Every day, the newspaper landed like a missile at his door. ELDERLY WOMAN PROFESSOR BLUDGEONED TO DEATH, the headlines screamed. CHIEF MINISTER IMPLICATED IN FINANCIAL SCANDAL. ARMED GUNMEN FLEE AFTER BANK ROBBERY.

Leaning on the railing of his third-floor apartment's balcony, Rusi surveyed the chaotic scene around him. Bicyclists weaved in and out of heavy traffic. The street department had once again dug up the sidewalk, so that it lay open like a mouth. Many of the balconies of the adjacent buildings had clothes hanging out to dry, so that denim jeans and white *kurtas* fluttered like flags in the wind. Involuntarily, Rusi smiled to himself, remembering how the unseemly sight had never failed to exasperate his mother. Khorshed Bilimoria had always raved about how uncooth it was to hang clothes out to dry in public, for the world to see. "Uncivilized *junglees,*" his mother used to mutter. "These people have no class at all." It had been one of Khorshed's many peeves. If she'd caught some insolent youth peeing against a public building or a *paan*-chewing passerby spitting a stream of sticky red betel juice onto the sidewalk, Khorshed had not been above going after them, armed with a lecture about cleanliness being next to Godliness. Then she'd come home, muttering about how the country had gone to hell after the British left.

Today, you can't even yell at someone for pissing or spitting near your apartment building, Rusi thought. They're just as likely to turn around and spit on *you.* Or worse, they'll come back with their *goonda* friends and create God knows what mischief. Mamma was lucky to have died when she did, may her soul rest in peace.

Thinking about the city of his birth made Rusi tired. He wondered if he and Coomi should just stay home tonight and send the wedding gift tomorrow. But his conscience pinched at him. Mehernosh's father, Jimmy, was an old friend and a good neighbor. Besides, Mehernosh was a childhood friend of Rusi's daughter, Binny, and had practically lived at the Bilimoria apartment when the kids were young. He had to be there.

Rusi left the balcony and knocked on the bedroom door. "The first shift must be close to finishing dinner by now," he said to the closed door. "At this rate, if we're lucky, we'll be in time for the third shift."

"I would've been ready by now if you weren't knocking on the door every two, three minutes," came the shrill reply. "It's like the All India Radio news bulletin every two minutes, telling me what time it is."

You should leave, Rusi thought to himself in disgust as he headed back to the living room. If you were half a man, you would not say another word, just get a cab and go alone. Would serve her right, to sit at home one evening, all dressed up. Would cure her of her tardiness in one quick stroke.

But even while he thought about it, he knew he would not do it. For one thing, he knew that Coomi would never let him forget the incident, would bring it up and throw it in his face like a dirty plate every chance she got. Besides, all their neighbors and friends would be at the reception and he'd have to come up with some excuse to explain Coomi's absence. And if he lied, told them she had the flu or something, they'd all know by noon the next day anyway. Because Coomi would be up early the next morning, visiting Dosamai, the old widow who lived on the second floor, telling her about her shock and fright at finding that Rusi had "abandoned" her, had left for no reason at all, without a warning or anything. Then the two women would speculate about Rusi's strange behavior, not once mentioning the issue of Coomi's tardiness, which was legendary among those who had ever made plans with Coomi. Dosamai had herself arrived at the same system of calculation that Rusi had, so that whenever the old woman wanted Coomi to escort her to her doctor's office, she always told Coomi to be ready an hour ahead of the time they had to leave.

But Dosamai had decided years ago that it was not in her best interest to encourage harmony between Rusi and Coomi. After all, why would Coomi come and spend half the day with an elderly widow if she didn't need someone to whom she could spill the bitterness from her heart, like water from an urn? And so it was that each day Coomi arrived at Dosamai's apartment, carefully carrying her urn heart, which had filled up again overnight, and the old woman eagerly waited for that gush of bitterness and anger that announced Coomi's arrival.

If Rusi had walked out, Coomi and Dosamai would spend happy hours the next morning sticking motives on him like postage stamps. Rusi could imagine their conversation, sure as if he were present.

"This is the utter limit," Coomi would say. "How many more insults have I to bear in this lifetime? That man is making it hard for me to hold up my head in public. Just because he has no *abroo-ijjat,* he must think I don't care about my reputation, either."

"What can you do, *deekra*?" Dosamai would say in her most fatalistic voice. "Who knows what's inside the heads of these menfolk?"

They would be silent for a minute. Then Dosamai would play her ace. "What time did he get to the wedding hall—can you call someone and find out? Maybe he stopped to see someone first. Met somebody or went somewhere he didn't want you to know."

Rusi could see it now: Coomi would be sitting in Dosamai's dark living room, a pained expression on her face. "Dosamai, even if he is running around, what can I do? I cannot go around following him all over Bombay like a stray dog. To tell the truth, that thought has also crossed my mind."

Dosamai would sit still for a moment. Then she would speak as slowly and gravely as any prophet ever did. "If this *dookh,* this suffering, is also in your *kismet, deekra,* you will have to bear it. What I say to you is go to the fire temple and light a *diva* for five days in a row

and pray for good luck. And keep an eye on Rusi's con
I've known that Rusi since he was born. He's alwa
the womenfolk."

"Rusi always did like women," Coomi had mu
keep the huskiness out of her voice.

But Dosamai didn't hear her. "I remember, ever since
little boy, he was always telling big, big stories," she continued. "How he was going to drive an imported car and buy a house at Worli and God knows what all other nonsense. Once, I caught him talking like this to my little Zubin, filling my boy's head with this foolish nonsense. Straightum-straight, I said to him, '*Ae* you, Rusi. Your mummy may allow you to tell these foolish stories in your house. But my son is not interested in your Cadillac or your Buick cars. We are poor people, but my Zubin is a good student and he goes to school every day. I don't want anyone filling his head with dreams of big houses or big cars. The house his old mother raised him in is good enough.' "

"So what did Rusi say?"

"Say?" Dosamai cried. "What could he say? Walked away *chup-chaap,* without another word."

For a second, Coomi's face softened at the memory of the restless, ambitious young man Rusi had been. Oh God, that was whom she had married—that thin, fierce man whose dreams had rattled around in his head like silver coins in a tin can. Who was this broken, cautious, grief-bent man she found herself married to these days?

Coomi still remembered an evening from the first year of their marriage, when she was pregnant with their daughter, Binny. She and Rusi had gone to Chowpatty Beach, sitting on the gritty brown sand as they watched the pepper red Bombay sun go down. Rusi had been in high spirits that evening, talking about how his new son—it had never occurred to him that he might have a daughter—was going to bring him good luck, how he'd work even harder now that he had a whole family to support, how he wanted at least five more children (Coomi had rolled her eyes in mock horror), how he would take his son to the factory with him as soon as the kid could walk, train him, groom him to take over the family business someday. *Saala,* he'd pull

, out of school and make them join the business as soon as they ed some arithmetic. He'd laughed then. "You'll see, Coomi," he d, his face as bright as the moon that was beginning to peer at them through the trees. "I know you don't believe me and that you think I'm telling these tall-tall stories, but I'll show you how successful I can be. I may not have gone to the university, but I'll still put all those college graduates to shame."

The light of his ambition had dazzled her. It was so overpowering that it burned away her words, her protests. So it remained unsaid: that she would be as happy with a baby girl; that coming from a large family herself, she didn't particularly want six children; that it didn't matter to her how successful or rich he was, she'd rather have him home in time for dinner; that she would fight him tooth and nail if he ever encouraged one of her children not to finish school. What she actually said to him was, "I know, Rusi, I know. I know all your dreams will come true someday. I just wish you didn't have to work so hard, darling."

Later that evening, they had walked up to the food stalls on the beach and each had two plates of *panipoori.* As always, Rusi was incredibly generous with his money, urging her to eat more, wanting to walk over to Cream Centre for ice cream. But she wanted a *lassi* instead, and Rusi made sure that the *lassiwalla* washed her glass twice, wiped the edge of the glass with his handkerchief "for germs," and only then was Coomi allowed to sip the frothy milk drink. While she drank, she eyed her dandified young husband in bemusement, thinking how different he was from the rough-tough men she had grown up around. Even then, in his white shirt and blue tie, he looked more like an energetic schoolboy than the businessman he was. It was the long, thin neck, she decided, that gave him his lost, innocent look. It was the cleanest, most vulnerable-looking neck she had ever seen, though she was at a loss to explain how a neck could so break your heart. And those eyes! They burned like coal in the gaunt cave of his face. All of him is in those eyes, she thought, all his hurts, all his losses, his father's death, his fierce ambition, his burning desire to be somebody. To do something large.

Dosamai's grave voice shook Coomi out of her reverie. "Don't just sit there like a dumb statue, Coomi. You listen to old Dosa—watch that husband of yours like a hawk," she said. "This is exactly the age when they get bad ideas, as soon as they are having too many white hairs to count. And enough wicked women are out there, only wanting a man to take them to nice-nice restaurants and to buy them new clothes and gold jewelry and whatnot."

Dosamai warmed to her subject. "*Arre,* Coomi, I used to watch my dear Sorab so carefully, he used to tell me it was good training for him for when he was dead. He would say, 'Dosa, all your staring and watching is building me up for the final hour. When I am dead and they finally lay me in the well in the Tower of Silence, naked as the day I was born, and I'll see all those vultures staring at me, I'll yell at them, "You black devils, you think your evil eye has the power to scare me? *Arre,* one look from my Dosa darling is more powerful than all your hungry looks put together." ' "

The two women laughed. After a few minutes, Coomi reluctantly got up to leave. "Don't worry, Coomi," Dosamai said. "I will make a few discreet inquiries about Rusi myself."

If Rusi had indeed gone to the wedding without Coomi, Dosamai would have been true to her word. Those discreet inquiries meant the old woman getting on the phone and calling on her small but loyal army of woman warriors in the neighborhood. "Amy," she would have said. "This is Dosamai speaking. Heard that Mehernosh's wedding reception went well. Though why Jimmy must spend that much money on the flower decorations onstage, God only knows. Jimmy Kanga was always a big show-off, *na?* I say if people have money to waste, give it to charity, like the Parsi Panchayet Fund. Still, it is their business. Some people have money to burn."

After a few minutes of speculating about the nefarious ways in which Jimmy Kanga made his fortune, Dosamai would cut to the chase. "Poor Coomi was here a minute ago, crying her eyes out. That husband of hers left her at home all dressed up and went to the reception alone. Coomi says he came home, got dressed, and left the house, only. She sat for an hour thinking he would come back. Afterward, she removed her sari and just went to bed, all hungry. And you know how much Coomi likes the *lagan-nu-bhonu,* especially the Mughlai chicken and the *pallao-daar.*"

"Oh, the bleddy liar," Amy would say. "He told me Coomi had the flu. But right away, I was knowing he was lying, because he turned his face away while he was talking."

"What time did he come in?" Dosamai would ask eagerly.

"He was late. I know the first *paath* had finished eating before he walked in."

"Ummmm," Dosamai would mutter. "Something is as fishy as a pomfret. I think Rusi has some woman on the side."

"*Bechari* Coomi," Amy would say. "Does she know?"

Soon, rumors would run from home to home like a telephone cable; idle speculation would harden into suspicion; suspicion would crystallize into truth, till half of Dosamai's guerrilla army would be willing to swear that they had glimpsed Rusi hopping out of the taxi at Cama Baug, with a strange young woman blowing him a kiss before the cab carried her away.

Rusi Bilimoria was of an age where it mattered what the neighbors said about him. For many years, his naked ambition and the fact that he owned his own business, no matter how erratic his fortunes, had attracted their envy and attention. Gossip buzzed around him like flies at a picnic; rumors danced around him like ghosts. But unlike the days of his ambitious youth, Rusi no longer wanted their awe or admiration. Now all he wanted was their approval. And failing that, he wanted them simply to leave him alone. So Rusi Bilimoria gritted his teeth and waited for Coomi to get dressed.

Despite himself, he could not help the rush of admiration when Coomi finally emerged from her room, wrapped up in her rose-colored sari. After all these years, Coomi was still an attractive woman. Unlike most of the women he knew, her body had not taken on the doughlike softness of age. The once-black hair was now splecked with gray but the darting dark eyes were as sharp as ever. The long nose was even more prominent now as it hung over the full, sensual lips. And yet, as he discreetly studied that face, Rusi wondered at the loss of the cheery, openhearted woman he had once loved. They used to laugh so much in the early days. Their entire group of friends had been drunk with youth and madcap playfulness, it seemed, the older members of the group as ready for a laugh as the younger ones like Rusi and Jimmy. Practical jokes, daredevil stunts, outrageous dares had made up their days: Zarin Kanga refusing to marry Jimmy until after he'd caught a stray pig for her. Soli Contractor drinking twelve Cokes on a dare and then retching at the sight of the soft drink for years. Bomi Mistry walking down the street wearing glasses with no lenses and scaring passersby when he scratched his eyes through them. How he himself had loved playing tricks on Coomi, how he'd loved it when she'd pretend to scold him and he'd pretend to be chastised. And the inevitable moment when her mock anger would be eaten up by her involuntary smile.

Like the time they'd all gone to Khandala in his car. Six or seven of them, all packed into his tiny Fiat. They were approaching a particularly steep hill when the devil got into him. He winked at his male friends, Jimmy and Bomi, silently asking them to play along. Halfway up the hill, he made the car splutter and then come to an abrupt halt. Somehow, he convinced the girls that they had to push the car uphill. The boys scattered, pretending to flag other cars down. And when, at the top of the hill, the car magically started and he finally let the women in on the joke, he thought he would die laughing. God, they were angry! Coomi especially, her dark eyes flashing as she lectured him on his bad manners and twisted sense of humor. But later, he looked at her in the rearview mirror and she smiled at him and then quickly looked away before any of the others could notice. Something lurched in his chest then, like a muscle spasm. After that, he began to pay special attention to her, noticed how quick she was to laugh and how she stood up to him in a way the other women did not.

Since Coomi lived in the same neighborhood as Rusi, he had seen her around for years. But until they were in their twenties, they had never exchanged a word. Coomi was never part of the group of boys and girls Rusi had been friends with his whole life. It was only after

Coomi met Sheroo Mistry in college that Sheroo brought her into the group. Still, Rusi never paid her much attention. At that time, he had a crush on Tina, a voluptuous girl with fierce dark eyebrows and lips soft as red cushions. Tina was a wonderful cook, and every Sunday Rusi went over for lunch to eat Tina's legendary chicken *dhansak,* under the watchful eye of Tina's father and hovering great-aunt. "Here's a nice fat piece of chicken. Eat more, *na,* Rusi," the girl would urge him, heaping more of the delicious rice and spicy *daal* onto his plate. In this way, Rusi figured out that Tina liked him. But when he tried to talk to her about how he felt, she would giggle and move away from him. "Enough, *na,* Rusi. All you boys want to do this *kissy-koti*, only. I am a girl from a good family, *baba.*" One Sunday afternoon, smarting from having lost a bid for a job and fired by the determination to try even harder, he poured his heart out to Tina. But the fire of his ambition singed her. "Hey, Rusi, stop this crazy big-shot talk, *yaar,*" she said. "I swear, sometimes you scare me. Why are you always wanting what's not there? Everybody says you are a show-off, and they are correct." Her words hurt him more than they'd any right to. His mouth suddenly tasted of dry ashes and the Sunday meal lasted forever as he went through the motions of praising Tina's cooking and making small talk with her father. When he left that day, his heart was cold. He never went back.

Coomi was different. He felt she understood him, understood that all he had were his dreams. Even when she teased him, there were places she never went to. "It's funny," he once said to her. "You are the only person I know who is not afraid of my dreaming. Even my mamma sometimes looks at me like I'm mad." She looked him right in the eye, then. "I'll be afraid the day you stop dreaming," she said seriously. He knew at that moment that he would someday marry her, that he had found a woman who would carry his boat to the shore.

So many hopes we had, he now thought. Each one of them dashed. What happened? Why did we let it? Would it have been different if Mamma had not lived with us? So many of our early quarrels had to do with Mamma. Or maybe I really did have an unrealistic expectation of marriage, like Soli says. "Too many Hollywood movies you are seeing, *bossie,*" his best friend, Soli Contractor, always told him. "After all, what do you expect? That all bloody women will be Ingrid Bergman, or what?"

After all these years, it came down to this: They were different. After marriage, Coomi showed a side he'd never seen before. She could be moody, cruel, caustic. And since he had never grown some essential layer of protective skin, her words directly pierced his bones, settling there like cancer. Coomi used words like razors, as weapons with which to cut. To Rusi, words were like the offerings of sandalwood he took to the fire temple—scented, delicate, beautiful. Coomi always claimed that the words she said in anger were pieces of paper that flew away once they left her mouth. But to Rusi, they were poison darts, powerful enough to destroy a man.

Coomi had grown up with several older brothers, all of them big, burly men whose favorite pastime was cutting one another with an insult or a crude quip. Rusi was an only child, raised by a genteel widowed mother whose only mode of chastisement was a disappointed silence. Hurts stuck to Rusi like fat to the ribs. Rusi's warehouse of resentments bewildered Coomi. But he was devastated by his wife's careless, cruel words. He was especially hurt when those words were directed toward his mother. Coomi tried to tell him she didn't mean what she said in moments of rage, that her temper flashed and died out like a match struck in the wind. He tried to tell her that he was a different kind of man, that he felt defenseless against the gust of her anger.

It became a pattern. Coomi would erupt. Rusi would withdraw into his shell. Sometimes, they went months without talking to each other. As their only child, Binny, grew older, she ran around like a mail carrier, relaying messages from one parent to the other. Then, in his desperate need for comfort, sex, love, kindness, he would go to Coomi again. After months of distancing, she would make him smile again with a sharp, witty observation. Or she would roll toward him in the middle of the night and hold him close until lust melted his resentment. For many years, each reconciliation was loaded with hope. Maybe she's learned her lesson this time, he'd think. And after all, she's basically a good woman. In later years, he went to her, while hating himself for his weakness, for needing her so.

Neither one of us realized how vital Binny was in keeping our marriage afloat, Rusi now thought. If Binny had not left for England, I wonder if the boat of our marriage would've ever leaked this openly? And then Mamma dying a few years after Binny moved out. Rusi remembered how in the weeks after his mother's death, Coomi had tried hard for a reconciliation with her husband. But it was much too late. By then, Rusi had learned how to harden himself to Coomi. He taught himself how to rearrange his face, made it go blank in Coomi's presence, as if it were covered by a translucent plastic sheet. He knew it scared Coomi, this blankness, this cool detachment. The bewildered hurt, the wounded expression in his eyes, the occasional outpouring of his bitterness, Coomi was used to those. But this indifference was something new and dangerous. Rusi himself thought he acted like a virgin each time Coomi touched him, flinching at the most casual contact. But he couldn't help it. He was polite to her, considerate even. But the light had gone out of his eyes. He treated her as if they were strangers sharing the same train compartment.

Some days, Rusi found this indifference the easiest thing in the world to stick by. Other days, he had to force himself to carry out the part he'd taken upon himself. Seeing the wound in Coomi's eyes, watching her struggle to match his frostiness with her own, his heart ached with regret and sorrow. He believed that Coomi had destroyed his life, and yet, despite himself, he did not relish the thought of destroying hers. In his heart of hearts, he believed Coomi was the reason he had never been wildly successful in his business. "You ruined me," he once said to her. "I could have been as successful as the Tatas or Birlas by now, but how could I concentrate, with half my mind always worried about you and Mamma fighting at home?"

She looked at him with contempt. "Everybody is to blame but yourself. You started with no college degree, no business contacts, no money in your pocket, but still *I'm* the reason you failed? No, I'm just a convenient scapegoat, Rusi. All you had were your ridiculous dreams. But you can't feed a family for even a day for the price of a dream."

Even now, the memory of that conversation made his eyes sting. Hearing Coomi's impatient tapping of her feet, Rusi forced himself back into the present. No use ruining this evening with ghosts from the past. Besides, he could tell that Coomi was waiting for him to say something, to comment on her appearance. He opened his mouth to compliment her but decided he was too tired to make small talk. "Ready?" he asked.

As soon as they stepped outside of Wadia Baug, they were cornered by Bhoot, the one-armed man who was Rusi's favorite resident beggar. "Rusi *seth,*" Bhoot said in his usual ingratiating tone. "May Allah shower his blessings on you. Some money, *sahib,* so that old Bhoot can eat some *daal-roti* tonight."

Rusi reached for a one-rupee coin and carefully dropped it in Bhoot's dented bowl, making sure he didn't accidentally touch it. Bhoot braced himself for the inevitable lecture that followed. "Make sure you use the money for food, not for your cheap country *daru,* you hear?" Rusi said in his sternest voice. "*Saala,* if I found out you're using the money to drink . . ." The rest of his sentence was drowned out in Bhoot's vehement shaking of his head, no, no, no. Every day, they went through this charade, both knowing that once Rusi turned away, they would each go back to occupying their very different worlds, without the slightest chance of Rusi being able to monitor how Bhoot lived in his own subterranean world.

It took them fifteen minutes to get a taxi. They were turned down by three cabdrivers before the fourth one told them to get in. Rusi climbed in with relief, but a second later, he screwed up his nose. On the dashboard, amid taped pictures of Hindu gods, were two sweet-smelling sticks of incense. The smoke made his nostrils tickle and he rolled down his window as fast as he could. He knew better than to ask the driver to put out the incense. In America, they ask your permission before they light a cigarette in their own house, he thought.

Here, these fools burn these sticks in a public vehicle. He stared out of the window in mute frustration.

Last year, he had decided to sell his car. He was getting too old and irritable to drive in a city where thousands of snarling, noisy vehicles attacked one another daily. The sweat, the grime, the black exhaust fumes of the double-decker BEST buses, the bleeping horns, the constant stream of people who darted in front of traffic—all were too much for him. The end of his driving life came on a Monday morning as he sat stuck in a traffic jam at Bori Bunder. The chaotic scene before him hit him with all the power of a blow to the head. "This is like hell," he said out loud. "No. This *is* hell." He sold his car the next week.

Still, there were times when he missed the exhilaration of driving—those heavenly nights when traffic moved briskly down the wide lanes of Worli Sea Face and he felt the spray of the sea across three lanes of traffic; his first glimpse of the setting sun as he flew down the flyover bridge at Kemp's Corner; the dexterous weaving in and out of traffic that he did on his way to an important meeting.

When they finally got to Cama Baug at 8:30 P.M., after having dodged the bony outstretched arms of the beggars in the alley, they were both already sweating from the Bombay heat. Rusi felt nauseous. To divert his mind, he thought of Binny, happily married in London. Rusi had visited her once and had fallen in love with the city—its broad, clean roads, its green parks, even the damp and chilly weather that everyone else detested. I may have been a flop as a husband and an unsuccessful businessman, but one thing I did successfully, he now thought. I got Binny out of this city that's going to hell. At the thought of his daughter, he felt a familiar ache in his heart. He knew that in her own way, Coomi missed Binny as much as he did. Now, he wondered whether she, too, was haunted by those dreams in which Binny was back at home and he was hugging and kissing her—sweet dreams that were invariably encroached upon by the thudding footsteps of reality. He wondered if Coomi, too, experienced the loneliness of waking up from those dreams and staring at the long black night that lay like a lonely, deserted alley before him. His heart wobbled from its usual hardened stance when he thought of Coomi missing Binny as ferociously as he did. In some ways, Binny was now his only way home to Coomi, not the stern-faced woman at his side, but the warm, impulsive dark-haired woman he had married. He longed to say something to his wife but was reluctant to break the silence that had engulfed them since they had left home.

Besides, he knew that Coomi blamed him for Binny's leaving. On the way home from the airport years ago, Coomi had turned to Rusi and said fiercely, "You chased my daughter away from me. Filling her head with all these big dreams. As if this city wasn't good enough for her. You stole my only child away from me, don't forget." For once, he was not hurt by her words, because he heard the loneliness behind them. Coomi's heart was breaking, he knew, just as his was. This was simply her way of dealing with her pain.

There was nobody at the front gate to welcome them. Rusi was both relieved and embarrassed. Obviously, the Kangas were not expecting any more visitors. A woman with waist-length black hair was crooning some song. "How deep is your love?" the singer asked. Rusi vaguely recognized the song as something Binny used to play when she lived at home. Behind the singer stood three overweight middle-aged musicians in tight dark suits, men who had abandoned all stabs at youthfulness. The husky-voiced woman singer was their sole concession to ornamentation.

Still no sign of Jimmy and Zarin Kanga. Rusi glanced at Coomi to see if she looked as embarrassed as he felt. But Coomi's face was impassive as she looked straight ahead, her eyes searching for a familiar face in the brightly clad crowd the Bilimorias were walking toward. As they approached the group of men and women sitting on the wooden chairs in the open air, there was a rustle of silk and chiffon saris, a glint of gold and diamonds as the crowd turned its collective head toward the newcomers.

"Rusi. Coomi. At last. Come, come. We were wondering whether to call or what. Bomi was getting worried." Sheroo Mistry's smiling face and welcoming arms drew the Bilimorias into the fold.

People moved their chairs to expand the circle to include the newcomers. After a few moments, Rusi noticed Jimmy and Zarin Kanga heading their way. Jimmy kissed Coomi on the cheek and then took Rusi's hand in both of his. "Hello, *bossie.* We were worried you were not going to make it. Mehernosh just asked a few minutes back whether you and Coomi were here."

Rusi could tell that Jimmy was in a good mood. "Zarin and I were just remembering how your Binny used to tease Mehernosh with that silly nursery rhyme," Jimmy continued. "Seems like yesterday, doesn't it? Can you believe that little boy is now a married man? Or that my beautiful wife is old enough to be a grandma?"

The Kangas exchanged a quick, intimate smile. Watching them, Rusi felt a momentary stab of envy. It was well known that the Kangas had a good marriage. They made a handsome couple. Jimmy Kanga, tall, well built, was one of the city's top lawyers, and everything about him, from his gleaming, healthy face, to his clean, well-manicured fingernails, was proof of the fact that he had transcended his humble beginnings. Zarin, too, had a quiet grace and authority, which made her the perfect companion for her wildly successful husband. In all these years, Rusi had never heard Zarin raise her voice. She's the kind of woman I should've married, he thought. My life would've been different then.

Now Zarin was smiling at him. "Rusi," she said. "Why don't you go indoors to the bar with Jimmy? I hate seeing any of my guests without a glass in their hands. Coomi and I will go get some soft drinks."

"Of course, of course," Jimmy said. "Rusi, my apologies. I'm forgetting my manners."

At the bar, a man with a handlebar mustache was pouring drinks. "Fali, a scotch for my dear friend here," Jimmy said. "Make sure it's the *asli maal,* the good stuff," he added with a wink. "None of that Indian brew for Rusi."

The man gave Rusi a quick look of approval as he fixed him a drink behind the table. Rusi understood that the Kangas had a two-tier system—cheaper Indian alcohol for most of the guests and the imported stuff for the important ones. Even as he appreciated being in the latter category, he felt a sense of distaste at this caste system of favorites. If Binny had gotten married in India, he thought, I would've served imported drinks to all my guests.

When they went back outdoors, Rusi noticed that Coomi had been cornered by Shirin, a spinster who lived in the vicinity of Wadia Baug. Despite himself, he felt a twinge of pity for Coomi. Shirin was invited to social functions so rarely that she reentered human society with all the subtlety of Hitler invading Poland. How that woman can talk, Rusi thought. Too bad they cannot power motorcars with Shirin's words. India would surely rule the world then.

"My God, remember in the old days when we would get hard rolls and real cream for five paisa, only?" Shirin was saying. "Today, the bread alone is costing as much as a whole chicken used to cost in the old times. Am I saying the truth or not?"

Bomi Mistry nodded. "This inflation is like a runaway horse. Nobody can keep pace with it. Why, I remember a time when—"

"Come on, come on, you two," Sheroo said. "You are sounding like old farts. What's the use of this remembering? The *banya* still charges me today's prices when I go to his shop, so what's the use of crying over spilt milk? Next thing, you two will be starting a petition to bring the British back to India."

"*Arre,* the British are not so crazy as to be returning to this wretched country," Bomi replied. "You could beg them and shower them with rose petals, and still they would refuse to come back."

Sheroo frowned. "*Besharam.* Shameless, you are. Have some patriotic sense. You think things cost much only in India? Inflation is a fact of life worldwide."

Bomi Mistry's eyes were already bloodshot, his face bearing the sentimental, puppy-dog expression that his friends knew so well. Bomi had already consumed four or five pegs, Rusi concluded. Four or five stiff ones, same amount of whiskey as water. "No country going to hell like this one," Bomi replied. "I tell you, until Rusi arrived a few minutes back, my heart was going thump-thump. I was wondering whether some *mawali* had cut his throat and stolen all of Coomi's jewelry or what."

Rusi laughed. "*Saala,* your imagination is as active as ever. No trouble with *mawalis.* After all, this is not New York or L.A. We were just—"

"Imagination-fimagination, nothing," said Bomi, interrupting angrily. "My dear fellow, where do you think you're living, in Switzerland? You know Kashmira, *na,* my Sheroo's brother's wife's niece? No? Anyway, she's a nice sweet *chokri,* twenty-three or twenty-five years old. Fair-skinned, but not stuck-up like many of these modern girls today. Anyway, two, three weeks ago, she was at an office party at Cuffe Parade. Nice, posh area. Her boss, Mr. Gandhi, was giving a party for all employees.

"Anyway, Kashmira and a coworker leave at about nine o'clock and get a taxi. Her friend is getting in first, then Kashmira. And while she's giving the *taxiwalla* directions, you know what happens? A man leans into the window and puts a knife at Kashmira's throat and demands her watch and gold earrings. The poor girl's hands are shaking so badly, she can hardly get the watch out, staring at this knife at her throat. The *taxiwalla* is also shaking; if he tries to drive off, the knife will be inside Kashmira. "*Memsahib,*" the poor *taxiwalla* says. "Please to give him anything he asks for."

Bomi paused for dramatic effect. Slowly, he finished the rest of his whiskey. He knew he had a captive audience now. Many of those around him had stopped talking and were listening to the story. They were all of an age and a class where stories of attacks on middle-class people fascinated and chilled them. Such stories put into high relief their love-hate relationship with the city of their birth.

Eyeing his audience, Bomi picked up the story. "So anyway, she gives him her watch—a gift from her dearly departed father, by the way—and then she's fidgeting with her earrings. Kashmira's friend helps her get the right one off. But while she is trying to get the left one, the *goonda* becomes nervous. She had on these dangling earrings, twenty-four-karat gold. He grabs at the earring, almost tearing the poor girl's ear out, and runs away with all the loot. He's gone, just like that. Disappears into the crowd before you could say one, two, three. And to top it off, he calls her a 'fat bitch' before running away—ladies, please to excuse my French. Now, if you knew Kashmira, you would know that whatever she is, she is not fat. Why, such a slim, good-looking girl you—"

"Bomi," someone hissed. "What happened to the girl?"

"What happened? *Arre,* her poor ear was spurting blood like Flora Fountain used to spurt water in the days of the British. Now, of course, the good old Bombay Municipality cannot even afford to keep the fountain running. Bombay Loonycipality, I call it." Bomi grinned at his own joke.

"Did she—did she lose her ear?" a woman asked in a low voice.

"No, luckily, the bastard had only ripped it badly. Took six to seven stitches, though. They took poor Kashmira back to the party, all bleeding and crying. Gandhi's wife called their family doctor. And the next day, Kashmira was more worried about spoiling the party than about her own condition. That's the kind of noble girl she is."

The group was silent. A few feet away from them, the longhaired girl was still singing. "C'mon, everybody," she cajoled. "Join in." But they scarcely heard her, lost as they were in their own thoughts. "How things have changed," Rusi said finally, and a dozen heads nodded in agreement. They were all old enough to remember a different Bombay, the Bombay of their youth, when marine bands played at night at Victoria Gardens and the city streets had belonged to them and not the shadowy, vicious creatures who now prowled them.

This sweet nostalgia was followed on its heels by another feeling, a feeling they couldn't name. Just a dull, flush-faced recognition that in a city of hunger and rampant poverty, their world of silk and gold was a glass house that others could not resist throwing stones at. That their very lives were an open invitation to violence. In the long moment that they were silent, they knew all this. But then the moment passed and their angry words rose and swarmed like bees.

"Why don't they get a job, instead of preying on women and young girls. . . ."

"Lazy, just lazy and dirty . . ."

"Once I stopped my car at Marine Drive and asked a ten-year-old beggar boy to get in. 'Come on,' I said, 'we need a servant at home. Pay is good, three meals provided, better life than this.' He ran away without another word. Just shows, *yaar,* they don't want to work. . . ."

"*Arre,* why should they work when they can beg? Some of them earn hundreds of rupees this way, I've heard. . . ."

"Some of these beggar women have more gold than I do. . . ."

"Now, the ones who are blind or crippled, I can understand. . . ."

"*Arre,* don't you know, they cripple their children at birth so that we'll feel sorry for them. That's how they earn so much. . . ."

"Right near our building, there's a case like that. Crippled his own flesh and blood. . . ."

"Any mother who would mutilate her own child . . ."

"Oh, they are not like us. Producing children like rabbits, how can they have the same love for their children that we do? . . ."

And then, like a Greek chorus: "Ah, Bombay."

Ah, Bombay, Rusi thought. What a place. City of dreams and city of awakening from dreams. Home of Dharavi, Asia's largest slum and home of the genteel, pristine Cricket Club of India. Birthplace of Zubin Mehta, world-famous music conductor, and of Ragu, the beggar boy blinded at birth by his father, who hoped this act of love would increase the flow of coins of pity into his son's begging bowl. City of savage love and savage hate. City where the golden skyscrapers kissed God in heaven and the black slums found hell on earth.

Somebody handed Rusi another glass of scotch, on the rocks. He thought of asking for some club soda but then thought the better of it. The whiskey tasted like golden threads of fire in his throat. For the first time all day, he felt himself relax. He thought about the poor girl with the six or seven stitches on her ear. He wondered idly about her attacker and where he had disposed of the watch and earrings. He tried to imagine someone attacking Coomi in such a violent way and was amazed at the hot rush of anger that accompanied that image. He had a passing urge to tell Coomi this, but he wasn't sure whether to share with her his reaction to that thought or his reaction to his reaction. So he said nothing.

Rusi Bilimoria sat back in his chair. The whiskey was making him feel melancholy and terribly alone. A cool breeze had started up from the bosom of the Arabian Sea. He looked at the people around him, many of whom he had known all his life. So many of them had lost their sons and daughters to America or England. They had worked hard all their lives, saved their pennies, complained about the rising prices of milk and chicken and sugar, postponed their own dreams—and still they couldn't hold on to their children or give them the lives they would have in the West. And so they performed the ultimate act of love—they unclasped their children from their bosoms and let their children go. Even the few among them who were genuinely rich, men like Jimmy Kanga, who could afford to keep their children with them—how could they enjoy their wealth, watched as they were by the accusing eyes of naked and hungry children?

Rusi gazed up at the starless sky, as if searching for an answer. We are all living on top of a ticking bomb, the Bomb in Bombay, he thought. Waiting for it to detonate. Our lives spent waiting. I wait two hours for my wife to get dressed. Then I wait for a cabdriver who will agree to bring me here. The beggars outside are waiting for us to leave, so they can feast on our leftovers. Like the vultures wait, patiently, at the Tower of Silence to feast on our remains. And all of us here, we are waiting for something to happen. For someone to light the first match. For someone to set off the bomb. For something that will either save us or destroy us.

The whiskey was transporting him, taking him far away. For a moment, he felt like a stranger, a detached observer among people who were his lifelong friends. But the next second, he felt a terrible mix of pity and affection and fear for them all. He wanted to gather them up in his arms and keep them safe and young. He wanted to ask someone's forgiveness and he wanted to absolve someone. He just didn't know who. He wanted to evoke a prayer for them all. He looked up at the moonless sky and felt a strong desire to sing a mournful, plaintive song. A dirge that the wind would carry all the way back to the waiting sea. But he just sat there, saying nothing.

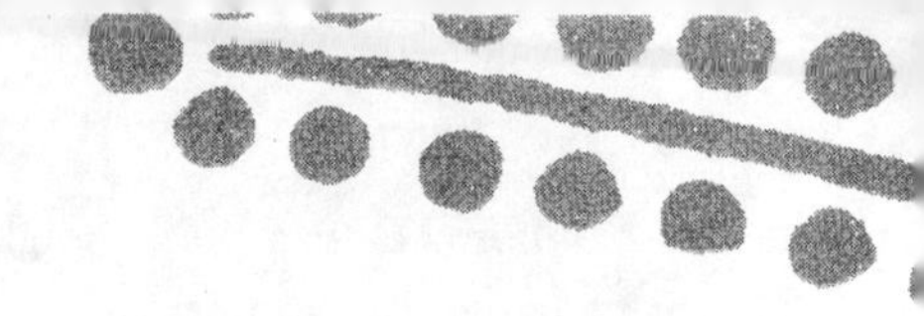

Two

Dosa Popat turned off the light in her living room and scuttled in her bare feet across the tiled floor. Crossing the dark, cluttered room, she headed for the window overlooking the street. Parting the curtains with practiced ease, she poked her head out, surreptitiously as a mole. Her nose twitched with excitement.

Dosa had raced across her room as soon as she heard Rusi and Coomi Bilimoria's footsteps descending the wooden steps of Wadia Baug. As she peered from the slightly parted curtain, she saw the couple step into the street. Instinctively, Dosa held up her left hand to her face and squinted at her watch. A few minutes before eight. As always, Coomi had taken her own sweet time getting ready. As always, Rusi must be seething with anger. A swift, experienced glance at the couple confirmed her suspicions. Dosa noticed the space between Rusi and Coomi as they walked down the street and the stiff, starched way in which Rusi was carrying himself. Coomi was taking small half steps, trying to keep up with her husband's stride, as if to appease his clenched anger by advertising the fact that she was hurrying up at last.

On their way to Mehernosh Kanga's wedding they were, Dosa knew. Tomorrow morning, she would get a full report about the wedding from the many foot soldiers in the army of gossip Dosa had carefully built over the years. From their reports, she would be able to piece together not only how much money Jimmy and Zarin Kanga had spent on their only son's wedding but who had gotten drunk and made a perfect fool of himself and who was not on speaking terms with whom. Dosa's pulse quickened at the thought of the pleasures that awaited her tomorrow. Most of the morning would be spent on the phone, she knew, and then the stream of neighbors would arrive, mostly housewives eager to strew their resentments and outrages like roses at Dosa's feet.

But that would be tomorrow. Tonight, Dosa felt a pang of loneliness and hunger at the thought of the festivities and the food the Bilimorias would soon partake of. In the last three years, Dosa's arthritis had gotten severe enough that she left her home only to attend an occasional funeral. Prior to that, she used to make it a point to attend the weddings of close friends and relatives. But as age drew her away from the pains and pleasures of married life and closer to the seductions of death, Dosa had given up celebrating marriage in favor of paying tribute to death. On more than one occasion, mourners had seen Dosa in her plain white sari at the Tower of Silence, seen the hunched figure with the beaklike nose and the cunning, darting eyes, and they had involuntarily shuddered at the resemblance between Dosa and the patient big vultures who would soon devour the body of the dead person. Even Dosa's last name, Popat, or Parrot, had a fowl-like association that was eerie.

Dosa had waited all day for her doorbell to ring, announcing the delivery of an order of the wedding dinner to her home. But the food never arrived, and now Dosa reconciled herself to making a scrambled egg for dinner. If old man Hosi Kanga, Jimmy's uncle, were still living, he would've definitely sent a *lagan-nu-bhonu* over today, Dosa thought. But Jimmy Kanga was like the rest of them—money minus manners.

Thoughts of the younger generation's shabby ways put Dosa in a reflective mood. She had not heard from her son, Zubin, in over three weeks. Ten years ago, Zubin had been offered a posting in Pune and had, in Dosa's estimation, accepted it all too eagerly. She always blamed her daughter-in-law, Bapsi, for the fact. Now, as she checked the calendar to see when she'd last received a letter from Zubin, she thought darkly about her daughter-in-law. That *daakan* has worked her *jadoo* to bewitch my poor Zubin, Dosa thought, not for the first time. Must be putting something in his food to make him forget his poor widowed mother.

Each Friday, Dosa wrote her son a long letter, brimming with the latest neighborhood gossip. Although she wrote mostly in English, Dosa lapsed into Gujarati whenever she was outraged about something or wanted to take a jab at Bapsi. When, during one of his visits, Zubin pointed out to her that he couldn't read Gujarati, Dosa put down his inability to a defect in his character. "If you were wanting to know what was happening in your poor mother's life, you'd be able to read not only Gujarati but German and Italian also."

"Now, Mamma, be reasonable," Zubin protested. "First, you send me to an English-medium school and then you expect me to read Gujarati. You think I'm Einstein, or what? And what does poor Bapsi have to do with this anyway?"

"Bas, bas, deekra," Dosa intoned. "No need to put down your poor crippled mother for the sake of your wife. Big and strong as an ox, she is. But far be it from me to say anything against your fair princess. What they say is one hundred percent correct—a son is a son until he gets his wife, but a daughter is a daughter all her life. But the good Lord didn't see fit to give me a daughter, someone who would have loved her old mother in her old age. *Chalo,* we have to bear silently whatever life throws at us."

Zubin stared at his mother with the same bewildered expression his father, Sorab, used to wear in his dealings with Dosa. Noticing the look, Dosa turned away with satisfaction.

Dosa had not had Zubin until she had been married for about eight years. This was not due to the whims of an unkind God or a defect of Sorab's, as Dosa wordlessly intimated to the people around her. For a woman who made it her calling to know the neighborhood's business, Dosa carried an astounding secret—in the first seven years of her marriage, she had had sex with her husband exactly three times. It had been her decision. It was the only way she knew to keep control over her life, to reclaim her body, which had been traded like a sack of flour.

From the day she entered St. Anne's School for Girls as a kindergartner until the day she was pulled out of high school, Dosa was the brightest student in her class. Her short stature assured that she would never be a good athlete and her high-strung nature guaranteed she would never be popular with her classmates, but nobody could deny that behind the plain face lay a brain as sharp and lethal as a bomb. When anyone asked her what she wanted to be when she grew up, Dosa replied that she would be happy being a teacher or a housewife, but she secretly always believed she was destined to be a doctor—the first Parsi woman doctor. At a young age, Dosa learned that ambition was more unattractive in a girl than pimples, but that did not prevent her from working hard toward a secret goal.

It all changed in one evening, when she was twelve, though it would be several more years before the consequences of that evening caught up with her. Her parents had left Dosa to watch her younger siblings and gone over to have dinner with the Popat family. The Popats were old friends and they were celebrating their son Sorab's eighteenth birthday. Fueled by the cheap whiskey he was consuming, Dosa's father, Minoo Framrose, got progressively more sentimental and bombastic. "You are my oldest friend, Darius," he said expansively, while his embarrassed wife tried to shush him. "So much we've been through together, *bossie.* Like a brother you are to me. Say the word, brother, and anything that's mine is yours."

Darius Popat looked at him steadily. "One shouldn't say things one doesn't mean, brother," he said.

"No, no. I mean it. Anything that's mine is yours. My word is as good as gold, Darius. You know that."

The room suddenly grew quiet. "Okay, then, *salaa.* Promise me one thing. That when Dosa, your oldest, turns sixteen, you will give her hand in marriage to my Sorab. We are honorable folks, would not want dowry or anything. I know your money situation. After all, you are having four daughters to marry. We would not ask for any dowry for Dosa. In fact, you know that apartment I have in Wadia Baug?

I'll present that to Sorab and Dosa as a wedding gift. So what do you say, *bossie?*"

For a split second, Minoo Framrose hesitated. Then he said, "Darius, you are indeed a great man, a true gentleman. My Dosa would be fortunate to be married into a good family like yours. I give you my word of honor, *bossie.* Now we will truly be brothers."

On the way home and all of the next morning, Shenaz Framrose berated her husband. She was more angry than Minoo had ever seen her. "What is my daughter, a pair of shoes, to be traded back and forth between two drunken idiots? You go right back to that shameless Darius and tell him it wasn't you speaking; it was the alcohol. Giving away your twelve-year-old daughter as if she's a prostitute. God will never forgive you if you do this, Minoo."

As his hangover loosened its grip on him, Minoo himself was awaking to the enormity of what he had done. In his heart, he knew his wife was right, which is why he allowed her to vent her anger at him without saying a word back. He had made a terrible mistake, and it was his daughter who would have to pay for it. But he also knew that despite Shenaz's protestations and his own doubts, he would never go back on his word to Darius. He had shaken his best friend's hand over their agreement. Not paying a dowry for Dosa increased the marriage chances of the other three girls. Besides, Sorab was a good man from a good family. The way Shenaz was going on, you'd think he'd sold Dosa to a brothel or something.

When Shenaz understood that he would not change his mind, she turned away in disgust. "Somehow, whenever you men make a gentleman's agreement, it is always us women who suffer," she said bitterly. Later, she made her husband promise not to mention his deal with Darius to his daughter. Shenaz wanted her daughter to have a few more carefree years before her life changed irrevocably.

Dosa learned about the arrangement the day after her sixteenth birthday. Her first reaction was to blame her mother. Dosa adored her father, hero-worshiped him, and instinctively faulted her mother for what she imagined was an ill-fated attempt to domesticate her. But Minoo spoke up. "Dosa. Baby. This is all my doing. This was my promise to my old friend Darius. Mummy was not having anything to do with it. But I've given Darius Uncle my word. And Sorab is a nice young man, intelligent and hardworking. And darling, I'm also having three of your sisters to marry off, don't forget."

She had turned on him with a look that chilled his blood, a look he knew he would remember on his deathbed. Her mouth opened and he waited for the black gusts of fury and despair to burst out, but she made no sound. She opened and closed her mouth, fishlike, three times. Then, she turned around and locked herself in the bathroom. He could not meet his wife's eyes.

When Mother Superior heard that Minoo was pulling her star student out of school to get married, she went ballistic. Just plain refused to let Dosa go. Threatened to visit Minoo at his office if he didn't show up in her principal's office right away.

When he went, he noticed that her face, usually so cheery, was flushed the color of a bruise. "Mr. Framrose, I want to hear for myself your reasons for pulling Dosa out of school in the middle of the year," she began. "I have heard some rumors and, frankly, they are so preposterous that I can scarcely believe them."

Before her intent gaze, Minoo felt the same quiver he used to when he had been hauled into the principal's office as a young boy. But his voice was calm when he spoke. "Well, Mother, the rumors are true. Dosa is getting married. And her husband does not want her to carry on her education after marriage."

Mother Superior's composure broke. "But, good God, man. Do you not understand what you're doing? Your daughter has a wonderful intellect and great curiosity. Dosa's thirst for knowledge is a beautiful, rare thing to behold. Believe me, Mr. Framrose, I've taught students in many schools, and Dosa can hold her own against the best of them. Your daughter has a great future ahead of her."

Guilt made him defensive. "With all due respect, Mother, my daughter is a *woman,*" he said, spitting out each word for effect. "Her choices are to become a nurse or a teacher—that is, cleaning up someone's vomit or teaching children who don't want to be educated. Instead, her husband can give her a life of comfort and ease. Besides, I have given her in-laws my word of honor."

They went back and forth for half an hour. When Mother Superior knew she had lost Dosa, she tried another tactic. "Mr. Framrose, I've always considered you a modern, honorable man. I realize there is nothing I can say that will change your mind about Dosa. But you have three other daughters at this school. Before you leave, will you make me one promise? That you will let these three girls fly as high as they want to without bargaining away their futures?"

His face flushed. "I promise," he said quietly. "The other three can study as much as they want to. I have always been a believer in girls' education. I'm . . . I'm just sorry Dosa won't have the same chance."

He had been true to his word. All three of Dosa's sisters went to college, a fact that gnawed at Dosa's heart her entire life. On her wedding day, she turned to the sister closest to her in age and said, "I suppose Daddy has made me the sacrificial lamb so that the three of you can build your lives on my broken back. Think of your poor sister when you are studying in a beautiful college library."

As the family prepared for the wedding, Dosa promised herself that she would never again be caught unawares by what people around her were saying or doing. The betrayal by her father crystallized her natural curiosity, so that soon after getting married, Dosa started prying, digging and unearthing all the hidden lives of the people in her new neighborhood. It was surprisingly easy. Most people long to talk about their lives, she found. Within weeks, she learned about who hated whom, which resident was in love with someone she shouldn't love, which husband was abusive, and which mother-in-law was tyrannical. Bad marriages, alcoholic husbands, errant children, problems with domestic servants, chronic illnesses, failed business ventures, sibling rivalry—Dosa's new neighbors brought the newcomer their litany of griefs, until she knew their lives as well as they did.

Over the years, she became the neighborhood's midwife of information—gossip was born in her apartment and was carried like a baby into the neighborhood by the battalion of housewives who visited her daily. Mothers would come to her to complain bitterly about their uncaring children; wives would bring to her their daily offerings of their husbands' infidelities or alcoholism or abuse. On rare occasions, the husbands themselves would march in unannounced to denounce their wives angrily and then appeal to Dosa to knock some sense into their silly, feminine heads. And Dosa herself would nab the errant children as they tried to creep past her apartment and lecture them how God was watching their every move. "Satan has been tied by God in thick-thick chains. But Satan is all day long working on these chains, making them thinner and thinner. Every time you are being rude to your Mummy, you know what's happening? You are helping that Satan make his chains thinner. Now, once Satan is free, who do you think he's going to come for, straightum-straight? For you." It was hard to say whether the children were more afraid of Dosa's twisted theology or of the sight of the short, pencil-thin woman with the long, clawlike fingers who peered at them with her beady eyes. But in either case, most of them went home after one of these encounters and sobbed their apologies to their wondrous mothers.

In this manner, Dosa found a way of realizing her lost ambition to be a doctor. Instead of fixing their broken bodies, she attempted to fix their broken lives. But Dosa never handed out enough medicine to actually cure them, just enough to keep them believing in her powers, to keep them coming back. Dosa's credo was not familial reconciliation, but wifely dominance, and she trained her army of frustrated housewives in that philosophy. Some of them took her message to heart, while others toyed with it, staying away from Dosa's venomous presence during periods of reconciliation with their husbands and then dragging themselves back in her lair during times of marital discord. Always, she took them back.

Dosa herself was not exempt from the neighborhood gossip—in the early years, there was much speculation as to why Sorab's young wife had not borne him a child. Few knew of the uneasy agreement

Sorab and Dosa had reached on their wedding night. Few suspected that Sorab was being made to pay for the ugly betrayal Dosa had suffered at the hands of her father. In this, Dosa was lucky. Sorab was essentially a weak, mild-mannered youth, who was easily cowered by his strong-willed, fiercely intelligent wife.

Dosa allowed Sorab to inflict himself upon her on their wedding night. He was an uninspired, inexperienced lover, and she willed herself to stay still under his chaotic, frenzied thrashings; tolerated silently the sharp pain and the feeling of disgust that ran through her body when he entered her. She even allowed him to pull her close to him and stroke her hair as he whispered his apologies for having hurt her. She waited for his breathing to get back to normal, heard his thudding heart slow down to a normal rate. Then she went to the bathroom, shut the door, and vigorously washed herself. You will not get pregnant, she told herself fiercely. You will not.

When she got back, Sorab was curled up in sleep, looking like a warm, happy puppy. Steeling herself to this sight, Dosa sat on the edge of the bed and shook her husband awake. For a minute, Sorab looked at her blankly, as if he had no recognition of the fact that the woman on his bed would be the one he would share his life with. Then his face broke into a beaming smile.

But then he saw the look on Dosa's face.

"Darling, what's wrong?"

She looked at him steadily, her eyes steely as the knife she was about to plunge into him. "Sorab, I will only say this once, so listen carefully," she began. "From this day forth, I will never have marital relations with you again. I will happily cook for you, keep your house for you, polish your shoes for you. But if you are so much as touching me with a fingernail, I will go to the fire temple and jump in the well there. I will be dead before the frogs in the well even know I'm there. This is my promise to you."

He looked at her and for a moment he thought he was asleep and dreaming. "Dosa, I'm not knowing you well enough to know . . . If this is a joke, darling . . ."

"No joke." And then, to make sure he understood, she repeated, "No joke. And another thing. I am not wanting anyone to know about this talk. Let them wonder why there are no children, let them do their *guss-puss,* I don't care. If anyone asks, tell them to mind their own business."

"But I want children," he cried. "Always I've been wanting children."

"Then you should have been a man enough to stand up to your *pappa* and told him you would find your own bride," she cried fiercely. "Instead of ruining my life, you should have spoken to *him* about wanting children. I don't want children, not now, not ever. All I wanted was to finish school and go to college. Instead, I have *this.*"

"But . . . but I had no idea. Millions of people have arranged marriages, after all. And I am a young man. It is impossible, what you are suggesting, Dosa. I have my needs, if you understand what I'm saying. All these years, I waited for you to become a woman, waited patiently. I'm a twenty-two-year old man. What am I supposed to do with my normal needs?"

"Go see a prostitute, if you have to. But I'm telling you Sorab, if you ever touch me again, the next time you touch me, it will be my cold, dead body."

She could not be reasoned with. For the first few months, Sorab pleaded with her, prayed to God for guidance and understanding, shed hot tears of bitterness and frustration, but it was to no avail. At times, his desire for her was so acute that he would leap out of bed in frustration and spend the night sleeping in the easy chair in the living room. Several times, he thought of leaving, but he knew that a divorce would break his mother's heart. And part of him felt sympathetic to the bright, fiercely intelligent woman whose life he had unwittingly destroyed.

Finally, in the seventh month of their marriage, he went to Dosa, the usual torment in his eyes replaced by something that approached calm. "Dosa, sit down," he said, motioning to a chair in the kitchen. "In all my nightmares, I never thought I was having to talk to my wife in this way. But you have left me no choice. Dosa, I am a man.

If you will not fulfill your wifely duties then I am going to start visiting prostitution houses. Do you understand what I'm telling you?"

For the first time in months, her face softened. She reached out and took his hand in hers, so that for one quick moment, his heart was alive again. "I do understand," she said softly. "It was never my intention to deprive you of your normal urges. You have my blessings to visit as many prostitutes as you want to."

He hit her then, hard, across the face, this man who had never gotten into a fistfight even as a young boy. "*Saali besharam.* I have married a demon, not a woman. You are lower than a common prostitute, talking to your husband like this. I should've let you jump into that well when you promised to. Should've pushed you in myself. At least then you could've inflicted your *dookh* on those poor frogs, instead of on me. What happened in November was not my wedding; it was my funeral."

She sat before him motionless, willing her already-swollen face to remain calm, willing her hands not to touch the blood on her upper lip. She waited for the thundercloud of his dark fury to pass and for Sorab to turn back into the kind, apologetic man that he was. She didn't have to wait long. His eyes widened at the sight of her swollen face as he emerged from the fog of his anger and his lower lip started to tremble. "Dosa. Darling. Oh, Dadaji, what have I done? Oh, Dosa, say something, please. Oh God. May my hands be chopped off for this. Oh, Dosa, forgive me, forgive me, please."

He never bothered her after that. But by their second wedding anniversary, he was making discreet visits to prostitutes, although he never told a soul about these visits. Whenever his mother asked him about grandchildren, he found a way of laughing off the question. He grew used to seeing the curious, slightly pitying look in the eyes of his neighbors. Strangely, their secret bound him to Dosa, gave him a sense of connection with his wife, whom, paradoxically, he loved more the more she scorned him. Dosa, too, found a way of dealing with the unspoken question that she knew was on the minds of her friends and neighbors. Without ever saying so, she lightly hinted at

Sorab's "problem," and she expertly made her husband the focus of their unspoken pity and derision and herself of sympathy and admiration. "Whatever God puts our way, we must accept," she said stoically, while her audience nodded and tsk-tsked in sympathy.

Seven years passed in this way. Each day, after Sorab left for work, Dosa cleaned house and prepared dinner. Then, her wifely duties done, she spent a few hours reading about the medicinal benefits of herbs, a topic that had piqued her interest a few years earlier. Often, a neighbor would stop by to pick up some of Dosa's home remedies for colds, fevers, burns, joint pain, alcoholism, infidelity. She never accepted money for her medicines; instead, the visitor had to repay her with nuggets of gossip and information. While she treated their physical ailment, she also counseled them on their career choices, parenting skills, and marital relations. Despite her youth, Dosa's reputation grew. Every woman she helped sang her praises to others. Women like Yasmin Shroff, who was five years older than Dosa but respected the younger woman's formidable will and intelligence.

"Go get a job," Dosa told Yasmin after the woman showed up at Dosa's apartment with bruises on her arm. "The more you are staying at home, the less he is respecting you and the more he's beating you. You have a good mind. Go use it. And don't worry about that *besharam* husband of yours. Leave him to me."

She was good to her word. Dosa visited the Shroff residence three days later to meet with Gustav Shroff. After some small talk, she got to the point. But Gustav was adamant about his wife not working. He spoke of manly pride and honor and family name. Dosa sighed. Gustav was not making this easy. She stared at him appraisingly. "Gustav, listen quietly for a minute," she said at last. There was a long pause. "Because you are my dear friend's husband, I will say this once," Dosa said softly. "Better if you heed my advice. . . . You don't want to have to worry about every meal you eat at home, Gustav. A man's home is his castle. He should not worry about something being in his food. You know what I'm saying? Better to let Yasmin find a job so she can be happy, too."

Gustav blinked. "You are threatening me, Dosa?"

"Threatening you? *Baap re,* Gustav, I am just a poor ignorant housewife. I just spend my time mixing my herbs and all. Some say they help; some say they don't. What do I know? And who am I to threaten you? No, as your well-wisher, I am just giving you some good advice. Follow, don't follow—your choice."

Before Dosa left that day, an agitated Gustav agreed to let his wife get a job and even offered to walk Dosa home. It was later that evening that he realized that the woman who had broken his will was a full twelve years younger than he was.

As Dosa grew confident that Sorab did not need her sexually, she warmed up to him in other ways. On weekends, she and Sorab went to the seaside and ate *bhelpuri* and *panipuri* for dinner at the beachfront booths. Or they caught a movie at the Bombay Film Society. They both loved movies, and on the way home, they excitedly discussed what they had seen. These were the times Sorab loved best, when his wife looked happy and alive. At such moments, he thought of her as a good friend, rather than as his wife, and forgot the great wound she had inflicted upon him. In his most forgiving moments, he even told himself that he had a better marriage than most of his friends, freed as it was from the tyrannies of wailing infants, sexual jealousies, petty grievances. Dosa kept a clean house, had dinner ready when he got home, loved going to movies with him, never fought with him about how he spent his time or his money. Besides, he was now getting sex on a regular basis. Two days a week, Sorab returned home late from work. He never explained where he had gone; she never asked.

A few weeks before their eighth wedding anniversary, Minoo Framrose died in his sleep. Sorab had just reached his office when he received the phone call; he turned around immediately and headed home. He found Dosa as he had never seen her before—distraught, hysterical, alternating between raging at her father and torn with remorse at the thought of seven years of bitterness and estrangement. Together, they attended the four days of ceremonies at the Tower of Silence. In those days, Sorab found his manhood. He was firm with Dosa when she refused to eat, he was gentle with her when she couldn't sleep, and he held her tightly when her body racked with sobs as they carried Minoo's body away to be lowered into the well where the vultures waited.

At home, she was exhausted, spent, as if grief had wrung her dry. "Go to bed," he said gently. "I will bring you some toast and butter for dinner."

But when he entered the bedroom, she was sitting on the edge of the bed, a thoughtful expression on her face. "Thank you for the last few days. What I would have done without you, I don't even know."

"Shh, shh, Dosa. Not even to mention. After all, you are my wife. It is my responsibility to take care of you. I just wish I could take your pain away, put it on my head instead."

Her eyes filled with tears again. "How can you love me still, after how I have treated you? I have destroyed your manhood, turned you into a shrimp. Any other man would have left years ago. All my *khoonas* against my daddy, I took out on you. Oh, Sorab, I should've jumped into that well years ago."

"Now, Dosa. No sense in crying over spilt milk. What use bringing up old ghosts? You are needing rest, darling. Just sleep now."

But she was inconsolable, and he soon realized that what Dosa needed was not sleep, but absolution. So he let her talk and she told him everything: How she'd won a book as the first prize for reading in second grade. How she still had the blue ribbon her book had been wrapped in. How she had been the best student in her class, always. How, although she had told not a soul, she had always believed she would be the first female Parsi doctor in the city. How her father had always encouraged her to do well in school, which was what had made his betrayal even harder to take. How she had loved and worshiped her father and how it tore up her heart to think he'd traded her future away like a pair of shoes. How he had come into her room the night before her wedding and told her he was sorry and how he had finally left when she didn't say a word. How, even in her darkest rage, she had understood why her father couldn't go back on his word to Darius, admired him for it even, and how she'd hated herself for loving him still. How it killed her, even today, to hear of her sisters' accomplishments and how she hated herself for resenting the very people she loved. How she had been scared of having children at a young age, how she had hated Sorab because she was terrified of his power to make her pregnant. How she'd seen him as the embodiment of the trick fate had played on her, how she'd vowed to make him pay for her father's mistake. How she had tried to continue hating Sorab and how she had failed. How his kindness, his mild temper had won her over. How lonely she felt when he was at work and how she looked forward to his footsteps each evening. How her terror of having children had dissipated, now that she was older, and how her heart warmed at the thought of having an infant to love. How she was tired of fixing everybody else's problems when her own marriage was a lie. How she, yes, how she wanted love, needed it, needed to be able to give it and receive it. How she was terrified that she was too late, that she had chased love out of Sorab's heart, just as she had chased him into the arms of strange women. How wrong she had been to punish him for another's mistake, how terribly, horribly wrong, and how she regretted it now.

He looked at her with incredulity, afraid of trusting what he was hearing. Some ancient instinct told him that this was not the time for words, and so he took her in his arms. For a moment, she stiffened, as if by habit, and then he could feel the slow thawing of her frozen heart. After years of sleeping with women he did not care to hold a second longer than necessary, Sorab Popat held on to his tiny, fierce, willful wife like a man clinging to a lifeline.

Zubin was born a year later. He was a cheerful boy with his father's easy, mild temperament and his mother's intelligence. Dosa was a zealous mother and doted over her only child with a ferocity and protectiveness that amazed and exasperated her husband. Zubin was not allowed to join the other neighborhood kids when they played on the sidewalk, because Dosa was terrified that her little boy would get struck by a car or, at the very least, stumble and bruise his knee. She took every cut or bruise or fever the boy ever suffered as a reflection of her poor mothering. When Zubin came down with the inevitable illnesses of childhood, Dosa would sit up with her ailing child all night long, covering him with blankets, opening and closing windows, putting cold rags dipped in Tata's eau de cologne on his fevered brow. It was as if the dark-haired boy with the ready smile had unlocked all the love that Dosa had kept hidden in her heart for seven long years. And strangely, there was enough love left over to include Sorab, so that some days, Sorab found it hard to remember the drought years. As the years rolled by, he thought of the time spent visiting prostitutes while his young wife slept virginlike in their bed, with the unreal air of a man struggling hard to remember a long-forgotten dream.

Once, on one of the rare evenings that they went to dinner without Zubin, Sorab decided to take a shortcut through the red-light district. As they rode down the street where Sorab used to visit his favorite prostitute, he slowed down his scooter ever so slightly to glance at the third-floor apartment he had visited for so many years. He thought he'd barely turned his head to sneak a look, but Dosa, eagle-eyed as ever, noticed.

"Someone you are knowing lives here?"

"Oh no, nobody. I mean, just someone from, you know . . ."

"I see."

Later that night in bed, Sorab opened his eyes to find Dosa peering closely at his face.

"So, do you ever miss them, miss her?"

It took him a minute to understand who she was referring to. "Miss them? Not for an hour, not for a minute. Why should I? My whole world is right here, under this very roof."

"Sure?"

He had never seen her like this, and his heart swelled with tenderness and pity. "Dosa, my Dosa. You are my wife as well as my life. The others were . . . paper. Understand? Paper. Whereas you are velvet—rich, heavy, dark. Something a man can hold in his hand and feel satisfied with."

Two days before Zubin's tenth birthday, Sorab decided to stop at Best Cake Shop to buy for his son and wife the chocolate éclairs they both loved so much. Since Zubin's birth, it had become a ritual that every payday, Sorab would come home with a small surprise for his family. Before he left the shop, Sorab placed an order for Zubin's birthday party. "Make sure it's freshum-fresh," he instructed the clerk. "I want the cake to melt in my son's mouth. See you day after tomorrow."

It was dark when he left the shop, and Sorab was filled with a longing to get home quickly to be with his wife and child. He decided to take a different route home. Balancing the small cake box on the front of his scooter, he cut in front of a motorist, who panicked and stepped on the gas pedal instead of the brake. It was a fatal mistake. The car hit the small scooter with an impact that lifted Sorab's slight body like a kite and threw him over two lanes of traffic. Passersby who saw the broken, twisted body instinctively prayed for his death. Two minutes later, their prayers were granted. Sorab's eyes fluttered for a moment, his mouth shaped into a wordless O, and then he was dead. Other witnesses shooed away the street urchins who had crawled under the flattened scooter in hopes of rescuing the enticing cake box.

Dosa refused to believe the news when it reached her. She could not accept that her life had taken yet another unexpected turn and that this time there was no ready target to blame for yet another betrayal, yet another delinquent promise. All the bitterness that Sorab's steadfast love and decency had drained from Dosa's heart now came pouring back, as did Dosa's sense of persecution, of injustice. She shocked her mother by reciting the names of all the people she wished had died in her Sorab's place. Her old mother, already guilt-ridden from a past mistake, tried desperately to help her bereaved daughter cope with this latest twist of fate, but Dosa was inconsolable. All three of her sisters rallied around her, including the youngest, Banu, who was in law school, and estranged from the eldest sister, who never let Banu forget that she was standing on the ashes of Dosa's dreams. Two years prior to Sorab's death, Banu had had it out with this eldest sister, whose grief had followed her like a shadow throughout her life. Dosa and Sorab had invited the entire family over to dinner, and, as was her habit, Dosa had made some barb about the "cushy" life her younger siblings led. But this time, Banu did not remain silent. "*Bas,* Dosa, enough is enough. Daddy's dead; you are having a sweet little son and a good husband. Still it's not enough. What happened to you is ancient history. *Baap re,* at this rate, the Hindus and Muslims will be friends before you forgive and forget. The rest of the family can keep saying, 'Poor Dosa,' but personally, I'm sick and tired of your *nakhras* and your caustic remarks. Don't ever invite me to your house again, because I won't be coming."

Seeing Banu at her husband's funeral made grief rise like bile in Dosa. She was on the verge of lashing out, of somehow blaming Sorab's death on Banu, but Shenaz Framrose restrained her. "*Deekra,* don't defile the memory of your saintly husband," she murmured. "This is a time for family to be together. You are suffering enough *dookh.* No need to spread it further."

After Sorab's death, Dosa became obsessed with her son. "You are now my son and my sun, the only light in my life," she would say to the bewildered boy, who was torn between wishing to protect his mother and wanting to run from her omnipresence.

Until Sorab's death, Dosa had showered her son with books, so that some of Zubin's earliest memories were of reading in the living room while the cries of the neighborhood children playing outdoors at dusk wafted in through his window. If he felt a pang of loneliness then, the novels and textbooks that he read more than compensated for it. Zubin had turned into a bookish, cautious young boy, more at home in a library or classroom than on a cricket field.

But now, Dosa wanted to talk to her son in the evenings, rather than have him bury his nose in a book. All day long, while Zubin was at school, Dosa would scour the neighborhood for nuggets of gossip, which she would then hoard and offer to Zubin at the end of the day. If the boy showed his boredom at the comings and goings of the adults around him, Dosa would chide him. "Just like the rest of them you're becoming, Zubin," she would say. "Not a care for your poor widowed mother." It was both Dosa's fortune and ill fortune that between Sorab's pension and investments and Darius Popat's generosity, she did not have to work for a living. Darius Popat had announced at his son's funeral that he would die before he would let his daughter-in-law get a job. Dosa was happy with that. After years of relative quiet, her apartment once again hummed with the sound of gossiping visitors. While Zubin was away at school, Dosa sat on her couch like royalty and made her pronouncements while her visitors brought her the juiciest tidbits of information.

A year after Sorab's death, Dosa found Zubin in the kitchen, taking apart a dead cockroach, a look of fierce concentration on his face. "My goodness, Zubin. What are you doing, looking like a murderer? Drop that dirty thing and go wash your hands, *fatta-faat.*"

"Is okay, Mamma," the boy said importantly. "I'm just practicing for my biology class. If I'm going to be a brilliant doctor, my teacher, Mr. Pinto, says I have to get over my *soog* and be ready to cut up people and all. But first, I start with insects."

This was the first Dosa had heard about Zubin's desire to be a doctor. The boy's words stirred up the envy that lived right below the surface of Dosa's skin. And on the heels of that envy came fear. Fear that her son would burn with the same ambition she had and then get destroyed by the fire of that ambition when it was snuffed out, as Dosa superstitiously believed it invariably would be. The envy alone, she would have been able to conquer, because Dosa genuinely loved her little boy. But the combination of fear and envy was toxic. She convinced herself that Zubin was about to make the same mistake she had, that his dreams were too large for his puny, middle-class life to hold. Her heart ached for her son, as if the disappointments she believed awaited him had already occurred.

In a panic, Dosa called Yasmin Shroff at work. Yasmin was now a secretary at Tata Industries and worldly in a way that Dosa admired. "Yasmin? Dosamai here. Sorry to disturb you at work, but I am having a problem. No, no, everybody is fine. It's just that—Zubin told me today he is wanting to be a doctor."

Yasmin sounded bewildered. "That's great, Dosa. But what about your problem?"

Dosa was impatient. "But that is the problem, stupid. At one time,

I also was wanting to be a doctor. But my dear departed father had other ideas. Instead, I married Sorab. I don't want my Zubin to go through the same disappointment that I did."

"Well, Dosamai, it's not as if you will marry Zubin off against his wishes. Also, children want to be different things at different ages. But if Zubin is serious, I think it would be so wonderful if he could actually live out your dream. In a way, Zubin could keep your dream alive. See what I mean?"

Dosa hung up from the conversation angry at herself for having called Yasmin. "That stupid Yasmin," she said out loud. "Has scrambled eggs for brains. Thinks because she works for Tata, she is as smart as Mr. Tata himself. Stupid fool."

Dosa did not want to realize her own aborted dreams through Zubin's achievements. Rather, she saw her role as protecting Zubin from future heartbreak. And if that meant she had to be the one to break his heart now, she was willing to pay the price. That evening, for the first time, she pushed Zubin outdoors to play cricket with the other neighborhood kids. "Enough of this mugging and studying. A real bookworm you are becoming. Sitting home all day and tearing apart poor little cockroaches. How you think the baby cockroaches' mummies and daddies must be feeling?"

Zubin, who had grown up hearing his mother curse daily the roaches that infested their kitchen, stared at his mother openmouthed. He had never so much as owned a cricket bat and had no idea what he would do among the tough, tanned, muscled neighborhood kids he was now being encouraged to socialize with. He put his mom's strange behavior down to her ongoing grief at his father's death.

From then on, Dosa embarked on a plan to save Zubin from his own intelligence. In a total reversal of her former behavior, she now encouraged him to do less homework. She extolled the virtues of humility, praised the holiness of small things. Why, working as a clerk with other Parsis at the Central Bank of India was as good a job as any other. A steady paycheck, good benefits, job security, long lunch breaks. She took to scanning the newspapers for any accounts of doctors who had killed patients through negligence, conducted weird experiments on them, stabbed their wives, or been involved in scandals. Any such nugget, she placed where Zubin would be sure to see it.

One day, she opened her front door to call Zubin in for dinner and saw that he was in an animated conversation with Rusi Bilimoria, who lived one floor above them. Rusi was already a legend among the neighborhood kids because he had a part-time job and was talking about buying a motorcycle with his own money. "When I buy a big house at Worli or Marine Drive, you can come visit me," Rusi was saying to Zubin. "Should be in a few years, *bossie.* What I say is, if you are willing to work hard, anything is possible, *na*? The sky is the limit, then."

His words frightened Dosa. She could see Rusi's self-confidence unravel all of her careful plans to ensure that Zubin grew into a modest, cautious man who did not aim too high. For six months now, she had worked to suppress her son's natural curiosity and native intelligence. And now, a young neighborhood show-off was about to wreck her scheme by instigating her son to dare to dream his way out of his middle-class existence.

She flew toward Rusi like a mother lion protecting her cub. "*Besharam,* stop filling my son's ears with all your *dhaaps,*" she cried. "Wadia Baug is good enough for us simple folks. You can go to your Worli and live with those Gujus and Sindhis, if that's what you want. We are happy being with our own kind."

"Mummy, Mummy, stop it," Zubin whispered. "We were only talking, that's all."

Rusi looked stricken. "I'm sorry, Dosamai," he said. "I didn't mean anything by it." He fled up the stairs.

From that day on, Dosa made it her business to know Rusi's business. For years, she watched him because she was afraid he would contaminate her son, who, with each passing year, was becoming the dull, mild man she wanted him to be. She often told Zubin to be thankful that she had saved him from Rusi's seductive but foolish dreams, especially in light of the fact that Rusi's business never quite took off the way he had predicted. "Remember what I told you years ago, *beta*?" she said when Zubin became an officer at Central Bank at age twenty-nine. "Look at the hours Rusi works, dragging himself home late at night, looking as tired as a mouse chased by a cat. And look at you, coming home by six-thirty sharp, in tip-top condition. And what for Rusi works so hard? Still stuck in Wadia Baug he is, same as us plain folk."

Dosa's victory was complete a few years later, when Zubin came home and recounted a conversation he had had with Rusi earlier in the day. Rusi had applied for another loan from Central Bank and Zubin's boss had just turned him down.

A teary Rusi poked his head into Zubin's office on his way out. "*Arre, bossie,* what's wrong?" Zubin said, rising to his feet. "What brings you here? Come in, come in."

Rusi's eyes were bloodshot and his usually neat hair looked disheveled, as if he had run his hand through it one too many times. "I'm sunk, Zubin," he whispered. "My boat is sunk. I have creditors in the market from whom I've borrowed money for the business. Twenty-eight to thirty-one percent interest they're charging me, boss. I came to see your branch manager for a loan at a regular interest rate, so I can get these bloodsuckers off my back. I'm expecting a big order soon from Sharma Enterprise. Big concern. With one order, I can wipe out my debts. But what to do? Your boss says he won't loan me another paisa. I don't even have the money to buy some inventory."

"But Rusi, are you mad? Doing business with these loan sharks? They'll bleed you dry. Plus, you owe *us* money. But how did you get yourself in this mess anyway?"

Rusi's lower lip moved, but his eyes were steady. "Just years and years of problems catching up with me. Always trying to stay one step ahead of failure. I started my business with no capital, Zubin. Do you understand? Nobody to back me up, nobody to teach or guide me. Every mistake I made, I paid for it myself. All by trial and error. I was a young man and impatient. Those American books I read, like *Think and Grow Rich,* made it look so easy. It wasn't. And trying to remain honest in business in this corrupt country . . . But forget it. I myself don't know what went wrong. Whatever it is, here I am now.

With a young child and a wife and mother to support. I tell you, Zubin, if I don't get this loan, I'll have to close the business down. Don't know what I'll do then—probably drive a taxi or something."

"So what did you say?" Dosamai asked her son eagerly.

"Say? Nothing," Zubin said with a shrug. "He went back in to see Mr. D'Souza, the branch manager." He did not tell his mother that he had personally implored his boss to extend Rusi another loan. And that D'Souza had reluctantly agreed.

And he did not tell Dosamai when D'Souza came into his office sixteen months later, all smiles. "That Bilimoria chap. Amazing fellow. Came in earlier today with the last payment on the loan. We were pretty sure he was putting some money aside, y'know, taking his cut before paying us back. So we did an audit on him, and guess what? Came back clean as a whistle. Turns out he was paying us back every penny he owed. Damn honest bugger. Guess I wouldn't be too happy if I were his wife. But since I'm his banker, I'm delighted."

Zubin's heart swelled with pride. "Yah, he's a good man, that Rusi. Known him my whole life, sir." But part of him also thought Rusi was foolish. So he's averted one crisis, Zubin thought. But without any money put aside, he'll be in the same boat next time. He's still living from one contract to another.

Dosamai did not share her son's affection for Rusi. When, after years of tracking him, she was convinced that Rusi would never be the success he had predicted, that his star did not burn as brightly as it had once seemed, she continued to watch him out of habit. And when Rusi's wife, Coomi, began to visit her with her litany of complaints against her husband, she became the jewel in Dosa's crown. Now, Dosa had an inroad into the innermost chambers of Rusi's red heart.

Dosa shuffled into the small dingy kitchen to take out an old battered frying pan in which to make her scrambled egg. She wished Zubin would call her tonight from Pune. With so many of the neighbors at the Kanga wedding tonight, the apartment building felt uncharacteristically empty and silent. Even that recluse Tehmi had decided to attend the wedding. I wonder if that drunken Adi is at home, she thought to herself. Or did Jimmy also invite him? I wish Bapsi had married him instead and left my darling Zubin alone.

Zubin's decision to marry at thirty-five had shocked Dosa, who had been lulled by the long years of living alone with her only son. Dosa immediately told her son he was too old and too bald to marry, but for once, Zubin would not listen. He was head over heels in love with the jovial, hardworking bank teller who had just been transferred to his branch. When Dosa met the strong, vibrant, buxom woman her son brought home, she regretted the many times she had talked her son out of marrying the insipid, pale, unthreatening women he had previously expressed an interest in. Those women, Dosa would have been able to control; one look at Bapsi told Dosa that she had met her match. Bapsi charged into Dosa's wiliness and guile with the open honesty and the head-on innocence of a young bull. All of Dosa's surreptitious ways, her slyness and penchant for troublemaking, now lay naked under Bapsi's unwavering gaze. Her new daughter-in-law blew Dosa's cover with alarming regularity. "Mamma, come away from that window," she would say in a loud voice as Dosa would discreetly part the curtains to spy on someone. "None of our business what others are doing." For Dosa, whose business *was* other people's business, Bapsi's words were blasphemy. To make matters worse, her daughter-in-law also refused to nurse Dosa's lifelong sense of injury at the cruel trick fate had played on her. "Come on, *na,* Mamma," Bapsi would boom in her good-natured way. "Who even knows if you really would have been a doctor? Anyway, you had a good man for a husband and your Zubin is a sweetie pie, and now you have a daughter who takes care of your every need. What else are you wanting? Let bygones be bygones."

It was like two continents clashing. And Zubin soon became the territory they each wanted to colonize, so that he was increasingly torn between the two strong women in his life. He spent years trying to build bridges between the two of them, to get them to speak a common language, but to no avail. Bapsi resented the fact that while she and Zubin were at work all day, Dosa invited a steady stream of neighborhood women into their home for hours of gossip and conversation. "An idle mind is the devil's workshop," she would say. "Why don't they do some social work or something instead of spying on one another and poking their noses in other people's business? Some people have too much time on their hands." Dosa saw this as a challenge to her life's work and reacted with the ferocity of a businessman whose lease has just been canceled. "You'd think she was president of the bank instead of just a common clerk," she'd complain to her many admirers. "The Queen of Sheba, my son has married."

The situation at home reached a point where when his branch manager offered Zubin a transfer to Pune, Zubin had to stop himself from kissing the man on both cheeks in gratitude. "Sir, I accept," he said. "No, no, nothing to think about. As long as Bapsi gets a transfer also, I accept."

Still, leaving Wadia Baug was not easy. On his way to the railway station, Zubin encountered Rusi Bilimoria coming up the stairs, and he thought back to a conversation from decades ago. Strange it is, he thought. For all his talk, Rusi never left Wadia Baug. And here I am, the one who is leaving. "Best of luck with the business, Rusi," he said, surprised at the tremor in his voice. "Thank you for all your help," Rusi replied, taking Zubin's hand in both of his. "You're a good man, and the building people will miss you. Good luck in your new life."

As he stepped out of the building, Zubin had felt a pang of fear and guilt at leaving behind the woman he loved and hated more than any other. But then he glanced at his wife, saw the gray streaming through her hair and how her mouth now curved downward, and he knew he had to give her a chance. Bapsi had put up with so much for his sake. Now it was his turn to make her happy. His mother would be safe, buffeted by the friends, neighbors, and even the foes that she had cultivated over the years. Out of fear, gratitude, admiration, boredom, and even love, they would flock to Dosa's home, seeking her advice on things, picking up the herbal tinctures that she brewed, dropping off an occasional box of sweets or a plate of mutton chops or *biryani* for her.

But tonight, there was only a scrambled egg and a slice of Modern bread for dinner. Dosa chewed slowly as she ate directly from the pan she had fried the egg in. Then she hobbled into the living room and turned on the TV, not bothering to flip channels. It would help kill the evening, pass the time. She intended to stay up until all the neighbors returned home from the wedding, intended to mark what time each couple or family got in.

But within moments, there was an odd whistling sound in Dosa's living room. She was in her shabby armchair, her feet curled up under her thin thighs, her head tilted back, her mouth open, a thin ribbon of drool curling on her chin. She was fast asleep.

Three

The wedding reception was going swimmingly well. Jimmy Kanga surveyed the bejeweled crowd before him, his chest sticking out with involuntary pride. Like a *jadoogar,* he, Jimmy, had turned the squalor of Bombay into something beautiful and refined. A shimmering refuge from the outside world. What were the lines from that song *Camelot*? Something about a brief shining moment? That is what he had created at his son's wedding—Camelot. Unconsciously, he hummed the tune to himself. From the elegantly dressed women in their jewels and silk saris, to the twinkling lights on a stage decked in rose petals, to the food and drink that were flowing as freely as the Ganges, everything was perfect. Perfect. No hint of the menacing, shadowy city that lay outside the tall iron gates. Jimmy Kanga had, with one wave of his magic wand, made that world disappear.

Jimmy felt the eyes of his guests follow his every move. Some of those eyes were wide with admiration, some narrow with envy, others wet with affection. Usually, the envy that he sensed in his friends and neighbors at Wadia Baug made him adopt a humble, quiet posture in their company. Not a trace of the roaring, competitive corporate lawyer who paced the corridors of the high court like a lion. Jimmy knew that many of his less fortunate neighbors masked the sourness of their own puny lives by ridiculing the successful and the powerful. It was their way of coping with the disappointments of their lives, and Jimmy respected that. He had learned the lesson of humility the hard way. But tonight was different. His only son had gotten married, and Jimmy relished the multiple roles he had to play—the proud, adoring father; the gracious, attentive host; the affectionate, doting husband; the sharp, charming business associate; the teasing, cussing good old Wadia Baug boy.

Surrounded by his immediate family, Jimmy felt blessed. Looking at them now, he felt the same appreciation and joy that he felt when he looked at a work of art at the Prince of Wales Museum. He reveled in the sight of them—his wife Zarin's trim, well-maintained figure; Mehernosh's handsome profile, which was fit to adorn the side of a coin; his new daughter-in-law Sharon's young, radiant face with its stubborn, pointed chin. Jimmy Kanga himself felt extraordinarily fit and youthful. Each morning before going to the office, he walked for an hour at a park in Breach Candy. The result was a body that did not squeak and creak with middle age the way so many of his contemporaries' did. He knew he looked good tonight. He had forgone the traditional Parsi *dagli* in favor of an elegantly cut dark brown suit that Zarin had picked up for him during her last trip to the States. *"Saala boodha,"* Soli Contractor had said, complimenting him earlier in the evening. "You are looking more like Mehernosh's older brother, rather than his father. What, is the law business not doing well these days? You looking for a second career in Hindi films? I heard Dev Anand is finally retiring." Dev Anand was the perennially youthful movie star, who, thanks to the twin blessings of genetics and face-lifts, had defied time and gravity.

Jimmy laughed. "*Saala,* Soli," he said in a mock whisper. "Don't let my son hear you say that. Especially in front of his young bride."

He had spent Rs. 3 lakhs on the wedding. At one point, Zarin had tried to curb his extravagance, but the pleading look on his face had stopped her. And now, Jimmy was glad he had not listened to his wife. Mehernosh is worthy of this party, he thought. After all, his Harvard-educated son had turned down several job offers in America to join his father's law firm. Not too many Parsi children disregarded the siren call of America these days. Just as he, Jimmy, had returned from Oxford to set up his law practice in Bombay, so had Mehernosh returned, all these years later. Both father and son had bucked the trend.

Though truth to tell, he could have happily stayed on in England, if it had not been for its awful racism. He had loved Oxford, its tree-lined streets, its quaint buildings, its ridiculously stuffy traditions. In the few years he had been there, he'd felt a loyalty—no, a *patriotism* toward the university that he had never felt toward any country. Some days, as he walked down the cobbled streets, breathing in the crystal-clear air, he felt as though he could go to war for Oxford, lay down his life for it. Oxford, after all, had given him a full scholarship, and the deans and professors had never made him feel anything less than welcome, had treated him no differently from the sons of lords and barons.

The problem was on the streets. There, he could not escape the color of his skin. In Bombay, Jimmy's light skin had been a sign of privilege, a status symbol. But in England in the late 1960s, his skin was not good enough. Not light enough. Although most people did not guess he was Indian, being mistaken for a Middle Easterner was not much of an improvement. Nothing overt ever happened—he was never verbally insulted or physically attacked. Just a slight chill in the air whenever he was around and that hard, appraising glance that lasted a second longer than it should have. Still, it was enough to make Jimmy bristle. He was simply not used to being looked down upon. That was the reason he called it off with Karen, the ruddy-cheeked, boisterous woman whom he had spotted in the library during his second term at Oxford. They had liked each other immediately, and Karen was miraculously free of the subconscious superiority he detected among almost every white person he encountered. But even Karen's devotion was not enough. He was painfully aware of how he and Karen were watched every time they entered a pub or walked down a street together. Although Karen never said a word, he knew that she was aware of it, too, and the thought made him feel small and weak. And Jimmy never wanted to feel small and weak again. He had spent too many years getting away from that feeling. All the time he was in England, he lived with the fear that if anybody ever said anything snide to him, the street punk that he had once been would come to the forefront and let his fists do the talking.

Also, there were whispered horror stories about the work experiences of other Indian students, once they left the cocoon of the ivory tower for the bullring of the corporate world. About inequities in pay, skipped promotions, discrimination, and harassment.

Jimmy decided early on that he would rather be a big fish in a small pond than a small fish in a big pond. He returned to Bombay soon after he graduated. His old college friends were incredulous at his return. "*Arre, yaar,* every day we are hearing stories about how the British government needs workers, how they're welcoming educated people with open arms," said Nasir Hussein. "People here are selling their houses, furniture, cats, dogs, parents—everything—and migrating. And you came back? Didn't they teach you basic geography, your East from West, at Oxford? Why are you going in the opposite direction?"

But Jimmy knew something they didn't. In England, he would be a dime a dozen, one of hundreds of brilliant Oxford graduates. In Bombay, his uncle's contacts, his Parsi heritage, his light skin, his fluent English, his Oxford education—all these would make him a star. Unique. A big fish.

Then there was the other reason, one that he was even more reluctant to talk about. Quite simply, Jimmy missed Wadia Baug the longer he was away from it. Walking past the gorgeous ivy-covered buildings, eating in Oxford's ornate dining halls, stepping into an icy night after a theater performance, he would suddenly be hopelessly homesick. At such times, Oxford seemed too dignified, too stuffy, too bloodless a place. He missed the Wadia Baug gang, their brashness, their nonchalance, their practical jokes and general irrelevance. It dawned on Jimmy that he would always be looking for a way to get back home. That was the side effect of being an orphan. More than most of his friends, Jimmy needed to have a place to call home. He had never forgotten those three months spent going from one relative to another, after his parents had died in a train accident when he was nine years old. His need for security, for permanence, for stability was infinite. He also felt he owed his uncle Hormazd his return. After all, it was his bachelor uncle who had stepped forward and proclaimed that he would care for his dead bother's son. It was Hormazd who had taken the train to Hyderabad and brought back to Wadia Baug an angry, bitter, confused boy of nine.

Looking at the hundreds of people gathered for his son's wedding, Jimmy Kanga repeated to himself the old, familiar words: Not bad for an orphan. The words were his rosary, the beads on which he measured his successes. He had said those words as he stood looking at the festive, cheerful crowd at his graduation from Oxford. After he had argued his first case before the Indian Supreme Court. After Peter Silk, his old roommate, phoned him from London asking for advice on a particularly difficult case. Not bad for an orphan, he thought, sitting in his big air-conditioned office at Breach Candy.

And after he married Zarin. Jimmy told all his friends that his luck changed after he married Zarin, that his wife was his reward for returning from England.

To Jimmy's chagrin, his law practice did not take off like a rocket after his return. He discovered that a degree from Oxford had not prepared him for the sluggish, bureaucratic Indian legal system. His clients were intimidated by his crisp, brisk manner; the judges were offended by what they considered to be his arrogant *phoren* ways. To his astonishment, Jimmy found himself losing a fair number of his cases. Despite Hormazd's best efforts, Jimmy's practice shriveled up as word spread about the young barrister's short temper and impatience with ill-prepared clients. Jimmy had been a young man in a hurry, but now he had nowhere to go.

The only bright spot in Jimmy's life during his first year back was Zarin, the daughter of Hormazd's family doctor. Jimmy had been interested in Zarin even before he had left for England, but had never had the nerve to ask her out. Although they were part of the same gang of Parsi boys and girls, Zarin Chadiwala was unapproachable, a member of a family of doctors who were legendary in the Parsi community. Although she lived only two streets down from Jimmy, she might as well have lived on the moon.

It was Rusi Bilimoria who had encouraged Jimmy to ask Zarin out. For weeks, Rusi had noticed the surreptitious glances that Jimmy threw Zarin's way, noticed the bead of sweat that trickled down Jimmy's face when Zarin stood close to him. He finally cornered Jimmy at Soli's birthday party. "*Saala*, here you are, a foreign-returned lawyer and you're frightened as a baby around a woman?" Rusi chided him. "If you don't talk to Zarin today, I'll march up to her and tell her how she makes your heart melt like ice cream."

"Don't you dare. I'll talk to her in my own sweet time. Approaching a woman is like approaching a judge—you have to lay the foundation down properly."

"Two hours," Rusi said, grinning as he walked away. "If you haven't laid the foundation in two hours, Mr. Big Shot, I'll speak to Zarin myself."

When Jimmy finally screwed up his nerve and approached Zarin, her reaction stunned him. "Gosh, Jimmy," Zarin replied. "Sure took you long enough. I've only waited for three, four years for you to ask."

By their fifth date, Jimmy knew that Zarin was the woman for him. On that date, he shared with her the perplexing dilemma of why his law practice was not soaring, why he seemed to be chasing his clients away. By this time, Jimmy had already told Zarin about the circumstances that had brought him to Wadia Baug, about the unhappy, terrified kid he had been. Zarin listened to his complaints wordlessly. When he was done, she spoke. "Remember what you told me about how hurt and lost and bewildered you were when you first came to Bombay?" she said. "Well, the next time you have a new client, try and remember how you felt as a boy. Your client probably feels the same way about the court system, I'm guessing. Like he's drowning in unknown waters. Your job is to be the guide, the strong anchor that Hormazd Uncle was for you."

He stared at her, knowing instinctively that it was perfect advice. After that day, he never lost a client because of his temperament.

Now, Zarin was walking up to him. "Hello, darling," she said, a smile drawn over her dimpled face. "This is quite a party, no?"

He put his arm around her and held her to his chest for a quick moment. "Yes. Looks like everybody's having a good time. Even Tehmi seems to be enjoying herself."

"Speaking of guests, why are you standing all by yourself, looking like the lord of the manor, master of all you survey? Come mingle with your friends, *janu.*"

"Oh sure, sure. I was lost in my thoughts, is all."

Arm in arm, they strolled toward where their son was sitting, surrounded by his father's old friends. Rusi Bilimoria looked up at Jimmy. "Hey, Jimmy." Rusi grinned. "We were just telling your son stories about your wild youth."

Jimmy made a face. "Okay, Mehernosh. As your legal adviser, I ask you to leave this group of crackpots this very minute."

"Oh, Mehernosh," Sheroo Mistry broke in. "You should've seen how *lattoo-fattoo* your daddy was over your mummy before their marriage."

That comment triggered a common memory. "*Ae,* remember when Jimmy first proposed to you, Zarin?" asked Soli Contractor. Except for Mehernosh, the rest of them laughed at the memory.

The whole gang had piled into Rusi's car and gone to Khandala for the weekend. Zarin and the other girls had lied to their parents and told them they were going on an all-girls picnic. On their first day there, inspired by the beautiful red hills of Khandala, Jimmy proposed to Zarin. Confident that she would accept, he waited until all of them had finished lunching on the hotel's veranda and then dramatically went down on one knee.

"*Ae,* Jimmy, what happened? You broke your knee, or what? Get up from that dirty floor," someone had said.

A look of disdain came over Jimmy's face. "Stupid donkey," he told the offender. "*Gadhera.* Can't you see what I'm doing? I'm proposing marriage."

At the word *marriage* conversation at the table came to a halt. Somebody let out a nervous giggle, but the offender was immediately shushed into silence by the rest. Zarin looked mortified.

Jimmy turned to Zarin. "Zarin darling. Love of my life, apple of my eye. I humbly beg you to make me the happiest man on earth by marrying me. If you say, 'I do,' I promise to love and cherish you till . . . till . . . the cows come home," Jimmy finished lamely. It was a surprisingly inarticulate speech for a lawyer.

There was a snicker at the table. Jimmy did not dare meet anybody's eye. Zarin felt, rather than saw, the smirks and shuffling of the people around her. She could not imagine what had possessed Jimmy to propose to her in such a public way. For a moment, she thought he was pulling her leg. But Jimmy's raised, glistening face, his flared nostrils, and his trembling body told her this was no joke.

With a start, Zarin realized they were all waiting for her to say something. More than anything, she wanted to cut the tension that was building. "Okay, Jimmy, I'll marry you. On one condition," she added quickly. "You see that little pig running around in the courtyard? You catch that little *dookar* and bring him to me. If you succeed, I'll marry you."

Slowly, Jimmy got to his feet. He stared at Zarin, aghast, while the others exploded in hoots of laughter. Zarin obviously has a well-concealed streak of meanness in her, Jimmy thought. Here she was, treating a man with aspirations to sit on the Supreme Court someday as if he were a common coolie.

Bomi Mistry leaned over the table to congratulate Zarin. "Well said, Zarin, well said," he cried.

"Why are you still standing here, Jimmy?" asked another boy, laughing. "Your fat little piggy is waiting for you."

"*Ae,* if Zarin won't marry you, maybe the pig will," Sheroo hooted.

Jimmy caught Rusi's sympathetic gaze, but Rusi turned away in embarrassment. A red-faced Jimmy turned to Zarin. "Consider your wish to be my command," he said in a stiff, pinched voice. He stepped off the veranda and into the courtyard. He looked evaluatingly at the resting pig for a second and decided that a swift offense would be his best strategy. When the pig saw the tall, intent-looking youth rushing straight toward him, he gave a squeal of surprise and moved hastily away, shaking his behind as he ran. Jimmy gnashed his teeth. The damn thing moved fast for something that looked like a coffee table on wheels. He tried again. And failed. Tried again. Lunged toward it. But he stumbled and the pig moved away again. But this time, it gave a grunt of annoyance rather than a squeal of surprise. Angry at being disturbed from his afternoon siesta, the pig rushed toward Jimmy, charging like a miniature bull.

Perspiration rolled down Jimmy's face. He'd have to marry Zarin from a hospital bed if that monster got hold of him. Abandoning all pride, he lifted his baggy pants from the waist and ran for the safety of the veranda. The pig followed at his heels, then stopped a few feet before the veranda, frightened by the noise coming from it.

"C'mon, Jimmy, run," his friends cried. "Watch out. That little *soovar* looks really mean."

At the veranda, Jimmy had a few minutes to consider whether he really wanted to marry Zarin after all. Any woman with such a cruel sense of humor was dangerous. But then he saw the bemused way in which she was looking at him, and his pride stirred. If, for centuries, men had hunted wild animals to feed their families, surely he could capture a stupid pig for Zarin.

"Where you going, Jimmy?" the people on the veranda asked in wonder.

"You all go in. I won't stop until I catch that *madaarchot* pig."

All that afternoon, Jimmy chased that pig. When he got tired and took a break, the pig chased him. At one point, he actually got his hands around the pig's rump. But the animal felt so fat and greasy that Jimmy loosened his grip in a gesture of involuntary recoil.

For an hour or so, the others sat watching the show, until one by one they left to take a nap. Each time someone left, they'd say, "*Chal ne,* Jimmy. Enough now. Just come in, *yaar.*" But it was no use. He was determined not to quit. Besides, Zarin never once asked him to quit, Jimmy observed. Rather, she gave him an intense, glistening look that made Jimmy go weak in the knees. It was a look of pure sexual desire. He wondered if the others noticed. But soon, there was no one left on the veranda to watch Jimmy's strange courtship of Zarin.

Later, Rusi offered to take the others for a drive. They urged Jimmy to accompany them, but he only looked at Zarin, a wild, primitive expression on his face. Zarin looked back at him coolly. Rusi got the distinct impression that if Zarin had at that moment asked him to quit, he would have. But Zarin said nothing, and Jimmy returned to his task.

When they finally got back at 7:30 P.M., a strange sight greeted them. Jimmy was stretched out on the long wooden bench on the veranda, his face streaked with dirt and gray with fatigue. His crumpled white shirt was as brown as the earth and hung over his torn pants. Jimmy was fast asleep and breathing so hard that even their start of surprise did not awaken him.

The reason for their cry of surprise was the pig. He lay on the first step of the veranda, a few feet away from his would-be captor. Like Jimmy's, the pig's face was streaked with dirt. Like Jimmy, he, too, was fast asleep.

Zarin went up to the sleeping man and kissed his forehead. "Wake up, my Oxford-returned *bevakoof.* You are a crazy man, but pig or no pig, I'll marry you."

Mehernosh Kanga was laughing as heartily as the old men and women surrounding him. "Wow, that was quite a narrow escape I had," he said. "If Mummy hadn't taken pity on Dad, I wouldn't be here today."

"Hats off to your mummy," Coomi Bilimoria said. "She knew how to handle your daddy from the start." Everybody in the crowd picked up on the implied dig at Rusi.

Looking at Rusi's flushed face, Jimmy felt a rush of pity. And amazement at his good fortune. In the old days, all the bets were on Rusi to be Wadia Baug's most successful resident someday. When Jimmy and the other neighborhood boys were spending endless hours standing at street corners, Rusi was already reading books on how to start a small business. While Jimmy couldn't remember whether he had even bathed that day, Rusi was begging his mother to buy him a business suit. While Jimmy was lost, bitter, and trying to decide what to do about the chip on his shoulder, Rusi was single-minded, focused, and determined to succeed by his own efforts. When they were younger, Jimmy had felt that he and Rusi were in some kind of invisible race, and now he wondered if Rusi had felt that way, too. Of course, Jimmy had stopped thinking that years ago, after he had left his opponent in the dust. Jimmy remembered a conversation with Rusi a few days before he left for Oxford. "You go and study everything that you can, *bossie.* By the time you come back, who knows? If my business is successful, *Inshallah,* maybe you won't need too many clients other than me. We could even form some kind of a partnership, maybe." Jimmy had wanted to laugh at the thought of an Oxford-trained lawyer being on exclusive retainer to a small businessman, but the look on Rusi's face stopped him. He realized that Rusi was not being funny.

Still, even after he'd returned from Oxford, it was far from clear that Jimmy would be the more successful of the two. Rusi, after all, had his paper factory by then. Both their lives had taken sharp, divergent turns. Jimmy had attended one of the most distinguished universities in the world. Rusi, on the other hand, had refused to go to college because he was much too eager to jump-start his destiny.

Now, Jimmy wondered if Rusi's life would have been different if he'd had a mentor. Someone who could have helped him realize what was possible for a middle-class Parsi boy and what was not. Instead of looking to multimillionaires like the Tatas and Birlas for inspiration, perhaps Rusi should have lowered his sights a bit, Jimmy thought. He had always believed that Rusi had made a mistake by not going to college or working for someone else before he launched his own business. All the things that the rest of the gang had learned in college or at someone else's expense, Rusi had had to learn the hard way. Jimmy remembered the first time he had an inkling that Rusi's business was in trouble. Rusi had approached him to ask him a simple accounting question. "*Saala,* this is the kind of thing that a professional would know like the back of his hand," Jimmy said. "Why don't you hire someone to do the books? I can get you some good names." He was unprepared for the sheepish look that crossed Rusi's face. "Jimmy, to be honest, I don't even know what I should know and what I'm expected not to know. I'm so afraid an accountant will swindle me if he knows how ignorant I am about financial matters. Besides, who has the money to hire someone like that? No, I'm just going to have to teach myself this, like everything else."

Perhaps if Rusi's father had lived, it would have all turned out differently, Jimmy now thought. He would have insisted that Rusi go to college. And with his bank experience, he could have guided his son in the business. After all, Khorshed Auntie could not be expected to have played both roles. She adored her only son too much to deny him anything. Jimmy felt a rush of compassion toward his neighbor, although he knew that Rusi believed that Jimmy had usurped his destiny, that Jimmy was somehow living Rusi's life. Don't ask how Jimmy knew that. He just picked up some dissonance, some envy, on the finely tuned radar developed by the very successful. Still, Jimmy had a reservoir of good feeling for Rusi. After all, it was Rusi's mamma who had first befriended the little orphan boy. Rusi had a birthday party a month after Jimmy arrived at Wadia Baug, and Khorshed Bilimoria had personally come to Hormazd's flat to invite the building's newest resident. Jimmy had been painfully shy during that meeting, speaking only in monosyllables, but Khorshed had bribed him with gifts of marbles and a spinning top. Before she left, she made him promise that he would attend the gathering. And he was glad he went. It was at Rusi's birthday party that Jimmy had begun to make the friendships that had lasted a lifetime.

Remembering Coomi's snide comment from a moment ago, Jimmy felt a renewed sense of gratitude toward Zarin. I've had two great people in my life, Jimmy thought. Zarin and Cyrus Engineer. At the thought of Cyrus, Jimmy's probing eyes searched the crowd to look for Cyrus's widow, Tehmi. He was surprised but glad that the reclusive Tehmi had accepted their invitation to Mehernosh's wedding. Perhaps this event would draw Tehmi out of her shell, much as Cyrus had once drawn him out of his. Cyrus had cracked open the shell that covered a sullen, moody boy. Jimmy could count on one hand the number of actual conversations he had had with Cyrus. But as a teenager, Jimmy observed how infectious Cyrus's enthusiasm and zest for life was. He noticed how people lighted up around Cyrus, and it made him want to be like the older boy. What a lawyer Cyrus would have made, Jimmy now thought. It was Cyrus who had persuaded Jimmy not to quit school, and he had been helpless against Cyrus's charm offensive. And once Jimmy made the decision not to quit, a funny thing happened. He realized that he really enjoyed learning. And that he enjoyed succeeding, being on the top of every list.

But God, it hadn't been easy. Losing his parents like that. More than three hundred passengers died in that train crash, but all he could do was feel the enormity of his own loss. He could still recall the screams of his ayah when the policeman came to the door with the news. And the first time he heard someone use the word *orphan* and realized with a thud that they were talking about *him*. And those awful three months when he was moved from the home of one relative to another, like a parcel. *"Dhobi ka kutta na ghar ka na ghaat ka,"* one of his older cousins said about him. "The washerman's dog belongs neither in the house nor outside." Which was pretty much how he felt. Uprooted. Even after Hormazd Uncle brought him to Wadia Baug, it wasn't easy. Grief had crystallized into anger by then. Hormazd was a bachelor and had no experience with children, let alone an angry, brooding nine-year-old nephew whom he barely knew. You had to give Hormazd credit for trying, but God, the poor man was so out of his element. While his uncle was at work, Jimmy spent the day on the streets. When the other Wadia Baug boys refused to skip school, he mocked them and then hung out with the street kids. The boy who had grown up in a genteel, solidly middle-class home in Hyderabad now came home bloodied from yet another street fight. Hormazd was beside himself, threatening to beat Jimmy, threatening to turn him out of the house. But he was constrained by the enormity of the tragedy that had befallen his nephew. And whatever his flaws, Hormazd provided Jimmy with the stability that the boy had so badly needed. No matter how far Jimmy wandered, he always had a home to return to.

During his visits to America, Jimmy was always struck by the proliferation of therapists. "A child falls on a playground in America and the parents rush her first to her therapist, then to her lawyer, and last to her doctor," he often joked. But he was also envious. There had been no counseling or any other help for him when he was growing up. He had wasted precious years acting out his anger on the streets, punishing others for his parents' death. No adult ever sat him down and asked him to tell them how he felt. Instead, they lectured him on how he ought to be feeling and behaving. "Be a good boy now, Jimmy," they said. "Poor Hormazd has been very good to you. Don't make him regret his kindness." He'd felt a murderous rage then, felt like spitting on their scrubbed, righteous faces, felt like annihilating them. Instead, he rushed back out on the street and tried to annihilate himself. Cyrus had entered his life at exactly the right time. Saved him from self-annihilation. Cyrus, too, had never talked to him about his feelings. But he could tell that Cyrus knew how he felt. While the adults seemed oblivious to the fact that rage can be as comforting as a blanket, Cyrus understood. He never tried to talk Jimmy out of his anger. He just urged him to rechannel it, use it to his advantage.

In a sense, that's what Zarin had done for him, too. Told him not to take his anger out on his clients, but on his opponents. In the courtroom, Jimmy's thundering oratory, his deliberate pacing of the floor, his exaggerated mannerisms were legendary. The older judges smiled knowingly at Jimmy's trademark lines and gestures—the clenched teeth, the long, thoughtful pauses, the elucidating of various points on all five fingers—but lawyers facing him for the first time were petrified. But Zarin had taught him to be compassionate toward his clients. Although most of his clients were big corporations, on the rare occasions when he represented an individual, Jimmy made sure that he did not intimidate him or her.

What a difference a good marriage makes, Jimmy thought. Zarin had brought him nothing but good luck. And with Mehernosh now working beside him, his joy was complete. Hard to believe that his only son had given up the lures of America to come home to practice law with his dad. Hard to believe that his only son was now a married man. It seemed only yesterday that Mehernosh was running around the playground near Wadia Baug in his khaki shorts and that cute yellow Bugs Bunny T-shirt. Although they became best friends only a few years later, Binny Bilimoria and Mehernosh had hated each other then. Every evening, Binny would go up to Mehernosh and greet him with an innocent "Hey, Georgie Porgie. How are you today?" As Mehernosh would stomp his foot, Binny would solemnly recite:

"Georgie Porgie pudding and pie
Kissed the girls and made them cry.
When the girls came out to play,
Georgie Porgie ran away."

Mehernosh hated that nursery rhyme, hated that nickname. Every evening, he would come screaming into the house, tears running down his cheeks, while Binny continued to play outside, looking like butter wouldn't melt in her mouth. The Bilimorias and Kangas tried hard to repress their smiles as Coomi chided Binny and Zarin consoled Mehernosh.

Jimmy could remember it all so clearly—attending Mehernosh's kindergarten play and laughing at the sight of his son dressed as a red lollipop; attending his son's sixth-grade awards ceremony, where Mehernosh won more prizes than any boy in the history of the school; sitting up with his boy all night, after his son broke his arm playing hockey; traveling through Germany with Mehernosh and watching the local girls fawn over his handsome teenaged son.

Thinking back on Mehernosh's youth made Jimmy think fondly of the old Wadia Baug gang. Jimmy had come to Wadia Baug as a stranger; his son ran around it as if it were his private kingdom. Mehernosh had the run of the building, going in and out of the houses of most of his neighbors. In those days, many of the neighbors kept their front doors open all day long. Jimmy and Zarin never had to worry about attending one of Jimmy's many business parties—they knew Mehernosh could sleep over at a neighbor's house. Whenever Sheroo Mistry made the bread pudding that Mehernosh loved, she would nab the boy and insist that he have dinner with them. Knowing full well that Mehernosh would beat him, Soli Contractor still agreed to one-on-one games of basketball with the young boy. And after Binny and Mehernosh stopped being mortal enemies and became good friends, Mehernosh practically lived in the Bilimoria apartment, refusing to come home even for dinner. "Leave him, leave him," Rusi would say. "He can just eat with us."

During the summer holidays, Rusi occasionally took Mehernosh and Binny to the Bilimoria paper factory for a few hours. An excited Mehernosh would return from those trips singing the praises of the "big-big" machines that Rusi owned. "Hey, Daddy, Rusi Uncle promised me a job at his factory when I grow up," he told his father importantly. "He said I can start as the night watchman."

"And I will be the foreman, so I can dismiss you if you don't do a good job," Binny added.

Jimmy still regretted the move to Cuffe Parade when Mehernosh was eleven. Looking back, he wondered what on earth he had been thinking. Truth of the matter was, Jimmy had gotten a little puffy with pride. He was at the peak of his powers; his practice was booming. He had just argued and won his first case before the Supreme Court, which had resulted in a landmark decision about corporate liability. The case made him the darling of the business community. *The Illustrated Weekly of India* did a short piece on him. He was turning away more clients than he was accepting. Money came pouring in like the rains during the monsoon season. Some of it, he gave away. Twice a year, Jimmy and Zarin went to Udwada and fed a lavish dinner to the impoverished Parsi families living there. He established a Parsi Panchayat scholarship that each year paid for a deserving Parsi student to study law or engineering in America. A lot of the money, he spent on his family. He remodeled the apartment, bought a new car, got Zarin a membership at the Taj Health Club. And still there was plenty of money left over.

So he bought a flat in Cuffe Parade in a skyscraper owned by one of his clients. He told Zarin it was a good investment, that his client was selling it to him at a price he would be foolish to refuse. And the view of the water from the sixteenth floor couldn't be beat. They would be far removed from the nasty pollution, from the noise of the Bombay traffic. The move would be good for their health and their sanity.

But the truth was, Jimmy had grown a little too big for Wadia Baug. He felt much more comfortable among his associates from Breach Candy and Marine Drive and Cuffe Parade because, among them, his wealth and success did not make him stick out. Especially after the *Illustrated Weekly* article appeared, his old neighbors seemed unsure of how to act in his presence. Some of them fawned over him, and their ingratiating manner annoyed him. Others acted nonchalant, and their refusal to acknowledge his success irritated him. He also became sensitive to the sting of their envy. Before, he could brush off their poison darts with a breezy, careless flick of his hand, but now they burned him for days. Once again, he began to feel like a stranger at Wadia Baug. The final straw came when he overheard Dosamai lecturing his son one evening. "Now that your daddy has become a big shot, don't you be all stuck-up around us," she told the teary boy. "Never forget where you come from, understand? Remember, what Ahura Mazda gives, Ahura Mazda also takes away." Jimmy flew up the remaining steps and pulled his son away from the venomous old woman. "Please, Dosamai," he said, choking on his anger. "Nobody has become a big shot. Whatever little I have, it's through the sweat of my brow. Everyone here is free to work that hard, if they like. Anyway, I don't like to involve my son in adult matters. I would wish that you wouldn't, either, ever again." Like a roach under the glare of a flashlight, Dosamai scuttled wordlessly into her dark apartment.

"I want to move," he said to Zarin that night. "I don't want my son growing up feeling like he can't enjoy the fruits of his father's labor. I can have the Cuffe Parade flat in move-in condition in two months." Zarin tried to talk him out of it, but Jimmy's mind was made up.

"Promise me this much at least," she said, when she knew that she had lost. "Let's keep this flat also. After all, it's paid for and we don't need the money. This way, we can come back occasionally to visit our friends and still have a place to stay."

He was so relieved at her assent that he readily agreed.

Good thing, too, Jimmy now thought. The year they had spent in Cuffe Parade was the worst period in their marriage. Mehernosh was miserable. He pined for his old neighborhood friends and hated his new school. "Such snobs, they are," he told Jimmy vehemently. "I told them where we used to live and that boy Ramesh said, 'Where is that? Out of Bombay?' I was ready to give him one big whack on his backside." Zarin, too, was silent around her neighbors and reluctant to get involved in neighborhood projects. Jimmy fumed about it to himself, convinced that Zarin was punishing him for making her move. But when he confronted her about not making an effort to get to know her neighbors, Zarin looked at him sadly. "I'm really trying, Jimmy," she said. "It's just hard. The people here are so different. They don't welcome Mehernosh into their homes, and everybody keeps their doors locked. The building association does not even allow the *pauwala* and the *doodhwala* to deliver groceries to the door. I just miss Wadia Baug. I can't believe it myself, but I even miss Perin and Villo fighting with the milkman every morning. Even the constant ringing of the doorbell. Here, you could go for days without anybody stopping by."

He turned away angrily from her. The truth was that Jimmy felt the same way, but he was loathe to admit it. Returning to Wadia Baug would be much too embarrassing. He had hoped that Zarin was not missing the old gang as fiercely as he was. "Maybe it's an adjustment period," he told her. "After all, we didn't make our Wadia Baug friends in one day, either. As newcomers, it's up to us to be more friendly. Maybe we should throw a party or something."

And so they did—the first of many parties. Their neighbors came, admired their flat, ate their food, said hello to them the next time they saw them in the elevator, invited them to their own parties. But somehow, it didn't take. Jimmy realized what the problem was one day: The people who lived around him were too much like the people he worked with. They had the same interests, the same ambitions. Compared to the eccentric zaniness, the melodramatic passions, the free-ranging diversity of the Wadia Baug crowd, these people seemed too narrowly focused, too bloodless. Too intent on holding on to what they had. This is exactly how I felt in Oxford toward the end, he realized with a start.

But it wasn't until Zarin's breakdown that Jimmy decided that his family's happiness was more important than his bruised pride. He came home late one evening to an astonishing sight. Zarin was sitting on the sofa, sobbing softly to herself. Her hair was uncombed and her dress stained with tears. He was stunned. "Where's Mehernosh?" he asked reflexively. "Is he okay?"

"He's out. I paid the ayah to take him to a movie. I just needed some time by myself. And I couldn't bear for him to see me like this."

"But darling, what's wrong?" he said, taking a step toward her. "Is it bad news about your mummy or daddy? Why didn't you call me at the office?"

"No. Nothing like that. Everybody's okay. Except me. I'm just slowly-slowly going out of my mind. Cracking up."

"But . . . what?" he spluttered. He felt breathless, as if he had taken a hard blow to the stomach.

"Jimmy, I can't take it anymore. I'm going. I'm taking Mehernosh and going back to Wadia Baug. You can come visit us there on weekends, if you like. I'm sorry, *janu.* I tried, I really did. But I can't live here anymore. You don't know what it's like during the day. The quiet. When the wind blows from over the sea, it moans, like an old woman crying. I just miss the hustle-bustle of our old building. I miss our friends, all the joking around. I miss the smell of Parsi food being cooked next door to us. No, those people weren't perfect, but at least they cared about things other than the price of gold and the share bazaar."

"Zarin. What are you saying? Leaving our marriage, leaving me over a lousy flat? You are obviously under a lot of strain. I'm sorry, darling. I've left you alone at home far too much, I think. Come sit with me. We'll deal with this problem, I promise."

They went to bed that night without the issue being resolved. But lying in bed that night, Jimmy had a revelation. Even the strongest of marriages were made up of more than just the two people involved, he realized. He had foolishly thought that Zarin and he were married only to each other. In reality, they were married to an entire group of people, a neighborhood, a way of life. Despite his love for her, he alone could not save Zarin. She needed all those others, their friends and relatives, in order to be whole and happy. Tears rolled down Jimmy's checks and onto his pillow. He suddenly felt incredibly lucky. All these years, he had been surrounded by a wealth of people, and he hadn't even known it. Had taken them for granted. Oh sure, they were irritating at times—Dosamai, with her penchant for gossip; Bomi and Sheroo, with their *koila* jokes; Rusi, with his ill-concealed competitiveness. But they were his community. His people. They had befriended him when he hadn't had two nickels to rub together, cared for his only son, sheltered his wife, held up his marriage. And he had left them behind like yesterday's newspaper. He had pulled his son out of a school he loved and his wife out of a community she cared about, all so that they could go and live among people who didn't care if they were alive or dead, as long as they paid their association fees on time. He had sacrificed a year out of their lives to the altar of his ambitions. He rolled over to face Zarin. "Sweetie, wake up," he whispered. "I've something to say to you."

When he casually told a client the next morning that he had decided to return to his old neighborhood, the man understood at once. "Of course, of course, Jimmy," he said. "You are a Parsi, born and raised among Parsis. Here at Cuffe Parade, you are forced to live among Gujus, Punjabis, Sikhs. Very hard adjustment to make, I'm sure."

Jimmy was shocked. Like many post-independence Bombayites, he was wedded to the idea of a secular, nonsectarian city. He resented his client's casual assumption that his discomfort with Cuffe Parade had to do with religion. After all, he was always telling his Parsi friends to think of themselves as Indians first, to divest themselves of their superiority and smugness. But driving home that evening, he forced himself to confront his own prejudices. He decided that he could not be certain that religious difference had played no role in his disenchantment with Cuffe Parade. So often, he had come home in the evenings and involuntarily screwed up his nose at the smell of unfamiliar food being cooked next door. Was that religious insularity? Or merely a cultural difference? Was he splitting hairs? What distinguished one from the other? And while he was on the subject, he dissected the guiding principle behind his philanthropy: Charity begins at home. This is how he had justified donating money exclusively to Parsi causes. Was that chauvinism? Or merely looking out for an incredibly small ethnic minority? He was only one man, after all, with a finite amount of money. And there was nothing wrong with helping your own. That's what the Marwadis and the Gujus did, and look at how those communities were prospering. Bombay was fast slipping into the gutter, and he could not pull it up by himself. What was wrong with trying to save just a tiny bit of it? And if he had to choose, why not save the ones he loved? And yet . . . If everyone felt that way, who would take care of those who needed the most help? By the time he got home, Jimmy had a ferocious headache.

But if Jimmy was unsure of his reasons for disliking Cuffe Parade, he was certain of his reasons for loving Wadia Baug. Their return to Wadia Baug was the mirror image of their departure a year earlier. Then, the neighbors had been awkward and tentative when it was time to say good-bye. Their departure had bruised their neighbors' pride, but they were not about to show the Kangas that. The farewells had veered from the hearty to the plaintive.

"Heck, we lived with you being gone to England; we can live with this," Soli said. "Just across town you are now. Be forewarned—the entire gang will be descending on your flat if our mouths water at the thought of Zarin's cheese *pakodas.*"

"Don't forget us," Coomi cried. "Oh, what are we going to do without our little Mehernosh here? My poor Binny is going to miss him so. Promise you'll keep bringing him back for visits."

"Make new friends, but keep the old. One is silver and the other gold," recited Dosamai in that righteous voice that made Jimmy bristle.

Their arrival was a different story. Their return was universally hailed as a triumph, as if Wadia Baug had won a secret war with its Cuffe Parade rival. "The Russians are coming. The Russians are coming," Binny cried, mocking the adults' fawning over the prodigal son's return, but her sarcasm could not mask her pleasure at being reunited with Mehernosh. "Hi, Georgie Porgie," she said softly, reprising their childhood association. Mehernosh beamed with joy.

Pooh-poohing Jimmy's decision to hire professional movers, Soli insisted that he and the other neighborhood men would move the Kangas back into their flat. Neither Jimmy nor Zarin had the heart to interfere with Soli's obvious pleasure, although Zarin had to look away when Soli handled her china. Three days after they'd moved in, Zarin looked around her flat and said what Jimmy had been thinking earlier that day: "Gosh, it looks like we never left."

Jimmy often thanked his lucky stars for his wife's minibreakdown. It had taken that, to bring him to his senses. Bombay's social fabric had frayed so badly in the years since their return to Wadia Baug. Every few days now, Jimmy heard of some millionaire or businessman being kidnapped at gunpoint, read about some retired executive found murdered by a house servant. So many of these incidents occurred in the rich parts of town, it seemed. Despite his wealth and prominence, Jimmy Kanga felt anonymous and safe in his old neighborhood. It was too middle-class a neighborhood to attract the attention of the gangsters who were constantly on the lookout for prospective targets. In the last ten years, Jimmy had stopped doing newspaper interviews for this very reason. He did not want to be trapped in the net of a gangster's attention. He had even given up his old habit of buying a new car every three years. New cars attracted too much attention. And truth to tell, driving in Bombay was no longer a pleasure. Each trip felt like a survival test. Mehernosh still had the driving bug, but Jimmy constantly lectured his son about the virtues of nonostentatious living. "Times are different, sonny," he told Mehernosh. "Better to fly under the radar these days. Too many Mafia types around now."

Looking at Mehernosh sitting comfortably between his elders, watching as they adored his son with their eyes, Jimmy Kanga knew that he had made the right decision. Mehernosh had grown up knowing the difference between how much something cost and what it was worth. Despite his American education, despite the sophisticated circles that Mehernosh moved in, his son had learned to value his heritage, Jimmy realized. He might spend his day among combative lawyers and tight-lipped, tightfisted businessmen, but at the end of the day, he came home to the down-to-earth reality of Wadia Baug. Of course, that was about to change. Jimmy had given Mehernosh and Sharon the Cuffe Parade flat as a wedding gift. Jimmy knew there was some dissent among the neighbors about whether Mehernosh should move out of the building. Dosamai, he knew, was spreading a rumor that Zarin was behind the move because she and Sharon had had a falling-out. Jimmy took such speculation in stride. After his return to Wadia Baug, he had decided that the occasional spurts of pettiness and jealousy were the price he would pay for the security and community the building provided his family. No, Jimmy was more concerned about Mehernosh's safety away from Wadia Baug. Still, Jimmy was a reasonable man. His son had argued with him that, statistically speaking, Bombay was a pretty safe city and that one could not stop living because of fear. After all, it wasn't as if nobody ever got killed near Wadia Baug. It was just that those stories attracted less attention. Mehernosh had assured his father that he and Sharon had no interest in an ostentatious, flashy lifestyle. And that they would take all reasonable precautions to be safe. Looking at his responsible, thoughtful son, Jimmy knew he had made the right call. Living in Cuffe Parade would make it so much easier for Sharon to commute to her job. Also, the newlyweds needed their privacy. Hopefully, they could make a go of it in their new home. If not, they could always sell the flat in a few years and buy something closer to

Wadia Baug. The Cuffe Parade flat that he'd bought for a song years ago was now worth over Rs. 1 crore.

As if he had conjured her up, Jimmy's sprightly daughter-in-law came up behind him and started rubbing his shoulders. His heart swelling with love for her, Jimmy took her hand and kissed it. "Come sit with me, my dear," he said. As Sharon took her seat in the circle, Jimmy thought about the years that Mehernosh had been at Harvard. How worried Zarin and he had been that Mehernosh would find an American girl and break off his engagement with Sharon. There were so many such cases. Surprisingly, they did not worry about Sharon getting tired of waiting for Mehernosh. As if it were unthinkable that anyone could dump Mehernosh, he now thought guiltily. But both children rose to the occasion. They stayed in touch by phone and letters and Sharon and her sister visited Mehernosh in Cambridge at the end of his first year. They loved Cambridge—the street musicians and the eclectic shops in Harvard Square, the long row of exotic restaurants in Inman Square, the quaint bridges that linked the banks of the Charles River—but Mehernosh scared them with stories about Boston in the winter—how the bony trees lost their green flesh and stood naked and shivering; how the frozen ground beneath his feet was as hard and uncompromising as some of his professors at the law school. Before she left, Sharon made Mehernosh promise not to sleep with the many women she saw lusting after him. He readily promised. And as far as Jimmy knew, Mehernosh had stayed faithful. From his own experiences, Jimmy knew how tempting it was for Indian men to go crazy when they left India for the sexually permissive West. He had seen some unbelievable things at Oxford. Men who returned to India with Ph.D.s in fucking. And that was during the ice age, as far as sex went. He could scarcely imagine the opportunities available to a handsome fellow like Mehernosh in America in the 1990s. He hoped for his son's sake that Mehernosh had had some experiences with American women. Jimmy was a great believer in broadening one's horizons. But he also knew that he would admire his son more if Mehernosh had resisted temptation.

As if he knew his father was thinking of him, Mehernosh got up from the circle of friends and strolled over. "Hey, Dad, just wanted to remind you. You better let people know about the surprise before they start to take off. The third *paath* will be sitting for dinner pretty soon."

Jimmy nodded. "Yah. I've already said something to a few of them. I need to tell the rest." He dug into his suit pocket and pulled out a short list of names.

Sitting back in his chair, Jimmy smiled to himself. He was glad that he had planned this little surprise for a few select friends. Nothing fancy, just a little something to top things off. Just a way to make the evening last a little longer. Jimmy sighed. This was the happiest day of his life. He wished it would never end.

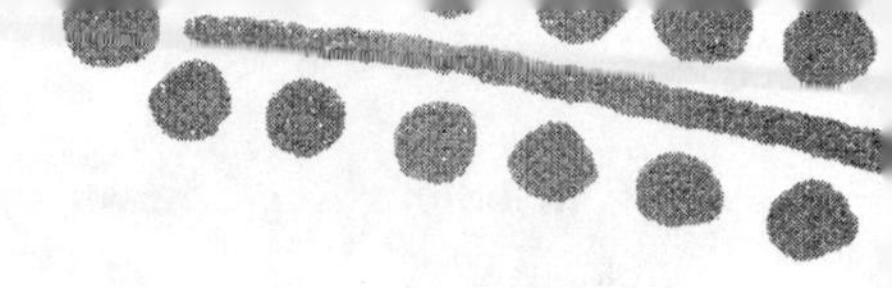

Four

Coomi Bilimoria surveyed the scene before her eyes and blinked. *Click. Whirl.* She turned her head ever so slightly and blinked again. *Click.* Another photograph of another scene, this one of Mehernosh Kanga holding up a glass of whiskey to his new bride's face as she screwed up her nose in disgust. It was a game Coomi played with herself every time she wanted to memorize something, this blinking of the eyes, as if for a moment she was not Coomi Bilimoria, wife of Rusi, mother of Binny, but, instead, an inanimate object, a camera. Someone who stood slightly outside the circle, watching, observing everything, in the hopes of repeating it all faithfully the next day when she sat on Dosamai's old stained sofa. Fodder for the gossip mill. Fuel for the fire. I am a camera. Watch me explode in a whiff of smoke and light.

It had started innocently enough, this habit, this obsession with mental photographs. After Binny left for England, Coomi waited for those weekly phone calls from her daughter. For the first few months, she wrote daily letters to her daughter in her head, letters that she somehow forgot to set on paper and mail to Binny. Soon, she added pictures to those letters. Oh, I must remember to tell this story to Binny when she calls, she said to herself. And to help herself remember, she took a picture of the scene. *Click.* Happy pictures. Sad pictures. A picture of Nillo Vakil's kidney stone floating in a glass of water by her hospital bed. A picture of Dosamai the first time Coomi saw her without her dentures on. A picture of Sheroo Mistry showing off the new gold necklace her husband had bought for her. A picture of Rusi praying out loud along with the *dastoors* at his mother's funeral, his melodious singsong voice overshadowing their professional, nasal chanting.

But Binny seemed strangely disinterested in her mother's pictures. Coomi could hear the impatience in her voice as she told her daughter about someone's appendectomy, somebody's Navjote ceremony, someone's broken hip. Binny only wanted to talk about Rusi and Coomi and about Khorshed, when her grandmother was alive. "Mummy," she said through gritted teeth, "enough of how the neighbors are doing. I want to know how *you* are." Binny was simply not interested in hearing about everyone else's life. That fact never ceased to amaze Coomi. She had an insatiable curiosity about the people around her and could not understand how her daughter could survive without such vital air. "I'm fine, fine. *Chalta hai.* But enough about me. Did you hear about . . ."

There were other things that made Coomi blink. She clicked on the fact that no matter how rushed and annoyed Binny seemed with her, she always had the time and money to talk to her father. Binny bristled when Coomi talked to her about trivial things, but she hung on to Rusi's every word as if he were King Solomon. When Coomi complained about Binny's favoritism to Dosamai, the old woman sighed deeply. "What to do, *deekra*? Such is the way of the world. Us womenfolk hold our children to our breasts, go through a lifetime of 'Drink your milk' and 'Do your homework' and 'Go do *soo-soo*' and whatnot and then these menfolk come around and, *bas,* the children flock to their daddies like the Pied Piper. Girls always love their daddies more. Fact of nature." As the silence grew between her only daughter and herself, Coomi stopped taking pictures for Binny and instead started collecting them for Dosamai. Over the years, she built a photo album of angry, bitter pictures. Of Binny's husband, Jack, looking at Rusi with raised eyebrows after Coomi snapped at Rusi at a restaurant during their trip to England. Of Rusi glaring at her while his mother complained about something Coomi had done earlier that day. Of Soli Contractor's shocked expression when he realized Coomi had overheard him commiserating with Rusi about his marriage. Every morning, after Rusi left for work, she took the album over to Dosamai's flat, where the two women pored over the pictures, revisiting the old ones, looking at the new ones with a fresh sense of injury and insult.

When Binny was younger, Coomi had laughed off her daughter's devotion to her father. Binny's fierce love for Rusi reminded her of how she had adored her own father, and she was proud of the fact that Rusi delighted in his daughter so much. She and Rusi had laughed uproariously the day their six-year-old daughter looked solemnly at her father and declared that she would marry him as soon as she was old enough.

"But *I'm* married to your daddy." Coomi laughed.

Binny looked at her with those big hurt eyes. "Oh no," she said, as if the thought had never occurred to her. "Oh no." And then, fiercely she added, "But Daddy loves me best of all. I'm correct, *na,* Daddy?"

As Rusi nodded, Coomi felt nothing but joy and gratitude. Not a bit of the jealousy that she now felt.

Those were the good years. In the early years of their marriage, she and Rusi had fought, but somehow there was enough elasticity in their marriage that it could snap back together. Sexual attraction, the optimism of youth, their hopes and ambitions, the desire for companionship—all covered up the basic differences between them. Like boxers, they withdrew from each other as far as they could to nurse their wounds, but they always made their way back into the ring. Yes, those were the good old days. Despite the fact that by then both she and Rusi realized how different they were from each other. Despite the fact that Coomi believed that Khorshed Bilimoria was waiting for their marriage to fail, that her earlier doubts about the suitability of her daughter-in-law had now crystallized into open contempt and hostility.

"Khorshed Mamma can't wait for me to walk out, so she can get you married to that Mani who lives in Paradise Building," she once cried to Rusi as they were driving to a work party. They had been married about three years by then. "Don't think I don't understand all her *tingal-tangal.*"

Rusi looked bewildered. "Mani? Who—what are you talking about? You think my mamma wants her only son to be a divorcé? What has gotten into your head to make you think like this, Coomi?"

"Yah, take your mother's side blindly. What else did I expect? God forbid that my husband would ever side with me. What do you know about what goes on in that house while you are at work all day long? Perhaps I should put on pants and go to work, while you stay at home with your sneaky mother."

"How dare you talk of my mamma in that tone. I want you to apologize to her, Coomi, when we go home tonight. Don't you think my poor widowed mother has suffered enough in her life already?"

But Coomi was not one to apologize. On rare occasions, she felt a twinge of regret and cursed herself for her careless words, for her awful ability to sting both Khorshed and Rusi with the lash of her tongue. But that night was not one of those occasions. "Over my dead body, I'll apologize to that woman," she said. "It would just give her more ammo against me."

" 'That woman'? This is the woman who never raised her voice at me, who raised me with love and respect, and my wife refers to her as *that woman*? Like she's a commonplace *ganga* or street sweeper?" Without warning, Rusi's body began to heave with sobs. "I married you with such hopes, to bring joy and good fortune into our house. Instead, I have a wife who acts as if my mother is her bitter enemy."

His tears shattered her anger and she reached for his hand. "Oh, come on now, Rusi, you know me and my temper. You know I didn't mean anything against your mamma. She's a good person. I know that. How many times must I tell you I don't mean anything by my words. Dangerous to drive a car this way, crying and all. Stop, *na.*" After he dabbed his eyes dry with his starched handkerchief, she put her arm around his neck and massaged it. "Sometimes I feel I've married a woman, I swear," she murmured. "Whoever heard of a man being so sensitive? Delicate as bone china, you are. One stern look and you can crack. But I didn't mean anything, honest."

More than once, she found herself longing for the brusqueness and bravado of her three brothers. The very things she had once loved about Rusi—that ridiculously long, vulnerable neck, the softness of his tone, his loving, thoughtful words—all irritated her now. Or rather, Coomi took it all personally, as if Rusi's quiet dignity, his soft-spoken words, his sensitive nature were all ways of showing her up, an affront to her loud and boisterous family.

Like the time before her marriage when she and Rusi were having dinner at her mother's home. Rusi was in the middle of a sentence when Sorab, her youngest brother, let out a loud fart. "What was that?" Fali asked, while the others burst into laughter. "Sounded like an earthquake in here."

Coomi noticed the look of shock and disgust on Rusi's face. At that moment, she was ashamed of her brothers, hated them for their rude manners and juvenile ways. "My God, Sorab," she chided. "That was so rude, even for you."

Before Sorab could respond, Fali turned to his sister, his face gleaming with malice. "Not even married yet and already acting like a madam?" he said softly. "*Arre,* Coomi, for your wedding, we're not going to hire a band. Sorab will play the trumpet with his bum only." Only Coomi and Rusi did not join in the laughter that followed.

Now, the memory of that dinner made Coomi feel defensive and protective of her brothers. Who did Rusi think he was? she fumed. Acting like a *bara sahib,* like he was royalty or something. Sorab and the others were just being boys, having fun, that's all.

Still, it was hard to know whom she should blame for the fizzling out of her marriage. They had started out with such promise, after all. She had liked Rusi months before he ever took notice of her, before their eyes met in the rearview mirror of his car. He was in love with whatshername—that plump woman—when Coomi first met him. Tina, that was her name. A girl with caterpillars for eyebrows. Still, Rusi'd had eyes for no one else at the time. But once he noticed Coomi, once their eyes met in the rearview mirror of his car and she smiled at him before looking away, he pursued her vigorously. Not that she had fought him too hard. In those days, Rusi had been like lightning in a bottle, dazzling. Aflame with ambition and guts and fire. None of this weakling stuff, this obsession with failure that dominated his life now. Once it was known that they were a couple, they were the envy of all their friends. How strange, how wrong it was that it was the others who had ended up with the good marriages, Coomi thought. After all, who would've bet on Bomi and Sheroo? Two nice but inconsequential people. Lightweights. She and Rusi had been different—smart, dynamic, ambitious. That was the big secret: She had been ambitious, too. Nobody saw it because she wasn't loud about her ambition the way Rusi was. He would talk about his dreams to a stranger at a bus stop, Coomi often thought, affectionately at first, then contemptuously. Anybody who knew Rusi for five minutes knew he wanted to be successful in business, own a factory with a huge, well-manicured front lawn like the one he'd seen in a German magazine, have lots of children, and, someday, have his sons take over the family business.

But Coomi's dreams remained unsaid, even to her closest friends. When she was a young girl, she had wanted to be a hero. As a small child, she believed that being a hero was a profession, so that one could choose to be a hero in the same way one could choose to be a doctor or a tonga driver or a banker. She spent hours daydreaming in the bathroom, ignoring her mother's incessant beatings on the door. "You selfish girl, I want you out, in one, two, three," her mother would scream. "Who you think you are, the Maharani of Jaipur? Using up all the hot water, you shameless thing." But Coomi barely heard her, dreaming as she was of rescuing infants from burning buildings, of stopping old people from getting evicted, of leading the Indian Army into glorious battle. She was a naturally curious child, and all her dreams were about exploration and adventure. She wanted to discover everything—from lost tribes in dark continents to what lay inside people's heads. Her father came home one evening, to find his six-year-old daughter sitting on the floor with the two dolls that she owned. Coomi had smashed their wooden scalps and was pulling out the stuffing with a pair of scissors. "Oh my God," he muttered. "Daughter, are you mad? What are you doing?"

"Oh, nothing, Daddy," she answered. "I am just wanting to see what their brains look like."

Surrounded by her teasing, boisterous brothers, Coomi grew up knowing that dreams had to be zealously guarded and kept secret. One day, when she was eight and Sorab six, she asked her younger brother to reverse the usual order of their play. Today, she would be the policeman and Sorab would be the thief, Coomi declared.

Sorab stared at his sister uncomprehendingly. "We cannot do that," he said.

"Why not? Why do I always have to be the poor thief? I'm older than you, even."

"Because you are a *girl.* Everybody knows a girl can't be a policeman." Sorab giggled at the silliness of the idea. "It is my job to catch you."

As she grew older and her dreams became more subversive, she hid them even more carefully. By the time she reached college, Coomi already understood how little value she had as a woman. She noticed how her mother unconsciously served the largest portions to her brothers, gave them the pieces of meat with the fewest bones. She observed how all her professors assumed that she was in college to find a suitable husband. "Miss Katpitia," her beloved professor Krishnamurti said when she went to his office in tears over an average grade. "What would I give to have my male students be as diligent as you are. It's so nice to see a student work so hard. Such a shame you will settle down any day now with your own family. Such a waste for a woman to be as smart as you are." She left his office, shaking with frustration. But Krishnamurti had done her a favor. She saw her earlier dreams of heroism and adventure for what they were—a child's fantasy. After that, she aspired to something even more fantastic—marriage to a man with prospects and with the good manners and culture that her family so badly lacked. Plainly said, Coomi was determined to marry above herself. It was painfully clear that she could not pull herself out of her lower-middle-class origins by the sweat of her own brow; no, she would need to perch a ride on the shoulders of a man who was unafraid to work hard himself. This was not the path Coomi would have preferred—she was too intelligent and proud for that—but it was the only path that would lead from her small, noisy, sweaty house to the outside world.

Rusi met her needs perfectly. It was too good to be true that she also found him easy to love. She liked Rusi the first time she met him. She had known about the Bilimorias for years, but she and Rusi had never really talked until the night of the New Year's Eve dance at Parsi Gymkhana. She had seen Rusi across the room and asked Sheroo to introduce them. After a moment or two, Sheroo disappeared, leaving them to chat for about ten minutes. Despite the fact that Rusi seemed distracted, despite the fact that most of their conversation revolved around Tina, the woman he was in love with, Coomi felt a sense of loss when Rusi finally excused himself and left her side. "It was nice chatting," she said as he got up to leave. "Nice to have finally met you." He nodded absently, but his eyes were already on Tina, who had walked in the door. Although they ran into each other regularly after that first meeting, it was about six more months before he noticed her again, during the car trip to Khandala. But Coomi was smitten. Everything about Rusi—his excruciating sensitivity, his gentleness, his moodiness, his relentless desire for self-improvement—was new and foreign to her. "That Rusi Bilimoria," she said to Sheroo, "he's different from the other chaps, no? Like he's made of milk and cream or something. So soft."

"And what are other men made of? Wood and bricks?" Sheroo laughed.

But it was true. Rusi was so different from the men she'd known that she could scarcely believe they had grown up in the same city, much less in the same neighborhood. He seemed untouched by the realities of common life, somehow. In some ways, he reminded Coomi of herself when younger. Then she, too, had lived in a fantasy world of dreams and ambition. But there were two vital differences: Unlike her, Rusi had a plan to turn his dreams into reality. And unlike her, Rusi was a man.

Her oldest brother, Fali, was appalled when he had found out that his sister was dating Rusi. "Of course, my only sister had to go and find the weakling of Parsi Gymkhana. *Arre, yaar,* your boyfriend doesn't even know how to bench-press, such a dandy he is. So many of my friends are interested in you, good strong he-man types, and you have to go out with a homo. Ever seen his legs? *Saala,* they're like two pieces of sugarcane. And how he speaks? Like he was educated in fucking Oxford or Cambridge instead of at the same *ghaati* schools we all went to. All because his daddy was having some nice post at Central Bank. No, Rusi isn't our type of folk, Coomi. You better think twice before you go *paagal* over him."

It was good advice, Coomi often thought in later years. But it came too late. She was already crazy about Rusi by then.

It was Dosamai who had bumped into Khorshed Bilimoria on the street accidentally on purpose one evening and told her about Coomi and Rusi. Khorshed, who prided herself on being an involved parent, was peeved to hear about Coomi from Dosamai. She was hurt that Rusi would keep his girlfriend a secret from her. Also, she was perturbed at the ominous tone Dosamai used to describe Coomi's family. "A little different from the people who live in Wadia Baug," Dosamai said. "The brothers, I've heard, are a little wild. All kinds of mischief making they are into. But they are boys, after all. Nothing to do with the *chokri* your Rusi is interested in. Also, what can their poor mother do? People say her husband was a drunkard. Just took off one day, only, and, *bas,* they never saw him again. How can such fatherless children not be *junglees*? Far be it from me to judge that poor woman."

Khorshed went home that evening with a heavy heart. But she hid from Rusi what she had heard, merely telling her son that she would like to meet the woman he was seeing, now that the whole building knew about it. She just wished he had heard it from Rusi, instead of an outsider, Khorshed said. And no, she would not tell Rusi who had told her the news.

The following Saturday, Coomi visited her future home for the first time. She was a little disappointed at how bare the rooms were and how simple the furnishings. Somehow, she had expected Rusi's home to reflect the largeness of his imagination. There were no pictures up on the walls, other than a large portrait of Khorshed's dead husband, no trinkets in the living room. Silence was a living thing in this apartment, she felt, and the thought made her shudder. But Coomi also noticed how gloriously large the rooms were compared to her cramped little flat, how high the ceilings were and how neat and tidy everything was, compared to the messy chaos that reigned in her home. She liked the orderliness of things in the Bilimoria household, but it also felt a little too sanitary and antiseptic, so that she felt a twinge of affection for the glorious mess that was her brothers' bedroom. At least you know that flesh-and-blood people live there, she thought, a little defensively. People who bleed when you cut them. But then she felt ashamed of this involuntary put-down of Rusi. Rusi was very much a passionate man, and she had the love bites to prove it.

Coomi could feel Khorshed Bilimoria's eyes on her and she fought the urge to shuffle in her seat. Khorshed was an imperial-looking woman with garlic white skin and thoughtful brown eyes. Next to her, Coomi felt gauche, awkward, and dark. Something about the old woman's regal bearing made her feel inadequate and nervous. She jumped as she realized Khorshed was saying something to her.

"I'm sorry?" Coomi stuttered.

Khorshed laughed and glanced at her son. "I just said, 'You will have some *chai,* correct?' " she repeated. "I have brought home some *daar-ni-pori* from the Ratan Tata Institute to have with tea."

Coomi stammered a yes and then was unsure whether she should offer to make the tea. She looked to Rusi for help, but he was staring resolutely ahead. "May I help?" she asked timidly.

Khorshed shook her head. "Oh, no, no need. The kettle's already on the stove. It will only be another minute."

Willing her hands not to shake, Coomi sipped her tea. Looking over the rim of her cup, she saw Khorshed staring appraisingly at her. She's trying to decide whether I'm good enough for her son, she thought. The thought made her bristle and, involuntarily, she sat up a little taller in her chair. If she asks anything about my daddy, I'm going to walk out of here, she decided.

But Khorshed did not ask her any personal questions that day. Instead, she talked about the price of fish, the recent bus strike, her deceased husband and her strong-willed son. "Put some sense into my stubborn son's head, if you can, *deekra,*" she said. "Tell him to give up these mad ideas of being a businessman and to allow his mother to find him a decent job at Central Bank instead. My husband, God bless him, was well regarded at his job, and I still have some good contacts there. Soon, with these Hindu politicians wanting to take over everything, I won't even be able to do that for him."

Rusi stiffened beside her and Coomi's heart ached for him. But she was afraid of interfering in what was apparently an old conversation between mother and son. "Rusi does what he wants, Auntie," she said finally. "He has a mind of his own. And I'm sure if he changes his mind in a few years, you will be able to help him still."

Khorshed smiled a wan smile. "Hard to say. If these politicians don't mess everything up, then it's a possibility. I tell you, I still mourn the day the British left India. Took with them the last remnants of decency and culture. The worst mistake we Parsis made was to join the freedom movement. We bit the hand that fed us. Our community had prospered and grown under the British. And this is how we repaid them, by marching in the streets and screaming, 'English, go home.' The height of ungratefulness. And look at the result. All these years of Hindu raj, and everything is falling apart. Nehru is a good, sophisticated man, but what can one man do alone? I tell you, India is at least lucky that it was Nehru who survived instead of Gandhiji. Mind you, Gandhiji was a great man, but he would have destroyed even a modern city like Bombay and turned it into a village. You know what he used to say about *khadi* and village industries and all that, no? If Gandhi had lived, I would probably have had to learn to wear a *khadi* sari and use a weaving loom."

Rusi rolled his eyes, as if he had heard this tirade numerous times before. He knew that part of his mother's opposition to the Indian leadership was purely aesthetic—in the early days after independence, Khorshed had feared that she would have to give up her precious silk saris and wear *khadi* instead. Rusi simply considered Khorshed's obsession with the British to be an eccentricity, rather than a political stance. But Coomi was shocked, and for a moment, she forgot her nervousness or the purpose of her visit. "But Khorshed Auntie, how can you miss the British? After all, India belongs to us. For years, those *goras* told us they were God, and we believed them. We let them into our country as guests and they acted like common thieves. I don't care how many blunders our leaders make, at least India is our own now. If I'd been a little older, I would've joined the freedom struggle, for sure."

Rusi tensed, because he knew what was to follow. He was angry at himself for not preparing Coomi any better for this first meeting with his mother and for not steering the conversation away from controversial subjects. After all, his girlfriend and his mother were the two most stubborn people he knew.

Khorshed spoke in a soft, choked voice. "My dear girl," she said. "With all due respect, you don't know what you're talking about. When we say *sir* to an Englishman, it's more than his white skin we're respecting. We're respecting the most civilized nation on earth—the birthplace of Shakespeare and Dickens. Where would India be without the British? You answer me that. Still a backward nation of bullock carts, that's where. No trains, no motorcars, no electricity. Can you imagine? They have given us all these gifts. Now that they've pulled out of here, you mark my words, life will continue to get miserable for us Parsis. Soon, we will curse the day we ever came to this country. I can see a day when even the Hindus and Muslims will unite and send us packing all the way back to Persia."

Rusi and Coomi exchanged wry looks. Khorshed caught the look and said, "You youngsters think I'm doing all *fekhem-fekh.* Think what you will. But I tell you, this is the voice of experience talking." She turned to Rusi. "Did you ever tell Coomi about what happened to my Hilla's husband?"

"No, Mamma, I didn't. We've had . . . more important things to talk about." Rusi's voice was teasing but affectionate.

Khorshed smiled. "Yes, of course. No need to bore you youngsters with ancient history. Pardon the ravings of a middle-aged woman, Coomi."

There was a brief, awkward silence. In an effort to end it, Coomi said, "No, please, Khorshed Auntie, of course I'm interested. Who is Hilla? And what happened to Hilla's husband?"

Rusi groaned, but the two women ignored him. Khorshed leaned forward in her chair. "Hilla is my older sister. Her husband's name was Pervez. They were well-off. No children, and Pervez had a good job selling insurance. He was a good husband—my Hilla would just have to look at a gold bangle or a silk sari and, *bas,* Pervez would buy it for her. Treated her like a queen.

"But then Pervez fell in with this group of friends and they started turning his head with silly notions about Gandhiji and home rule and all. This was around 1945. They gave him all kinds of fanatical books and pamphlets to influence him. The freedom bug bit him hard. Stopped wearing a shirt, tie, and pants and started wearing those uncomfortable *khadi kurtas.* Can you imagine a Parsi dressing like that? Looked ridiculous in them. He and Hilla used to come over and he'd sit right where you're sitting on that sofa. Pervez and my husband would argue for hours. My husband would remind Pervez that he was a married man and that he had a responsibility to his wife. But he was like a man possessed. Wanted to give up his job and work full-time for independence only. 'Pervez,' I once said to him. 'Have you no *akkal* left? You think they'll make you prime minister or something if we get independence? Can't you see these people are making a fool out of you?' Well, he huffed and puffed and walked out of my house. Called me a traitor to my country. Can you imagine? Me, a traitor. What state secret did I ever sell anybody? But I made up with him the next day because of my poor sister. My Hilla was beside herself. Bit by bit, he was making her sell the gold *daagina* that she had brought as her dowry. All the money went to the Congress party. Finally, he did what she had long feared—left his job. One fine day, he left work at noon and never went back. Hilla begged him, but he had taken leave of his senses. While he was having fun with his sit-downs and hunger strikes and what all, Hilla was the one sitting at home, having to deal with creditors. I used to slip her a note out of my household expenses whenever I could."

Khorshed paused for a minute, but neither Coomi nor Rusi had the nerve to interrupt her. "Anyway, this went on for months. Then one day, they were having another pro-independence demonstration at Flora Fountain. Hilla begged Pervez not to go. Despite having little money, she even suggested going to the cinema, because before this madness gripped him, Pervez loved movies. 'Let's go to the pictures today, Pervez,' she said. 'Just spend the day together, the two of us.' But he looked at her like she had insulted God or something. There would be time for movies-fovies after independence, he said. And so off he went, dressed in his white *kurta*-pajama costume. Well, it was as Hilla had feared. The crowd got out of hand and the police opened a *laathi* charge. They say a policeman was beating one of the demonstrators, and Pervez, of course, had to jump in. From what we heard, he was cursing and attacking the *hawaldar* with his bare hands. Well, the fellow just swings his baton and brings it crashing down on Pervez's head. Just one blow. But Pervez was down."

"Baap re," Coomi said. "The poor man. What—did he die?" She looked at Rusi, but he sat with a deadpan look on his face. He'd heard the story numerous times before.

" 'Poor man'? If you're going to feel sorry, my dear, feel sorry for my innocent sister. No, Pervez didn't die. Not right then anyway. But the blow to his head made him go mad. Just cracked up, you could say. Hilla tried taking care of him at home, but it got too dangerous. Once, he came after her with a kitchen knife. That same day, my husband got him admitted to the hospital. Poor Hilla used to visit him every day, although she had to change two buses to do so. But then Pervez took to tearing his clothes, and he turned even more violent when he saw Hilla. They had to keep him strapped to the hospital bed whenever we would visit. But he was like a mad dog. Even now I can remember the *khoonas* with which he would look at Hilla, like he wanted to kill her. It was horrible. 'Pervez hates me,' she would sob. '*Mera khodai,* I don't know for what *paap* I'm being punished that my husband hates me so much.' Once, I walked into his room and caught him spitting at my Hilla. Spitting. I lost my temper. 'Pervez, stop this behavior this very minute,' I said. And you know, he stopped immediately and smiled this angelic smile. It was enough to melt even my heart. 'See, Hilla,' I said. 'He's not as mad as we think. Mostly, he is just acting.' But then he started crying softly. Even today, my hair stands up when I remember it. He cried as if his heart were a shattered windowpane. Somehow, I knew right then that he would not live too much longer. And surely, less than two weeks later, we got a call saying that Pervez was dead. He hung himself with some wire that he found."

There was a long silence. Coomi groped around for the perfect response to the gloomy tale, but she was at a loss for words. Fortunately, Rusi cleared his throat and seized hold of the conversation. "Speaking of the British, my daddy was quite a collector of things from the British time," he said. "*Ae,* Mamma, will you show Coomi some of Daddy's old currency notes?"

Mother and son got up to get the photo albums in which Khorshed kept the notes. Sitting alone for a moment in the living room, Coomi looked around at the austere space, idly thinking of how she would redecorate it. She heard a murmur of voices from the next room and strained to hear. "Seems to be a nice girl," Khorshed was saying. "A little *saamli,* not very fair-skinned, but nice all the same."

On that day, Coomi was relieved to pass muster. But in later years, as relations worsened between her and her mother-in-law, Coomi would remember Khorshed's mild criticism as something more emphatic and ominous. "Your mummy didn't like me from the first day," she once accused Rusi. "Blamed me for not being as light-skinned as you Bilimorias. Thought I wasn't good enough for her golden boy, at the first meeting, only."

"That's not fair, Coomi. Mamma has gone out of her way to accept you into the family. Besides, I had warned you."

They both knew what he meant. Before they married, Rusi made it clear that he expected his wife to respect his mother as much as he did. "My mamma raised me with love and kindness," he told her. "In return, I love and respect her. See, Coomi, all these years, it was just the two of us. Naturally, when a new person comes in, there will be some adjustment. But my mamma is basically a good and decent woman. You will have no problems with her. I don't even know whether to say this to you or not, but I believe in being honest, so I'll say it: I want none of the problems that other people living in joint families have. If you ever have a disagreement with my mummy, I will take her side. Blindly. I'm telling you this now because I don't want problems later. Even if I think you are right, I will back her up. Out of respect for her age. I love you very much, darling, but please don't ever make me choose between the two of you."

Bathed in the golden light of a Chowpatty Beach sunset, warmed by the ocean breeze, dizzy with love for this skinny, fierce young man by her side, she agreed. She understood. After her father left, she, too, had been raised by a single parent, after all. In her case, there had been three other people in the house. She could hardly imagine the closeness between Rusi and his mother, the two of them alone in that big flat all these years. "I love you because you love your mummy so much," she said. "Rusi, I promise. I will never make you choose. You'll see, we'll all live like one great big family. I am already having one mother. Now, I'll have another."

But it didn't work out that way. Khorshed was awkward and distant in Coomi's presence and seemed quite satisfied playing mother to only Rusi. Although Khorshed seldom said a critical word to Coomi's face, Coomi could never escape the feeling that Khorshed was watching her every move, waiting for her to stumble, ready to judge and criticize. If Coomi left the lights on in the kitchen or the dining room, Khorshed silently came up behind her and turned them off. Or she went over Coomi's housework after Coomi had already cleaned the house. Khorshed also kept control of the household finances and always seemed critical at the amount of money Coomi spent when she went grocery shopping. "That's all the change left?" she asked in a mild voice. And Coomi bristled, sensing an implicit criticism in her manner.

She could have dealt with Khorshed's wrath or open hostility, because Coomi knew how to use words like swords. But she was helpless against Khorshed's imperial gaze, the silently contemptuous way Coomi felt she looked at her. "I swear, my mother-in-law speaks with her eyebrows," Coomi complained to Sheroo. "Anything I do—sleep in late one day, yell at Binny, or, God forbid, forget to iron my husband's shirt—and that eyebrow gets raised. I wish whatever that woman was thinking, she'd say to my face. Instead, she waits till Rusi gets home and then complains to him. *He* must then talk to me. Heaven forbid that Queen Victoria of Bombay could tell me something directly. Khorshed Mamma thinks this is a civilized way to handle things, but I think it's plain underhanded and sneaky. Poisoning my husband against me."

Khorshed's manner grated especially when Coomi's brothers stopped by her house for a visit. "*Saala,* I feel like I'm walking into a morgue or an ice factory when I enter your house," Fali said jokingly. But there was enough truth in the statement for Coomi to feel the sting of his words. She seethed over how frostily Khorshed greeted her brothers when they stopped by, how primly she talked to them, until they shuffled awkwardly on the sofa, suddenly aware of the breakfast stain on their shirts, their dull, unpolished shoes, their loud, gruff voices. She was angry at her brothers then. Don't let her intimidate you, she wanted to shout at them. She's no better than you are; don't let her convince you otherwise. But she could not embarrass them by telling them she had noticed their embarrassment. Instead, she indulged in small talk, laughed and joked with them as if blissfully unaware of the tension in the room, all the time painfully conscious of Khorshed's watchful gaze.

"Why do you always sit there when my brothers come to visit me?" she said to Khorshed after she had been married for two years. "After all, it's *me* they come to see."

Khorshed's eyes brimmed with tears. "I didn't know it was causing you a problem. After all, they are visitors in my late husband's house. It is my duty to see they don't misbehave."

" 'Misbehave'? What are my brothers, wild dogs? What do you think they'll do, Khorshed Mamma, steal your dead husband's picture from the wall?"

"Don't you dare. Don't you dare take my husband's name in vain. He was worth more than you will ever know."

When Rusi came home from work that night, he went directly into his mother's room, as was his practice. It was a custom Coomi hated. Khorshed often relayed the events of the day to Rusi, and Coomi felt cheated at not being the first one to have her husband's attention and ear. Then Rusi came into their room, a worried look on his face. "Mamma tells me there's a problem," he began.

Coomi let out a shriek. "*Bas,* enough, no more. Mamma always tells you there's a problem. And usually the problem is me. Why doesn't she talk to me *khoollam-khoolla* about what troubles her?" Before Rusi could stop her, she rushed into a startled Khorshed's room. "I thought our little argument today was over, but of course it wasn't. Why is it that you never say anything to my face, even though we are alone all day long?" she asked, her eyes blazing. "Why do you do this *guss-puss* with your son every evening, poisoning him against me? If you didn't want him to marry me, you should've said something earlier. Lots of others would've gladly married me. This plotting behind my back, I cannot stand. From this day on, whatever you want to say, you say directly to me, you understand?"

Khorshed looked from one to the other and then burst into tears. Rusi was transfixed at the sight of his mother's tears, horrified at the pain and hurt he saw on her face. Khorshed's tears reminded him of those awful days after his father's death, and he was furious with Coomi for making him relive those days. Placing himself between the two women, he turned to his wife. "Coomi, enough," he said in a fierce low voice, which scared Coomi. "Don't you dare stand here and insult my mummy. You better control your bleddy tongue, right now." It was the angriest Coomi had ever seen Rusi and it shook her up. It was also the first time that Rusi spent the night away from her, sleeping on the couch in the living room.

The next morning, Coomi rose early and prepared *rava* for breakfast. Khorshed loved the sugared wheat dish, and Coomi fried a liberal amount of golden raisins and cashew nuts to sprinkle on top. She waited until mother and son joined her at the breakfast table. "Khorshed Mamma, I'm sorry," she said. "I don't know what got into me. I've been emotional lately, I think. Please to forgive me."

Khorshed looked embarrassed. "Please, please. We're family members. Sometimes, angry words are spoken. This has been a hard adjustment for all of us. Let's carry on. Everything is okay."

But a week later, there was another fight. Over lunch, Khorshed commented on how high the previous month's water bill had been, and Coomi immediately assumed the comment was directed at her. "If you like, I will start taking baths at my mother's house," she said. "That way, it will save you a few paise each month."

"Coomi, stop this nonsense. All I was saying was how expensive everything has become in Bombay."

"Oh, change your story, change your story. But Khorshed Mamma, you can't fool me anymore. I know your barbs and cuts well by now."

This time, Coomi waited for three days before making up with Khorshed. Other bursts of anger followed, along with bouts of recrimination and apologies. Over time, the quarrels grew more frequent and the apologies never followed. "I don't know what to do, *bossie,*" Rusi confided to Soli Contractor. "Coomi is more and more convinced that Mamma hates her guts. And Mamma, God bless her, says she's bewildered by that, but frankly, *yaar,* she does little to change Coomi's mind. Some days, I feel like a bone being pulled at by two dogs."

"Women," Soli said. "Women."

Busy with their own lives, Coomi's brothers began to visit the Bilimoria home less frequently. But Coomi was convinced this was because of Khorshed's intimidating presence. As Coomi grew more defensive about her own family, she brought more and more of her old habits and behaviors into her new home. "So what if we shout and scream at one another like savages?" she told Rusi. "We are *bhola-bhala* people; we don't carry a grudge like some people I could mention. *Bas,* we say what's on our minds and then it's over. At least our hearts are clean, even if our fingernails may not always be."

"It's over for you, maybe," Rusi said excitedly. "But what about the person at the other end? You release the arrow from your bow and, you're right, you no longer are carrying the arrow around. But what about the person whose heart it is now stuck in?"

But no matter how hard they tried, neither could make the other see his or her point of view. Once, frustrated and hot from one of their many agonizing arguments, they made love, furiously, desperately, silently struggling like wild animals in each other's arms. Afterward, with Rusi cradling her, Coomi broke down hard. "I don't know why we can't go past a few weeks without a fight. So different we are—like two people speaking different languages. But wasn't there a time when we spoke the same language?"

After her birth, three years into their marriage, Binny became the glue that held her parent's marriage together. They both adored their little girl, and Binny was an instinctive peacemaker, a child whose need for love was so great and naked that it often shamed them into making up with each other. Once, after a particularly heated argument with Rusi, Coomi was busying herself in the kitchen, when she felt a tug on her dress. "Come on, *na,* Mummy," Binny said, dragging Coomi from the kitchen. "Daddy has a headache. Let's both of us give him some *kissy-koti* to help him feel good." Reluctantly, Coomi allowed herself to be pulled out of the kitchen. By the time they reached the bedroom, Coomi was smiling despite herself. When Rusi looked up at them, she shrugged. "What to do? Little lovebug here won't leave me in peace until I give you a kiss." They grinned over Binny's head, their argument forgotten. When they went to bed that night, they let Binny sleep between them. Coomi fell asleep marveling again at her daughter's peacemaking abilities. Before Binny drifted off to sleep, Coomi whispered to her the song she'd made up when Binny was six months old:

> *"Good night my darling and God bless you*
> *And happy dreams and angels guard you*
> *And I love you and I love you*
> *And pom pom pom pom pom pom POM."*

When they didn't feel anything for each other as man and wife, Coomi and Rusi were still proud to step into the world as Binny's parents, each of them holding one of her hands. Binny was wise. When she was three, she looked up one morning from the banana she was eating for breakfast. "Mummy," she said seriously. "Who put the banana inside the peel?" Coomi felt such tenderness for her daughter at that moment that she thought her breast milk was going to start flowing again. Binny was funny; she made her parents laugh. She also made them angry, frightened, worried, sad, proud, joyous, giddy. Together, they attended her parent-teacher conferences and school plays. Together, they chided her when she occasionally brought a bad report card home. Together, they anxiously paced their apartment the night Rusi finally allowed Binny to attend a late-night party when she turned seventeen.

"You know that famous line from that movie: 'We'll always have Paris'?" Rusi said to his wife that night as they waited for their daughter to come home. "I feel like that about Binny. That no matter what happens, we'll always have Binny. I'll always love you as the woman who gave me Binny."

"*Bas,* that's all? That's the only reason to love me?" she asked playfully.

Rusi sighed. "No, Coomi. Many other reasons to love you. But darling, that temper. You must promise to control it better."

"I promise, Rusi. I'll try harder."

"Sometimes, I look at our daughter, and although she's almost a grown woman and all, I feel the same magic I did the day she was born. As if I still cannot believe that she's here. That we made her. My one true, unqualified success."

But then Binny grew up and went away. Then it was the original triad again—Coomi, Rusi, and Khorshed, older now and even more dependent on her son. Khorshed had tried to prevent her beloved granddaughter from leaving Bombay to go study in England, but Rusi understood that the old woman was working from a place of fear and need. "Let her go, Mamma," he said to his mother. "Give her your blessings. No opportunities for her in this city. Let her go and explore her options." He held back his own tears, wrestled with his own fears and needs while he said those words.

"All those years ago, everybody wanted the English out of India.

Now we are willingly sending our children to England and America. What a strange world," Khorshed whispered.

But under her son's cajoling, Khorshed relented. Coomi was a different story. The thought of losing Binny, and of living in the Wadia Baug flat with only Rusi and Khorshed, was unbearable to her. "Why must Binny go abroad?" she asked Rusi. "Binny is like a plant we have watered and fed daily, and now, when it's ready to bloom, it must be transplanted in someone else's garden? She is our only child, Rusi, our own flesh and blood. It's not like we have ten other children. You may be so hard-hearted, *baba,* but I cannot bear to be parted from my only daughter."

She and Binny had not really been close since the time Binny had turned thirteen, but that inconvenient fact was now forgotten as Coomi rallied to persuade Binny that Bombay was good enough for her. "Millions of people live here, go to school, get Ph.D.s., become lawyers and doctors. Our colleges are second to none. Why do you need to go abroad to be successful? That father of yours has filled your ears with all his nonsense."

Binny listened. She did not contradict her mother. She did not say: I am tired of being the glue that holds you and Daddy together. I have already given you my entire childhood. You do not have the right to expect more than that from me. I am afraid that as long as I live here, you will keep using me to patch your marriage together. Now it is time for you to find out if the two of you have a future without me. I will no longer be the third leg that holds your marriage up. And there's more. I, too, have my own dreams and ambitions. You see, I love physics. After I stopped believing in God as a teenager, I would stand at the window at night and talk to the stars. Do you remember? I want to learn everything there is about the universe. And if I live here, in this house, with its walls dripping with your frustrations and Dad's sorrow, I will never know another universe. Wadia Baug will consume me, be the only reality I know. And I must know more. Do you understand? I must, for the sake of my soul, for the sake of my life. My life. Do you understand?

Binny heard her mother out in silence. Then, when the time came, she fled.

Two years after Binny's departure, Khorshed Bilimoria got sick with the flu. A week later, she died at Parsi General Hospital. Suddenly, there was a funeral to plan. Binny wanted to fly back, despite the fact that she had exams that week. Coomi agreed, glad for a chance to see her daughter, no matter what the circumstances. But Rusi put his foot down. "Your studies are the most important thing right now, Binny," he said. "You loved Granny while she was alive, and she knew that. Take satisfaction from that. Nothing you can do for her now. I know she would want you to concentrate on your studies. Do well in your exams, for her sake."

Khorshed's funeral. The hunched men in their white *daglis,* the wailing women in their white saris, the mumbling, shuffling *dastoors* who prayed in their nasal twang, the moth-eaten, sunken pallbearers, the sandy-colored dog who was made to circle the dead body ritualistically. It was all so heartbreaking.

But Rusi's farewell to his departed mother was more heartbreaking than anything else that day.

An hour before the actual ceremony, Coomi followed Rusi as he walked aimlessly around the Tower of Silence, waiting for the funeral to start. She understood that Rusi had to get away from the wailing women, all of whom tsk-tsked and talked endlessly about poor Khorshed and what a sad life she'd had, losing her beloved husband so young. Coomi followed her husband down the green trails. Located in the heart of Bombay, the green acres of the Tower of Silence were an oasis of tranquillity, an almost surreal contrast to the noise and snarling chaos that lay outside. Trees and wildflowers grew everywhere and muffled the distant sounds of traffic. As they walked, they spotted several of the wild peacocks that lived on the grounds. Coomi drank in the serenity of the place with the fierce, intense thirst of a city dweller whose landscape usually yielded only cement and plaster. She noticed the red cloud of dust that they made as they walked, noticed the deep blue of the cloudless Bombay sky. Despite the slight incline of the terrain, Coomi could feel herself breathing deeper, could sense her heart rate slowing down. "It's peaceful here," she murmured, and Rusi nodded. But even as the words left her mouth, Coomi heard a flutter of wings above them and looked up, to see the sinister wings of a large vulture as it flew overhead. She half-turned toward Rusi, knowing instinctively that her husband was thinking the same thought that had flashed through her mind—that this bird and its companions would soon feast on Khorshed's shriveled flesh. Since only the professional pallbearers were allowed to approach the huge well into which the dead bodies were lowered, neither Coomi nor Rusi had actually seen the site. But they had heard enough stories to have a good mental picture of vultures greedily circling the well, and upon seeing one of those birds, she knew that Rusi, too, had felt the horror, the same sickening pit in the stomach. Coomi remembered that a few years ago, some of the non-Parsi tenants of the wealthy neighborhood that surrounded the Tower of Silence had complained about what they considered to be a barbaric custom. At a public meeting called by the Parsi Panchayat, these residents told horror stories about birds dropping off objects that looked suspiciously like a finger or a toe on the windowsills of their expensive high-rise apartments. Some of the younger Parsis had shared their revulsion, had argued that this ancient way of disposing of the dead might have worked on the open plains of Persia but was unsanitary and dangerous when practiced in the middle of a bustling city. But as usual, the doddering old men prevailed. As usual, custom and tradition triumphed over common sense.

But no time now for these thoughts, because upon seeing the vulture, Rusi had stopped abruptly and was gazing off into the distance. As Coomi watched, his face folded with grief and he began to cry in great heaving sobs. His anguish was so immense that Coomi knew that he was doing more than saying good-bye to his mother. Rusi was also crying for the father he had lost so unexpectedly, for the marital bliss he had barely experienced, for the daughter he had sacrificed, for the business that had never soared, for a life that was a litany of griefs and disappointments. The sound of his sobbing merged with the twitter of the birds. Coomi tried to say something kind and comforting, but her words shriveled under the force of his immense grief. Instead, she took the two steps that separated her from her husband and merely held him, held him tightly, as if to protect him from the intruding world. But this only made him cry even harder. "Oh my God," Rusi sobbed. "Oh my God, this awful pain." It had been a long time since Rusi had cried in Coomi's presence, and the sound of his sobbing shocked her. As Rusi trembled in her arms, Coomi felt as if she were holding a proud but broken animal. But despite her sadness at seeing her usually remote husband so helpless in her arms, some part of Coomi sang. It's not too late, she said to herself. All I have to do is reach for him and he comes. Still. And another, more fierce thought: I can help him. I can save him.

But the moment came and went. Seconds later, she felt Rusi's heart hardening like cement as he realized that he was in the arms of the enemy. He strained against the arms that only a moment ago had provided such comfort, and when he detached himself, his face bore the distant look she had come to know so well. "Sorry, so sorry. Um, probably should go back," he said stiffly. "People are waiting. The *dastoors* must have come by now."

As they walked back, Coomi grew cold and afraid at the thought of attending her mother-in-law's funeral. She was suddenly very aware of the long and terrible history she shared with Khorshed. About the many times she had wished for the old woman's death, the numerous times she had told Rusi that his mother was a thorn in her side. She wondered if Rusi was remembering all this now. If so, he would not be the only one. Coomi had shared her bitterness with so many of the neighbors, friends, and relatives who were gathered for the funeral. Instinctively, her eyes searched for Dosamai, before she remembered that the old woman was at home nursing a cold. But many of the people gathered here knew about Coomi's complaints. Just a week before Khorshed got ill, Coomi had complained about the old woman to Amy. "Old as the hills, she is, but still she pokes her nose into my business," she'd fretted. For almost twenty-five years, the mourners at the funeral had been divided into two camps, hers or Khorshed's. For decades, they'd heard her tearful stories about how Khorshed had stolen her husband from her, how she would not find any peace until one of them was dead. And now Khorshed was dead. And the eyes of all the relatives and the neighbors were upon her. To see how she mourned. And Rusi was leaning away from her, remote as a star, acting as if the woman beside him were a distant acquaintance. He would be no help at all.

Somehow, she got through the funeral. She sat in one of the middle rows, surrounded by members of her own family, trying to look as small and invisible as possible. It was easy, too, because all eyes were fixed upon Rusi.

Because throughout the ceremony, Rusi stood not too far away from his dead mother and prayed out loud for her soul, prayed the Avesta, the holy book of the Parsis, in that deep, beautiful, melodious voice of his. Somewhere between a song and a chant, Rusi's hypnotic rhythm drowned out the petty, mumbling prayers of the hired priests and cast such a spell on those gathered that even the white-saried old women were too stunned to wail. It was beautiful. It was profound. And they had never seen anything quite like it. There stood Rusi, gray-haired, erect, proud and dignified as the stone lions at the entrance of Wadia Baug. An old warrior, praying out loud for the soul of his dead mother. Singing out his love, his ancient grief, not afraid of sharing this thick love with the world. Even Zenobia, the neighborhood atheist, was moved. This is the power of the true believer, she thought to herself. This is the power of love. And for a moment, she was envious.

Rusi's loud singsong chant reached even the non-Parsi guests sitting on wooden benches outside the cabin where the ceremony was going on. Parsi custom did not allow them to witness the ceremony. Rusi apologized to them before the start of the ceremony, but they put their hands on his shoulder and said they understood. When Rusi's eulogy for his mother reached them, they, too, felt the power of those mysterious ancient words that few knew the meaning of. "When I die, I also want somebody to pray over me like this," Maniben whispered to her husband. "Khorshedben's soul will go straight to heaven after this."

Coomi was relieved that Rusi's performance had taken the focus off of her. But now, with the ceremony over, she could feel everybody's watchful eyes on her. She missed Binny dreadfully at that moment. The others waited as she and Rusi went up to pay their last respects, to bow before Khorshed's body and put *lobaan,* frankincense and sandalwood, into the small fire that blazed in an urn before the body. "She looks peaceful," she murmured to Rusi, and he nodded, his eyes filling with tears. As they got up in unison, she could feel all the narrow, penetrating eyes riveting back on Rusi, and she was grateful.

But Coomi was also embarrassed by the nakedness of her husband's love for his mother. This was the final display of that love, and it had been for the world to see. Despite her death, Khorshed had once again managed to steal Rusi away from her, and this time in the most public of ways. Even in death, Khorshed had triumphed. She had had the last laugh. As Coomi bowed her head in respect before Khorshed's sleeping form, she could not shake off the feeling that she was also bowing her head in submission and in defeat.

It was eerily quiet in the apartment in the days that followed the funeral. Rusi sat in his rocking chair and gazed out of the window for hours, never once initiating a conversation. Or he busied himself sorting his mother's papers and going through her things. Coomi was at a loss as to how to help him through his grief. "Anything for me to do?" she asked as she stood at the entrance of Khorshed's room. Without Rusi's having said a word, Coomi got the strong impression that he did not want her to enter his mother's bedroom, did not want her to defile it with her presence. He stared at her uncomprehendingly for a long moment. "No, nothing to do," he answered at last.

Coomi suspected that Rusi was silently blaming her for his not being present when his mother died. She chaffed at the injustice of that unspoken accusation. I was not responsible for what happened on that last night at the hospital, she told herself. "It's a pity, what happened in the hospital," she ventured to say, still standing in the doorway. He sat still for so long that she thought he hadn't heard her.

But just as she was ready to repeat the sentence, he said, "Wasn't meant to be. Just my *naseeb.*" Instead of reassuring her, the words made her feel defensive.

Her need to talk to someone about the events of that night wrestled with her new resolution to attempt a reconciliation with Rusi. Ultimately, habit won over good intentions and drew her to Dosamai's house a week after the funeral. It was Coomi's first visit since Khorshed's death and Dosamai was eager to critique Rusi's performance at the funeral. The old gossip was annoyed at Rusi because his eulogy for his mother had touched and silenced even his usual critics, depriving Dosamai of her favorite target. Just a few days before, Jiloo had cut Dosamai off by saying, "Say what you will, Dosamai, that Rusi is a good man. How many men you know who are loving their mothers so openly and proudly? Yes, his marriage may be a flop, but he's not the *badmash* we make him out to be, I don't believe."

So Dosamai greeted Coomi eagerly, hoping for news she could use to counteract this new feeling of goodwill toward Rusi. "How are things at home?" the old woman asked.

"Fine. The house feels a little empty. Rusi's been very quiet, so even when he's home, I feel like I'm all alone all day." Coomi knew better than to tell Dosamai her hopes of reconciling with Rusi.

"Speaking of Rusi, I was thinking, It's good that Rusi loves his mummy and all, but it was a little too much at the funeral, no?" Dosamai said. "Meaning, why hire *dastoors* to pray if he was going to drown out their voices with his praying? Such a show-off, your husband."

Coomi knew better than to contradict Dosamai. So, although her heart rebelled at this mischaracterization of Rusi's motives, she remained silent. Besides, she needed to empty herself of the bubbling resentment she had carried to Dosamai's flat.

"I keep thinking of the last night that Khorshed Mamma was alive," Coomi said. "Being in the hospital with her, watching that respirator go up and down, up and down. The noise of that machine. Never will I forget it. And Dosamai, this part I haven't told you about yet. Khorshed Mamma opened her eyes once at about three A.M. and groaned Rusi's name. Just an hour before that, I had reasoned with Rusi, told him there was no need for both of us to be sitting up all night on those hard wooden chairs. You know what those rooms at Parsi General are like. Told him to go get some sleep on the bench in the hallway. And look at my *kismet*—an hour later, Khorshed Mamma asks for Rusi and I run to the hall and wake him up. But by the time we get back to the room, she has her eyes shut and is sleeping peaceful as a baby. Rusi calls her name several times, 'Mammaji, my mamma,' he calls, but she doesn't open her eyes. And Rusi gives me a look of such *khoonas* and distrust that I wished I were the one dying instead of Khorshed Mamma. As if I did something deliberate to keep him away from his mother. He just sits up in that chair the rest of the night, not daring to leave his mother's side. But she never opens her eyes again. And you mark my words, one of these days I'm going to be blamed for that, too."

"What to do, *deekra,*" Dosamai said. "For some of us, it is just our lot to get blamed for other people's mischief. Same thing with that cow that my son has married. Somehow, I only get blamed for everything that happens to her. Anyway, I have made some new mixtures. Take some with you; they'll help you sleep better."

Coomi left Dosamai's flat that day carrying one of Dosamai's herbal tinctures for anxiety and stress. But she also left without the usual satisfaction she got after letting the venom and anger seep out of her heart. She took that to be a sign of progress. If she were to make up with Rusi, Coomi knew, gossiping about her husband to Dosamai was a habit she would have to wean herself off. The fact that she felt dissatisfied after visiting Dosamai was a good sign. It was time to stop perfecting her outrage, polishing it like a stone, under Dosamai's careful tutelage. She resolved to avoid visiting the old gossip for a few weeks.

Despite Rusi's disinterest and absentmindedness, a tattered hope fluttered in Coomi's heart, like a piece of paper blowing along the sands of Chowpatty Beach. In their middle age, perhaps she and Rusi could finally learn to be man and wife. Nobody stood between them now. No longer did she have to feel as if a pair of eyes was watching her every move, waiting for her to fail. She could—would—rescue Rusi from the whirlpool of grief he had been drowning in since his mother's death. Coomi knew better than to console her husband with the easy patter of professional mourners: She was old. At least she didn't suffer. She died a peaceful death. All of us have to go sometime. She noticed how Rusi gritted his teeth when well-meaning neighbors recited these rehearsed lines. No, she would not say those words, because she understood that death at any age is still an insult to life, an affront to those who must keep living. Instead, she would rescue Rusi a day at a time, until someday he would have a treacherous thought: Is this how it would have been? Could marriage have really been this wonderful, this smooth, happy ride, if Mamma had never been in the picture?

Once Rusi had time to come to terms with his mother's death, perhaps they would patch things up. Start life again, just the two of them, in a way that had never been possible until now. Maybe they could go to Khandala or some nearby place for a few days, just to get away from the hurt and grief that hung like lanterns from the walls of their flat. Something like a honeymoon period. After all, despite all his faults, Rusi was a good man. As much as Coomi had resented her husband's devotion to his mother, she also admired it. Not too many of the men she knew would have taken care of an elderly parent the way Rusi had. Her own brothers, for example, loved their mother, but they were not above yelling at the old woman to shut up when she got on their nerves. And now, with Khorshed out of the way, maybe Rusi could learn to transfer all his love and caring to her. God knows, she had prayed for that long enough.

So Coomi went to work. At night, she held Rusi in her arms, trying to ignore the fact that he moved stiffly away from her the first chance he got. Using Khorshed's old recipes, she cooked Rusi's favorite dishes, despite the fact that he ate little. Within his earshot, she described her dead mother-in-law in affectionate, nostalgic tones, trying to ignore the look of amazement on the face of the person she was talking to. On Khorshed's first-month death anniversary, she got up early in the morning and silently accompanied Rusi to the fire temple. She tried not to notice, willed her eyes not to click on the picture of Rusi sitting on the wooden bench, as far away from her as he could. Instead, she closed her eyes and tried to pray for her husband to thaw toward her. Please, God, she thought. Please, please, please, please. Coomi even tried to fight against her chronic tardiness, so that when they went out, Rusi had to wait only a half hour for her to get dressed, instead of the usual hour or two. This last change was dramatic enough that several of their friends commented on it.

But there was a harsh fact to be faced: They had forgotten how to be a couple. There was no longer any shared intimacy between Rusi and her. No matter how hard she tried, Rusi was as stiff as a marble statue around her. All his responses to her were forced, his words stilted and abrupt. "Rusi," she said one afternoon. "I bought some fresh pomfret today. A good price, it was. What dish would you like for dinner?" He looked at her disinterestedly. "Doesn't matter," he said with a shrug. "You cook whatever you're fond of. I can eat anything."

For weeks after Khorshed's funeral, Coomi sifted through the sands of time to rediscover the fierce young man she had loved and married, but the tide had washed him away. In his place was a gray-haired man with eyes that were unbearably sad. She had to look away from those eyes because of the piercing knowledge that she was at least in part responsible for that sadness.

"Yahoo!"

Rusi and Coomi both turned toward the stage to watch the singer. As they turned, their eyes met and, for an unrecognizable moment, they smiled at each other. Coomi knew that she and her husband were briefly united by the same happy thought: Binny. *"Yahoo! Chaye koye muje jungalee kahe."* "So what if someone calls me crazy." The middle-aged singer with the thinning hair sang the popular movie hit from the 1960s with a desperate stab at exuberance that normally would have made Coomi turn away in embarrassment. That was the trouble with Parsi weddings, Coomi often railed. Everybody concentrated so much on the menu that nobody paid the slightest attention to which musicians they hired. Even a man as sophisticated as Jimmy Kanga had hired a two-bit band for his only son's wedding.

But right now, Coomi approved of the choice of song. Although Rusi was currently standing a few feet away from her and talking to a tall, handsome-looking woman whom Coomi did not recognize, she knew that the exuberant chorus of the song had transported her husband to a happier time. It also connected Rusi to her, no matter how briefly. They had exchanged a look, a smile of recognition, had both thought of Binny at the same moment. That made her glad, so much so that she forgot to blink and take a snapshot of Rusi talking to a strange, attractive woman.

It was a nice song, a little manic, brimming with energy. Sort of like Rusi in his younger days. Coomi remembered that a young Binny had pleaded with them to take her to see a rerun of *Junglee,* the movie the song was from. Binny loved the old song, would stand in front of the mirror wriggling her hips and singing the words in her broken Hindi. And when Rusi came home from work, Binny hurled herself at her father, letting out a bloodcurdling cry of *"Yahoo."* No matter how often Rusi pretended to jump and quiver with fright, the joy of scaring her unsuspecting father never dimmed for Binny.

In the movie theater, Coomi and Rusi laughed in delight, watching Binny bop her head and sing along to the song. Throughout the movie, which Rusi and Coomi had first seen years ago, Rusi kept a restraining hand on Binny's knee. It was Rusi's job to make sure Binny stayed in her seat during a movie. She was at the age where she took movies literally, believed that the actors were flesh-and-blood people up on a stage. If a screen character said, "Let's dance," that was all the invitation Binny needed. She would turn to her father, tug at his tie, and say loudly, "Come on, Daddy. He's asking us to dance."

It was worse during the barroom fight scenes. Binny tried valiantly to help the good guys. Turning around in her movie seat, she tried to pry it loose, so that she could hurl her chair at the bad guys, as everybody in the bar seemed to be doing. Binny never understood why her parents did not do the same.

Coomi's task was even more demanding. Binny could not distinguish one actor from another. However, she did understand that most movies had a good guy and a bad guy, and since Rusi mostly wanted to see Westerns or World War II movies, that was a helpful insight. Problem was, the good guys and the bad guys looked the same to Binny. If the bad guy had a mustache or an evil scar, that helped. But the war movies were perplexing. To Binny's undiscriminating eyes, the Germans didn't look any different from the Americans. The adults understood that the Germans were the ones who mostly said just one word, *"Ja."* And sometimes, when they were really pushed, *"Ja, ja."* But to Binny's unsophisticated ears, all foreign accents sounded strange.

For Coomi, this lack of discrimination was an unhappy state of affairs. Minutes into a movie, Binny fixed her big unblinking eyes on her mother. Then the dreaded question rolled off her tongue. "Mummy, is this a good man or a bad man?"

"Good man," Coomi answered, hoping to nip it in the bud. "Can't you see, *beta,* he's the hero?"

A second or two passed.

"And this man, Mummy. Who's he? The good man or the bad man?"

"Same man, Binny. The hero, I told you. Be quiet now and watch the picture."

A moment of blissful silence. Then the little voice again, insistent as a hammer at dawn. "Who is this man, Mummy? Good or bad?"

Rusi leaned over. "So sorry. Tell you what, Coomi. If you just answer her questions today, I promise we'll come back next week to see the film again. I'll talk to Mamma about keeping Binny for a few hours."

And so Coomi spent the movie saying alternately, "Good man. . . . Bad man. . . . Bad—no—good man. . . . Good man."

After awhile, they stumbled upon a cure. Coomi figured out that if she kept an endless supply of potato chips ready, she could intercept Binny's merciless questioning. Carrying a handbag with bags of chips in it, Coomi waited for the movie to start and then handed Binny the first bag. The more chips she popped in her mouth, the fewer questions popped out. When Binny was done with one bag, Coomi swiftly took the empty bag away and handed her a new one. A few weeks later, Coomi read a magazine article about Chinese peasant women who drugged their infants with opium while they worked in the fields. She felt a twinge of guilt before she could even remember why.

Wish I could get those years back, Coomi now thought. No matter what kind of a husband Rusi had been, he was a good father. And Binny had been a lovely child, not a trace of the sullen teenager she would become. How close she felt to Rusi the day Binny was born. How shimmeringly fragile and sweet that moment when Rusi lay beside her in her hospital bed and they looked at their strange, beautiful daughter in awe.

No hair. That's the first thing she noticed about Binny. Bald as a spinning top. Good lung power, too. Amazing what a din someone so small could make. With the nurse's help, she held the baby to her breast for the first time and felt a tremor run through her. After the feeding, she insisted on holding her baby some more. Her daughter felt so good in her arms as she lay sleeping. And she was hers and Rusi's. She had given birth to this healthy, pretty, greedy baby in her arms. That was the amazing part. She got to keep her. She was going to take her home.

Rusi was anxiously waiting for them in their hospital room when Coomi was finally wheeled in. She smiled at her husband as she entered the room. Rusi's eyes were bloodshot and he looked as tired as Coomi felt. "Good job, Coomi," he said inanely as he bent down to kiss her, and despite her fatigue, she felt an urge to laugh. For a second, they grinned at each other like conspirators. But Coomi could tell that Rusi was dying to hold the baby, so, reluctantly, she parted with her.

For a moment, Rusi looked lost, as if he didn't know what to do. Then instinct took over. He cooed at the baby as he paced the hospital room. Next, he tested all of the baby's fingers one by one, wriggling them up and down. Then he tested the ears, clicking his fingers on each side. "She's a perfectly put together baby," he declared happily. "If she has her mother's looks and her mother's brains, she will be all right."

Later that day, with both of the baby's grandmothers in the room, Rusi leaned over his daughter's crib. He fished into his pocket and took out a bunch of keys. He jingled them near the baby's right ear and then laid them down in the crib. "These are yours, sweetheart," he whispered to her. "These are the keys to the house, to the factory. Everything I own now belongs to you. You already have the keys to my heart."

Coomi smiled now, thinking of those happy times. At that moment, they knew so little about what awaited them. No knowledge then about the fact that Coomi wouldn't be able to have any more children. About how valiantly Rusi would try to fight his disappointment at the wilting away of yet another dream; about how miserably he would fail at hiding his disappointment at having no more children. No idea then that Khorshed, not content with having the devotion of her son, would also lay claim to Binny's heart. No hint of the fact that the triad of Khorshed-Rusi-Binny would make her feel like a stranger, an outsider in her own house.

It was Khorshed who named her first grandchild. During the ride home from the hospital, it was Khorshed who rode in the front seat with Binny, while Coomi alternately dozed and gazed out of the window in the backseat. Before Coomi and Rusi entered the flat with their precious cargo, it was Khorshed who performed the Parsi welcoming ceremony for Wadia Baug's newest resident. Khorshed put a small red *tikka* on her granddaughter's forehead. Then she took a raw egg and circled it around Binny's tiny head before smashing it on the threshold. Next, she took a dried coconut and cracked it at the side of the door. Finally, the house was ready for Binny. "Enter with your right foot," Khorshed told Coomi.

In the euphoria of those early days, Coomi was expansive, generous, ready to share her daughter with her widowed mother-in-law. She welcomed the fact that Khorshed watched Binny when she and Rusi went out in the evenings; basked in the glow of Khorshed's unabashed pride in her granddaughter. But as Binny got older, Coomi began to see the trinity of Khorshed, Rusi, and Binny as a threat, in collusion against her. If she threatened to whip Binny for bringing home a poor report card, the old woman would intervene. Would get emotional, right in front of the child. If Binny needed extra lunch money, she took to asking her grandmother. Khorshed complained about Coomi's extravagant household budget, but she always had a rupee or two for Binny. But what really dismayed Coomi was that, like her father, Binny was also sensitive, moody, easily devastated by an unkind word. She tried to toughen up her daughter but came up against the raw power of genetics. She could not diminish Binny's tendency to be hurt any more than she could change her own capacity to wound her daughter unwittingly with her words. Coomi deeply regretted her teenaged daughter's growing estrangement from her. But to have acknowledged her role in that estrangement would have devastated her. It was less painful to blame Khorshed for the distance between them. She complained to whoever would listen that she had given birth to Binny and Khorshed had adopted her a few hours later. Just like that. Without asking for permission, without any words exchanged. No contract, no signature. Just the authority of blood. "They stole my only child away from me," she hissed to Dosamai. "Mother and son, they stole my daughter, until she, too, acts like a stone statue in my presence. Even Binny's husband, Jack, was reserved with me when they were visiting us here a few years back. Polite but reserved. Not jovial the way he is with Rusi. They think I don't notice, but I notice everything."

Coomi watched as Bomi Mistry slid up to where Rusi was talking to the unknown woman. Before she could check herself, she felt glad that Bomi had interrupted Rusi's conversation. Rusi had been standing a little too close to the woman for her liking. That sudden spurt of jealousy did not take Coomi by surprise. She wished she could feel toward Rusi the same frosty indifference he exhibited toward her, but she couldn't. Whether she was blaming him or praising him, loving him or hating him, Coomi was still very aware of her husband's presence in her life. She often prayed to be blessed with the kind of deadness that Rusi showed in her presence, but her prayers were not answered. Coomi needed to feel *something*—even if only self-pity and bitterness and a sense of being aggrieved—in order to stay alive. Years ago, she had come across the phrase "a strange and tangled love" and had immediately thought how well it described her feelings toward Rusi. She'd grimaced, knowing how startled Rusi would be to hear that his wife felt any kind of love toward him. But then, Rusi had never understood her, never appreciated the red-hot blood that pumped through her heart. That thought made her feel superior.

Another thing Rusi didn't know about her: that she watched everything. Took pictures with her eyes. For instance, Rusi did not know that she had been watching his face while Bomi told that horrible story about poor Kashmira being robbed. She had read every expression on Rusi's face—his disgust at the savagery of the robbery, his loathing of a city where such events occurred daily, his sudden, awful gladness that Binny had escaped Bombay. She could read him like a book. All the while she had been talking to "Killer Breath" Tehmi, trying not to breathe while Tehmi talked, she had been following Rusi with her eyes. She had seen him glance up at the pitiless sky as if asking for help, had known from the bright, wet, expansive look in his eyes that he was slightly drunk. Rusi always got sentimental when he was drunk. She was sure he didn't know that about himself.

Khorshed had been dead for six years now. Binny had been gone for eight. It was just Rusi and Coomi in the house. Her prayers about wanting to be alone with her husband had been answered, but they had been answered by a God with a twisted sense of humor. Coomi had never been more angry at Rusi than in the weeks following Khorshed's death. She had really tried to win him over, but Rusi had rebuffed every overture. A missed opportunity. And now, a gap that stretched between them, wide as the Arabian Sea. And in the middle of this gap, a question mark: Why had things gone so horribly wrong? If dolts like Bomi and Sheroo could have a happy marriage, why not them? For all her faults, Khorshed had not been mean or tyrannical, the way so many Parsi mother-in-laws could be. Binny had been a beautiful child—curious, brimming with zest and laughter. Rusi was basically a kind, decent man. And she, Coomi, had come to this marriage with so much hope and expectation. She had been given so much. Why had she ended up with so little?

A few weeks earlier, Coomi had visited the fire temple in the afternoon. There was no one else there. Something about the thick old walls darkened from years of smoke, the tranquil silence that hung over the place, and the steady flame of the eternal fire that burned in the large urn made her acutely aware of how alone she was. Before she knew it, she was sobbing hard. "Please, Dadaji," she prayed. "Help me. Forgive me for all the times I wished Khorshed dead. I would give anything just to have her company again. Living with Rusi is like living alone, almost." It was true. The business still took so much of Rusi's time. Rusi still spent an average of ten hours a day at the factory. Coomi knew that part of the reason Rusi worked so hard was simply to stay away from home. With Khorshed gone, Coomi now blamed Rusi's business for the breakup of her marriage. She believed that Rusi brought the frustrations of his business home with him. Rusi believed just the opposite—that he took the frustrations of his marriage to work with him. "If I had just had a little encouragement at home, who knows where I could have been today?" Coomi once overheard him say to Soli Contractor. "In England, they have a saying—ninety percent of your success depends on whom you marry. So true, so true." As always, Coomi had felt revulsion. She hated to hear Rusi admit to any weakness. The men she had grown up around remained stoic and *bindaas,* no matter what setbacks they faced.

Sheroo Mistry was saying something to Coomi, but she did not hear her. She was still watching her husband. Bomi had whispered something to Rusi and Coomi watched as Rusi threw back his head and laughed his familiar high-pitched laugh. It was a sound she heard so rarely these days. For a moment, she saw the outline of Rusi's head—the broad, glistening forehead, the big Roman nose, the prom-

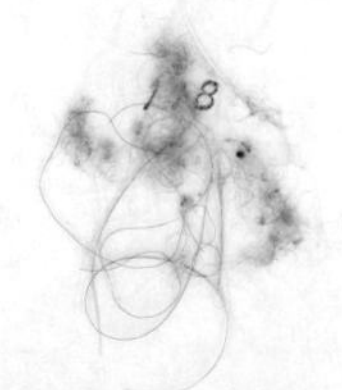

inent Adam's apple—framed against the black canvas of the sky. Quick as a breath, Coomi blinked. *Click.* She would save this picture, sharing it with neither Binny nor Dosamai. Something about the way Rusi looked right then reminded her of a younger, brighter face, and the memory made her smile.

But the next moment, her smile faded. Rusi had caught her staring at him, and the laughter that had bubbled in him like a spring froze as abruptly as a stream in winter. His face closed like a door and Coomi watched as the wary, guarded expression she hated took over.

Rusi was looking at her, a look of studied indifference on his face. Coomi turned her camera on herself. *Click.* She watched herself dissolve into nothingness.

Five

All through the evening, Soli Contractor had waited impatiently for Rusi Bilimoria to arrive. "Please God," he murmured. "Just for today, let that slow coach Coomi be dressed on time." But it was not to be. By the time Rusi and Coomi finally walked in, Soli felt as if the letter had burned a hole in his pocket and would at any minute drop to the floor.

Soli was a short walnut-colored man with twinkling light gray eyes that would've been more appropriate on a schoolboy's face, rather than on his own wizened one. Someone had once told Soli that his smile was wider than the distance between Bombay and Calcutta, and sometimes when Soli caught himself smiling, he told himself, I am bridging an entire subcontinent with one smile.

But Soli was not smiling today. Throughout the wedding reception, old friends had teased him for not following his usual practice of eating dinner in the first shift and then going home for his "beauty sleep." Soli's rigid habits caused much merriment among his friends. "A *pucca* bachelor, you are, Soli," a neighborhood wag once told him. "You've successfully managed to resist the demands of a wife, and you know what? You've instead succumbed to the tyranny of an alarm clock."

Bomi Mistry was among those surprised to see Soli still at the reception. "What happened, Soli?" he boomed. "Bad case of diarrhea? Never heard of you refusing *lagan-nu-bhonu.* Or did you already eat at home?"

"Who said anything about refusing? Everybody is a joker today. If you are wanting the truth, Mr. Charlie Chaplin, I have decided to wait for my good friend Rusi, who is as always fashionably late. *Arre,* if I'd had dinner, I would be belching so loud, they'd hear it from here to Chembur."

Bomi winked conspiratorially. "No use waiting for the Bilimorias. Mehernosh will be a grandfather before they show up. You know that Coomi."

"Right you are, *bossie.*"

But Soli could not prevent his head from shooting up every time there was a movement near the entrance to the reception hall. The other guests exchanged quizzical looks. "*Baap re,* Soli," Sheroo Mistry said. "Who are you expecting to roll in through those gates? Queen Victoria? Or some secret Juliet?" She laughed at her own joke, her flabby, sleeveless arms flapping at her side. Soli scowled.

When he finally saw Rusi and Coomi walk in through the big iron gates, Soli heaved a sigh of relief. He intended to corner Rusi soon after he sat down, but then Jimmy walked Rusi back to get a drink and the opportunity was lost. Throughout the evening, he kept waiting for a chance to pull Rusi aside, but there never seemed to be a moment when the two of them were alone. Soli was beginning to think he would have to return home without having shown Rusi the letter.

Finally, he got his chance. As the remaining guests rose to dine in the third and final *paath,* Soli got Rusi's attention. "*Bossie,* just one minute," Soli said, casually pulling Rusi aside and letting the other guests walk past them. "Before we sit down to eat, something I have been wanting to share. Been troubling me for days now. Read this and tell me what I am to think about it."

Rusi put on his reading glasses. It was a short, neatly typed letter.

Dear Soli:

It is with some trepidation I write. I know you still live at the same address because I checked with a mutual friend. It's interesting—you have stayed at the same address all your life and I have moved so much. Strange how life has treated both of us so differently. Still, all circles must come to a close. Which is why I am writing my first letter to you in almost forty years.

My son, Moshe, and I are planning a trip to Bombay in the next few months. Hard to believe, but my son is now older than you and I were when my family lived in Bombay. Moshe is a serious young man and recently he has gotten it in his head that he wants to visit his mother's birthplace. He wishes for me to accompany him. My husband, Nizzim, died last year of heart failure and I am ready for a vacation. Besides, it has been too many years since I have visited the city that I still think of with much affection.

But I'm rambling. The fact is that of all our old friends in Bombay, Soli, you are the one I would like to see the most. In fact, being in Bombay and not visiting you seems absurd. But that must be your decision, too, and if you would prefer not to disturb the sleep of the past years, I will understand.

If you do wish to get together, drop me a line. We can finalize plans.

Best wishes,
Mariam

Rusi looked up from the letter. Soli and he had not talked about Mariam in decades. There was a moment's silence as he tried to figure out what response Soli wanted from him. "It's a nice letter," he said lamely.

Soli looked incredulous. "Nice? 'Nice letter'?" he cried. "This letter is costing me four nights of sleep. As soon as I saw who it was from, I should have torn it up. Like a ghost, she is entering my life after all these years. I tell you, Rusi, a letter is like a *bhoot.* It enters your home silently, slipping in through the mail slot of a closed door. And then it haunts you and haunts you. Four nights, and I tell you, *bossie,* not a wink of sleep."

"But Soli, why? You can ignore it if you don't want to see Mariam again. Though it may be good to see her again."

"Why? I'll tell you why. Because this letter is like walking through a graveyard and opening all the graves. Do you know what's inside these graves? Coffins filled with memories. Memories, all buried and sleeping for years and years. Then what happens? Some woman in Israel is deciding to open up some graves in Bombay. Next thing, all the memories that were so nice and quiet begin to rattle around like bones. And the noise of their rattling is keeping me awake all night."

Rusi had never seen Soli this upset—except for one other time. That time, too, it was Mariam who had been responsible. "But Soli, surely you're not in love with her after so many years?"

"Love? Who's talking of love? I'm talking about hate. Is the lion at Victoria Gardens loving the zookeeper? Are the fish at Tata Aquarium loving their tanks? Why, then, should I be loving the woman who trapped me years ago? No, I am older and wiser now, Rusi. Then, I was still a *baccha,* compared to what I am knowing now."

Rusi blinked. He suddenly saw another, younger face transposed over Soli's old wrinkled one. It was the face of a young man with disheveled hair and bloodshot eyes. A face from that night, so many years ago. They had all been so damn young then, he even younger than Soli. Still, he had been able to help his friend that night. Involuntarily, he sighed. So much pain in this world, he thought. So much damn pain.

Soli must have seen the look in Rusi's eyes, because he said, "Rusi, do you remember that time I came to you after Mariam had left me?"

Rusi nodded. As for Soli, he remembered the day as if it were yesterday.

After Mariam left, Soli turned from the window to face Jamshed and Mehroo Katpitia's suddenly shabby-looking room. The evening shadows on the wall reminded him of the way in which Mariam's hair had fallen across her tear-streaked face. A clock ticked tormentingly; flies buzzed around the untouched tandoori chicken; the fizz in the raspberry drink sank into impotence. Slowly, heavily, Soli made his way across the room and sat at the edge of Jamshed's bed. It was still warm from where Mariam had sat on it minutes earlier. He could still smell her perfume in the air, so that if he shut his eyes, it would be easy to pretend that Mariam was still here, that the world still spun as reliably and faithfully on its axis as it had an hour earlier. That nothing had changed. But the cold, empty feeling in his stomach told him differently. Fear and grief rose like vomit in him as a dark loneliness fell over him. He felt completely and utterly alone in that room, as if he were the only living being on the planet. As though if he never left that room, nobody in the outside world would miss him. For a long moment, he thought of that outside world—a sunlit world of jokes and love and hope—with something approaching nostalgia, the way an amputee misses a leg he no longer has.

He felt as though, on a whim, some cruel God had revoked his citizenship from that golden world. That he had been deported to a land of frigid temperatures and long, dark evenings, spent endlessly alone. That alone could explain the manner in which he was shaking, rustling like a piece of paper in the wind. But then a great sob rose like a black bubble inside him, started deep in his stomach and floated upward to his chest, and then the sob was in his throat, so that when he tried to swallow, he could not; pain was lodged in his throat like a pebble. Now the dark bubble was in his mouth, a sob so big, it felt like an extra tongue, so big that it forced his mouth open and then he had to let it out, a black apparition pouring out of him, like the water bubbles that gather at the mouth of a drowning man. It was then that he knew that the shaking of his body had been a prelude to the bubbling grief that was now spilling like sour milk from him.

With amazement, he listened to the wild, guttural noises he was making—he had never suspected that he, Soli Contractor, neighborhood clown, was capable of so much emotion. And he had never known that human misery could so much resemble animal pain, that howling at the moon was not merely the domain of the animal kingdom.

But as his initial wonderment passed, Soli began to wonder whether these strange animal sounds would ever cease, how he would ever reenter the world of human beings. He felt a moment of panic at the thought of that world. He had left it only a few hours ago and yet it already felt distant and strange, like a country he had not visited since childhood. What citizen from the outside world could he reach out to? Which friend would reach into this cold room and pluck him out of the darkness? Jamshed and Mehroo Katpitia were in Udwada, members of the outer world.

Rusi, he thought suddenly. Soli felt a moment's hesitation at the thought of confiding in someone so much younger than him, but his desperation overrode his hesitancy. Rusi was sensitive and mature for his years. Besides, Rusi had lost his father at a young age. He knew what it was like to watch love vanish from your life. Yes, Rusi would be much more sympathetic than someone like, say, Bomi. He could not risk that buffoon Bomi making one of his *koila* jokes at a time like this.

As he made his way toward Wadia Baug, Soli prayed he would not run into his mother. Creeping past his own flat, he reached the Bilimoria apartment at 9:00 P.M. His shiny round face was smudged with tears, his hair wild and uncombed, and his eyes red and unnaturally large, as if the tears had forced them wide open, had made him see things he did not particularly want to see. When Rusi answered the persistent rings of his doorbell, he saw a small hunched figure leaning against the wall, as if he hoped the wall would hold him up.

Rusi, who was nursing a cold, had fallen asleep listening to the radio. The persistent bell jarred his sleep and he sat up in bed for a full moment, with a strange icy feeling in his stomach, before he recognized the source of the sound. Rusi's knees were weak as he slipped out of bed and into his slippers. Who the hell can it be? he wondered as he walked to the front door, trying to get there before his mother did.

It was a moment before he recognized Soli, and when he saw the tearful face, his stomach lurched, so that he thought the flu was making him nauseous. "Soli," he cried. "*Su che?* What's wrong, boss? Is your mamma sick?" And then, in a flash of blind panic, he remembered Jamshed and Mehroo were out of town. "Is it Jamshed? An accident?" he cried.

"No, no, nothing like that, Rusi. Please, sorry, I was not meaning to upset you. I was not knowing it is so late at night. Khorshed Auntie, my apologies. I just wanted to see Rusi."

Khorshed Bilimoria had come to the front door to see what the commotion was about. She gazed at the distraught young man quietly. "No harm done. I was just reading in bed. Would you like to come in, Soli? I was saying to your mother only today that I haven't seen you in a few weeks."

Soli smiled in gratitude. "No thanks, Auntie. And Khorshed Auntie, please to not say anything to Mamma about this. But please, may I disturb Rusi a little more and go get a cup of tea somewhere? Just for a short time only? It's urgent, Auntie. I am needing to talk with a friend," he added, his eyes filling up again.

"Ja," Khorshed said to Rusi. "Go get dressed, *beta.* But you boys don't walk the streets at night. I will give you money. Go take a taxi and find a restaurant that's open. Get something to eat. *Dosas* or *samosas* or sandwiches. Both of you have red noses, all congested. Get some good food. It's my treat."

But at the restaurant, the sandwiches remained untouched as Soli recounted the details of his five-month love affair with Mariam. He ended the story by telling Rusi about his breakup with her earlier in the day. Concern for Mariam's reputation made Soli skip over the part about their lovemaking.

"Israel? Why are the Rubins moving there?" asked a bewildered Rusi as he picked at a pimple. "*Arre,* those Arabs will make mincemeat out of all of them."

"She said all the Jews were her people," Soli said in a choking voice. "That Israel was where her home was."

"How can her home be where she has never even been?" Rusi cried. This time, he was genuinely puzzled. "Mariam is like us—Bombay-born and -raised. Forget Israel—if I had a chance to go to America or England even, I would not go. And Israel is like a newborn *bachcha*—who knows if she will walk or fall? I tell you, Abe Uncle's brains must be getting all scrambled."

"Rusi, you are saying word for word what I said to Mariam. But she is acting so strange—nothing I can say except 'Yes, madam. Yes, madam.' She was not listening to me whatsoever. I think even if I had said, 'I am killing myself, Mariam,' she would still be talking about

Israel and Germany and that bastard Hitler and I don't know what all." And Soli felt the horrible shaking start again, so that he set down the teaspoon he had been holding.

Rusi reached over and firmly clasped Soli's cold, quivering hand. Absently, he remembered Miss Desai, his fourth-grade science teacher, saying in her prim, high-pitched voice, "Heat flows from bodies with high temperature to bodies with low temperature." He hoped his warm hands could warm up the hand that shook like a rattle inside his. But he knew that it was more than just Soli's hands that had to be warmed up, that some essential fire had gone out of his friend, that this shaking was the outer manifestation of something thin and icy that moaned like the wind inside Soli. He remembered how he had felt when his father died and his heart ached at the memory.

Soli had seen the pity in Rusi's eyes. "I must be catching a cold," he said self-consciously, trying to explain away the wretched shaking. He started to say something but then stopped, a look of mortification on his face. He stared at the object of his shame, at the large silver tear that glistened on Rusi's hands as they lay covering Soli's. "It's . . . something . . . water leaking . . . ceiling," Soli stuttered.

"Soli. *Bossie.* You listen to me. Nothing wrong with how you are feeling. In your shoes, I would be the same way. That Mariam treated you badly. You are upset, that's all. Better to cry than to keep it all inside. Tomorrow, it will be fifty percent better, you'll see. My mamma says tears are the jewels of God. *Arre,* even a he-man like Bogart would cry if his girl were to leave him."

His reward was the tiniest of smiles. "Rusi. A friend in need is a friend indeed. Thank you, *bossie.*" And without warning, Soli's body heaved with sobs. A waiter rushed up to the table, but Rusi fixed a fierce gaze on him and nodded for him to leave them alone. "Cry away Soli," he murmured. "Good for the soul. Clears those sinuses also. But don't worry, *bossie.* Tomorrow, you will wake up feeling like a new man, you'll see. No shame among friends, Soli, no one here to hear, keep crying."

Rusi gazed at the bald old man standing next to him in his starched white *dagli* and wondered what had happened to the slender, grief-stricken man he consoled at that restaurant decades ago. Time had kidnapped that youth and the years disguised him, stolen his hair, bent his back, yellowed his teeth.

But as if that were not mischief enough, time left the inside of this old man intact, so that the mischievous gray eyes contradicted the yellow teeth; so that the constant jokes that bubbled like a hot spring inside Soli were at odds with the slow, careful way in which he walked. Most of the time, Rusi noticed only his friend's irrepressible spirit, admired how time had not dulled the wit and the humor. But today, he noticed how much Soli had aged and realized with a start that the same criminal who had stolen Soli's youth was beginning to steal his own. Despite the fact that Soli was older, Rusi suddenly and acutely felt his own years.

Rusi knew Soli was waiting for him to say something. "So what are you going to do, Soli?"

"I don't know. Rusi, you won't believe—years and years it took me to forget that girl. For God knows how long, I would be seeing her in my dreams night after night. When all those Arab-Israeli wars were going on, I would light a special *diva* and pray for her safety. Not only for Mariam but for Abe Uncle, the whole family.

"But then, bit by bit, I was forgetting her. Some days, I was trying to remember her nose or her mouth and nothing is coming before my eyes—just air. And I am happy. Dadaji, I say, you are hearing my prayers. Help me to forget this woman, who has gripped me worse than the devil."

Suddenly, Rusi knew exactly what Soli should do. In his own life, he had left too much unsaid, had run away from too many ghosts. He hated to see his friend make the same mistake. "Soli, listen," he said urgently. "Write to her. Or, if you like, come to my factory tomorrow and call her from there. But *bossie,* face this situation. Mariam ran away from you once; don't you run away from her." He wanted to tell Soli more about his own regretful life, the silences that populated his days, but this was not the appropriate time. So he simply said, "*Bossie,* not too many of us get a chance to enter the past. Yes, you cannot change the past, I agree. But at least you have a chance to understand it. Take it.

"*Arre,* Soli, how can she hurt you any worse than the first time? And you lived to be an old *boodha,* didn't you? Men can live with a broken heart, it just goes to show. Who knows why Mariam is writing to you? Who cares? The point is, you need to bury her ghost once and for all. And that can only happen if you meet her."

Soli listened silently. "Maybe you have a point. I will think about it." Suddenly, his demeanor changed. "She's probably looking like an old *boodhi* now. May help to see her like that, with dentures and wrinkles. Whereas I'm still Prince Charming—and your own wife told me so, when we were in bed yesterday."

They grinned at each other, now that Soli was once again in his familiar jostling element. Rusi felt relieved. Soli's sense of humor would be his salvation.

Out of the corner of his eye, Rusi saw Jimmy Kanga headed their way. "Here comes Jimmy," he said hastily. "We'll talk more, okay? Stop by the factory tomorrow."

Before Soli could reply, Jimmy Kanga had reached them. "Okay, you two lovebirds. Enough of your *guss-puss.* All of us are waiting for you two, to start dinner. Rusi, you disappeared for so long, poor Coomi thought she was a widow. She just agreed to marry Dolly Dingdong." The three men chuckled. Dolly, who lived in a nearby building, was a tall man, thin as a wafer, who at some point had hit upon every woman in the neighborhood. Their responses to his overtures were identical: They laughed.

Rusi suspected that Jimmy was a little drunk. And why not? he thought. It's not every day that a man is lucky enough to have a son getting married.

"Hey, Soli. To mark the historic occasion of your waiting until the third shift for dinner, I have arranged a special tribute." Jimmy grinned. Soli immediately smelled a rat, but Jimmy would not say anything more except a cryptic "You'll see." As they passed the band, Jimmy winked at the musicians. Rusi and Soli had barely sat down to dinner when the band leader leaned into his microphone. "We have a special request from the father of the groom. This one is in honor of his good friend Soli." With that, the band launched into "Here Comes the Bride."

The diners roared. "You stupid swine, Jimmy . . ." Soli began. But Jimmy thumped him hard on his back, his face red with glee. "Come on, Soli, be sporting. It's just that everybody in the third shift was eagerly awaiting your arrival, as if you were the damn bride. None of us can remember another day when you waited this long for dinner."

"You see this?" Soli said to Rusi in mock anger. "This man is one of Bombay's leading advocates, Oxford-returned and all, but his brain is still like a common *ghaati*'s. Oh God, save us from all these middle-aged clowns and their not-funny jokes, and God save the queen. And you, Rusi, you *bevakoof.* What for are you showing off the three teeth in your head? Only encouraging Jimmy's stupidity, you."

Bomi Mistry got unsteadily to his feet. "To Soli," he said. "May he still get his beauty sleep tonight and wake up tomorrow transformed from the Ugly Duckling into the Golden Swan."

Amin, Rusi thought to himself. *Amin, amin, amin.* May my poor friend wake up tomorrow morning with a healed heart. He watched silently as Soli slipped effortlessly into his usual role of court jester. He wondered if any of the others saw past the banter and jokes to Soli's cracked and hurting heart. Surely, Jimmy had wondered what they had been discussing so intently. But maybe not. Jimmy had other, happier things on his mind tonight. Rusi whispered a silent prayer for his friend, wished him a good night's sleep after four nights of wrestling with Mariam's memory.

After dinner, the waiters came out with aluminum bowls and a pitcher of warm water. Moments before, the gaunt-faced men had expertly folded the large banana leaves that the guests had dined on into a long roll and swept them from the table. Now the waiters poured warm water and liquid soap onto the diners' hands. After drying them on their white linen napkins, they were ready for ice cream. "Hope it's *pista* ice cream—my favorite. Or tutti-fruitti," Soli said.

Immediately after dessert, the diners rose as one, as if commanded by some unseen hand signal. On the way out of the dining area and into the reception hall, the conversation revolved around the meal, as if scores of restaurant critics had all converged on the same spot.

"Chicken could've been little more tender."

"Fish was good though—nice big pieces. Chutney was delicious."

"*Pallao-daar* was excellent, too. Nice-nice pieces of mutton in the rice. Very tasty."

"Good *achaar,* also. Nothing like that carrot pickle to complete the *lagan-nu-bhonu.*"

"I tell you, that Jimmy knows how to celebrate a happy occasion with *dhoom-dham.* Rare to see such a lavish wedding in these tight times."

"Yah, but he should've cut that Adi off when he reached his limit. That boy missed a great dinner. Serves him right for drinking so much. Misbehaves every time, that Adi. An embarrassment to Wadia Baug, that's what he is."

"Somebody said Soli's gone to check on him. Hope he doesn't throw up all over poor Soli's *dagli.*"

"Yah, that will make him regret waiting till the end for dinner, for sure."

"Now, you men leave poor Soli alone. Enough *maasti* you all have done for one evening, at his expense."

Outside the entrance of the reception hall, scores of dark, hungry eyes followed their every movement. The children on the street involuntarily licked their lips in anticipation of the leftovers they would soon be devouring. For today, at least, there would be no need to dive into the large city Dumpsters in search of pieces of bread or bits of bananas left inside the peel. Tonight, they would eat well.

As they left the dining area, the diners were oblivious to the wave of anticipation that went through the huddled crowd. The combination of food, drink, music, and companionship had momentarily transported most of them to a state of well-being and comfort. The reality of the hungry children a few feet away from them was the last thing they wanted to confront.

Jimmy Kanga had already cornered several of them and asked them to stay on after dinner. "Zarin and I have planned a surprise for a few of our special friends," he whispered mysteriously.

With the dulled curiosity of the overfed, they wondered what the surprise was.

Six

Soli had first met Mariam when he was twenty years old and she was seventeen. Soli and the other neighborhood boys used to hang out at Cream Café, where they would kill the hours ordering mutton cutlets, *samosas,* and chicken patties. One evening, Soli was holding court, entertaining the others with his jokes, when his eyes fell on a young girl sitting a few tables down. She had long brown hair, which she wore in two thick braids that came to rest just under her breasts. Soli thought she had the pinkest lips he had ever seen, and her skin was the color of butter. But what made Soli's heart lurch so violently that for a moment he thought he had the hiccups were her eyes. They were the kindest eyes Soli had ever seen. He had seen such eyes on old, sweet-natured dogs, but never on a human being. Right now, those eyes were focused on the short gray-haired man sitting at the table across from her. Whatever he was saying to her in an urgent, emphatic whisper was making those brown eyes brim with tears. "I'm sorry, Daddy," Soli heard the girl say. "I'll try and do better, honest." Soli felt a gush of anger at the middle-aged man for making such a pretty girl cry. Gazing at the girl, he felt as if he had been transported from the restaurant into a museum, where he was staring at a most beautiful portrait.

Reluctantly, he tore his eyes away from the other table and concentrated on what his friends were laughing about. Looking at their pimpled young faces, he noticed with a shudder, for the first time, their bushy eyebrows, their scraggly mustaches, their bad haircuts, their irregular teeth. Even the handsome ones among his male friends, he suddenly found ugly, compared to the smooth, regular lines of the girl sitting a few feet away. And at that moment, rough-and-tumble Soli Contractor, neighborhood clown, the boy who could spit farther and fart louder than any of his friends, felt an overpowering desire for something finer and smoother than the coarse life he had always known.

Easing back on his chair, he turned to the boy next to him and asked in a discreet whisper, "You know who that *chokri* is, the one in the green blouse?"

"That? That's the new Jew girl. I'm thinking her name is Mariam or Maryann or something. Her family just moved into Norman Building from Bandra. Her brothers go to the same school as my brother Baman. Nice boys. Both were boxing champs at the school they went to in Bandra. Baman says they used to have a nice big bungalow in Bandra. But then Abe Uncle—that's the father sitting over there—Abe Uncle's business partner swindled him big-time. So they had to sell the bungalow and move into our area. See what a wonderful area we live in? Bankrupt people come here to enjoy the fine air."

"Our area is any day as good as Bandra," Soli answered automatically.

For the next fifteen minutes, Soli kept glancing at the other table. But the girl did not look up. Her eyes were now dry and she spoke to her father in low tones, much like his own. Soli strained to hear what they were saying but was unable to catch more than a few words. He was suddenly ashamed of the loud crackles of laughter, the mimicking sounds of farts, the competition to see who would belch the loudest, all of which were coming from his table. As he watched, Soli noticed that the girl frequently moved her hands in expansive, graceful gestures as she spoke. He thought it was the prettiest thing he had ever seen and wondered if it would look strange if a man moved his hands about when he spoke. He decided to try it when he got home.

At last, the man at the other table pushed back his chair, brought out his wallet, and stood up. With an affectionate arm around the girl, he walked out with her.

In that instant, Soli knew that this was the girl he would marry.

He had a sudden picture of them walking at Chowpatty Beach at dawn, both of them barefoot in the sand, his one hand holding his shoes and the girl's sandals while his other arm was draped around her neck. If there were not too many people around at that hour, he would give her an occasional kiss, just a quick peck on the cheek, just so that he could watch the slow rise of her smile, as beautiful as the movement of the sun as it rose each morning.

Soli had pushed his chair back and risen. As his friends looked up in surprise, he put a crumpled note on the table. "That's my share, plus tip. I . . . I just remembered I have an appointment somewhere." He ignored their howls of protest as he ran out of the restaurant.

Out on the street, he had a desperate moment when he thought he'd lost them. But there they were, a few yards ahead, walking in brisk steps, the man's arm still around his daughter's shoulder. Soli followed them at a distance. He felt as if the two strangers had cast a spell over him and were pulling him along with an invisible leash, like the family dog. He had no idea what he would do if they were to stop suddenly and ask him why he was following them.

When they got to Norman Building and went up the stairs, Soli stood weakly outside, leaning against a lamppost. What to do next? He didn't have a clue. Finally, he went inside the apartment building and gazed at the wooden board that displayed the names of the tenants. He scanned the board, looking for an unfamiliar name, different from the Christians and Parsis who occupied the building. At last, he found it, tucked between Patel and Verghese. Rubin. Surely that was a Jew's name. Third floor. He felt a sudden burning desire to see the inside of their apartment, to see how they lived, to find out whether their surroundings were as refined and graceful as the occupants themselves.

There was a small *lassi* shop across the street. Soli went in and ordered a *lassi.* Holding a glass of the sweet yogurt drink in his hand, he gazed toward Norman Building, half-hoping that the mystery girl would appear at a window facing the street. But nothing stirred. Several times, the *lassiwalla* asked him if he was all right and several times Soli irritatedly brushed him off, not wanting the *lassiwalla,* with his enormous paunch and red *paan*-stained teeth, to intrude upon the sweet fantasy he found himself engulfed in. "Come on, come on," he murmured, trying to will her to the window. He waited for an hour, slowing sipping the *lassi,* licking his upper lip to remove the milky white mustache that had formed. At last, he rose and went home, disappointed but strangely exhilarated.

A week later, the image of the girl rose before his eyes again. Soli was at home reading in bed after having had dinner with his widowed mother. But the lines on the page kept rearranging themselves into the shape of the girl's slender face. Soli shut the book with a thud. "Mamma," he said. "Too hot in here. Going out for a few minutes to get fresh air."

When he arrived at Norman Building, the street was busy, as usual. Soli leaned against the same lamppost he had leaned against the day he had followed the Rubins home. For a second, he had a vision of himself as a bronzed statue, one hand in his pants pocket, leaning his right shoulder against the lamppost, a dull notch where his shoulder rubbed daily against the post. A bronzed Romeo, pining away for his Juliet to appear at the window. The vision made him feel very old and sad, and in order to get rid of that feeling, he shook his head swiftly from side to side, like a dog emerging from the ocean.

Then he heard it. From the third-floor window, music was floating down toward the street like a single feather, the plaintive notes of a violin sounding as sweet and lonely as the lullaby Soli's father used to sing to him when he was a boy. He knew with absolute certainty that the music was coming out of the Rubin apartment. He also knew with terrifying certainty that he was about to make a fool of himself, that he would not return to his depressing, quiet apartment tonight without getting a glimpse of the people who played such holy, heart-piercing music. Like a man in a dream, he entered the building and walked up the stairs. At the door, his index finger trembled in the air for a moment but he rang the bell.

"Just a minute." A patter of feet, and then Abe Rubin's round gray-haired face peered at him blankly. "Yes? Can I help you?"

Soli suddenly realized that he was unable to speak. Abe was staring at him with a puzzled expression on his face, clearly waiting for him to say something, and *he could not speak*. His mouth was so dry that no words would emerge. He opened and shut his mouth a few times and tried to fight the urge to flee down the stairs two at a time.

To Soli's mortification, Abe Rubin began to laugh. "What is it, son? Can I help you?" he repeated, a kindly expression on his face.

Soli gulped. And plunged. "That music?" he stammered. "I was just walking by—I told my mamma I was going on a short walk only, you know? And I am hearing this music, just walking by your building for no reason, you know. I . . . I . . . What record is playing, sir? It is quite . . . beautiful," he said finally.

Abe gazed at the boy, trying to place where he had seen him and to discern the reason for his nervousness. "Do you live in the building?"

"Me? No, sir. That is, I live just around the corner, only. In Wadia Baug. The Contractors, you know? My daddy was a higher-up in the postal service, may God bless his soul. Good family, sir."

"All right, all right." Abe laughed. "I don't mean to give you the third degree."

"Third degree, sir?" Soli blinked. He wished he had never knocked on the door of this strange man. Although he had read about the Jews and how Hitler had killed them by the millions, he had never met a Jewish family before, and now he racked his brains to remember what he had heard about the Jews in Bombay. He had read *The Merchant of Venice* in school, but the man standing in front of him looked nothing like Shylock. He wondered if this man, who was using expressions he had never heard, was typical of other Bombay Jews.

"Abe, who is it?" An intelligent-looking woman, her hair tied up in a scarf, came to the door.

"Oh, just a boy from the neighborhood. He's a regular musical aficionado. Says he heard the music on the street and was curious to know what it was."

"Why, that's lovely." The woman's face lit up. "Do come in, Mr. . . ."

"Contractor. My name is Soli Contractor." Although they were very dissimilar, something about this cultured woman with the big brown eyes reminded Soli of his mother and made him feel at ease. Compared to his robust, boisterous father, Abe Rubin seemed like a man from a different planet. But this woman felt familiar, and Soli gave her a warm, grateful smile.

"Well, Soli—may I call you that? You're as young as my children, after all—Abe will be glad to have another classical music fan. You're a Parsi, yes? In Bandra, we had many Parsi friends. In Bandra, we knew many families who were interested in the same things we are, but here—" She stopped abruptly.

Soli noticed a shadow cross Abe's face. "Now, Emma. We have to stop thinking like that," Abe said softly. She nodded, a beatific smile on her face. Standing on her toes, she gave her husband a quick peck on the cheek. Soli was startled. In his whole life, he had never seen a woman kiss a man in public. His own parents, for instance, had pulled away like guilty children the one time he had entered their bedroom and found his father resting his head in his wife's lap. Emma's gesture just added to his conviction that he had entered a new world, more dazzling and sophisticated than the one he lived in just a few streets away.

Soli followed Abe into the living room. For a moment, he was disappointed. In his imagination, he had pictured a fairy-tale apartment straight out of *Arabian Nights,* exotic and sensual, with velvet couches and silken drapes and Persian carpets. He had heard that the Jews were rich people, and he was ready to be dazzled by an apartment that he thought would be as foreign to him as the people living in it. The soulful music that wafted onto the street, the way Abe's daughter spoke with her hands, these things had accentuated their strangeness, their difference. He thought of himself as cotton and of the girl as satin, and he expected an apartment that exaggerated those differences. But the Rubins' apartment looked fairly similar to the apartments in Wadia Baug, other than the fact that it had more artwork on the walls and two built-in bookshelves that were filled with Abe's record collection.

And there was one other vital, happy difference between this apartment and the ones in Wadia Baug. The woman he would marry lived in this one. She was in the living room, reading, her feet up on a coffee table. She had on a blue cotton dress and her thick hair was free from the braids he had first seen her in. She looked up when he came in, her face echoing the mildly curious expression on her mother's face from a moment ago.

"Mariam, this is Soli Engineer. This is my daughter, Mariam."

"Contractor. My surname is Contractor, sir. Soli Contractor."

"Pardon me. I stand corrected," Abe said, a slight, ironic smile on his face, which left Soli feeling flushed and confused. Should I not have corrected the man? he wondered. Was it some breach of etiquette he knew nothing about? He felt small and lost among these people. But then he thought to himself, If this girl is to marry me, she better learn my correct name right now. After all, that will be her name someday. Mrs. Mariam Contractor. He swirled the name in his mouth like rock candy.

Mariam had risen from the couch and was holding out her hand to him, a quizzical expression on her face. They shook hands. Mariam's hand was smooth and small, and Soli was suddenly ashamed of his big coarse hands. He wished he knew what she was thinking, what impression he had made on her. He wished that Abe Uncle would disappear and leave the two of them alone to talk. He wished that he had met Mariam years ago. For a moment, he felt a pang of regret at the years spent with his pimply-faced school friends, playing aimless card games and holding spitting contests. And all that time, this girl had been alive, had lived in the same city. And he had not known her. Now, Soli searched her face for some sign of interest or friendliness, but he saw nothing there except a formal politeness. She was treating him as if he were her father's friend, and his heart dropped at the realization. He stood there blinking at her, wishing he could make her laugh as easily as he could his friends, but after a second, Mariam turned her attention away from him and to her book. He was suddenly as jealous of the book as if it were a rival vying for Mariam's attention.

Soli came to life again when he saw Abe's eclectic record collection. Hundreds of records. How did he find the time to listen to all this music? Soli did not even own a phonograph. All he had at home was an old radio. The idea of choosing what music one wanted to listen to at a particular moment was a new and wonderful one.

The next two hours were a blur. When Soli finally staggered down the steps of Norman Building, he felt breathless and spent. When he had rung that doorbell, he had entered a magic kingdom. He had heard of Beethoven, Mozart, Chopin. Now he could pluck the fruits of their genius. Abe Uncle had whispered the magic password to him and let him into an exclusive, secret club. A club whose membership merely required an open, vulnerable heart. The way Abe explained it, music belonged to everyone. Beethoven was merely a man, a man who apparently felt the same whirling joy and the same sweet, exquisite grief that was running up and down Soli's body like mercury.

Out on the street, he felt like skipping, shouting, singing at the top of his lungs. If a friend had told him just then that his mother had died in the time he had been away, Soli would've been hard-pressed to return to his apartment, which suddenly seemed dull, dark, and boring. He felt as if someone had parted a curtain and revealed a shiny world that had always existed but had been kept from him. His ears ringing with the holy sounds of the music he had heard and with Abe's erudite explication of that music, Soli walked the streets for an hour that night before his racing heart slowed down enough to allow him to go home and face his worried mother.

He was a regular visitor to the Rubin household from that evening on. It was ironic—he had mustered up the courage to enter that apartment to seek out Mariam, but it was Abe with whom he spent most of his time. Instead of speaking his love to Mariam, he had to be content with learning another kind of love—the love for beauty, art, books, music. It was Abe who took him to his first classical music concert. From the moment the crisply dressed musicians tuned their finely honed instruments until the rousing finale, Soli sat transfixed, the music alternately breaking his heart and making it turn cartwheels. When the concert was over and the others got up to leave, Soli sat still, staring at the now-empty wooden stage, discreetly wiping away the tears from his eyes. "Ahem," Abe said. "That was a pretty amazing evening, eh? Looks like the music got to you." Soli's lips moved, but no sound emerged. Abe chuckled, a soft, knowing sound. "I'll wait in the lobby for you, son," he said. "Give you a few minutes by yourself."

On the way home that evening, Soli told Abe that he had decided to buy a gramophone. He would need Abe's help in starting his own record collection. And while he was at it, perhaps Abe would recommend some books for him to read.

But Soli's body never let him forget the true reason he had entered the Rubin household. When Mariam was at home during his visits, he was as achingly conscious of her presence as he had been that very first night. From Abe, Soli learned the second-greatest passion of his life—music. From his own untrustworthy postadolescent body, he learned his greatest passion: Mariam. The sight of her never failed to tug at his heart, made him aspire toward a life that was pure and fine.

And yet . . .

She was so young. Just a child really. And he was barely a man himself, still in college. And Abe and Emma Rubin were so good to him. In them, Soli had found the kind of surrogate parents that he would have killed for as a boy, if only he had known that people like them existed. Soli was terrified of making any move toward Mariam, for fear of offending either her or Abe and thereby being banished from the Eden he had stumbled upon. And Mariam never gave any indication that she liked him. Not enough for him to hang a hat on anyway. One day, he arrived at the Rubins' flat, to find Mariam home alone. "Daddy just phoned," she said. "He and Mummy are running just a tad late and asked you to wait." He thought she meant for him to wait outside the apartment, and so his heart flipped like an omelette when she held the door open for him to enter. He immediately wished that Abe would be held up for hours, so that he could finally spend some time alone with Mariam. He was determined to make the most of his sudden good fortune. "There's a good concert next Friday," he began, and was glad that his voice came out smooth and steady. "All Cole Porter songs, they are playing. I was planning on going, and I was wondering if you would be . . ." But here his nerve gave out. "But you must be busy," he added vaguely. "Sorry to keep you from your work." Mariam looked as uncomfortable as he felt. She stared at him for a full moment, an expression on her face that he could not read. "Actually, I do have an exam tomorrow that I'm studying for," she said. "But please feel free to sit here and wait for Daddy. I'll be in my room, if you need anything." She was almost out of the room when she turned to look back over her shoulder. "And thanks for that . . . half-baked invitation," she added, making a sound that was part snort and part laugh.

"Mariam, wait," he called after her, knowing now that she was angry at him, but not exactly sure why. But she did not look back. "Stupid donkey," Soli said, pinching himself hard on his left arm. "One chance, and you had to make a total idiot of yourself."

After that evening, Soli would sometimes catch Mariam looking at him with a strange gleam in her eye, but when he would return her glance, she would simply smile and look away. Most of the time, she barely noticed him, absorbed as she was in the enchantment of her own growing womanhood. Mariam. The word soon became a groan, a sigh that contained all of Soli's unexpressed, unfulfilled desires.

Thus, in this way, Soli spent the next seven years of his life. In those years, he went out with a few other girls, nice Parsi girls from good families, the kind of girls his mamma approved of. At his mother's urging, he reluctantly allowed a matchmaker to introduce him to a few girls. But he was adamant about one thing—he would not say yes to marrying a girl until he had spent some time with her. Most of the time, the girl's parents would refuse, afraid of ruining their daughter's reputation by allowing her to consort with a young man who made no promises of marriage. But a few agreed, and Soli went out with them. He also dated a few of the women he worked with. There was nothing wrong with these girls, except for one thing. They were not Mariam. They didn't have the kindest eyes in the world. Their smiles did not carry the sun. They did not talk with their hands—hands that he imagined covering with silver bracelets—like Mariam did.

And without Soli's ever having to say so, the girls he dated realized that something was missing, a certain ardor that they needed. Soli was kind to them, affectionate even. But he did not look at them the way a lover should. Some of them accepted this; others tried to arouse his passion with every trick that they knew. But they were young and inexperienced and, of course, didn't have a clue about his obsession with Mariam. "*Baap re,* Soli," one of them once said. "I used to think you were a thorough gentleman, but now I'm thinking you're more like a pitcher of cold water. You are more passionate about your precious record collection than about me."

As the years passed, Soli stopped visiting the Rubins as much as he used to. The silence that he had built around Mariam threatened to choke him. Also, his job in an accounting firm kept him busy and his own record collection was fast catching up with Abe's. He joined a musical society and found friends his own age to go to concerts with. Still, as a sign of appreciation for everything the older man had taught him, Soli would go over every Christmas with a brand-new record for Abe. For weeks, he would search for some obscure recording he was sure Abe would not have, and on Christmas morning, he would ring their doorbell and drop off the gift. Abe and Emma, as gracious as ever, would insist he come in and take a cup of tea with them. The couple seemed to accept the fact that Soli's new life did not permit him to visit them as often as he once had. If, while looking around the living room for Mariam, Soli noticed that the apartment was bereft of a Christmas tree, it never occurred to him to question it. Soli knew all about Christmas trees and Santa Claus and mistletoe from the books he had read as a child. But he knew nothing about Judaism, and to him, Jews were just another kind of Christians. And Abe and Emma, touched as they were by Soli's annual gift, never had the heart to tell him that in some parts of the world, his innocent gesture would be enough to ignite a neighborhood.

Eventually, Mariam went from being a sharp stab to a dull ache in Soli's heart. When his mother begged for a daughter-in-law, "so that I can rest these old bones and die in peace knowing someone will take care of my son," he would smile and give her a quick hug. "Find me a beautiful *gori-gori* girl like you and I'll marry her this minute," he would say, and then quickly turn away before she could answer.

Or he would joke, "Why *khaali-pili* you are wanting to invite trouble into our house, Mamma? You know the Mahabharata wars that a daughter-in-law can create. What's the saying? No wife, no strife in life."

After a few years, he came to believe his own words.

One Sunday morning, Soli heard a horn toot under his window at 6:00 A.M. Grabbing the plastic bag that held the mutton cutlets his mother had prepared, he kissed her and quickly ran down the stairs. Two carloads of friends had stopped to pick up Soli on their way to Juhu Beach. He opened the front door of the second car and got into the passenger seat. His friend Dinu was squeezed in between Soli and the driver of the car. As the car took off, Soli turned around, careful not to knock Dinu's glasses off by making any fast moves. As he recognized the woman sitting between the two others, he gave a start of surprise.

"Oh, Mariam," he said. "You coming with us to Juhu?"

"No, Soli," Dinu said with a sarcastic laugh. "Mariam will drop us off and continue to Paris."

Still, his surprise was understandable. Mariam did not really hang out with his crowd. What Soli did not know was that Mehroo Katpitia, who had recently married his friend Jamshed, had struck up a friendship with Mariam in the last two years. It was Mehroo who had invited Mariam to the picnic. Mehroo had thought nothing of it when Mariam had casually inquired if Soli would be there.

Soli spent as much time around Mariam as he could that day without making the rest of them suspicious. He knew that if his friends got a whiff of the fact that he was interested in Mariam, they would be merciless in their teasing. He glanced at her every chance he got and realized that she was even more beautiful than when he'd first known her. Time had burned the puppy fat off her face, leaving behind something sad and authentic, and the dark circles under her eyes gave her a haunting beauty she had not had before. He noticed that her hands were as lovely as ever, the rich blue vein running like a river down its length. He longed to speak to her alone but didn't know how. Impatience made him restless and he shifted on the sand until one of his friends asked, "*Su che,* Soli? You need to do *soo-soo?*"

His chance came in the afternoon, when the others were napping under the shade of the coconut trees that lined the beach. Mariam got up and declared she was going to walk the length of the beach. Soli rose casually to his feet. "Can't let you walk alone," he said lightly. "Sea may come and kidnap you. Then Abe Uncle will be after my *boti.*"

They had barely moved away from the sight of the others when Mariam turned to him. "So you've forgotten the Rubins, eh? We don't see you much anymore. Mommy and Daddy still miss you, *men.* But you must be busy now, what with working and all."

Soli looked away to where the thrashing Arabian Sea seemed to be imitating the turmoil he felt. He didn't quite know how to answer Mariam's half question, half accusation. Suddenly, he remembered the first time he had seen her. He had visualized a similar scene, the two of them walking side by side on a beach, their bare feet leaving small dust clouds behind them, the sound of the waves a soft lullaby. But wait—he had imagined her walking closer to him than she now was, and the arm that should have been affectionately around Mariam's waist was instead hanging miserably by his side. He remembered, too, his foolish optimism of seven years ago, when he had believed that he would marry her someday. Well, life had certainly played referee to that fantasy, had sent him back to his corner, empty-handed.

But then he asked himself, What does this mean, her sudden appearance at this beach, in my life? Have the past several years merely been a detour and is this really the path of my true destiny? In his confusion, he started walking faster. "Soli, wait up," he heard her say. "Are you angry with me? I wasn't trying to offend you. I just wanted you to know that you were . . . that I . . . missed you."

His laugh sounded more bitter than he intended. "How can you miss me?" he cried. "You were barely noticing me all these years."

She looked at him appraisingly for a full moment, as if trying to decide how honestly to answer his accusation. "Oh, I noticed you all right," she said finally. And then, in a voice so soft that he had to strain to hear, she added, "I noticed you the very first time you came over."

"Ha-ha. That's a laugh. Very funny, Mariam."

"Except I'm not joking."

Now he was confused. "Are you saying . . . You couldn't possibly be . . . Why, you never even looked up from your books when I came over. And there I was, dreaming of you each and every night." He stopped, mortified, waiting for her to react with shock or anger, but her face was gentle and wistful, and it gave him the nerve to go on. "Now you are knowing the truth. All these years, I've been in love with you."

She was silent again. Then came a torrent of words. "I know. I just kept waiting for you to say something. It was awkward. You being Daddy's friend and all. Besides, I wasn't sure. I mean, you never said anything. How could I know? And I was shy. Don't think I haven't regretted it all these years. Anyway, I really didn't know. Whether you felt anything, I mean. I mean, I *suspected.* But hard to know for sure, you know? First time I knew one hundred percent was today. From the way you kept plotting to sit next to me. But even now, I could be wrong. You're probably over it by now anyway. Seven years is a long time. In which case, I'll feel very, very foolish by the time this day's over."

Her words reached him from a great distance, a solitary beam of blue light that pierced a hole into his heart of darkness. The light spread through his body, so that his face lit up like the sun and Soli Contractor smiled his Bombay-to-Calcutta smile.

"Mariam," he said. "How I have missed you, I can never tell. Just imagine . . . Imagine America without the Statue of Liberty. India without the Taj Mahal." Hearing her giggle, he went on. "Louis Armstrong without his trumpet. Tarzan without his Jane. That's how much I have missed you."

Her smile matched his. "Oh, Soli, that is so good to hear. But then, Soli, why did you stop visiting us?"

"How to explain?" he cried. "At your home, I never got to see you alone. Never only the two of us. And you were only seventeen, just a little girl. What could I say to Abe Uncle? Then also, I am Parsi, as you know. My mamma is wanting me to settle down with a nice Parsi girl. And your religion is different from ours. Your parents are probably wanting you to marry your own kind, no? So for all these good reasons, Mariam, I decided to stop torturing myself by going over there."

Her eyes were suddenly inexpressibly sad. "You're right," she said with a tight laugh. "These are all good reasons. Well, we should probably turn back. I don't want these Parsi tongues wagging."

He could feel her pulling away from him as the sea was pulling away from the beach. He felt a sudden panic. If he lost her now, he would never find her again. "Mariam, wait. I'm sorry I've been such an *ooloo.* This is all such a shock, and I'm such a blunderbuss. What I want to say is . . . Oh, to hell with what I want to say. What I'm wanting to do is kiss you. May I?"

Months later, they were still arguing about which one of them had first stepped into the other's arms. But at this moment, all Soli knew was the reality of finally having his arms around a woman who had begun to seem mythical to him. But Mariam was delightfully, gloriously real. And he was, against all odds, kissing the lips that he had fantasized about for seven long years. In the midst of his delirious joy, Soli had a thought of utmost clarity—that from this day forth, his life would be divided into before Mariam and after. Mariam was the dividing line that separated a world of listlessness and loneliness from a world of love and happiness. "Oh, Mariam," he whispered. "What if you had not come on this picnic today?"

As he said the words, he felt little stings of icy pain on his lower back. Turning his head, he saw a group of young urchins throwing pebbles at him and imitating his hushed whispers and puppy-dog expression. *"Saala badmash,"* he roared at the giggling children in mock anger. "*Chalo,* get out of here." The chattering children ran away, squealing at the unexpected pleasure of being chased by an adult.

But the mimicry had made the two of them self-conscious.

"Everything okay?" he asked awkwardly. "Good. Let us hurry back to the group. We don't want any silly talk to start about us." But he was still holding on to her, his words and expression contradicting each other.

"Soli?"

"Umm?"

"If you really don't want them to gossip, you'd better wash your face in the water before we join them. There's a large streak of red lipstick from your lips to your chin."

They had been together for five months. In that time, they had shared the news with only three of their friends, Rusi Bilimoria and Jamshed and Mehroo Katpitia. Abe and Emma believed that Mariam was spending most of her evenings at Mehroo's home. If they wondered why a recently married woman would want to spend so much time with their single daughter, their relief overshadowed their suspicions. Since their sons David and Solomon had left for Israel, Mariam had few companions her own age. There were no Jewish families in their new neighborhood for Mariam to associate with. And this group of Parsi boys and girls seemed nice—a little young for their age maybe, but friendly and polite.

Soli didn't understand Mariam's desire to keep their affair a secret. He knew that both their families would have a hard time accepting that they were marrying out of their communities. But the Rubins had virtually adopted him a few years earlier. And he knew that his mamma would ultimately put his happiness over her own reservations. The sooner they confided in both sets of parents, the faster this transformation would occur. He decided to broach the subject with Mariam. "Darling, why all this *choop-chaap*?" he asked her one evening. "Sorry—Gujarati word. Meaning, why all this hush-hush stuff? I mean, I am so proud of you, I'm ready to take out an ad in the *Times of India,* declaring my love for you. Don't you feel the same?"

"Of course I do. But I don't want Daddy to find out. I need more time. It's . . . I dunno, it just doesn't feel like the right timing." Her words disappointed him, but he understood. She just needs more time, he told himself.

But Soli was frustrated. It was hard to find public places where the two of them could have some privacy. The thought of taking an unmarried girl to a hotel was unimaginable. Occasionally, they would climb down on the rocks near Marine Drive and find a secluded spot to kiss, but Mariam looked so tense and distressed that it took all the pleasure away. She was constantly afraid that one of her father's friends would see them. Once, Soli hired a taxi to drive them around as they sat kissing in the backseat, sheltered by the dark privacy of the cab. But even that was uncomfortable. For one thing, they had to be as silent as mice, afraid of drawing any attention to themselves. As Soli put his hand on Mariam's knee, he caught the cabdriver's leering eyes gazing at them in the rearview mirror. The cab gave a lurch as their eyes locked. Soli used that as an excuse to vent his anger. "That's how most accidents happen—by *gadheras* not keeping their eyes on the road," he muttered, loudly enough for the driver to hear. "Eyes everywhere excepting where they should be." He ignored Mariam's cautious squeeze on his arm, asking him to shut up. They left the cab that day more frustrated than when they'd gotten into it.

The next day, they had their first real fight. "Are we thieves or spies?" he burst out. "Are we planning a war with Pakistan or a bank robbery? If not, why do we have to do all this hush-hush stuff? For the first time in my life, I'm lying to my dear old mother. And for what reason? It seems wrong to lie about the thing I'm most proud of—my love for you, Mariam. How to make you understand this?"

"I *do* understand. I hate this, too. But I need time, Soli. Daddy had always wanted me to marry a Jew. I need to prepare him for this very slowly."

"But you won't even come and sit with me at Chowpatty Beach or go into a private cubicle at Café Paradise. For seven years, I waited to kiss your lips. And still I have to worry about some *soover* taxi driver spying on us in his cab. I'm a grown man, Mariam, not some six-year-old boy in half pants."

Then he caught a lucky break. Jamshed and Mehroo, who were

renting a one-room flat in Colaba, asked Soli to keep an eye on it while they went to Udwada for two weeks. Before leaving, they dropped the spare key off with him. "Mariam," he told her the next day. "It's a godsend. Let's spend a day by ourselves in Jamshed's flat. You have to come. Darling, I am wanting to talk to you and kiss you without worrying about Abe Uncle or God knows who else. Please, darling. I'll go up first and take over some snacks and all. You come later. No one will see. I'll wait at the window and open the door before you even knock. We'll have a little indoor picnic, yes? Please, Mariam. We hardly get to see each other."

On the day she was to come, he bought a dozen chicken sandwiches, potato wafers, and a bottle of wine. He took out one of Mehroo's bedspreads from the closet and spread it on the floor for a picnic. He put Louis Armstrong on the gramophone. True to his word, he looked out the window for her and opened the door before she rang the doorbell. It was 3:00 P.M. on a Saturday. She hurried in. Her hair was tied back in a scarf and she had on a purple dress with black patent-leather shoes. She swayed a little to the music and then undid the scarf with a jerk. Her brown hair fell across her face like a shadow across a mountain. He kissed her before she had crossed the room.

They sat on the floor, munching their sandwiches and drinking the wine, until they had only about half a glass left. Soli dipped a potato wafer into his wine and watched it swim in the colorless liquid before fishing it out of his glass with his fingers.

"Ugh. You Parsis are a strange lot. Imagine eating a soggy potato wafer."

He rose to his feet with the careful solemnity of a drunk. "Now that you have insulted the whole Parsi community, I feel responsible for defending their honor as well as the honor of all those who like wet potato wafers," he said with a flourish. He tried to say something more lofty, but the wine was squatting heavily on his tongue. Slowly, he made his way to the bed and sat on it.

Mariam giggled. "Whatsamatter? Cat got your tongue?"

"Not the cat. The wine." He thought hard for a minute. "It's funny, no, when you can actually feel your tongue in your mouth? Like a big sponge, it is. You know what that's like?"

"Can't say that's ever happened to me, Mr. Soli." Mariam's eyes were dancing.

"Mariam?"

"Um?"

"Know what I would like? To feel *your* tongue in my mouth."

Silence.

"Mariam?"

"Um?"

"Come and sit here next to me. Please? Now, isn't that comfy? Mariam. Darling."

The room was silent expect for the sounds of their wet, long kisses. Then, Mariam pushed Soli away. "Okay, Soli. Don't get me all hot and flustered. I've got to go soon. That's enough."

"Oh, Mariam, please. Just this one time. I am so eager for you. Please, darling. When will we get such a chance again?"

"Soli, I can't. My father will kill me if he finds out, and besides, what if there's trouble later?"

"Oh, Mariam, your father is not here. But I am, and madly, madly in love with you. Seven years I waited, darling. Seven years. And there will be no trouble. I can, you know, pull out before . . . before . . . Trust me, darling."

Her mouth tasted salty under his. Their bodies folded together as if a master architect had designed them for each other. Her long legs clung to his body like a vine on a tree. When she slipped off her dress, the slenderness of her shoulder blades reminded him of the neck of a violin. "Mariam," he whispered. "You are perfection."

Outside their window, the real world raged on—a lonely old woman peered through heavy curtains to spy on her neighbors; a street urchin tied a firecracker to a stray dog's tail and then laughed as the animal went crazy with fear; a young couple rushed their firstborn to the hospital after he mysteriously stopped breathing.

In the still-larger world, Europe slept a cautious sleep as the nightmare of World War II crystalized into the frostiness of the cold war;

on the Asian continent, China, India, and Israel hurtled toward their individual destinies. Baptized in the blood of the Hindu-Muslim riots, a young India struggled to emerge from the memory of the carnage. A short distance away, Israel flexed its muscles as it traded one set of enemies for another.

But inside this room, a different sort of blood was being shed. It was blood that would have to be washed off the blue sheet before Jamshed and Mehroo returned. Indeed, the sheet with its drops of blood was a kind of flag, the symbol of a new country. A country where the divisions of race and religion were melting under the heat of desire, melting into a new flesh, melting into a new four-limbed animal, an animal that was all mouth and tongue, all curiosity and all softness, all ache and all fulfillment of ache.

For Soli and Mariam were more than just lovers. They were citizens of a nation that had just been born.

Later, he lay on the bed with his hands knitted behind his head, listening to the sound of running water as Mariam took a bath. A lifetime of such joy awaits me, he thought, and shivered with pleasure. Mariam and I making love and then me lying awake, listening to the sound of the water running. When she stepped back into the bedroom, her face was damp and flushed from the hot water. She sat at the edge of the bed for him to zip her dress.

"Mariam," he said, sitting up on one elbow as he dropped tiny kisses on her bare, fresh-scented back. "I can't wait for us to be married. Then we will be having fun like this all the time."

She smiled at him, and he noticed that the dark circles under her eyes were lighter. "So much happiness—it's almost more than one has the right to ask for," she whispered, taking his hand to her eyes and holding it there.

"Oh, darling, no such thing. You watch. We are going to be the happiest, luckiest couple we know. We already are."

Two days later, Mariam left with her parents for their annual family vacation to Goa. Soli, who had never been to the oceanside Portuguese colony, wished he could have accompanied them, but he knew better than to suggest that to Mariam. He was loath to part with her, but Mariam consoled him. "Be patient, Soli," she said. "Our reunion will be the sweeter for it. I'll phone you at work as soon as I get back."

But the day of her return came and went without a phone call. A worried Soli left work a little early and headed directly for Mariam's apartment building. He was relieved but astounded to see the lights in the Rubin apartment. So they were home. He tried to think of all the reasons why Mariam had not called him, tried to decide whether to knock on Abe's door in the hopes that Mariam would answer. But his courage failed him. There must be a good reason if Mariam hasn't called, he told himself. Maybe she's tired or sick. Or maybe she's told Abe Uncle about us. If so, better for me to wait.

He was almost mad with worry the following day, as the expected phone call never came. Each time his phone rang at work, he would answer it with a thumping heart that almost stopped beating when he realized the caller was not Mariam. The tenuous nature of his relationship hit him as he realized that he did not have the authority simply to pick up the phone and talk to the woman he loved. Then, at 4:00 P.M., when he was sure that Mariam was dead, the phone rang again, and this time it was her. "Soli? Hi, it's me. Sorry for not calling yesterday. Things are a little topsy-turvy here. Listen, are Mehroo and Jamshed still out of town? . . . Great. Can we meet at their apartment again tomorrow evening? . . . Sure that's convenient? Okay, I'll see you there, around six-thirty."

Ignoring his boss's mutterings, he left work early again the next day. He picked up two bottles of Duke's raspberry and a full tandoori chicken for dinner. If Mariam was arriving directly from work, she would be hungry.

The dark circles were back under her eyes. In fact, Mariam looked two years older than when she had left for Goa a week earlier. Soli could not help the involuntary start of surprise. "Darling. Have you been sick while on holiday? Did the air in Goa not suit you?

"I'm fine," she said. "Just fine." But her manner was agitated and her eyes darted around the room.

She was making him nervous. In an effort to control his own agitation, he got up to pour her a soft drink. "Well, even if you're sick, luckily for you, the doctor's in the house." He grinned. "Here's some of my own, homemade *dava.*" He kissed her long and hard, and after a few seconds, she relaxed. "Aha. Better already. Here, come sit on this bed and I'll give you some more medicine. Or perhaps you'd like an injection? Just a few pokes?" he said, grinning lewdly.

Mariam let him pull her on the bed, but he could tell she was distracted. He held her for a few minutes, hoping to calm her down, but it felt as if he was embracing a stranger. At last, he held her at arm's length for a minute and searched her face. "Mariam, what is the matter?" he asked quietly.

"Something happened while we were in Goa," she said in a low voice that matched his own. "A decision was made, you could say." She bit her lip and looked away from Soli's concerned, anxious face. When she looked at him again, her eyes were red. "Soli, my whole family had decided to move to Israel." She heard him gasp, but she didn't stop. "Daddy says there's nothing left for us in India, that a Jew has no business living anywhere now except in our homeland. What happened during the partition riots really scared him. The way those Hindus and Muslims butchered one another. Almost like what happened in Germany with the Jews. I know partition seems like ancient history to you and me. But Dad remembers it vividly."

He started to protest, but she stopped him. "While we were in Goa, we met with two other Jewish families," she continued. "It was my dad's friend Nizzim, who lives in Goa, who convinced him that it was time to leave. Goa's a pretty safe place for Jews, but Nizzim still feels that his children would be better off in Israel. All three families have decided to leave at the same time, in maybe two months from now. Dad is already looking for a buyer for the flat."

His whole world was caving in. He felt as if someone had toppled the planet, so that grass was now growing on the sky and clouds floating on the earth. "Mariam, darling, please. If this is a joke, please stop now," he beseeched. "See how my heart is racing, like those horses at Bombay racecourse." But one look at Mariam's face told him that this was no joke, and his heart turned icy.

"Daddy says he is tired of how much we have to struggle here just to get by. He says that if we're going to work this hard, let's do it in a place that's at least attempting something bold and new. The British have been gone from India for over ten years and nothing has changed, he feels. Just last night, when the electricity went out, Daddy said, 'Damn it, if we're going to live in a country of power outages and shortages, we may as well put up with those things in a country where we are working for the good of our own people.' It just reinforced his decision. And I'm telling you, Soli, the partition bloodbath scared him. He says he's never been able to look at India the same way since then. It reminds him too much of what happened in Germany."

"*Germany?* You're comparing India to barbaric *Germany*? How can you even compare that *madaarchot* crazy Hitler with his toothbrush mustache to our decent Oxford-educated Nehru *chacha*? Nehru puts a fresh rose in his buttonhole every morning—that's how civilized and gentle he is. A man who loves nature, loves children. Not like that eunuch Hitler, with his silly haircut and a voice that's sounding like he always has hiccups. And besides, Hitler's dead. As for partition, that was years and years ago, and that, too, was between the Hindus and Muslims. Let me ask you, Mariam, has India ever hurt you? Was your father not having a big business and fine house in Bandra? Did anyone ever harass you here?"

Mariam looked at Soli over the gulf of history and memory. "Soli, Germany was a civilized country, too. So civilized that they designed gas chambers to fry people in, so civilized that they removed gold fillings from the mouths of the dead. Just think about that. Daddy says that the only way to ensure this doesn't happen again is to be among our own and to work for a strong Israel. And after all, that is our original homeland."

Fear and some vestige of national pride made his voice sound harsher than he intended. "What homeland? India is your homeland. This is where you were born, where you were going to school, getting a job, having friends, going to picnics and parties. That way, as a Parsi, I, too, can claim that our original homeland was all of Persia—what is now Iran, Iraq, Israel, everything. Zoroastrianism was the religion of the whole area, you know. We were the original settlers. But do you see us going to the Shah of Iran and asking for our homeland? Do you see us Parsis asking those Arabs to give us a new country?"

"And do you see you Parsis losing six million of your own people in the Holocaust?" Mariam said fiercely. "Six million dead bodies just because one German bastard was sick in the head?"

Soli stared at Mariam. He had never seen her like this. Something had happened to her while in Goa, something that had changed her in a way that put her out of his reach. Suddenly, he was battling for his life, for his future happiness. "Mariam, I'm not arguing with you. What happened in Germany was the worst kind of sin. God will never forgive those Germans, that much, I know. But darling, all those millions who died, how are they your people? You didn't even know them. Your mummy and daddy and your brothers and me—we are your people. All those who love you. And if you marry me, my mamma and my friends will become your people. And nobody will be hurting you here, I promise. After all, they will have to fight me first. India is your country, Mariam. You are a *pucca* Bombayite, born and bred here."

"Soli?" she said slowly. "What if I asked you to leave everything and everybody you know here and come with me to Israel. Would you do it?"

He looked shocked. "Now Mariam, be reasonable. My whole life is here. Who will look after my mamma when she is old if I go away? And what would I be doing in Israel anyway, among all those bearded Jews? I've never even left Bombay, let alone going to Israel."

"But you expect me to leave my parents and David and Solomon and stay on. I love you very much Soli, but I can't marry you. Something happened to me last week that I can't explain. It's almost as if my love for you has expanded to include millions of others. And yes, you're correct, they're strangers to me, but in a way they're also my family. We were always raised to think of ourselves as Bombayites first, but Nizzim Uncle says that's a mistake. That's how Hitler won, he says, because the Jews thought of themselves as Germans, even when nobody else did. There is a new country being built for Jews and by Jews. I want to be part of it."

His face turned dark with rage. "And what is India, then, just a dirty handkerchief for blowing your nose and then throwing away? It was good enough for you people all these years. And now that we are finally having our freedom, now that the British have returned to their cucumber sandwiches and fish and chips, now at the most exciting time, you all will leave India."

"Well, the Jews always were a wandering people," Mariam said with a sad smile he didn't understand. For some reason that sad smile, so remote, so timeless in its grief, upset him more.

"The Hindus always complain that the Parsis don't act like they belong to India, that they are always having their noses up in the air, but you people are the Parsi's Parsi," he said bitterly. Then his face collapsed with pain. "But Mariam, if you were leaving, why all this?" he said, his hand sweeping over the bed. "Why all the kissing and hugging and dating? Were you making a *chootia* out of me, or what? You didn't even give me a hint about what Abe Uncle was thinking."

"Soli, I swear to you that everything that I've told you has happened in the last week. Daddy says he and Mummy have been discussing the move for over a year, but nobody told me a thing. I guess they first wanted to see how David and Solomon would do in Israel.

"As for what happened in this room—I wish I could tell you that I'm sorry that it did, that I regret it. But I don't. Soli, you are the kindest, funniest man I have ever met. You have made these last five months magical for me. I am sorry that I seem to come into your life only to hurt you. Believe me, there's no one in this world whom I want to hurt less. And Soli, promise me this. Never forget that no matter where I'll be, I'll carry you in my heart. Always. You must believe me when I say this."

It was over. He had lost her a second time. He felt empty, past the point of rage and accusation. He wanted to say something, wanted to hold her in his arms one more time, but he suddenly felt so shy and awkward around her that he hoped she would leave.

Mariam must have sensed his discomfort, because she said she had to run along. When she stood at the front door with her hand on the knob, he walked over and kissed her lightly on the forehead. Mariam took his right hand in hers, raised it to her lips, and kissed it in such an intense, ritualistic way, that he thought it was some ancient Jewish custom he knew nothing about. It dawned on him how little he knew of Mariam, her religion and her history. He felt ashamed of himself. He should have asked more questions, learned more about her religion. How naïve he had been in thinking that love could build a bridge over history.

And then she was gone. His hand still tingled from where her mouth had been. He felt a mad, animal need to rush down the stairs and plead his case with Mariam again. He could not lose her like this, so easily, with so little of a fight. Surely there were some words that he could say that would make her realize what she was giving up. But when he thought of the specific words, nothing came to mind. He felt exhausted and spent. He had a sudden image of being seven years old and at school. An older bully was twisting his hand behind his back while Soli bit his lip from the pain. They were both engaged in a silent contest of wills. Pain filled Soli's body, but the older boy would not slacken his grip. Finally, bending over until he was down on one knee, his mouth tasting of salt, Soli cried out, "I give up." Immediately, the grip slackened and he felt better.

He went to the window and opened the curtain. Mariam was hurrying away, without a look back. "I give up," he whispered to her receding form. Then, again: "I give you up."

When he turned back to face the room, it seemed shabbier than it had an hour ago. He noticed the peeling paint, the cracks in the floor tile, the frayed corners of the lamp shade. A fly buzzed around where the tandoori chicken lay open and untouched. He heard his own footsteps as he walked toward the bed. He sat down at its edge. The bed still bore Mariam's imprint, and absently, he ran his hand lightly against it.

Then Soli Contractor put his head in his hands and wept. He wept as he had not wept since he was thirteen years old and he saw his father's still form laid out in white, knowing that in a few moments this big jovial man would be pecked at by vultures. He cried for himself and for Mariam, for the couple they might have been, for the children they would never have. He cried for his poor mamma, who would go to her grave asking for a daughter-in-law. He cried for the six million anonymous strangers whom Mariam had called her people. He cried for India, for losing a family as fine as the Rubins, and he cried in rage at Israel for stealing them away from him. He cried for the ghosts of history who had entered and destroyed his life in such a visible way.

Thinking back to the previous time he had been in this room, when Mariam and he had transformed it from a run-down apartment into a holy altar, Soli cried some more. He cried for the drops of blood on a blue sheet, which would never be shed again. He cried for the contentment at the sound of running water that he would never feel again. He cried for the singing of the flesh that he would hear no more—for his limp and useless hands, for his passive, tasteless tongue, for his yellow, dulled heart. He cried for the slow, dull trickle of blood in his veins and for his heavy and useless legs, which, disentangled from Mariam's, could no longer hold him up.

In the distance, he heard something breaking, like fallen china.

It was only the sound of his dying heart.

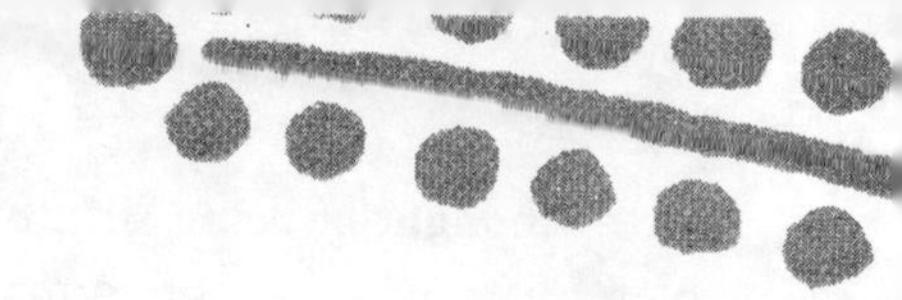

Seven

She couldn't help herself. For the seventh time that evening, Tehmi Engineer looked hurriedly around, making sure that no one was watching her. Coomi Bilimoria had been talking to her a few minutes ago but had now moved a few feet away, doing that strange thing with her eyes that only Tehmi seemed to notice. Confident that no one was paying her any attention, Tehmi let her right hand travel discreetly to her left armpit. Shifting her sleeveless blouse ever so slightly, she moved her middle finger in a circular motion until she found what she was looking for.

A lump. Probably the size of a small grape, Tehmi reckoned. But unlike a grape, this lump didn't feel soft and squishy. Instead, it was as though a hard pebble had made itself at home under her skin. She had accidentally discovered it while in the shower, about a week ago. But on that day, preoccupied as she was with shopping for a new sari to wear to Mehernosh Kanga's wedding, she hadn't given the matter much thought. But that night, she had accidentally touched it while falling asleep, and this time, the hardness of the lump against her fingers had jolted her awake. Curious, she'd pressed down on it, gingerly poking around its edges, ready to wince if the pressure hurt. But the lump was strangely painless. She racked her brains to remember if she had accidentally injured herself, but she couldn't imagine how she could have hurt herself in such an inaccessible place.

As the word *cancer* formed in her brain, she froze. That's impossible, she'd told herself, 100 percent impossible. But then, the second treacherous thought: Why impossible? Her stomach lurched violently at the thought of being sick, but it wasn't the illness itself that troubled her as much as the formalities of illness: the visit to her grave-faced family doctor, the mammogram, the referral to a cancer specialist, perhaps a biopsy. Tehmi knew of five Parsi women in the past three years who had had breast cancer. It was an epidemic sweeping through the community, like the influenza epidemic that had crippled her hometown when she was a little girl, three years before her family moved to Bombay. Tehmi felt overwhelmed and tired at the thought of spending the next few weeks in the waiting rooms of doctors' offices. Also, she thought, whom can I ask to go with me when I visit the doctor? Who will be there for me while I wait for the diagnosis? Automatically, Tehmi's mind leapt back to the dual tragedies that had befallen her over forty years ago. Those incidents had slowly banished her from the community and sense of engagement that the other residents of Wadia Baug took for granted. In fact, Tehmi was the only Wadia Baug resident who did not mind being the target of Dosamai's gossip, because it was proof that she existed, that she surfaced occasionally in the minds of people living beside her.

Lying alone in bed, her finger rubbing compulsively against the newly discovered lump, the loneliness that Tehmi's forced exile had bestowed upon her threatened to overpower her. Who would sit with her for long hours if she needed chemotherapy? Who would visit her in the hospital if she needed surgery? Who would take care of her when she returned home? What would be worse, she wondered—if her neighbors continued to avoid her as they had done in the decades since the day she learned that grief had its own peculiar stench, or if they suddenly came to her rescue, their newfound compassion a taunting reminder of the long, barren years when it had been lost? Which would be harder to bear, the sting of pity or the slap of indifference? The pain of continued exile or the pain of a prodigal's return home?

Then again, it could be nothing. Tehmi also knew of women who'd spent weeks believing they were staring death in the face, only to have death remove its mask to reveal a child's gleeful grin. It could all turn out to be so harmless, like stepping onto solid ground after a scary Ferris wheel ride.

Toward dawn, she had made up her mind: She would do nothing—yet. She would simply keep an eye on this strange fruit growing in her body, hope that it would disappear as suddenly as it had appeared. And if it didn't—well, she was sixty-three years old. She had already lived several times as long as Cyrus had. She had taken up space on this planet, drunk its water, eaten its fruits and grains, feasted on its animals, for over six long decades. Enough was enough. No need to be so pathetically invested in life. She remembered seeing Amy's chest after her mastectomy, the snakelike scar that ran across a chest as flat as the Deccan Plateau. She had forced herself to make one of her rare hospital visits to see Amy after her surgery because Amy had sent food for Tehmi and her mother for a week after Cyrus's death, and one thing about Tehmi, she never forgot a kindness. But seeing Amy with those plastic drain bottles coming out of her like drooping wings made Tehmi wish she had not gone. And when the sick woman unexpectedly asked her if she'd like to see the scar, some mixture of pity and morbidity made her say yes.

It was a mistake. The scar reminded her of why she had turned away from unpleasant things ever since Cyrus's death, why she had carefully built for herself a sanitary life, a life minus blood, urine, and pus, a life where children did not enter (because, after all, children get older and sometimes even die), where the tearings and brushings and bruisings of human intercourse were kept at arm's length. Of course, it made for a lonely life, but Tehmi felt she had ample justification for choosing a clean life. Once a woman has witnessed the human body distorted beyond recognition, once she has smelled the distinct, unmistakable smell of charred flesh from a body that used to smell of rose water and eau de cologne, then that woman has the right to turn away from all things ugly, Tehmi believed. And if that turning away required her to sacrifice most of humanity, so be it.

But some stenches never die. Once inhaled, they stay buried in the guts of the person inhaling them, sending up their ghastly vapors at inopportune times. Thus, Cyrus lived inside of Tehmi even after his death. On one hand, it made her feel close to him, as if he had never really left her. On the other, carrying around a dead man who stunk to the high heavens ensured that few of the living wanted to befriend her. Years ago, she had been confronted with a choice. She chose the dead.

It was a bright Tuesday afternoon in October, two days after Tehmi's twentieth birthday. She had been sitting in the Elphinstone College cafeteria with her friend Naju when she looked up and saw a handsome young man walking toward them. With a quick glance, Tehmi took in the straight back, the muscled, sun-kissed arms, the big brown eyes. But most of all, she was mesmerized by the mop of curly dark brown hair that shone like a halo in the afternoon sunlight. "Don't look now," she whispered to Naju, "but there's a real lollipop walking toward us."

As if on cue, Naju promptly looked over her shoulder. She let out a groan as the stranger reached their table. "Oh God, that's no lollipop, Tehmi," she said loudly. "That's just my idiotic older brother, Cyrus. This is my friend Tehmi. Say hello to her, Cyrus, and then tell me what historic occasion has brought you here." Even as she blushed and returned Cyrus's greeting, Tehmi could now see the resemblance between her friend and the man who stood grinning at his sister.

"Not even an offer to sit down and have a cup of *chai,* Naju?" he said in an ironic voice laced with laughter.

"If I offer you *chai,* I know I'll be the one paying for it, you loafer. So first tell me how much money you need to borrow and then I'll see if I can afford tea."

Cyrus pulled up a chair. "Such distrust," he said in a sad voice, although his eyes gleamed with mischief. "A pity, really, in someone of such tender years. Your poor husband is going to have a tough time. . . ."

"Not to worry about my nonexistent husband. I'm more concerned about my very existent brother, who I know hasn't come all this way to talk about my marriage prospects."

Cyrus smiled a slow smile, which made Tehmi's stomach flip in a way it never had before. Tilting back in his chair, he turned to face

Tehmi. "Miss Tehmi, it is, correct?" he said. "Well, Miss Tehmi, I appeal to your sense of fair play. Let us assume, for a moment, that a man does need a small loan. Notice, I said loan, as in something that will be repayed. Let's say that our man has finished a tough exam at his law college and in order to soothe his weary mind, he decides to take a walk down Colaba Causeway. There, he spots a pair of shoes, made of fine Italian leather. Now, this man could have instead gone to the Gateway of India and stared out at the water for a few hours to calm his tired brain. But fate decreed otherwise. It led him by the hand to a pair of fine Italian shoes. Can you blame the man for believing that it is his destiny to own those shoes? But fate, as we know, is cruel. And so it happens that when the poor, wretched man opens his wallet, he finds he is short by a few measly rupees. Then, inspiration strikes. He remembers that his younger sister—the same sister he has done countless favors for, I may add—is at nearby Elphinstone College. The tug of ancient bloodlines pulls him toward her college. He walks as if in a fog. Only she can help him fulfill his true destiny. Only she can—"

But here, Cyrus's voice cracked with repressed laughter and the three of them burst out laughing. "*Bas, bas,* Cyrus, even for you, this is too much," Naju spluttered.

However, Cyrus was not quite done. "And so, Miss Tehmi," he resumed. "I'd like you to be the judge. Is it such a sin for a poor law student to ask his prosperous younger sister for a small loan? Especially when it's for such a good cause? Tell you what, Miss Tehmi. I'll let you decide my fate."

Lust rose like steam within Tehmi. I'd like to decide your fate, you baby doll, she thought. I think you should marry me, myself.

She turned to Naju. "Come on, *yaar.* Give him a few rupees."

"Bravo." Cyrus beamed. "Good judgment call, Tehmi. A girl after my own heart. You heard her, Naju. What are you waiting for? Cough up the money."

Naju grumbled as she reached into her purse. *"Saala besharam,"* she said. "Turning my best friend against me. God knows how you do this, but you pulled it off again. Here, this money is just to have you shut up, you rascal."

"Thanks again," Cyrus said to Tehmi as he pocketed the money. He turned to Naju, poker-faced. "You know, I do all this for you. Buying good clothes, expensive shoes. All so that you have a brother you can be proud of. So many sacrifices . . ."

Naju rose with a roar. "You ungrateful scoundrel. Give me back my money right this minute. It's bad enough you buy those ridiculous, expensive Italian shoes, but then to expect me to lick your boots, now that's the limit."

Cyrus sat there, shaking with silent laughter, watching as his sister spluttered with indignation. Then, with a satisfied look, he rose to his feet. "Was very nice meeting you, Tehmi," he said. "You're a great partner in crime." He winked at her conspiratorially, and then he was gone. Tehmi felt as if he had sucked all the sunlight out of the room with him.

The darkness that Cyrus left in his wake stayed with her for the next three days. Out of that darkness, his shiny face would rise before her eyes at unexpected times. She was irritated at herself for this sudden infatuation, but irritation did nothing to dispel it. Finally, on the fourth day, she asked Naju if she could stop by that evening to pick up her philosophy notebook. They made plans for Tehmi to stop by at 6:00 P.M., but she deliberately showed up an hour later, when she knew the Engineers would be sitting down for dinner.

Cyrus answered the doorbell. He was wearing blue pajama bottoms and a thin white *saadra,* instead of a shirt. He did a double take when he recognized his visitor. "Why, hello. Come in, come in, please. We just sat down for dinner. Hey, Naju, it's your friend, that nice, generous girl from the cafeteria." He winked at Tehmi, a warm smile lighting up his face.

Naju's mother, Mani Engineer, insisted that she join them for dinner. "Naju, go get an extra plate and set it at the table," she ordered. Tehmi did the required amount of demurring, but her heart was singing. So far, her plan was working beautifully. Dinner at the same table with Cyrus seemed like bliss.

But to her horror, she found herself dumbstruck and unexpectedly shy during dinner. Each time she caught Cyrus's eye, he smiled, but she looked away sternly, certain that he could read her thoughts, could see on her flushed face three days worth of lustful thoughts. To make matters worse, Naju was looking at her curiously, even thumping her on the back once and saying, "Why so quiet, Tehmina? Has a great big black *bilari* got your tongue, or what?"

She sat through dinner dumb with misery, angry at herself for having connived this disastrous plan, unhappy at liking so very much a boy who seemed to be looking at his dinner plate with more interest than at her. Tehmi had always been proud of her slim, tall body, her fair skin, her straight, proud nose, but today she felt gawky and ugly.

So that when she saw Cyrus striding toward them as she and Naju sat in the college cafeteria two days later, she made herself look away and then focus on him again to make sure that her eyes were not playing tricks on her. Naju's groan at spotting her brother confirmed for Tehmi that the smiling man standing beside them was not a figment of her imagination. "Oh no, here comes Mr. Readymoney," Naju said. "Wonder what he wants from his sister this time—new shoes, new shirt, a vacation in Paris? Go away, Cyrus. You're going to make a pauper out of me, I swear."

Cyrus pretended to be hurt. "Such ingratitude," he said, addressing Tehmi. "Such suspicion. Here I am, all ready to repay the many favors my sister has done me. But I'm an unfortunate man, Tehmi. Bad *kismet. Chalo,* it's simply not in my *naseeb* to repay my debts to my sister." And with the same hangdog expression that Tehmi was coming to recognize, he turned away from them in mock dejection.

"*Arre baap,* what an actor he is," Naju said, rolling her eyes. "Not so fast, you ruffian. The sun must have risen in the north today, but if you are wanting to pay me back for my many kindnesses, I am ready, able, and willing. What did you have in mind?"

A slow grin spread like a sunrise on Cyrus's golden face. "I just thought I'd treat my beloved sister—and her best friend, of course—to lunch at the Leopold. But if you two ladies have a better offer, I'll understand." He was addressing his sister but was staring at Tehmi, an expression on his face she couldn't read. She looked uncertainly from brother to sister.

"I swear, Cy, if this is another trick of yours to *patao* a free meal off me, I'll kill you," Naju said. "Tell you what. Show me your wallet before I say aye or nay."

Wordlessly, he pulled out his wallet. "There. Unless you two *devis* order all the animals at Victoria Gardens for lunch, I should have enough money." Naju grunted in satisfaction and surprise at her brother's unexpected solvency.

At lunch, Tehmi was mostly quiet as brother and sister kept up their usual banter. But halfway through lunch, she looked up from her mutton *biryani* and caught Cyrus staring at her. The expression on his face made her stomach lurch, as if she were on a boat. In that moment, she knew for certain that lunch was a ploy to get to know her. A feeling of tenderness swept over her. She basked in the warmth of the knowledge that Cyrus had gone through the whole charade simply to get her to have lunch with him. One look at Naju's face told Tehmi that her friend was oblivious to her brother's intentions.

She could scarcely believe her luck when Naju rose and declared that she would use the loo while Cyrus settled the bill. "And Tehmi," she said, looking over her shoulder, "don't let this scoundrel trap you into spending a single *aana* on lunch. Not even the tip, *saamji ne?*"

Cyrus looked bemused. "*Baap re,* that sister of mine should be the lawyer in the family, instead of me. She should have been up there, along with Gandhiji and Nehru, negotiating India's independence. The British would've left India long before they did, just to get away from her, I swear."

Tehmi laughed and then stopped abruptly as she saw the flame that leapt into Cyrus's eye. He was silent for a moment, his face uncharacteristically serious. And then he said, "I'm not *maroing* a line or anything, Tehmi, but I must tell you. You have a laugh that a man would want to hear on his deathbed." The look in his eye was velvet and there was no trace of the mocking young man from a few minutes ago.

She felt uncontrollably shy and young. "You are so funny, I can't help but laugh," she said finally. "I like it when you make jokes and all."

"Thank you. I'm glad someone thinks my jokes are funny. Now, here's a confession to match yours. Tehmi, the reason for the lunch today is that I wanted to see you again. Do you understand what I'm saying? Um, see, I liked seeing you at dinner at our house the other night. Oh God, I hope I haven't embarrassed you or anything."

Somehow, it evolved into a weekly tradition, the three of them having lunch at the Leopold each Wednesday. Cyrus never asked Tehmi out by herself, but she was too happy at seeing him even once a week to care very much. They both got practiced at exchanging secret glances over Naju's head. It took Naju about three months to smell a rat. It simply wasn't like Cyrus to spend his money on her and her friends. And he was different around Tehmi, she realized, softer, more protective. Still, she knew better than to ask her brother and expect a straight answer. Instead, she cornered Tehmi on their way to college the day after. "Tehmi, don't feel bad, *yaar,* but I have to ask. Is there something going on between you and my brother?"

Tehmi tried to look confused, and when that failed, outraged, but she was a poor actress. Under Naju's steady gaze, she stammered, "I don't know about Cyrus, but I sort of like him."

Naju let out a hoot of laughter. "*Mara baap.* A sensible girl like you falling for a *badmash* like Cyrus? What lines has he been *pataoing* you with? Not loaning him money, are you?"

"How can you say that? That poor boy has been feeding us every week and never asked us for a paisa. You make him sound like some roadside beggar."

Naju made a clucking sound. "Poor Tehmi," she said gravely. "My brother has struck again, I can see. A goner, you are. Still, I'd rather see Cyrus with you than with some of those tarts who pant after him. So tell me. Have you two kissed yet? Is my dear brother a good smack-eroo?"

"Stop it Naju. I never should have told you. We've never even been out alone. I mean, I don't even know if Cyloo likes me."

"Ah, Cyloo, is it?" Naju teased. "And what do you mean, not sure if Cyloo likes you? Of course he does. Haven't you seen the way he looks at you? Like you're a piece of chocolate mousse?"

The next Wednesday when Cyrus arrived to pick up the two women, Naju faked a stomachache. "Must be the *bhelpuri* I ate last night or something. You two chickies carry on without me. I'm not eating lunch today."

"That's a first," Cyrus said automatically, and for one awful moment, Tehmi thought Naju would change her mind just to punish him for the comment. But Cyrus was already saying, "*Accha,* if you're sure you're okay, we'll carry on, then."

"Saala mawali," Naju muttered to Tehmi, who was trying to suppress a smile. "You'd think he'd protest even once, *naam ke vaste.* But this is what happens when you're an ordinary salad leaf sitting next to a chocolate mousse."

On the way to the restaurant, Tehmi was excruciatingly aware of Cyrus's every movement. She was terrified that once at the restaurant, they would find that they had nothing to say to each other. But she had underestimated her companion. Cyrus asked her questions about herself with a greater interest than anyone had ever shown in her. Under his skilled, gentle questioning, she found herself talking about things she had never shared with another human being. She told him about the death of her father when she was seven, how she could still recall the rattle of his keys as he let himself in after working the late shift at the mill. She recalled the mysterious time that followed her father's demise, how she had lost her voice for about seven weeks. Seven weeks spent in total silence, her eyes filling with tears as she heard her distraught mother's pleas, her teachers' stern rebukes but was unable to explain to them the terror she herself felt at this silence that draped over her like a sheet. Her mother had taken her to see her family doctor, who told Dinabai that Tehmi was simply seeking attention. After seven weeks, her voice came back, as mysteriously as it had disappeared, like a gold ring she had lost and found. But Tehmi never forgot the whiteness of that silence. And although it had terrified her, some part of her had grown to valorize that silence, so that even now she held on to some of it, like a childhood coat she had long outgrown but couldn't bear to part with.

It wasn't just Tehmi who had been traumatized by her father's death. Her strong, jovial mother had aged overnight. The first time Tehmi knew for certain that things would never be the same at home was when Dinabai forgot to bargain with her favorite fish vendor and automatically paid full price. Tehmi would never forget the look of pity that stole over the fish vendor's face as his eyes swept over Dinabai's listless body. And that sad listlessness had come to define Dinabai.

Under Cyrus's warm, watchful gaze, Tehmi described the small apartment in Wadia Baug, where she and her mother, Dinabai, had moved after her father's death. She told him how lonely she felt there, especially in the evenings, when her mother delayed turning on the lights until it was almost dark in order to save on the electricity bills. Sometimes they would sit in their darkening apartment, bathed only by the shaft of light from a nearby streetlamp, and Dinabai would suddenly whisper, "There. Did you feel it? Your father was here with us. He's watching over us still." At such times, Tehmi was filled with an inexpressible sadness and an unnameable terror, a feeling that most of life was being played out away from the main stage and that in the wings lurked unimaginable sorrows and heartaches. Then, everything cut her to the quick and she felt connected to the universe by its common pain. She became excruciatingly aware of the powerless pacing of the caged animals in Victoria Gardens; the longing in the eyes of a child whose parent had just refused her a ride on the merry-go-round; the sad lopsided face of the moon three days before it swelled into fullness; the pitiful shivering of the homeless men who slept on the streets, covered only by a worn cotton sheet. "I feel so responsible for my mummy's happiness," she heard herself say to Cyrus. "You know, after Daddy died, my mummy didn't touch any of his belongings for almost three years. It was as if someone blew a whistle and a certain part of our life stopped forever, just froze up. I try so hard to cheer Mummy up, and I know that she tries hard, too, for my sake, but when you have to *work* to be happy, it's not the same, *na,* as just feeling happy from the inside."

She looked at Cyrus, ready to stop if she saw the slightest hint of boredom or pity, but all she saw on his face was kindness. Encouraged, she went on. "You know the worst part about this? I feel guilty when I'm happy myself. I feel like, How dare I be happy when the person I love the most, my mummy, is so miserable? She thinks I don't know, but I've seen her sometimes just sitting on my daddy's bed, silently stroking the sheets, as if feeling for his shape, like she expects him to show up. After so many years, my mother misses my daddy as acutely as that. Then I think, What right do I have to any joy, in the face of so much suffering?"

He touched her then, for the very first time. Leaning forward, he gripped her arm, squeezing it until it hurt slightly. "Tehmi, listen to me. What you just said, that's a sin. A *paap,* do you understand? Tehmi, a person can only give to others what he himself possesses. So if you have happiness in your heart, you can share it with someone and make them happy. If you have only grief, that's all you can pass on to someone else. Your being unhappy or guilty does your mother no damn good. No good at all. If anything, it adds to her suffering. Please, you must change this way of thinking."

She was absurdly moved by the fervent expression on Cyrus's face. To lighten the mood, she said, "*Wah, wah.* Such a good barrister you will someday make, Cyrus. I can see you now, arguing at the high court and all."

But Cyrus was not done. "Tehmi, please. For my sake, change your thinking. It hurts me deeply, believe me, to hear you talk like this."

After their first date, they reached an unspoken agreement that they would no longer include Naju in their Wednesday lunches. They smiled at Naju's good-natured lamentations about how quickly her good fortune at eating at Cyrus's expense had vanished. But they were seldom moved enough to invite her to join them.

They had been dating for about seven months when Cyrus asked her to skip classes one day and go with him to Marine Drive. Sitting on the cement wall overlooking the heaving ocean, he turned to her. "*Ae,* Tehmi, a question for you. What will you be doing on this day a month from now?"

Tehmi smiled. "Silly man. How would I know?"

"*Wah.* I know, but you don't? Okay, I'll tell you. You'll be marrying me on that day, darling. And if you don't, then you'll be attending my funeral at the Tower of Silence. Either way, you're spending that day with me."

"*Ovariu.* What dirty things you say sometimes," Tehmi said, snapping her fingers three times to ward off the evil spirits.

Cyrus grinned. "So it's settled, then. In a month's time, we are getting married."

"But Cyloo, we have no money, no place to live. The pocket money you get won't keep us alive for two days even. And the main thing is, you have your big law exam to prepare for next year."

"Law can wait. I can't. Besides, I already spoke to a fellow in my class. He can get me a job as a foreman at Bombay Chemicals anytime I want. His uncle works there, and I'm to go meet him this week. Pay's pretty good, he says. As for a flat, I was thinking that maybe we could live with your mother until I save enough for our own place. That way, you won't worry too much about her, either. Think your mummy will say yes? But those are all *chota* problems, solvable. Main thing is, I wanted to know your answer before I tell Daddy I am leaving college."

"Leave college? But Cyloo, you have less than a year to go," she cried, horrified.

"One year? I think I will go mad if I have to wait ten more minutes to marry you."

She was flattered, bewildered, scared. The thought of telling her mother about her plans terrified her. Her mother didn't even know that Cyrus Engineer existed. She enlisted Naju's help, asking her to come over when she broke the news to her mother. She had expected the older woman to list a hundred reasons why wanting to marry Cyrus was a bad idea, but Dinabai withheld her judgment and instead expressed an eagerness to meet the young man who had stolen her daughter's heart.

She could tell that her mother liked Cyrus right away. He was at his best that day—warm, funny, deferential, sensitive. Tehmi felt her heart ache with love for this young man, who, seemingly without effort, could wipe the sadness off her mother's face. She had left it to

Cyrus to broach the subject of their living at the Wadia Baug flat after marriage, and it was gratifying to see the look of happiness on her mother's face when Cyrus proposed the idea to her. On one point she was adamant—under no circumstances would she allow the two of them to contribute toward the rent. "We are poor people, *deekra,*" she said to Cyrus. "Apart from some of my wedding jewelry, not much I will be able to offer by way of dowry. Instead, I want you to put away whatever money you were thinking of paying me as rent and save for a place of your own."

"Dina Auntie, you are wrong," Cyrus replied. "You have already given me a huge dowry, the biggest treasure that you possess—Tehmi's hand. What more can I ask from you?"

Dinabai's eyes filled with tears. "Live for a hundred years, *beta.* You have made an old lady happy with your godly words. May you and my daughter have long years of happiness."

Part of Dinabai's blessing came true. They did have years of happiness. They just weren't long.

In the years to come, Cyrus's father, Dali Engineer, told whoever would listen that he had never been opposed to his son's choice of a bride, just the alacrity with which his only son was willing to sacrifice his future as a lawyer to take up a mediocre job at Bombay Chemicals. "I only said to him, 'Get your law degree first and then marry,' " the distraught father would recount. "*Bas,* that was my only demand on him. We all liked Tehmi a lot, nothing against her. By the grace of God, we have enough; we didn't care about dowry or anything like that. Only reason I boycotted the wedding was that I hoped my absence would shock Cyrus into leaving his job and returning to college. Of course, if he'd never taken this job, my son would have someday prayed for his dead father's soul, rather than the other way around. May he rest in peace, my beloved Cyrus."

Three days after Cyrus's visit to Dinabai's home, he took Tehmi to his parents' home. The Engineers had met Tehmi several times before, but Cyrus was confident that once Dali really got to know

Tehmi, his father's objections to the marriage would disappear, that the older man would immediately grasp why his son would not want to waste another moment without being married to Tehmi. But Dali was not convinced. He remained opposed to them marrying this young—after all, Cyrus was only twenty-two and Tehmi even younger, a little over twenty. He also felt that Tehmi should finish her college degree before marrying. He said as much to Tehmi, who sat frozen, unsure of what to say or do. Naju and Mani tried to intervene on Cyrus's behalf, but Dali silenced them with a dismissive wave of the hand. "Does no one in this family have any sense left? What these two youngsters are proposing is foolishness, I tell you. Cyrus has a great future ahead of him, and it isn't at Bombay Chemicals."

A few days before it was time to enroll for the next term at Cyrus's law college, Dali made his son an offer. He would support Cyrus and Tehmi for a year if Cyrus promised to finish his degree. The older man was stunned when his son immediately dismissed the offer. It was his responsibility to provide for his wife, Cyrus declared. He wouldn't let his daddy deprive him of that pleasure, even though he appreciated the generosity of the offer.

And so there was a subdued, simple wedding in Udwada, attended only by Dinabai, Naju, and Cyrus's best friend, Percy. It broke Mani Engineer's heart to miss her only son's wedding, but, as she explained to the young couple, she would be disrespecting her husband if she went. Going to Udwada was suggested by Dinabai, who could not bear the thought of having a wedding in Bombay without the participation of Cyrus's parents. Cyrus himself remained unworried about the breach. "Just give them a few weeks," he told his new bride. "We'll take some *mithai* over to them in a few weeks. My daddy cannot resist Parsi Dairy Farm's *suterfeni,* I swear."

But things never quite got resolved between father and son. Despite Cyrus's popularity and success at his job, Dali could not make his peace with the fact that his intelligent son was working in a job that didn't make full use of his talents. And although he liked Tehmi, he couldn't help but subconsciously hold her responsible for his son's detour from his destiny. And as valiantly as Dali tried to ignore it, he was always aware of the differences between his son and the girl he had married. "Nothing against Tehmi," he once said to his wife, "but if she'd been a girl from a different family—you know, a family that valued education and culture—she would have never encouraged Cyrus to leave college." Mani had spoken up then. "Nobody encouraged our Cyrus to leave college. He's my son, too. But I have to put the blame where it lies, not on the shoulders of some poor twenty-year-old girl."

As the expected thaw never materialized, Cyrus grew finely attuned to every real and imagined snub or slight directed at Tehmi. Once, while they were over for dinner, Dali was speaking to Tehmi, when he had a momentary memory lapse and couldn't recall her name. Tehmi was about to make a joke of it, but Cyrus jumped in. "Tehmi. Her name is Tehmi and you know it," he said through clenched teeth. "She has only been your daughter-in-law for seven months. About time you committed her name to memory."

There was a shocked silence at the table. Then Naju spoke up. "Come on Cyrus, that's not fair. Daddy just had a minute's memory loss. Happens to me all the time."

"*Bas, beta,* save your breath," a hurt Dali interrupted. "Cyrus is all *gussa* and hatred these days. No point in saying anything to such a person."

Tehmi and Cyrus had their first fight that night. During the train ride home, Tehmi tried to explain to Cyrus that his father had meant no harm and she had not been insulted. Cyrus listened silently, but once they got home, he erupted.

"My daddy has even turned you against me, has he? First Naju and now you. Even if I'm wrong, so what? You are *my* wife, not his. Why are you *khali-pili* taking his side? Can I not count on even you for support?"

She was stunned. "Cyrus, what are you saying, darling? Of course I'm on your side. You know I support you cent percent. I just hate to see you and your daddy angry with each other, that's all. I know how much you love him." She saw a new side to him that night, a childish side that wanted blind, unquestioned devotion from her. Strangely, this vulnerability only made her love him more.

There were other fights, most of them involving Dali. Tehmi knew that Cyrus loved and respected his father, but both men were reluctant to admit this central fact to one another. Dinabai, too, was upset at the growing distance between father and son. But the one time she commented on it, Cyrus cut her off abruptly. "Dinabai, please. This is my family *mammala,* not yours," he snapped. The older woman was stunned at this uncharacteristic sternness and turned her face away before her son-in-law could see the hurt in her eyes. Later that night, a subdued Cyrus had apologized. She forgave him readily, but from then on, she didn't involve herself in the matter.

In his sane moments, Cyrus often told Tehmi how much he appreciated her efforts and overtures to his father, but the quarrel with Dali was never completely resolved. There were times, early on, when they left Dali's home with Cyrus vowing to never go back. But Tehmi prevailed on him. "We have so much love for each other, Cyloo, surely we have enough to spare for them. Soon, Dali Uncle will see how much we love each other and then he'll be happy for us. Remember, everything your daddy says, it's because he loves you. You don't know what I would give to have my daddy back. Let the small things go, Cyloo." Here, Tehmi got behind-the-scenes help from her mother-in-law. Mani, who was determined not to lose her only son to what she considered to be her husband's silliness, early on established a tradition that the young couple was to have dinner every Saturday at the Engineers' home in Flora Fountain. If it was a special occasion, Dinabai joined them, too.

At Wadia Baug, people marveled at the change in Dinabai. The bawdy, no-nonsense woman she had been before her husband's death resurfaced after lying dormant for years. Now, Dinabai joined her neighbors in bargaining with the fish vendor and participated with gusto in their ritualistic tirades against the butcher and the milkman. There was some good-natured neighborhood gossip about the fact that Cyrus had taken not one but two brides. Tehmi was aware of the gossip but paid it no mind. She was just awed that Cyrus could draw out a side to her mother she had given up as lost forever. "My God, Mamma," Cyrus once said after Dinabai had told a particularly bawdy joke, "how did your late husband ever manage you? You must have kept the poor man up all night." Tehmi was about to reprimand Cyrus, when she saw the coy look on her mother's face. "My husband was having no complaints about me in that department," she replied. Tehmi blushed.

Most evenings, Cyrus came home from work armed with sweets and stories, both of which the two women eagerly consumed over dinner. Despite Cyrus's protestations, Dinabai kept her part-time job as a cook at the Ratan Tata Institute, and Tehmi loved the days when both her mother and husband were at work and she spent the morning making an elaborate dinner for them. Sometimes, Cyrus had a friend from the factory call Tehmi from work. "Cyrus says he's having an emergency. He's not sure he can make it through the day without seeing you. Tehmiben, can you come meet him at the gates at shift change?" Invariably, Tehmi would drop whatever she was doing and go meet her husband. They would have dinner and then walk around Apollo Bunder before returning home. Dinabai, who, to Tehmi's relief, had turned out to be a most noninterfering mother-in-law, always encouraged her daughter to spend time alone with her husband. "My mother-in-law was a real *daakan,* possessive and jealous of her son. Didn't give us two minutes of peace or privacy," she told Tehmi. "I've always vowed I would not be like that."

Dinabai was not the only one to fall prey to Cyrus's charm. Wadia Baug's older residents lit up like hundred-watt bulbs when he stopped to talk to them in that teasing manner of his. Several of the girls in the neighborhood had secret crushes on him. "I swear, he looks like an Englishman," they said giggling. "Tehmi's fair-skinned also, but she looks like black carbon paper compared to him." Starstruck teenagers like Rusi Bilimoria followed Cyrus around like groupies. Jimmy Kanga's uncle once requested Cyrus to talk to his errant nephew about the importance of a good education, and young Jimmy emerged from that conversation dazzled. In later years, Jimmy always attributed his becoming a lawyer to Cyrus. "Changed my life, he did. I was much younger than he was, but he took me under his wing. I was a bad student, already headed for trouble. A bitter young man I was in those days. Didn't care about my studies, didn't care about anything. But he was so kind, so understanding, that Cyrus. Made me see the light. Of course, at that time, I was too young to know that he'd left law himself. That was the miraculous part—how a man who decided against law himself was responsible for me becoming a lawyer."

Within months of moving into Wadia Baug, Cyrus organized a neighborhood cricket league. Every Sunday morning, Rusi and the other neighborhood boys rode the bus to a nearby practice field, where Cyrus coached them in the intricacies of the game. The boys played their hearts out, for fear of embarrassing their coach with a poor performance. They returned home around 1:00 P.M., hot, sweaty, and happy. On rare occasions, Cyrus asked a bewitched boy to stay to eat the mutton *dhansak* and kebabs that Dinabai had prepared for Sunday lunch. The guests watched, mesmerized, as Cyrus ate potato chips along with his *dhansak*—a boyhood habit that he could not forsake. "Need something crunchy with the *daal,*" he'd say.

How can one person make a difference in so many lives? Tehmi wondered as she looked at her mercurial husband. She noticed how Pestonji, the eighty-year-old widower who lived on the ground floor, made it a point to look out of his window around the time Cyrus came home each evening. As soon as the old man spotted Cyrus, he opened his door and waited on the landing. "Good evening, Cyrus," he greeted him daily. "How was work today?" And no matter how tired he was, Cyrus would stop and chat for a few minutes. In the nearly three years they had been married, she noticed the change in her own mother, how Dinabai always combed her hair and changed into a fresh duster coat an hour before Cyrus was expected home. Until Cyrus came to live with them, Dinabai wore the same housedress for days, changing into her sari only when it was time to go to work. Most of all, Tehmi noticed the difference in herself, how the evening shadows did not make her cry anymore. Whereas once she had dreaded dusk, she now felt a quickened anticipation when the sun started to go down, because it meant that Cyrus would be home soon. The melancholia she had struggled with her whole life loosened its grip on her. Love was tearing holes into the veil of gloom that had covered her life since her father's death. And it wasn't as if Cyrus had coarsened her, made her lose her sensitivity. Quite the contrary. Cyrus often told her how much he loved the fact that she felt things deeply, that she was not like the silly, shallow girls that he had known. It was just that Cyrus had taught her that she had a responsibility to be happy, showed her how to look for pleasure in the small things, never to bypass a chance to laugh. Also, the world somehow seemed a little more ridiculous and funny and topsy-turvy when she was around Cyrus, not quite as filled with menace and sorrow as it had once seemed.

How long can this happiness last? she asked herself as she stood at the window, waiting for Cyrus's familiar shape to turn the corner and wave to her. Can life really be this easy, this effortless?

The night before Cyrus's death, Tehmi dreamed of a white tiger. In her dream, the tiger was standing in a clearing in the forest. Slowly, the animal raised its striped snowy white paw and held it out in a pleading, poignant gesture. Tehmi saw that the tiger's blue eyes were filled with tears. She woke up to a feeling of oppressive sadness, feeling crushed by the weight of emotions that were difficult to articulate. She tried falling back to sleep, but sleep had fled. Unable to face the long, cold night alone, she woke Cyrus up. But when he turned on the light and worriedly asked her what was wrong, Tehmi could not answer. Instead, she held him in her arms and kissed every inch of his face as lightly and tenderly as she could. She felt maternal, rather than sexual; she held his face as if it were the sacred, carved face of a deity. They made sweet, magical love that night, a love that transcended sex. Wrapped around him, she felt as if he was no longer simply her husband but her brother and friend, as well, that they had both shed their private skins, their gender even, to become an indivisible coiled entity, much like those indistinguishable male-female figures on ancient Hindu temples. "Nobody we know—none of our friends—shares what we share," Cyrus whispered to her later. "Nobody I know feels more loved by his wife than I do. And if I tried to love you more than I do, I would burst, I swear."

But even love couldn't wash away fate. Toward morning, a feeling of dark foreboding lingered. Twice that morning, she almost asked Cyrus not to go to work that day; twice, she told herself she was being silly and that Cyloo deserved better than a crazy woman for a wife. Finally, to shake herself out of the bleak mood the dream had placed her in, she impulsively told Cyrus that she had decided to go spend the day at his parents' house. He could pick her up there after he left work. Dinabai stood at her window and waved to them as they left the apartment together to catch the same bus. She got off at the Fort bus stop and turned around, to catch him waving to her, his sweet face divided into three parts by the iron bars on the bus window. Then the bus was gone.

She had hoped that her mother-in-law's bustling, good-natured presence would help her snap out of the foul mood she was in. But fear lingered in her heart that morning, like a kiss on the cheek. It was April 14, 1960.

The explosion that shattered Tehmi's life happened a few hours later. An hour earlier, the Engineers had sat down to a late lunch. Afterward, Tehmi was in the kitchen, preparing to wash dishes. It was warm in the kitchen, and Tehmi opened the large window behind the sink to let in some air. Naju was in the adjoining dining room, cleaning up the table and chatting to Tehmi about a mutual friend. "Anyway, like I was saying, Tehmi. That Shirin doesn't know how lucky she is to have someone as nice as Behram chase after her. The only offers I get are from gents like Pesi *Pipyoo,* you know, men who need their mummies to chase after them with their bibs and milk bottles." Tehmi opened her mouth to laugh and then felt her teeth rattle. As the deafening explosion assaulted her ears and made her heart thump furiously, her eyes widened with disbelief. A stream of objects—matchboxes, keys, the severed leg of a doll, a battered frying pan—flew into the kitchen from the outside, like small meteorites hurtling through space. The glass panes in the window she had just opened blew out like candles on a birthday cake. In the far right corner of the kitchen, a lightbulb shattered. Panic engulfed Tehmi. Oh Dadaji, it's an earthquake, she thought. We are all dead ducks. Beneath her, she felt her knees wobble, as if body parts once made of bone and muscle had given way to cotton wool. She could taste blood in her mouth, but her panicked mind had still not registered that she was biting down hard on her lower lip. From a distance, she heard Naju screaming. "*Mari gai, mari gai, mari gai.* Oh God, what is happening? Is Pakistan attacking us, or what?"

Then, Tehmi could hear Dali Engineer's voice over Naju's. "Naju, *deekra.* Calm down. Control your fear, I say. Get down on the floor, both you girls. If this is an air raid, better to be close to the floor." Despite her confusion, Tehmi could hear the struggle in Dali's voice as he sought to quell his own fear with calm authority. "Tehmi. Mani," he called. "Gather together now, everybody. But be close to the ground."

Following the last command was easy because Tehmi's trembling legs could no longer support her weight. She had no idea how much time had lapsed from when she had first felt the earth tremble. But a few minutes after she had made her way into the dining room, there was another explosion, louder than the first. More windowpanes shattered. Dali reached over and pushed her head down while his wife tried to console their hysterical daughter. But Naju was uncontrollable. *"Mara baap,"* she screamed. "If the Pakistanis are attacking, where can we go? Daddy, we should get out of this city, *fatta-faat.*"

Tehmi was forcing herself to think. "But if this is an air raid, why is there no air-raid signal?" she said. "This is an earthquake, not an attack."

Mani spoke up then, in a voice so thick with fear that it took Tehmi a second to place it. "But if it's an earthquake, where is my Cyloo? Oh my Lord, if even a *baal* on my Cyrus's head is affected, I will go mad."

And then Tehmi saw the white tiger again. He stood before her, as real as the matchboxes that had hurtled past her a short while ago. And for a moment, she knew the truth—that Cyrus was dead. But then denial, fear, and a stout loyalty to Cyrus took over. She was repulsed by the momentary betrayal of her own mind, took it as a sign of wavering faith. "Cyrus is okay," she said more fiercely than she intended. "My Cyrus is a king, a survivor. Nobody can touch him, not even God."

Later, she was haunted by that statement. She wondered over and over again about the conceit of that belief, whether she had not challenged and tempted the fates with her arrogance. Perhaps the white tiger had been a test, a test of her humility, of her faith. Perhaps, until she had uttered those words, Cyrus had been alive, injured maybe, but alive, waiting for someone or something to tip the scales of fate in his favor. Perhaps she had sealed his fate with those contemptuous words, banished him to a place where even God could not save him.

A chastised Mani Engineer stared at her daughter-in-law in shame and awe. "Right you are, Tehmi," she said at last. "My Cyrus will return home safe and sound this evening. I will light a *diva* in the *agyari* for seven days to celebrate his safe arrival."

Tehmi knew she needed to go downstairs and use the phone at the Irani restaurant to call someone to go tell her mother that she was okay. But she was strangely reluctant to move, to change this configuration on the floor that she was part of. As long as they did not let the outside world in through the front door, they were safe. Safe in their illusions maybe, safe in the cocoon of denial, but safe nevertheless. Outside lay reality, with teeth and claws as sharp as those of the white tiger from her dreams. Outside lay news that had the potential to destroy lives, news of Cyrus's fate.

But eventually, reality rang the doorbell and Dali Engineer got up from the floor to answer its call. It was Cyrus's boyhood friend Percy, who lived around the corner from the Engineers. "Dali Uncle, oh, please, I'm so sorry. Oh, Dali Uncle, please, give me some good news. Tell me Cyrus has not gone to work today."

Dali looked confused. "I'm sorry, *deekra.* If you are needing to talk to Cyrus, you'll have to wait until he returns this evening. Of course he's at work right now. Hope your problem can wait till evening."

Percy stared at Dali in mortification. "Dali Uncle . . . what are you saying? Cyrus at work? Then you haven't heard?"

"Heard what, Percy?" Dali said, an edge to his voice.

But Percy had spotted Tehmi behind Dali, and he lurched toward her, as if hoping that the same question asked twice would produce a different answer. "Tehmi, hi. Listen, Cyrus didn't go to work today, did he?"

But then Dali's legendary temper flared. "Percy, would you stop this nonsense and tell me what's going on? All of us have had enough excitement for today, what with the earthquake and all. We've already said that Cyrus is at work. Now, what's the problem?"

Percy raised his voice to match Dali's, but his had the thin string of hysteria running through it. "That wasn't an earthquake at all. That was a massive explosion at Bombay Chemicals. Most of the plant is destroyed. If Cyrus is at the factory, he's dead."

Dimly, Tehmi heard the shouting and then the sound of a scuffle. Mani had heard the last part of Percy's words, and before she could stop herself, she slapped the messenger. There were raised voices, screams, the muffled sounds of women crying. But Tehmi didn't care. She felt removed from the theater of grief around her, as if she were a visitor from some sunny, magical planet, untouched by the tyrannies of mortal flesh. Leaning against a wall, she felt herself sinking slowly toward the floor.

Percy caught her just before she hit the floor.

They had to wait four days before they got Cyrus's body. And when they finally did, it was scarcely worth the effort, because this ravaged, charred body was not Cyrus. Tehmi's mother had fought with her tooth and nail about not looking at the body, but Tehmi would not hear of it. "I looked at him while he was alive and I will not send him from this world without looking at his face again," she said. But she miscalculated. It did not occur to her that she would feel nothing but revulsion for the hideous black face before her, that she would fail to find a trace of the man she loved in the object she saw. The Cyrus she knew and loved had skin kissed by the sun and not lashed by fire. Cyrus had soft curly hair, but the body before her had burned hair stiff as paper. The Cyrus she had married smelled of roses and lavender, but the stranger before her emitted a smell that made her gag. Instead of pity or sorrow, she felt hate. She was unprepared for the sudden blinding anger she felt toward Cyrus for putting himself in this position, for allowing himself to die such an ugly, gruesome, unresisting death. "You let me down, Cyloo," she whispered as she flinched away from the shriveled piece of flesh before her. "You were supposed to teach me how to laugh, feel joy. Now you have stuck the sharpest knife into my heart. Less than three years of marriage and you have left. How do I laugh now? Now that the teacher has gone away, what is the student to do?"

They had already started the funeral ceremonies before they were given the body. Tehmi had wanted to wait, holding on to a vain hope that Cyrus was injured but alive, but the elders prevailed. "It's our Parsi custom, *beta,*" Dali Engineer intoned. "Without the proper ceremonies, my Cyrus's soul will be left to linger, not reaching its final resting place. Besides, the newspapers say there is no chance that anyone could have survived the blast."

All over the city, funerals were being planned. The first blast had been followed by a second, deadlier one. The Engineers never found out if Cyrus had died in the first or second explosion. But for the rest of his days, Dali Engineer prayed that his son had been killed instantaneously, as had scores of other workers.

Tehmi walked through the week as in a dream. The Engineers insisted that both she and her mother stay at their home until they received news about Cyrus, and she agreed because she was too tired to care. Besides, the thought of facing the Wadia Baug apartment, to which Cyrus had brought so much laughter and sunlight, was unbearable. Friends from Wadia Baug whom Cyrus had collected like trophies came to visit, to stand vigil with Tehmi, but still, she felt utterly alone. "Tehmi," fifteen-year-old Rusi Bilimoria whispered to her during that period. "You know, everyone always makes fun of me for being such a dreamer, but Cyrus doesn't. He understands. Besides, I really believe in the power of hope, you know? I feel it in my bones that Cyrus is okay. You keep hoping and praying, promise?"

Somehow, Rusi's words penetrated, probably because he referred to Cyrus in the present tense. That's how she thought of Cyrus, too, and it irritated her no end that everybody else had switched to the past tense in talking about her husband. "That's okay, Cyloo," she whispered to herself then. "They may be ready to turn on you, but I'm not ready to give up yet. I'll make those vultures fight with me for every piece of you, I promise."

Of course, those were the good old days. That was before she knew how little flesh there would be left to fight over.

Looking at Rusi now, still lean and straight-backed, but with eyes that seemed heartbreakingly sad and old, Tehmi felt a gush of affection and gratitude for the gangly, dreamy teenager who had tried so hard to console her during that wretched week. She remembered overhearing what Rusi said to a friend on the day of Cyrus's funeral. "We shouldn't be talking of Cyrus's death; we should be talking about his martyrdom. Our building has lost its crown prince today." She never told Rusi, but that snippet of overheard conversation put starch in her back that day, helped her go through her twenty-five-year-old husband's funeral with grace and dignity. Because his words so completely echoed what was in her own heart. She was just grateful that someone else knew the enormity of what was lost, that someone else understood that Cyrus's was no ordinary death because Cyrus was no ordinary man.

She wanted to tell Rusi this today, wanted to thank him for his kindness from decades ago, but then she remembered the days that followed and all the things that had happened since. She forced herself to remember that by the first anniversary of Cyrus's death, all the neighbors and friends disappeared, so that she and her mother were the only ones who left for the *agyari* at 5:30 A.M. that morning to meet with the Engineers and listen to a half-sleepy *dastoor* pray for Cyrus's soul. No one else came; no one visited. It was as if the happy times when Cyrus lived in Wadia Baug had never existed. The odor of her grief had chased them all away.

Three days after Cyrus's funeral, she fell into a deep sleep. She had barely slept during the days that she kept vigil for her doomed husband, afraid to miss that dazzling moment when she would receive word that Cyrus was safe, that somehow he had charmed or tricked death into letting him go. But then she slept for eleven straight hours. When she awoke, it was 7:00 P.M., and for a moment, she thought it was early next morning. As her heavy eyes searched in the dark for the clock, she became aware of a terrible taste in her mouth. It was not the usual sour taste of sleep. Rather, this was the taste of burned flesh, a taste so pungent and sharp that she was afraid to swallow. Leaping out of bed, Tehmi headed for the bathroom sink. There, she vigorously brushed her teeth, using more toothpaste than ever before. She ran the toothbrush over her tongue, scrubbing so hard that she spat tiny traces of blood. Next, she gargled with warm salt water. But it was of no use. The taste of charred flesh would not leave her mouth.

Tehmi's vigorous gargling attracted her mother's attention. *"Su che, deekra?"* she asked. "Your throat is hurting or something? Put on some Vicks if it is. So much tension you've been under, no wonder you're not well."

Tehmi opened her mouth to correct her mother and the old woman flinched as if she had been slapped with a dead fish. "*Baap re,* Tehmi," she gasped. "What is that smell from your mouth? What have you been eating, *beta*?"

She stared at her mother. So the taste in her mouth had an odor, could be spotted by others. She wondered if it smelled as bad to her mother as it tasted to her. Instinctively, she covered her mouth before she spoke. "Haven't eaten anything since that scrambled egg you made this morning," she mumbled. "That's why only I've been brushing my teeth. My mouth has a horrible taste."

Her mother looked worried. "Maybe the egg was rotten. But that was so early this morning. I didn't even wake you for lunch today. Thought you needed to sleep. Are you having motions, Tehmi? Perhaps it's indigestion or diarrhea."

But she was healthy in every other way. Her mother insisted that she go to a doctor, but Tehmi resisted. Dinabai had already spent too much money on Cyrus's funeral, and she hated to waste money on a doctor. Besides, Dr. Poonawala would ask to look down her throat, and she was embarrassed to expose him to an odor that made even her own mother cringe. In the weeks that followed, she took to speaking less and less at home and covered her mouth when she did speak. After a few feeble tries, Dinabai did not disturb her as she sat for long hours staring into space or writing in her book. The older woman had herself known deadly grief and she respected its authority. And truth be told, she was afraid of hurting her daughter's feelings with her involuntarily flinches each time Tehmi opened her mouth. Whatever deadly germ was lodged in her daughter's mouth gave Dinabai the dry heaves. Despite her best intentions, Tehmi's mother felt relief when her daughter did not open her mouth for hours.

Dali and Mani Engineer stopped by two weeks after the funeral to check on their daughter-in-law. They were shocked at the sight that greeted them. Tehmi's hair was disheveled, her eyes blank. There was a faint dry crust of white around her mouth. Tehmi saw the shock in their eyes and was mortified. She was excruciatingly aware of the damp patches of sweat near the armpits of her dress, her uncombed hair, her uncut black fingernails. Afraid of making them nauseous with what would escape from her mouth, she refused to speak to them, but this only bewildered them further. "Tehmi, *deekra,* don't be angry at us, please?" Mani said, misunderstanding her silence. "Only reason we haven't come sooner is Dali was unwell. But we pray to God twenty-four hours a day to give you strength, believe me." Tehmi tried to tell Mani with her eyes that she understood, but the occasion called for words. Finally, the Engineers got up to leave, hurt and bewildered by her strange behavior. Tehmi refused to see them out, so Dinabai slipped on a vest over her duster coat and walked them to the main gate. Dali, already racked with guilt, turned to Tehmi's mother on the way out. "I always liked your Tehmi," he said. "My objection to their marriage had nothing to do with her, believe me."

"I know, I know, Dalibhai," Dina cajoled. "Trust me, Tehmi is not angry at you. Far from it. It's just that—there's another problem. Nothing to do with what you're thinking."

"Problem? Any problem, Dinabai, I'm at your service. Tehmi is not just your daughter but our daughter, too. Tehmi is a proud girl; she won't tell us. But you tell us—what problem is she having?"

"Bad breath." The look of incredulity on Dali's face spurred Dina on. "It's not a joke. Something has happened to Tehmi. Three days after the last ceremony, she woke up with it. When she talks, it's a smell so bad that—God forgive me, for she's my own flesh and blood—even I have a hard time trying not to vomit. It's made her so quiet, my heart aches. And yet, God save me, I'm glad when she's quiet." Dinabai looked ready to cry.

The Engineers exchanged a glance. Dali cleared his throat. "But Dinabai, surely this is not a serious problem. We can take Tehmi to our family doctor. Probably just needs some strong *dava* to clear it up."

"I tried getting her to go to Dr. Poonawala," Dina said excitedly. "But what to do, Dali? She refuses to step out of the house."

Mani spoke up. "I'll have Naju talk to her. Better to have someone her own age talk to her. Naju needs to come see her anyway. It . . . it will be good for both of them."

Indeed, it took plain-speaking Naju to get Tehmi into Dr. Poonawala's clinic. "What are you going to do, sit in your flat like some old hag, waiting for the problem to go away?" Naju cried in exasperation. "What if it takes weeks to clear up, Tehmi? Why torture yourself and your poor mummy with this horrible smell? Stinks like you swallowed a dead rat or something."

Dr. Poonawala prescribed some medication, assured her the problem would be resolved within four days, and expressed puzzlement when she returned a week later. "Let's try it for another week," he intoned. "Some cases are more difficult than others."

But there was no improvement by the following week. A perplexed Poonawala switched medications. "This powder is ten times as strong as the last one. Should clear it right up. Sorry to have not tried this medicine the first time."

The next time she left to visit Poonawala's clinic, Rusi Bilimoria spotted her as she left Wadia Baug. "Tehmi, wait," he said, catching up with her. "How have you been? I've rung your doorbell many times, but your mummy always says you're sleeping or not feeling well. Anything I can do to help you, you have only to say."

Moved by his words, his warm, intense expression reminding her of Cyrus's kind, beloved face, Tehmi spoke before she realized what she was doing. "Rusi, hello. Thank you for your concern. I've been well, just resting. You know, I'm so—"

She stopped abruptly, having noticed that Rusi had drawn in his breath sharply and was looking away. Instinctively, her hand flew up to her mouth. "Sorry, so sorry," she muttered. "Some minor problem I'm having."

Rusi, realizing that Tehmi had noticed his instinctive reaction, looked mortified. "No, no, no, *I'm* sorry," he murmured. He stared at her, unsure of what to say next, willing his body not to react if Tehmi opened her mouth again. Suddenly, he wished his mother was with him. But Tehmi was done talking. After a few agonizing seconds, she nodded sharply and resumed walking. Rusi walked back home, furious with himself. Surely the smell was not as bad as all that, he said to himself. You behaved liked a bastard. But at the thought of the smell, his stomach heaved again.

Tehmi arrived at the clinic that day desperate to find a cure for this strange problem—she couldn't believe it was a disease; there were no other symptoms. She watched Dr. Poonawala closely to pick up on any signs that he was shunning her, but the doctor was a consummate professional. But his quiet, unflinchingly kind manner offended her that day. Of course he can tolerate me, she told herself as she left with yet another prescription. He's used to working with cadavers and God knows what other foulness. Compared to dead bodies, I probably smell like a rose.

And then she saw Cyrus's remains again, smelled again the terrible foul smell of rotting, burning flesh. And it clicked. She was tasting

Cyrus in her mouth. It was as if she had inhaled Cyrus that day at the morgue, taken him in through the pores of her skin and now he was lodged inside her, festering, smoldering. She was both repelled and comforted by the thought. It scared and disgusted her to realize what had happened, that somehow what she had seen and smelled at the morgue that day had followed her home, had lodged itself inside her skin, seeped into her bones, danced on her tongue, found its resting place inside her mouth. But it also comforted her to know that Cyrus was still with her, that she could call on him, talk to him whenever she wanted. *That she could taste him in her mouth.* She felt as if she had tricked death somehow, found a way around the finality of death to hold on to Cyrus. Yes, this was not the Cyrus of her dreams, but if she could not have the Cyrus who smelled of talcum powder, she would at least have the Cyrus who smelled and looked like burned rubber. Cyrus, too, must have missed her so badly, longed for her so very much, to have gone to such lengths to come to her. She felt gratified and humbled at the thought of her dead husband proving his love to her from beyond the grave.

As she walked, she felt a lifting of the thin, brittle feeling that had grabbed her from the day that Cyrus had not come home. The encounter with Rusi now seemed insignificant, as did her earlier desire to beg Dr. Poonawala for a cure. What did it matter if she lost a friend, one breath at a time? What did it matter who from the building still spoke to her? What did it matter that even her own mother turned away each time she spoke? Cyrus had not abandoned her. He had kept his promise never to leave her. She laughed out loud at the thought. Of course Cyrus had kept his word. When had Cyrus been anything but honest and loyal to her? Now it was her turn. She was only angry at herself for not recognizing earlier the extent of Cyrus's love for her. How sad Cyrus must have felt when she didn't recognize him right away, how hurt he must have been each time she swallowed one of Dr. Poonawala's powders or brushed her tongue with one of his pastes. As if she was trying to kill Cyrus, flush him out of her life, like an unwanted fetus.

No more. She said the words out loud. "No more." Said it as her grip loosened on the paper bag containing Dr. Poonawala's powders. *Cyrus over everyone else.* Repeated it as she dropped the bag on the sidewalk and kept walking, without looking back. "No more." In the battle between the living and the dead, it was no contest. Cyrus had come back to her, not abandoned her, not turned away from her. He had chosen her. Now it was her turn to choose him.

Now, at Mehernosh Kanga's wedding reception, Tehmi wondered for the umpteenth time whether she had made the right choice. She could still clearly remember the day she had decided to withdraw inward, to shun the living in favor of the dead. It had been so easy and clear-cut back then. In the weeks and months since that fateful day, how resolutely she had ignored Dali Engineer's pleadings that she see a better doctor than Poonawala, that she go see an ear, nose, and throat man. How easily she had ignored Naju's exhortations to go out with her occasionally, instead of spending her evenings at home with Dinabai. How firmly she had refused her mother's plea that she get a job, instead of sitting home crocheting all day long. Instead, she packed Dinabai's lunch each morning and waved to the older woman as she set out for the Ratan Tata Institute. Then she spent the day dreaming about Cyrus. Some days, she even forgot to take a bath. Often, she was interrupted by one neighbor or another attempting to check on her. Mostly, Tehmi ignored the doorbell until it stopped ringing. Or she acted so strangely toward them that it took them months to screw up the nerve to return.

Like the time she let Amy Gazdar in. Tehmi waited until Amy settled into the chair in the living room, and then she went into the bedroom to conduct the conversation from the adjoining room. "Mamma is not here. She will be home soon," she said to her visitor.

Amy decided to ignore the strange sitting arrangement. "I know. I came to see you, Tehmi. A few of us friends are thinking of going to Colaba Causeway tomorrow evening to do some shopping. I just thought maybe you would like to join us. You know, get some fresh air and stuff."

"Thank you for the food you sent after Mummy and I got back after the funeral," said the dull voice from the other room.

Amy felt a trickle of sweat run down her face. "Tehmi, did you hear what I said? About Colaba Causeway?"

There was a long silence. Then Tehmi replied, "Thank you for visiting. But I am tired now. Thank you for the food."

"No mention, no mention." Amy hurried out of the apartment and went directly to another neighbor's flat to relay her strange encounter with Tehmi. Months went by before she visited Tehmi again, and then she went on a Sunday, when she knew Dinabai would be home.

Tehmi was convinced that Amy's visit was an act of charity and she bristled at the thought. She constantly looked for signs of revulsion on the part of her visitors, hoping to support her belief that they stopped by out of morbid curiosity and pity. Once, she looked out of the window in time to see Dinabai, who was returning home from work, give a box of R.T.I. chocolates to the elderly woman who had just paid Tehmi a visit. Seething with anger, Tehmi waited for Dinabai to enter the flat. "So you now have to bribe your friends to come visit your foul-smelling daughter, uh? I saw you hand the chocolate box to that old woman who sat here wasting my time. Just dropped by for a visit, did she? What am I, the charity case of Wadia Baug?" A stunned Dinabai swore her innocence, but Tehmi remained suspicious.

Naju was the only visitor that Tehmi looked forward to seeing. But Tehmi's new passivity was too much for Naju. Once, in the days when she used to visit at least once a month, Naju lost her temper. "*Bas,* enough is enough, Tehmi," Naju said. "I love my brother very much also, but this is not what Cyrus would have wanted, you sitting at home like a *maharani* while your poor mother slogs all day to feed and clothe you. You are too young to be living off her widow's income. At this rate, even the money you got from Bombay Chemicals will be gone in no time."

But Naju's words had no effect on Tehmi. "Cyloo doesn't want me to work," she said in that dull voice she had developed since his death.

"Cyloo doesn't want you to work?" Naju repeated incredulously. "What, Cyrus just wants your mother to work, with her asthma and all? How are you knowing Cyrus doesn't want you to work? Did he come to you in a *sapana* and tell you? Come off it, Tehmi. Don't blame my brother for your laziness."

She did not talk to Naju for three full months after that, until Naju apologized. During those months, she also stopped visiting her in-laws, despite the fact that this meant forgoing the cash that Dali Engineer used to press into Tehmi's hand after each visit. When she finally made up with Naju and resumed the visits, the balance of power had shifted. The Engineers stopped begging Tehmi to go see another doctor for her problem and Naju gave up trying to get Tehmi out of her shell. All of them accepted that the dull, silent woman in front of them was a pale shadow of the woman their son had married. Watching her made Dali's and Mani's hearts ache even more for their lost son. Cyrus had left a half-dead woman in his wake, they realized.

Tehmi's isolation only exaggerated her melancholia. Once, she sobbed for hours after having spotted a crow peck on the remains of a mouse outside her window. Another time, she left Bomanji Pharmacy in tears because another shopper had refused her young daughter money to buy an orange ice-candy stick. At times, she worried that she was losing her ability to distinguish between griefs because every hurt and loss felt the same. But there was no one to confide such thoughts in. In the three years since Cyrus's death, she and Naju had more or less drifted apart. Naju had finished her B.A. and was now busy planning her wedding to a businessman from Surat. Besides, Naju was too down-to-earth and fun-loving to understand the pathos that Tehmi felt. That was the beauty of Cyrus—he was that rare man who could understand two women as diverse as Naju and Tehmi.

For Cyrus's sake, she forced herself to participate in the preparations for Naju's wedding. She owed the Engineers that much, she felt. They had been nothing but decent to her since Cyrus's death. So she accompanied Mani and Naju to pick out the saris and jewelry to be presented to the groom's relatives. The years had taught them all that as long as Tehmi looked away slightly when she spoke to them, Mani and Naju could tolerate the odor from her mouth. The salesmen in the shops were a different story. Tehmi was convinced that only the scent of money, even more powerful than the smell of her breath, kept them from asking her to leave.

"Tehmi, it's all in your head, *yaar.* Nobody was looking at you funny," Naju attempted. But a look from Tehmi silenced her.

The day before the wedding, she was helping Naju try on her wedding sari, when the latter turned to her, pulled Tehmi toward her in a tight hug, and burst into tears. "I keep wishing Cyrus were here," Naju sobbed. "God, I miss him so much, I can only imagine what you must go through. I keep thinking of what he would have been like today, older but as handsome as ever. Tehmi, I just want to say I'm sorry for every horrible thing I've said to you since Cyrus's death, about not working and all. And I feel so bad, I mean, about this bad breath problem. No, don't look away. I'm not meaning to embarrass you or anything. I just see how shy it's made you and it seems so unfair, on top of everything else you've had to go through in the last few years. It's like a dual tragedy, you know?"

Tehmi blinked. She hadn't known Naju had ever spared two minutes thinking about her. "You were my friend before I ever met your brother," she said finally. "I may not see you as much now, you being in Surat and all. But remember, you are more than my sister-in-law. You are my friend first and foremost. All the years that I didn't get with my Cyloo, I now wish for you, in your marriage. Be happy, Naju. Try to forget about the sad things, if you can. Leave your brother's memory to me—I'll guard it well. And don't you worry about your parents. I'll take care of them, I promise."

She was good to her word. Until Dali and Mani Engineer died in a car accident on their way to Pune in 1977, she visited them regularly. Twice a week, she would go over to their flat with a cooked meal. They, in turn, came to rely on her more than ever. "With Naju in Surat, you are the only daughter we still have in Bombay," Mani would say to her.

On the fifth anniversary of Cyrus's death, Dali told Tehmi he had a surprise for her. The Engineers had established a trust for Tehmi.

Each month for the rest of her life, she would receive a fixed sum of money from the trust. It wasn't much, Dali mumbled, but it was enough to make it possible for her never to have to work, if she didn't want to. Tehmi protested vehemently. "But I'm making some money now from my crochet work," she said, but Dali shushed her. "I'm not doing it for you; this is for my Cyrus," he said. "Besides, this is your fair share. If my Cyrus had lived, he would've inherited this flat and all that, after all. But fate had a different plan for us. My Naju is well settled and so are we, by the grace of God. No sense in making you wait to inherit things until after we kick the bucket. No, use it to enjoy your youth."

The Engineers watched in dismay as Tehmi's youth flitted past her. On her twenty-ninth birthday, Mani invited Tehmi and Dinabai to lunch. They had the celebratory *mori daar,* fried fish and *sev.* Mani served her famous *lagan-nu-custard* for dessert. "An auspicious meal for an auspicious occasion," Mani said. After lunch, they moved into the living room and Mani called for the servant to put on the tea. Finally, timidly, she broached the subject. "Tehmi, dear, Dali and I are having something to say to you. All we ask is you keep an open mind about the subject. Promise? . . . Okay. Do you remember our good friend Perin? Well, as you may be knowing, Perin has as a son, Viraf, almost the same age as you. He's a good boy, no bad habits, doesn't smoke or drink. Has a good job at Godrej. What we were thinking is, would you like to meet him? Viraf is looking to settle down, and Dali and I are so wanting you to be happy. We appreciate the devotion you have shown to our Cyrus, but, Tehmi, there's a time and place for everything, including mourning. We have watched Viraf grow up, so we feel like you would be in good hands. And as far as we are concerned, you will always be our daughter."

"But Mani. Tehmi is a widow. You know how people feel about that," Dinabai interrupted.

"Not these people, Dina. These are good, modern people. They know about Tehmi's situation and have no problem with it."

Tehmi could feel three sets of eyes staring hopefully at her. She turned to face her in-laws. "Thank you, both of you," she said simply.

"But I can't even consider what you said. I'm still married to Cyrus, you see. It would be cheating to marry someone else. Also, there is the other problem. Or have you all forgotten?" she said with a grim smile. "I wouldn't wish that on my worst enemy."

Dali cleared his throat. "Ah, yes. About that problem. Tehmi, I still believe there's probably a simple cure for that. We, after all, never really pursued a cure. Earlier, what with the shock of Cyrus's death and all, I could understand. But enough years have gone by now. Why suffer unnecessarily? Let us make an appointment to go see Dr. Udwadia."

Tehmi got up abruptly. "Nothing can be done about that. Not even the best doctors in England or America can help with that. *Bas,* that's in my *naseeb* to live with, just like Cyrus's death was in my *naseeb.*" She stared at Dali. "Don't ask me to take my bad luck to some poor man. I'll destroy him, too."

"What nonsense, what nonsense," Dali said, shaking his head vigorously. "You are an educated, smart girl. How can you think like some illiterate villager?" But Tehmi could tell that the fight had gone out of him.

Within her neighborhood, she achieved a kind of mythic status as she grew older. By the time she was in her forties, she became a figure of derision and pity, mystery and awe. Residents who had moved to Wadia Baug since Cyrus's death and only knew Tehmi as an elusive, shadowy figure cautioned their children to stay away from the strange lady on the first floor. Teenagers nicknamed her "Killer Breath" Tehmi. The older residents, dimly remembering those three magical years when Cyrus had shot through their lives like a bolt of sunlight, halfheartedly scolded the teenagers and appealed for empathy. But the truth was that they blamed Tehmi for their frightening inability to help her with either one of the two misfortunes that had so swiftly befallen her. People like Amy Gazdar, whose attempts to help had been so brutally rebuffed, soon forgot the sequence of things, so that they now believed that Tehmi had stopped speaking to them at Cyrus's funeral and that fate had punished her for her arrogance, that her foul breath was merely a symptom of her foulness of temper. "Pride,"

Dosamai intoned to her gallery of housewives. "God does not like proud people. See how swiftly He punished Tehmi, with breath worse than a stray dog's. I've seen chickens with their throats slit who smelled better."

It was only after Dinabai's death, when Tehmi was fifty-seven, that the enormity of her isolation hit her. The three years she took care of her bedridden mother gave her the perfect excuse for socializing even less than before. Caring for Dinabai took up all her time, so that whereas earlier Tehmi would attend the occasional funeral and pay the rare hospital visit, now even those interactions fell by the wayside. Dinabai's funeral was well attended. People Tehmi hadn't seen in years showed up at the Tower of Silence. She was shocked to see how much older everyone looked—children whom she remembered as seven-year-olds were now self-consciously introducing their young husbands and wives to her; men whom she remembered as middle-aged were now bent with osteoporosis. She realized that it had been years since she'd had a conversation with Soli or Rusi, that she had never really spoken to Bomi Mistry's wife, Sheroo.

A few days after Dinabai's funeral, Tehmi made two shocking discoveries. The first was that Cyrus had left her around the same time that her mother had. The second was that she missed her mother more than she did Cyrus. So many decades had passed since she had touched Cyrus's taut flesh, kissed those soft lips. By contrast, she could still feel the roughness of Dinabai's parchment skin, could still recall the outline of the bedsore on her back, which she cleaned several times a day with Johnson's baby oil and Cuticura talcum powder. She had taken good care of her mother. She was proud of that. Tehmi tried to remember whether she had been a good wife to Cyrus, whether she had cared for him as lovingly as she had cared for her mother. And she came smack up against a harsh fact: She did not remember. Too many years had gone by and too little of that time had been shared with Cyrus. She realized that what she had been holding on to for all these years had been the memory of a memory. The shadow of a shadow. "Cyloo, forgive me," she cried. "I cannot even remember what your sweet face looked like. Forgive me, my darling. You see, there are so few people left that I can talk to about you, what with your dear parents gone. And Naju comes to Bombay so rarely now because of her diabetes and all. No one left to remind me of you, Cyloo. With Mamma dead, the last person who knew you is also gone."

Cyrus had disappeared. Perversely, the bad breath remained. The tiny Wadia Baug flat now felt empty and big. Tehmi had never realized how much she relied on her mother for socialization and company. Even when the stroke rendered Dinabai speechless, she communicated with her daughter with the squeeze of a hand or the blink of an eye. And when she couldn't do even that, there was still the fact of her presence, the fact of a physical body that had to be bathed, cleaned, fed. Tehmi did all this without complaining. A servant helped her with the daily sponge baths and the bedpans, but Tehmi still planned and cooked their daily meals, tended to Dinabai's bedsores, prayed every evening at Dinabai's bedside in the hopes that the old lady could hear her. In those days, she didn't have too much time to talk to Cyrus. So that when he ignored her when she eventually turned to him again, she thought he was merely angry with her. But a few days after Dinabai's funeral, she realized, Cyrus has left me for good.

At Dinabai's funeral, Jimmy Kanga had offered to have Zarin stay at Tehmi's flat her first night home alone. Tehmi had refused the offer, but then the silence in the house felt oppressive to her. Swallowing her pride, she dialed Zarin's number and requested her to spend a night or two at her place. She could picture the look of startled surprise on Zarin's face, but to her credit, Zarin agreed immediately. Tehmi was amazed at how wonderful it felt to have a companion in the flat, even one who was a virtual stranger to her. The enormity of her loss hit her then. How abruptly my life changed, she thought, her mind going back to the day of the explosion at the factory. That night, as Zarin slept on the couch, Tehmi permitted herself to do something she never did—ask herself, What if? What if she had refused to marry Cyrus until he finished his law degree? He would have been safe when the chemical factory exploded on that fateful day. What if she had listened to her dream and begged Cyrus not to go to work that day?

She was sure he would have agreed, because Cyrus had never refused her anything. What if she had listened to her mother and not insisted on identifying Cyrus's remains? She would not have breathed in that horrible smell of death, a smell that had haunted her ever since and made her an outcast among her neighbors.

Toward morning, Zarin was awakened by a strange noise. Sitting up on the couch, she listened in silence. Tehmi was tossing and turning in her sleep, talking to herself. She was making a whimpering sound that made Zarin's hair stand on end. She thought it was quite possibly the most heartbreaking sound she had ever heard.

Zarin never went back to Tehmi's flat after that night. But from that day on, she never said a bad word about Tehmi. And every year on Mehernosh's birthday, she had a large box of *jelabis* delivered to Tehmi's home.

Standing by herself at Mehernosh Kanga's wedding, Tehmi idly wondered if Zarin would continue to distribute *jelabis* among the neighbors now that Mehernosh was married and moving to the Cuffe Parade flat that the Kangas owned. She wagered that the tradition would continue. The Kangas were generous people. It was not even that Tehmi cared for *jelabis.* Usually, she'd taste a piece or two of the sticky orange sweet and then cut the rest of it into tiny pieces for the crows to eat. But receiving the box of *jelabis* once a year made Tehmi feel part of the neighborhood, proud of the fact that there was at least one neighborhood ritual that she was part of. That was the main reason she had attended Mehernosh's wedding. Tehmi had never forgotten Zarin's one-night stay at her apartment in the days following Dinabai's death. She also had a warm spot for Jimmy because of how he had adored her Cyrus. Still, she was surprised—and moved—by the invitation. She suspected that the Kangas liked her, though she had no idea why they would. She had certainly not made any overtures toward them in the years since Cyrus's death. Despite herself, she was flattered by the affection that she suspected was behind the invitation. She was also amazed at how excited she had been in the days leading up to the wedding. She actually went out and bought a new sari for the occasion. Since Dinabai's death six years earlier, even the rare wedding and Navjote invitations had stopped. It was as if the neighbors expected to see Tehmi only at sad occasions such as funerals.

Out of the corner of her eye, Tehmi saw Jimmy Kanga approaching her. Her finger froze where it had been feeling the lump under her armpit. Casually, she let her right hand drop to her side. With a practiced eye, Tehmi noticed that Jimmy was standing as far away from her as he could and still be heard. She felt a rush of sympathy for him. Poor man, she thought. Of course he doesn't want to be showered with my dragon's breath. Not on his son's wedding day. One whiff of my breath will turn the expensive foreign perfume he's wearing into cheap *attar.* She giggled, and the realization that she was pleasantly drunk made her giggle some more. She never should have accepted that glass of whiskey Bomi had thrust into her hand. She tried to concentrate on what Jimmy was saying to her.

"Tehmi, just wanted to let you know. Zarin and I are asking some of our guests, mostly people from Wadia Baug, to stay on a little while longer, after the other guests leave. We have a little surprise for our special friends. And don't worry about getting back. We've rented a bus to take the Wadia Baug gang back home."

Jimmy saw her surprise at being included in this select group and felt a rush of guilt. Of course she was surprised. After all, she had only been invited to the wedding because they had invited the whole building. And now he was asking her to stay behind, presuming a friendship where none existed. He felt he owed her an explanation. "Tehmi, when you see our little surprise, you will understand. But, on this happy day, let me please just say what I have said to many others and what I should have said to you years ago. I am what I am today because of your Cyrus. It was he who directed my life at a very crucial stage. He was a great man, Cyrus. Hard to imagine that my Mehernosh is now older than Cyrus was when he . . . when he . . . well, you know. One more thing: Although I didn't know Cyrus well, I'm glad I knew him even a little bit."

He saw the tears well up in her eyes and panicked. "No, no, I didn't mean to upset you, Tehmi. No tears on this auspicious occasion, please. Let's all just have a nice time, okay?"

She forced the tears back and smiled. "Okay, Jimmy. Okay. No sadness today. But just one thing. Your Mehernosh reminds me a lot of my Cyrus. You and Zarin, you are good parents and good people. I may not say much, but I notice things, you know."

She saw the look of startled pleasure on Jimmy's face and was glad she had said what she did. She watched as Jimmy approached some of the others and wondered what the surprise was about. For a moment, she wondered if she could confide the news of the lump growing in her body to Jimmy and Zarin. She knew that if she asked Zarin to go with her to the doctor, Zarin would not refuse.

Then she remembered her earlier resolution to wait and watch. She would do nothing—yet. Nobody will pluck the strange fruit growing inside my body, she said to herself. The words sounded vaguely dirty and made her giggle. She had a sudden clear picture of herself: an old snowy-haired woman standing alone, holding an almost empty glass of whiskey and giggling to herself. The picture made her giggle even more.

People were staring at her. But she was used to that.

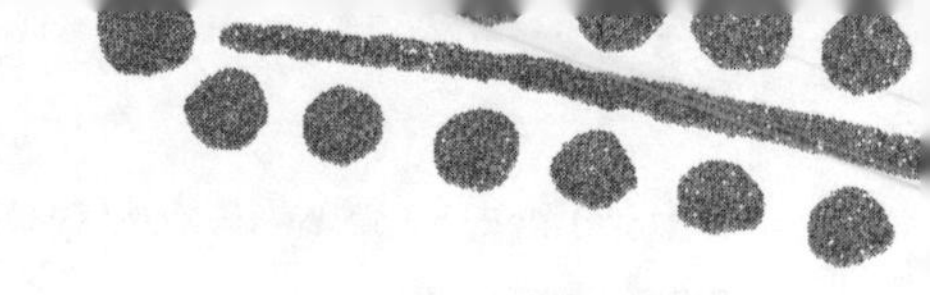

Eight

No matter how often it happened, the residents of Wadia Baug still got irritated at Adi Patel for his theatrics. Halfway through dinner, it happened again. A dark-skinned woman in a lime green sari was serving the guests *pallao-daar* from a large platter when her eye caught Adi's. You would've thought the woman had zapped him with electricity. Adi's head jerked backed and he let out a soft, strangling cry. For a long moment, he grabbed himself around the waist and rocked back and forth as the other guests watched, transfixed. Then, abruptly, he pushed back his chair, accidentally knocking over Katy's glass filled with Gold Spot, and walked rapidly away from the long row of seated guests. The wild, haunted look in his eyes so scared three-year-old Malcolm that the boy burst into tears. "*Mooa,* Adi," the boy's mother muttered. "Looking white as a *bhoot* and scaring my poor Malcolm. What for he drinks so much if he can't control himself?"

Adi walked rapidly to the large room inside the reception hall. He sat on one of the large leather armchairs, running his fingers through his thick, wiry hair. He should've known better than to attend Mehernosh's wedding. Any gathering of happy people depressed Adi, and weddings were the worst. To him, they were torture devices to remind him of how different his life was from that of normal men, how far removed he was from the ordinary dreams of wife, children, and home. Tonight, at least three of the women from the building had said to him, "Now, Adi, it has to be your turn next. You're not getting any younger, you know." But the pity in their eyes told him that they did not believe their own words, that they had no expectations that he would ever take a bride.

And they were right. Although he was only twenty-nine years old, he knew beyond a shadow of a doubt that he was doomed to remain single. Saraswati had seen to that. Philomena had revived some long-buried hope, had made him briefly dream of new possibilities, but all that was over now. It had been a year since he had broken up with Philomena and he still missed her terribly. And yet, even in the depths of his longing for her, he couldn't see how they could have continued.

Saraswati.

At the thought of her, the old nauseous feeling rose like a wave within him. After ten years of living with the thought of Saraswati, he knew that he would never be free of the dark-skinned woman who continued to haunt him after all this time. When he was younger, he had wrestled with her memory, telling himself that each thought of her was like taking a razor blade to his face. But it was no use. Saraswati stayed in his life. He felt as if some part of him were broken, that part that made other men brazen and nonchalant and unapologetic for their deeds. After all, most of his friends had done exactly what he had done and hadn't given it a second thought, joked about it even.

But tonight, Adi accepted that Saraswati was very much alive where it mattered—in his memory. He still remembered the musky smell of her and how her dark body, smooth as polished granite, had felt under him. Better than his own voice, he remembered the single sound she made in the back of her throat, a sharp, stifled sound, after he had finished making love—but no, he could not call it love; it had been more like the mad, demented thrashing of a large bird with a broken wing. She'd held still until he finished, the last convulsed spasm of delight drawn out from his tired body, until he was free from the blinding lust that had consumed him so briefly but completely. But as he lay on top of her, his breath still ragged and irregular, his mind already trying to process the experience, with half of him feeling a sad, bitter sense of letdown while the other half of him gloated and sang, she made that strange sound, that half sob. And when he raised his head at last to look at her, he expected to see—what? love? hate?—anything but the deadness, the passive muteness of a broken animal, that he saw in her face. Those large black eyes as blank as a wall.

He'd gotten away from her as soon as he could. He mopped his sweaty body with his shirt and pulled up his pants. Before he left the small hovel with the single cot, he glanced back at her. To his horror and revulsion, he felt his lust rise again. A nauseous blend of pity and self-loathing gripped him. He groped in his pocket and threw a coin on the bed, near where she was pulling her sari below her knees. "There," he said. "Buy something sweet for yourself. And now, get going. Come on, *jaao.*" He waited at the door, and when she walked past him on her way out, he smelled her musky scent again. He wanted to throw up.

He was nineteen at the time of the incident and she was probably a few years younger. It was Nari Uncle's idea, the episode with Saraswati. Nari was a neighbor who owned the largest *chikoo* farm in the village. Adi's father, whose farm was adjacent to Nari's, was flattered that the most powerful man in the village considered himself a family friend. Nari was a bachelor, and every Friday evening he would visit Adi's father and the two men would sit out on the front porch, drinking toddy and talking about the price of *chikoos.* Adi's mother, however, disliked Nari and privately called him a dirty old man, the kind of man who made a woman feel naked by just looking at her. Whenever Nari was over for dinner, Pillamai made it a point to send the young women servants away, in an attempt to protect them from Nari's lecherous eye. Despite her husband's protestations, she would serve dinner herself. Nari, in turn, was exaggeratedly polite and formal with her. "Hello, Pillamai," he would greet her. "*Tabeyet kem che?* How are you keeping these days? The asthma better?"

Nari was a tall, beady-eyed man in his fifties, with scanty hair and a slight stoop. His breath stank from the toddy and the cheap *bidis* that he smoked instead of cigarettes. Although he was the wealthiest man in the village, he dressed poorly, wearing the same half-sleeved shirts and khaki pants over and over again. *"Saala kanjoos,"* Adi's father would tease him. "No *bairi,* no children, nothing. Who are you saving your money for, a mistress? What, would it bankrupt you to be nicely suited-booted sometimes?"

But everybody knew that Nari did not have to save money to pay for a mistress. Like a predatory animal, Nari rode around his vast kingdom and eyed the wives of the impoverished, gaunt men who worked for him. When a certain woman caught his eye, he merely approached the hapless husband and told him to deliver his wife that evening to the small hovel with the single cot that stood at the south end of his property. Because even Nari had his standards. These women were good enough for him to sleep with, but the thought of having them inside his house, lying on his clean sheets, made him sick. The hovel did nicely for these expeditions.

On occasion, a hotheaded young laborer would balk at the thought of the slimy old man touching his young bride. In such cases, Nari merely smiled and walked on. But that evening, there would be a visit by three or four of the local *goondas* to that young man's hut. They would explain to him the customs of the place; they would educate him about the terms of employment; they would explain to him that fucking any woman Nari chose were the perks of being a *zamindar,* a landowner. If the young man still did not understand, they would let their fists and chains explain to him what their mouths could not. Sometimes, they would casually, disinterestedly, rape his young wife before leaving, just to emphasize their point. To make sure that the young man really understood that his employment had been terminated.

Once, a badly beaten young man named Rahul dragged himself to the local police station to file a complaint against Nari. A dumbstruck constable rushed in to tell the police chief about their unexpected visitor. The great police chief himself left his office to greet the young man. He personally escorted Rahul into the police station, whereupon he proceeded to have the reckless young man seized by his constables, hung upside down from his ankles, and beaten with rubber strips. They left him dangling there for almost twenty-four hours. The story was told with great merriment the next day, when the police chief was having dinner and drinks at Nari *sahib*'s home.

It was Nari who procured Saraswati for Adi. He had run into Adi one evening while the young man was working in his father's fields. *"Wah wah,"* Nari said. *"Deekra,* you're growing into a regular Tarzan. Look at those biceps. The girls around here must be mad about you, uh? Showing them a good time or what?" he asked, making a lewd gesture with his hands.

Adi blushed. It was one thing to talk about such things with the boys with whom he hung around. He was not used to such conversations with his father's friends. "No, Nari Uncle," he stammered. "It's . . . it's not like that."

Nari looked offended. "*Arre,* 'it's not like that' means what? What, are you a man or a *hijra*? A bleddy eunuch you are becoming. *Saala,* is that old father of yours teaching you anything except how to count *chikoos*? Did you not learn anything from all the animals around the farm? My God, when I was your age, I had more women than there are *chikoos* in these fields. What's the use of being a landowner's son if you don't take advantage of all the natural resources around you? I'll tell you what. Do this. Come by the house tomorrow evening at seven. I'll have a nice present for you." And with a wink, Nari walked away.

Adi decided immediately that he would stay away from Nari Uncle's house the next evening. The next day, he had almost forgotten the conversation. But at about five that evening, he remembered, and a strange, slow feeling rose in him. He felt anxious and excited and guilty. Besides, Nari Uncle would be angry if he didn't show up. He'd go visit the old man for five minutes and then leave, he decided. Even as he told himself that he would not stay, he knew that he was lying to himself.

Nari was waiting for him as if it had never occurred to him that Adi would not come. "Ah, there you are. Want a glass of whiskey or toddy before we go? No? You don't drink? That father of yours is raising a girl, not a boy. At your age, I could put down half a pint of brandy easy, straight from the bottle. Anyway, come on, that present of yours is waiting. Name of the present is Saraswati. Fat and juicy, she is," he added with a wink.

Adi followed the old man through the darkening fields as if in a dream. He felt possessed, as if something of Nari's foulness had entered his soul, gripping him like a vise. Nari was right, he decided. He was getting to be a sissy. Besides, he hated being the only boy in his group of friends who was still a virgin. He hated the loneliness of jerking off by himself in the fields at dusk while all his friends spoke about visiting prostitutes and finding women to have sex with, as if it was as effortless as dipping a cup into a pond. What was he waiting for anyway? His mother had told him never to sleep with a woman he didn't love. But what does she know? he asked himself. She was just a simple old woman who had spent too many years on a *chikoo* farm. Just look at Nari. He lived his life any way he wished, and there had been no bad consequences. No bolt of lightning had struck him down; no punishing God had put a pox upon his house. Mamma is wrong, Adi told himself. There was more to life than the strict, narrow way in which she had raised him. By the time Nari stood with him at the entrance of the hovel, Adi had worked himself up to a frenzy. And when he looked in and saw Saraswati lying on the cot, her green sari lifted to her knees, the madness fell upon him like a black rain, washing away his natural compassion and kindness. He forgot to ask himself whether he liked the woman before him, if he even found her attractive. All he had known in his life were the polite, clean, virginal Parsi girls. Despite all the macho talk among his friends, he had always supposed that when he first made love, preferably after marriage, it would be to one of these girls. But the woman before him was dark as the fields around them and smelled as rich and loamy. Everything about her was alien to him, as if a shadow had moved out of the background and was suddenly at center stage. Her unfamiliarity excited him.

Nari gave him a thump on the back. "Now we'll see if you're a girl or a boy," he said, grinning, his stained teeth glistening in the dark. "Enjoy your present." And Adi felt another push on his back. Then he was alone with the strange woman.

A nasty brew of grief and anger rose like bile inside the boy. For a moment, he hated the woman before him, as if she were his oppressor. Then the revulsion gave way to a chattering excitement. Or more accurately, his revulsion itself excited him. He was not used to thinking of women in such antagonistic ways. Approaching the cot, Adi fell upon Saraswati in a frenzy, like a hungry bird of prey descending on a small mouse in a field.

And when it was all over, she had made that one sound. And looked at him in that dead, lifeless way. He hurried away from her as quickly as he could, as if she were a fever he was in danger of contracting the longer he was near her. As he made his way home through the moonlit fields, his gait was slow and unsure, a stark contrast to the frenzied walk he had taken an hour earlier. His heart felt heavy and dull, as if all the blood had been drained out of it. He was not exactly sure what he had expected from the encounter with Saraswati but it was not this pitiful, lonely feeling that he was now experiencing. He was angry with himself, feeling that his sheltered, puritanical upbringing was interfering with what he fancied should be a triumphant moment, but the anger didn't change the fact that he felt as if he had made a mistake.

"How was she?" Nari asked Adi the next evening. "Should I try her out also, or do you want me to reserve her for you only? Or would you like to sample her younger sister?" he added with a wink. Adi did not know whether to burst into tears or strangle the salivating old man who stood before him.

In the weeks that followed, running into Nari became a torture. Adi felt as though he and the dirty old man he despised were now eternally linked, as if, in some perverse way, Nari knew him better than his own parents did. His mother still treated him the same way, asking him whether he had brushed his teeth before going to bed, and suddenly he despised and envied her innocence and goodness, her belief in God. Can't you see that I have changed? he wanted to scream at her. Can't you smell the foul air around me, the new scent of sweat and blood and semen that follows me everywhere? At the same time, he was terrified about her finding out. Nothing would break her heart more, he knew. Unlike his father, Pillamai was a city woman, and although she had little formal education, she had a stern sense of right and wrong. As a young bride leaving her beloved Bombay for her husband's *chikoo* farm, Pillamai had been horrified by how casually the male landowners slept with the female laborers and how carefully their wives looked the other way. "Don't know what you did before marriage," she told her husband soon after their wedding, "don't even want to know. But I promise you, if you ever look at one of those poor *ghaati* women wrong, I will be back in Bombay before you can finish saying my name." Having married into a social order where most human beings were either predators or prey, Pillamai was determined that her son would be neither. Mostly, she taught him by example. Ever since Adi could remember, Pillamai had treated the farmworkers with respect and they, in turn, trusted her. The women would often bring in their meager savings to Pillamai for safekeeping, because if they kept the money at home, their husbands would likely hand the cash to the local bootlegger.

But now, Adi felt banished from the purity of his mother's world. He tried to avoid Nari as much as he could, but the old man hovered around him like stale air. He hated his father for letting Nari into their home, noticed for the first time the weakness around his father's mouth, how he laughed a little too readily and eagerly at Nari's awful jokes. Until this time, his father had been a shadowy figure in Adi's life, a man who seemed as remote and distant as the trees on their farm. Adi had always identified much more with his softhearted, citified mother than his rustic, patriarchal father. Still, he had been proud of the old man, enjoyed his gruff humor and his capacity for hard work. But now resentment made him watch his father more closely. He noticed how his mother had to pester her husband for household money before he would part with it and how Pillamai treated her husband like a petulant child who had to have things his own way. He dimly remembered how independent and outspoken Pillamai had been when he was younger and was struck by how she now mostly kept her opinions to herself. The only time Pillamai spoke up, it seemed, was in defense of one of the poor tribal women who worked on the farm. Adi felt embarrassed at how dictatorial his father was to the men who sweated on his farm and how servile and eager to please he was around Nari. He saw the mute hatred on the ebony faces of the bone-thin farm laborers as they lowered their eyes when the old man walked past them and Adi saw how oblivious he was to their hatred. He both hated and admired his father for this oblivion, his supreme indifference—hated him for the arrogance that indifference implied; admired him because he read into that indifference a kind of manliness that he woefully lacked. He knew for certain that his father would never be haunted by the face of a woman he had abused, that it would never occur to him that he had done anything but exercise his natural rights. Some part of Adi longed to seek his father's confidence, to confess to him what he had done to Saraswati, but he knew that his father would laughingly slap him on the back, wink at him, and tell him not to tell his mother. That his father would misunderstand him and think he was bragging, rather than confessing. Or, worse, if he figured out that Adi was tormented by his action, he would mock him, say something unpleasant about not realizing he had raised a daughter instead of a son.

As for Nari, whom Adi began to think of as his evil, shadow father, Nari treated Adi like a co-conspirator, smirking at him, elbowing him in the ribs, smacking his lips when a young peasant woman walked by them. And he was in no position to tell him to stop, because, after all, hadn't he proven himself to be as dissolute as the ugly old man who stood before him?

About a month after his encounter with Saraswati, she came to him. It was a bright yellow day and he was walking in his father's fields, supervising the picking of the *chikoos,* when a movement to the right caught his eye. A woman in a rust brown sari was approaching him. He stared at her and for a moment their eyes met. He looked deeply into her face, searching for a sign that would tell him if this was the woman he had slept with, but the woman's face was blank as a sheet as she walked by him. And then it hit him: He didn't even remember what she looked like. He could pass her every day and not know it, for she was one of those interchangeable laborers, women who men like himself used and discarded like a piece of tissue. She was any of the women who surrounded him; she was all of them. Suddenly, he was reliving that night in the hovel. He felt dizzy, light-headed; hot vomit rose inside him like lava. The next minute, he was leaning against a tree, retching his insides out. From a distance, he heard the foreman's worried voice. "Adi *seth,* what happened? Go inside, *seth,* too much heat today."

The next day, he approached the foreman. "There's a woman who works on Nari *seth*'s farm," he said, trying to make his voice as casual as possible. "Name is Saraswati, I think. Maybe seventeen, eighteen years old? See if you can find out where she lives. Got a letter that came to the house to deliver to her."

He thought that the foreman looked at him strangely, but Adi told himself it was his imagination. In any case, he had directions to Saraswati's home the very same evening.

Two days later, he was standing before her hovel, screwing up his courage to enter. In all these years, he had never visited this part of the village. Finally, he bent and poked his head into the hut. When his eyes adjusted to the dark, he saw an old woman cooking at a kerosene stove on the mud floor. "Saraswati live here?" he asked her. At the authority in his voice, the old woman jumped to her feet. "Yes, *sahib.* But she's gone to the *baniya* to pick up some rice. Should be home any minute, *seth,*" the woman stammered. Although he had grown up hearing it, the servility in her voice set his teeth on edge today. "Is okay," he said. "I'll wait outside." Already, a group of curious children had gathered around him. The old woman peered anxiously at him from inside the hut. He felt like a foreign dignitary visiting a strange country.

Saraswati recognized him before he knew who she was. Her hand flew up to her face, which was neither beautiful nor ugly. He was startled and ashamed to see that she was terrified of him. He wished the children would disappear, but he did not want to attract any more attention by shooing them away. He took a step toward Saraswati. "It's okay," he said. "I want to talk to you. This your hut?"

Once inside, he politely asked the old woman to leave them alone for a few minutes. When she hesitated, looking worriedly from him to her silent granddaughter, he deliberately stiffened his voice and again asked her to leave. This time, she obeyed. Saraswati crouched in the corner, sitting on her haunches and whimpering to herself. She was steeling herself for another attack, he realized with dismay. With the veil of lust lifted from his eyes, he saw her fully for the terrified, pathetic woman-child that she was. His heart swelled with unbearable pity and he felt like flinging himself before her feet and begging her forgiveness. He swallowed hard to rid his throat of the lump that was hardening there. "Listen," he began. "What happened that n-night was a mistake. I'm sorry for it. I will never bother you again. You listening to me?" But although her whimpering had stopped, her eyes stared at him in the same unseeing way they had that night. He felt the chasm between them as acutely as if it were about to swallow him up. He wanted to grab her face, make her eyes focus on him, make her see how awfully sorry he was, but he knew that this would be yet another violation of her. Dumbly, miserably, he realized there was nothing else to say. He was suddenly unsure of his reasons for visiting her. Reaching into his pocket, he pulled out two one-hundred-rupee bills. "This is not to insult you," he said carefully. "Just a way of saying I'm sorry, that's all."

He left her then, feeling that he had not accomplished anything that he had wanted to when he had sought her out. But what did you expect? he argued with himself. That she'd forgive you? Welcome you with open arms? It went about as well as could be expected. At least she didn't make a scene, bless her. And you can send her more money from time to time. By the time he got home, he felt lighthearted, as if someone had excavated a boulder from his heart.

Two days later, he was working in the fields, when Nari walked up to him. The old man's eyes were blazing and his face was ugly with rage. "Get in the Jeep," he said. "We are needing to have a talk." Adi was about to protest, but the look on Nari's face stopped him. Nari drove for a few minutes in silence. Then, in a voice taut with anger, he said, "Heard you were out visiting that girl's home earlier this week. Heard you were poking your nose where it didn't belong. What were you doing there?"

Adi froze, wondering how Nari had found out so soon. Then a

wave of anger rose in him to match Nari's. "Nobody's business what I was doing there, Nari Uncle. I'm free to come and go where I want."

Nari let out a cry of rage. He pulled the car off to the side of the mud road and slammed on his brakes. Turning to Adi, he grabbed him by his shirt and pulled him toward him until their faces were a few inches apart. "You fucking swine, don't you ever talk to me in that tone. Only the fact that you're my friend's son keeps me from twisting and breaking your bleddy chicken's neck. Nobody's business what you do, you say? Well, it is my business when you cost me a laborer, that, too, during *chikoo*-picking season. A fine worker Saraswati was, too."

"What . . . what are you talking about? How does my visiting Saraswati cost you anything? Oh my God, did she run away or something?"

"Run away? You could say that. Yes, you bleddy bastard, she ran away from this world all the way into the next. She killed herself, you cowardly idiot. Poured kerosene over her own body and lit a match. Can you imagine how barbaric these people are? And you know why? Because Mr. Guilty Conscience here decides to go to her hovel and give her some money so that he can sleep peacefully at night. In front of the whole village, you exposed her. May as well have put a sign around her neck saying 'I'm a two-bit slut.' Her father had no choice but to disown her. In fact, if she hadn't killed herself, he'd have had to do it. Then, I would've lost *two* hard workers. And then I would have definitely killed you myself."

Adi felt numb, as if he had bathed in ice. He tried to feel something for the dead girl but realized that he didn't know her well enough to muster anything except a feeling of dread. He was only nineteen years old and he was responsible for the death of a woman. He had a sense that his life was galloping away from him, that someone had changed the script to his life while he wasn't looking. At last, he said, "I was only trying to help. I just felt bad for her is all."

"So our Prince Charming was going to help," Nari spat out. "*Arre,* why didn't you just marry her, then? See if your pious mother would have accepted that. Trying to help, my foot. *Deekra,* this system has been in place for thousands of years. It's our tradition—landowners are allowed to sleep with the wives and daughters of their laborers. One of the few rewards for how hard we toil. This is the arrangement, and everyone accepts it. But the key is, it is done in secrecy. You don't go around advertising the fact that you've slept with such and such woman. That way, her husband or father can still maintain his manhood, his family honor. Everybody knows and nobody knows. It's perfect. But then you had to come along and spoil everything. Now I'll probably have a bleddy union organizer coming in to exploit all this."

Adi sat there, mutely, miserably. First a rapist, now a murderer, he told himself. Because he had killed her, sure as if he'd lighted the match himself. No use pleading good intentions. Saraswati was dead, regardless. The thought of his mother finding out about his fall made Adi find his tongue at last. "Nari Uncle, Mummy must never find out about this. You can take whatever punishment you want from me, but she must never know."

Nari's expression changed. "Now, what's this talk of punishment-funishment? You are a Parsi, the son of generations of landowners. Who am I to punish you? Besides," he said deliberately, "this news would kill your poor mother, good, pious woman that she is. Far be it from me to give her such dangerous news. Also, there's no shortage of labor in India, thank God. Ten other Saraswatis to take her place. Just let this be a lesson to you, Adi. Never interfere with the natural order of things. Still, if you are feeling guilty about the loss you have caused me, perhaps you can help me out occasionally. I have no sons, and you are a nice strong boy. I'm getting old and could use some help."

Adi nodded mutely, not knowing that he was shaking hands with the devil. But he soon found out. For the next three years, Nari was like a dark, sinister shadow that he could not shake off. As if to rub salt in his wounds, the old man used Adi to procure women for him, loaning him his Jeep to pick them up and deposit them at the hovel. Once, he even suggested that Adi watch, but the look in Adi's eyes made the old man laugh nervously and pretend he had only been joking. Nari also used Adi to break up any efforts by his laborers to organize, to run the union leaders out of town. Adi hated himself for acquiescing to Nari, but the thought of Nari ever telling Pillamai about Saraswati's suicide (in his mind, he called it a murder) was even more unbearable than the humiliations he suffered. Also, to relieve the pressure, he began to drink, toddy at first, then whiskey, sitting in the fields after dark, alone with the stars and his blurry thoughts. He found that he had a natural talent for drinking, that he took to it like mother's milk, and pretty soon he was chased by the triple demons of Saraswati's memory, Nari, and alcoholism. Pillamai's father had been a heavy drinker, but she had kept that from her only son because the memory of how unpleasant her father's drinking had made her childhood was too hard to talk about, even with Adi, her closest confidant. Anyway, Pillamai's relationship with Adi had altered greatly, and when she allowed herself to feel her hurt, she was bewildered by the gap that had grown like a valley between them. At first, she tried talking to him. "Adi, are you sick, my darling? Is that father of yours working you too hard? Why these dark circles under your eyes? Adi, anything you are wanting to share with your mother? You know, we have always been able to talk with each other."

He remained silent. There was no way to tell her about those horrifying dreams where a dead woman visited him, dreams made more horrifying by the fact that they came to him in broad daylight. Also, he had begun to resent his mother because, by her very presence, she made him feel unclean. The more he pimped for Nari, the further he pulled away from Pillamai. They represented the two extremes in his life, the sun and the sun's shadow. And slowly, Adi was becoming a furtive creature of the shade, of the dark alley, of the hidden corner. He felt it had been a very, very long time ago that he had been young.

The first time he came home drunk, his father was gone on an overnight business trip. Pillamai smelled the drink on his breath as soon as she opened the door. She was too stunned to say anything. Instead, she beat him, lashed out at his impassive face, beat against his youthful body with hands made strong by terror and grief. He made no move to stop her. Her racking sobs pierced his frightened heart like a needle, but he steeled himself to her. He was distressed that his mother had found out about his drinking, but also relieved. He felt as if he were doing her a favor. He had changed. He was no longer her little Adi, innocent, pure. The sooner his mother knew that, the sooner she acknowledged the monster he had turned into, the better it would be for her.

Pillamai looked at her son's marked face as if she were waking from a dream. *"Maaf kaar,* Adi, *maaf kaar,"* she pleaded with her impassive son. "Forgive me, my darling. May God punish these hands that have struck you. But in my worst nightmares, I was not thinking my loving son would come home drunk like a common farm boy."

He looked at her in all his unsteady, drunken, imperial glory, for a full moment. Then, as if she were a fellow passenger on a bus, he walked by her silently and went to his room.

But that night, he lay awake in bed and knew he had to get out of the village, knew he had to leave the farm. He thought back to Pillamai's reaction at seeing him drunk and knew he had to get away from the shadow of bewildered pain that darkened his mother's face, get away from the knowledge that he was responsible for that shadow. That it was his lust, the tyranny of his howling body, that had smeared the sun. Above all, he needed to get away from Nari and his lewd, salacious suggestions, his assumption that Adi shared his heart of darkness. Adi had always assumed that he would live his life in the village of his birth, in much the same way that his forefathers had. But the lush greenness of the farm, the loamy brown soil, the splendid blue sky, all the things that had made him feel united with this land from the day he was born, all of this merely tortured him now, made him acutely aware of his disinheritance. Nari had sucked the green out of the earth and the blue out of the sky, leaving in their place a dark void.

Bombay. The word came to him like a beacon of light, like a shimmering jewel from out of the void. Bombay. A new city, a fresh start, a place to rest his head without the torment of dreams. He could live with his aunt and uncle, whom he visited every year and who loved him like a son. And why not? he thought excitedly. If ordinary *begaaris* and laborers can go to this city and become millionaires, why will I not be successful and happy there?

He was so caught up in the excitement of his new plan that it came as a shock when his father refused to let him go, saying that he needed his only son to work in the family business. "But I want to attend college there," Adi said, surprising himself as much as his father. He had never seriously considered college before. But the old man was unmoved. "Don't need a professor to teach you the price of *chikoos,*" he said flatly. "A boy like you doesn't need college. You have the farm." That night, Adi sat in one of the illicit country bars, downing glass after glass of cheap *daru,* denouncing his father to whoever would listen. A week later, as he stumbled home from yet another drinking binge, he passed out on the side of the road. When he came to, the morning sun was poking daggers into his eyes. When he got home, his father was standing by the door, his hefty body blocking most of the doorway. "*Saala* drunkard," the furious old man cursed. "Treating this house like a brothel, you are. You've made a laughingstock of us among the lowest of the low. For weeks, your mother has been crying at night and I haven't been able to understand why. Now I know. Your turn to cry now, you *besharam.*" Too late, Adi saw the whip in the old man's hand.

It was the first of many beatings. But the alcohol seemed to harden Adi's flesh as well as his heart, so that it was the father's hand that ached after the whippings, his voice that trembled with emotion, and his gaze that faltered. And soon, the old man realized the futility of the beatings. It was increasingly clear that if things did not change, Adi would not live to see his twenty-third birthday. More than once, the Patels heard stories about their drunken son deliberately walking into the path of a scooter or an autorickshaw or about Adi getting into fights with men he would have normally avoided locking glances with. Finally, unable to bear his wife's quiet sobbing any longer, Adi's father called his brother-in-law in Bombay and discussed the possibility of his son living with him and his wife. Two afternoons later, he found his son loitering in a toddy bar, lifted him by the back of his shirt like a wet rat, and told him to pack his bags. The train to

Bombay left in two hours. Pillamai was heartbroken, but she consoled herself by thinking that after a few months in Bombay, her son would return to her, recovered and healed from whatever it was that was tormenting him.

In his first month in Bombay, gratitude, relief, and excitement made him stay away from the bottle. But one evening, on his way home from picking up a college application form, he saw Saraswati again. She walked by him, her sweaty arm brushing against his shirt-sleeve. He spun around to look for her, but she had melted into the multiheaded crowd. His insides dropped; he felt weak. Only the momentum of the crowd kept him moving. Passersby cast strange looks at the young man talking to himself, but he didn't notice. So she had followed him all the way to Bombay. Even her death couldn't keep her away from him. Which meant there was no getting away from her. Which meant there was no safe hiding place. Which meant she was a germ, a virus that had entered his blood and would travel with him wherever he went. And the only way to check this virus, to keep it from entering his brain, dominating his thoughts, destroying his heart, was to medicate against it. Before he knew it, he was in a restaurant, ordering a beer.

To support the drinking, he needed a job. Which meant no college. His uncle, after unsuccessfully trying to persuade him not to throw his life away, got him a desk job at the Life Insurance Corporation. For a boy who had spent his entire life working in the aromatic open spaces of a *chikoo* farm, being locked up in a dingy office was a kind of death. But soon he discovered that the afternoons went faster if he secretly sipped on a bottle of brandy during lunch. He told himself that his coworkers did not suspect a thing, but the fact was that Adi exuded an air of hurt and vulnerability that made strangers want to protect him. He was oblivious to the fact that his bosses usually gave him the more challenging assignments in the morning, and Sushma, the kindly lady who sat beside him, usually went over his reports before they were turned in for the day.

His elderly uncle and aunt were happy for the company of their unassuming, if strange, nephew. But whenever they were in Adi's presence, they felt an inexplicable sadness, as if they were talking to a man doing his best impression of being alive. Their good-natured attempts to draw him out of his shell were usually met with a slow, sad smile that showed them the futility of their efforts. Pretty soon, the three of them slipped into a routine. Adi came home late in the evening with a slightly unsteady gait and ate a quick dinner, listening in silence while the two elders carried on a prattling conversation. Then he washed the dishes and retired to his room. Late at night, his relatives often heard the clinking of a glass bottle.

Each summer, Pillamai, who had finally made her peace with the fact that Adi would never return to the farm, visited her son for two weeks. Her husband refused to accompany her on those trips. "It's the law of nature that the young visit their elders, Pilla," he would say. "If he wants to see his old *baap*'s face again, let him come to me."

Pillamai, who had years ago learned not to contradict her headstrong husband, now spoke up, desperately attempting to bridge the divide that had sprung up between the two men she loved the most. "Why are you standing on such ceremony? What difference does it make who comes to whom? Adi's your only son. He's young and busy at work; he has limited vacation time. He's not his own boss, like you are. Come with me. He's so anxious to see you."

But in the end, Adi's father won their silent battle. Four years after he had left the village, Adi returned to his father's sickbed. The phone call from Pillamai told him that his father was critically ill with pneumonia. At first, he thought it was a ploy, a trick to get him to come home, but he immediately banished the thought. His mother was too honorable a woman to stoop to that. Besides, the fear in her voice was only too real. During the train trip home, he prayed that he was not too late to see his father alive. Regret swarmed around him like summer flies. He resolved to come clean to his father, to make him understand where and why his only son had gone wrong. Let my father live, he bargained with God, and I will give up drinking. I'll persuade Mummy and Daddy to sell the *chikoo* farm and buy a flat in Bombay. I'll change my ways, please God, I promise I will. All the way there, he rehearsed what he would say to his father, how much he would reveal about Nari's role in his dissolution, how much blame he would assign and how much responsibility he would assume.

But the man he found on his deathbed was not the hearty, stocky man he had left behind. This man was timid and weak and had eyes that brimmed with tears every time he saw his prodigal son by his side. Adi knew immediately that he had arrived too late, that instead of saving his father, he would be bidding him good-bye. There was to be no movielike reconciliation scene, no rising from the dead. Instead, Adi sat for hours by the old man's side, mutely holding his hand, trying to keep it warm with his own. Once or twice, the old man tried to speak, but a coughing fit interrupted his words. "Is okay, Daddy, is okay," Adi whispered. "You rest now. Nothing to say now. Just sleep."

They must have both dozed for a few hours, because Adi was suddenly awakened by the sound of his father whispering his name. "Adi," the old man whispered urgently. "Adi, *maaf kaar*. Forgive me, forgive." Adi knew immediately the old man was referring to the whippings. "Nothing to forgive," he said. "I deserved all that and more. No forgiveness needed at all." But the old man's eyes were still cloudy, his brow furrowed and his breathing labored. At last, Adi realized that his father needed absolution before he could die. "Daddy," he cried, his own eyes red now. "I forgive you. I forgive you, so that you may forgive me. I'm just—I . . . I never stopped loving you, ever." His reward was a tired smile. The old man turned his face to the wall. A few minutes later, he stopped breathing.

Suddenly, Adi was the head of the household, responsible for the farm and for his mother's financial security. Pillamai begged him to take over the farm, which had been in the family for generations, told him she would help him run it. He was amazed at her faith in him and annoyed at how little she knew of the man he had become. For several days after the funeral, he kept coming up with reasons why his taking over the farm was a bad idea, but she wouldn't let up. "Mummy," he said to her finally, hoping to shut her up. "If I have the farm, I'll drink up all the profits in six months flat." He knew he had hurt her, but she was quiet after that, as if she couldn't argue with the veracity of his statement. A few evenings later, he was walking around the farm. It was a warm, still evening and the dying sun had left a splatter of red in the sky. All around him, the world was bathed in gold, so that the treetops burned like candles. The last birds were chattering to one another, their voices sad and plaintive. He realized with an ache how much he missed the land of his forefathers, its deep silences and its simple beauty. In contrast, Bombay seemed like a heavily made-up tart—loud, brash, gaudy. Suddenly, the enormity of what he had lost, the full price of his disinheritance, hit him. He had lost not only this holy land but also the respect of his father, the bond with his mother. He looked around him and everything felt rooted—the tall trees that had dug their feet solidly into the earth, the vagabond birds who had come home to their nests, the dependable, darkening sky that covered him like a blanket. He alone was rootless, homeless. Instinctively, his hand reached into his pants pocket for the silver flask containing the golden liquid. But tonight, his loneliness was too deep for the alcohol to bore holes in it. Tonight, the loneliness engulfed him, tightened its coils around him. Adi felt as if he were in a movie running backward. He heard his father's piteous plea for forgiveness, felt the grip of his father's hand on his neck as he told him to go pack his bags for Bombay, saw the look on his mother's face the first day he came home drunk, remembered the first time he had tasted whiskey and thrown up immediately after. Memory upon sad memory, piling up like playing cards. He was sobbing out loud now, waiting for the movie to end, but inevitably, his mind raced down its familiar paths—Nari's debauched face loomed near his eyes; he recalled the fateful walk from Nari's home to the hut where Saraswati waited; he felt again the icy feeling that had lodged in his stomach upon hearing about Saraswati's death. And then, as if in response to his own sobbing, he heard that sound that Saraswati had made in her throat after he had finished raping her.

The idea of how to avenge himself on Nari hit him so hard that he stopped crying. He would turn the farm over to the people who worked on it. Some of them, after all, had slaved on that land for generations, so that the farm had been in their family for generations also. The farm belonged to them as much as it did to him. Besides, it would serve Nari right to have the land adjoining his owned by men he thought were dumber than cattle. Adi remembered how much the landowners had feared labor unrest, how ruthlessly they had crushed any attempts by the farmhands to band together. He himself had been used by Nari to quell such unrest. He could make Nari's worst fears come true, in an instant. Maybe he could gather up all the men whose wives and daughters had been humiliated by Nari and sell the land to them. The Society of People Fucked Over by Nari. Adi laughed out loud at the thought of Nari's face when he broke the news to him. The dirty bastard would never have another night's sleep, for fear that one of his new neighbors would slit his throat in the middle of the night. It would serve him right, this foul old man who had destroyed so many lives to feed his evil appetites.

For two days, he played with this idea, touching it like a piece of velvet whenever he needed comforting. On the third day, he got mightily drunk and slipped into his usual state of fatalism. The cold fact was that executing his plan would take the kind of clear-eyed discipline that Adi was no longer capable of. For two days, alcoholism competed with vengeance; in the end, the bottle won. He was too weak a man to withstand the force of Nari's fury, his mother's bewildered sense of betrayal, or even the gratitude of the farmhands. To carry out his plan, he would need the strength to bear the lifelong enmity of the landowners and the lifelong gratitude of the disenfranchised. And Adi was too weary and too drunk to want either.

It was also a shock to realize that, in a break with family tradition, Adi's father had bequeathed the farm to his wife and not to his son. As far as Adi knew, this was a first in the annals of the Patel family. For generations, the farm had passed on to the oldest son, with an implicit understanding that he would provide for the womenfolk and his other brothers from the profits of the *chikoo* trade. Adi tried to muster up some outrage when he saw the will, to call up some remnant of bruised pride. The will was a slap in his face, he knew, the ultimate statement of how unworthy he was in his father's eyes. But the fact was that he understood his father's reasons for entrusting his wife, rather than his drunken son, with his legacy. It was Pillamai who was angry about the terms of the will, swearing to Adi that she had no idea when her husband had changed it. But she had more pressing things to think about. Within hours of her husband's death, Nari had made Pillamai an offer to buy the farm. She had kept the news from Adi as long as there was any hope of her son agreeing to run the farm. Adi now understood the reason why his mother had been so desperate that he take over the family business—Pillamai detested Nari almost as much as he did. But Pillamai was a realist. When her son warned her that he would drink up the profits in six months, she believed him. Pillamai knew that Nari's offer was far below the market value, but she also realized that none of the other landowners would bid on her land now that Nari had expressed an interest. Also, Nari had promised that she could live in her house as long as she was alive. And with Adi's drinking, it would be nice to have some money to invest and bequeath to her prodigal son. God knows, he would need it to survive if the drinking ever got totally out of hand.

In the end, the Patel farm was sold to Adi's old tormentor. Both mother and son wept after the deed was signed. "Sorry, Mummy, sorry," Adi said. "I wish there had been some way to keep the farm." Pillamai opened her mouth to say the obvious but then thought the better of it. Besides, she could see that her weary son was ready to wash his hands of the whole matter and return to Bombay. Adi was relieved that the money from the sale would assure his mother a comfortable life. He had halfheartedly suggested to his mother that she move to Bombay, but she had refused. "This is your family home, *deekra,*" she said. "Even if the farm is no longer in the family, at least one Patel should still walk upon this land. After I'm dead and gone, it will be a different story. Besides, my beloved's spirit is still here."

Some part of him understood what his mother was saying. Also, perversely, he appreciated the awful logic of this final capitulation to Nari. He had fled the family farm because of Nari, had been driven from it because of events set in motion by the old man. The sale only legitimized that fact, brought out in the open what had happened years ago. Nari had owned his soul for years; now he would also own the soil that had nourished that soul. The trees that his ancestors had proudly planted had yielded bitter fruit for Adi; maybe it would take Nari's foul seed to make them sweet again.

He returned to Bombay even more quiet and inward-looking than before. The past engulfed him like a fire. He had daily conversations with Saraswati, angrily asking her to leave him alone or pleading with her to forgive him. He imagined Nari stalking across the farm, uprooting the trees he and his father had so lovingly planted. He tried hard not to think of his mother, living alone in that big house, surrounded by ghosts and the fragments of her former life.

It took Philomena Pinto to drag him into the present.

Philomena was the new clerk, whose desk sat diagonally across from his. She was everything he was not—gregarious, boisterous, sensual, assertive. The first time he saw her, he was filled with a lust that shook him to the bottom of his feet. He felt amazement and gratitude at the knowledge that he was capable of so much feeling. That the unholy trinity of Nari, Saraswati, and alcohol had not destroyed every nerve ending, every ounce of emotion in him. For days, he watched her out of the corner of his eye, followed the line of her legs to where it melted into her hemline, thrilled to the sound of her sudden spurts of laughter, noticed how she talked in the same breezy way to everyone, from the bosses to the teenaged boy who delivered tea to the office. He knew he had to talk to her, get to know her, but each time she glanced at him, he looked away hastily. For the first time, he wished he had a close friend in Bombay, someone who could advise him on the best way to endear himself to this girl who was driving him mad.

She saved him the trouble. One afternoon, when most of his colleagues were on their lunch break and he was chewing a dry *batatawada* at his desk, she approached him and stood in front of him with a hand on her right hip. "Say, *men,* whatcha staring at me all day long for? You want to talk to me, why don't you just come up and say hello, straight off, like a regular gent?"

He opened his mouth to protest, but no words came. She held his gaze and he was the one who looked away first.

Two days later, while waiting in line for the BEST bus to take him to his favorite after-work bar, he spotted her standing about twelve people behind him. Stiffly, he raised his hand in greeting and then immediately turned back around. Seconds later, he felt her tug at his shirtsleeve. "Move over, *men.* Why should I wait back there when I have a friend ahead in the queue?" When the man behind them muttered about people breaking the queue, she silenced him with a look.

"I'm sorry about the staring," he said to her after they had boarded the bus and he had paid for their tickets. "I meant no harm, I assure you."

She pinched his arm. "I know that, silly fellow. Okay, I meant to tell you, I'm sorry about my little lecture the other day. I don't mind you staring at me. Kind of flattering, even. You see, I just wanted to say hello, that's all. Didn't know how else to talk to you."

He laughed and then, amazed at the unfamiliar sound of his laughter, he laughed some more. He felt bewitched and out of his element, like a man breathing underwater. He was simply not used to a woman this warm, so disarmingly honest. When they first started going out, he was so paranoid about anybody at the office finding out that he would concoct elaborate schemes to throw them off. After years of secrecy, of living in the shadows, he was not ready to be pulled out into the blinding sunlight. At the office picnic, which he attended for the first time ever because Philomena was going, he refused to sit beside her, for fear that someone would read on his face how he felt about this woman. He did not trust himself to sit next to her without glowing. Philomena indulged his desire for secrecy for about two months. Then one day, she refused to speak to him at all. When he looked up from his paperwork to glance at her, she resolutely looked away. He went half-mad with apprehension, terrified that she would not show up at the Chinese restaurant they had planned on meeting at after work. But when he got there, she was waiting for him. The waiter had barely taken their order when she lit into him. "I'm telling you, *men,* I don't know how much longer I can take this. You act as if you're ashamed of me or something, like I'm some disease that has to be hidden. I'd rather die than go on like this. You make me feel like a common whore."

He flinched. "Philomena. Don't be silly. I was just thinking of you—you know, your reputation and all."

"Are you a politician or a Mafia man, that my reputation will be hurt if people know I'm going out with you? Come on, *yaar.* It's not like we're nine-year-olds or something. Anyway, Adi, I'm a frank, open person. I'm telling you, I cannot live like a thief. If you can't handle that, I'll just leave this very minute. Either you're proud to be with me or you're not. Besides, darling, I think it's *your* reputation you're worried about, not mine. Dating a non-Parsi and all."

"Not at all, not at all," he replied, shaking his head vigorously. "Not being a Parsi has nothing to do with it." And it was true. He had already decided that if his mother ever resented the fact that Philomena was a Catholic, he would play his ace. "Mummy, listen," he would say. "So Philomena isn't a Parsi. But this *chokri* is so good for me, I haven't touched a drop since I've met her." Which was not a lie. The urge to drink had dropped away from Adi like an old coat that no longer fit. And Philomena seemed to have exorcised Saraswati from his life, too.

Philomena brought back to life some part of him that the encounter with Saraswati had snuffed out even before it had fully bloomed. He marveled at how easily she awoke the dead parts of him. That day in the Chinese restaurant, he told her, "Darling, I am so proud of you, you have no idea. If I was hiding you, it was only because I don't want anybody to steal the treasure I have found. But if you want people to know, if you don't mind their stupid gossip, I don't care." To his astonishment, he found that he believed what he had said.

He began spending Friday evenings playing cards with her friends. He was amazed at how comfortable he felt with this boisterous, youthful group of people, at how easily they accepted him. His uncle and aunt made good-natured comments about how little they were seeing of their nephew these days and were rewarded by his happy, shy smile. He knew he would have to bring Philomena home sometime soon, but he was eager not to rush things, afraid of anything or anybody interrupting his period of hard-earned bliss. Some evenings, Adi and Philomena would go to Apollo Bunder after work and sit by the banks of the sea for hours. Or he would take her to Chowpatty Beach and they would find a secluded spot to neck furiously on the brown sands. Despite his incredible longing for this woman who gave herself so fully to him, Adi always managed to keep himself from going too far. When he made love to Philomena for the first time, it would be in a real bed with clean white sheets, he decided.

So he was stunned when, after a spell of frustrated necking, Philomena turned to him and said, "Adi, this waiting is getting too hard, *men.* Can we not get a hotel room or something?"

He stared at her. Where he came from, women who asked for sex were considered to be whores, loose women of poor character. It was the man's job to keep asking for it, to beg, plead, and cajole, until he succeeded in wearing the woman down. For a second, he was offended, as if Philomena had somehow stolen his role and his lines. But then he felt incredibly lucky and happy. A woman loved him enough to want to sleep with him. Instead of whimpering or cowering from him, a woman had openly, frankly expressed her lust to him. She had thought of herself as his equal and not as his victim.

That Saturday, they checked into a hotel on Juhu Beach. From their room, they could hear the tossing and turning of the sea. The sound steadied Adi, made him feel as though what they were about to do fit in with the natural order of things.

It was only his second time with a woman, the first having been the unhappy episode with Saraswati. Somehow, Philomena seemed to grasp how fragile and insecure the man she held in her arms was. In contrast, she seemed experienced and confident, guiding him, leading him on. He closed his eyes and told himself to concentrate on the wonderful things Philomena was saying and doing to him. But perversely, he kept seeing Saraswati's blank face in front of his eyes. Adi's body was hot, but his heart was ice-cold. Philomena was warm, passionate, trusting—everything that Saraswati had not been. She removed her clothes hastily, eagerly, and then undressed him—something that Saraswati had not done. Philomena talked during sex, told Adi how much she loved him, wanted him—something that Saraswati hadn't. The hotel room was cool, clean—unlike the fetid, steamy hut on the south side of Nari's fields. Their bed was soft, wide, solid—unlike the narrow, hard cot where he had destroyed Saraswati. But when it was all over, at the moment immediately after his climax, Philomena made the same sobbing sound back in her throat that Saraswati had. Or at least that's how it sounded to his hot, fevered ears.

Nothing to do now but to go through the motions. Nothing to do but smile and say, Darling, that was so good, hope you enjoyed it, too. Nothing to do but pretend to be spent and roll onto your side and take an afternoon nap. Nothing to do but to be wide awake, to feel a single line of sweat trickle down your face and know that you are doomed. To admit to yourself that even love cannot save you. To know that your sin is too great, the stain too deep, that even this sweet, generous, bighearted girl breathing next to you cannot save you from your old nemesis. To know that Saraswati is here, in this room, souring it with her presence, her blank dark eyes staring accusingly at you, ruining your only shot at happiness. To know that an illiterate peasant woman has finally managed to destroy you, you, the son of a landowner.

His mouth was so dry, all he could think about was that he needed a drink. He was suddenly irritated by Philomena's heavy presence next to him, as if he wanted her to read his mind and disappear. To leave this room, this hotel, his life.

He took her home as soon as he could tactfully do it. If she noticed his unease during the cab ride home, she didn't comment on it. After he dropped her off, he continued in the same cab to the bar he hadn't visited in months.

He went through the motions with Philomena for a few more days, answering her worried questions about his remoteness with a false heartiness. "Darling, what's wrong? You're not having any regrets, are you?" she asked him during a coffee break.

"No, of course not," he said, looking away from her. "It's just, I don't know, maybe I'm getting a cold or something. I better go directly home from work tonight."

He turned away from the suddenly knowing look on Philomena's face. And he was unable to look her in the eye when he called off the affair a week later. They were sitting in a private cubicle in their favorite Irani restaurant—the same cubicle where he used to take her over their lunch break to neck. "Something has come up," he mumbled. "I have to break off this affair, right now."

" 'This affair'? Is that what we've been having, an *affair*?"

He stared mutely at the cup of tea he had ordered, unable to look up.

Philomena laughed a contemptuous laugh. "Come on, *men.* Don't be such a damn coward. Nothing's come up, unless it's the fact that you've been coming to work drunk. Yah, don't think I haven't noticed your breath, stinking like a sewer. Or how you've been hiding from me like a little schoolboy. What it is is that you're just like all the other men. I was right after all. You had what you wanted from me, in that hotel room, and now that you've tasted the cherry, you want to go rinse your mouth. Saving yourself for some nice, virginal, innocent Parsi girl that your mummy will pick for you, eh?"

He looked at her then, his eyes flashing. "I'm not like all the other men," he said. "It's not like that, not what you're thinking at all. I still respect you, love you even. . . ." He stopped, frightened by the look on her face.

"My mummy always said, 'When a man talks about how much he respects you, beware.' Because, you coward, if you respect someone, you don't have to say it, *men.* You just do. You Parsi boys are the most hypocritical of them all. You try to act all sophisticated and free, but underneath, you all are more old-fashioned than the Bhendi Bazaar Muslim with his four wives."

He opened his mouth to protest, but she had risen from her chair and stood towering over him like a mountain—proud, imperial, wrathful. "I really thought you were different from other men," she said, her mouth twisting bitterly. "But you turned out to be a boy, just like the rest of them." For a moment, she looked as if she might cry, and his stomach clenched. He thought he would do something violent, smash some plates if she cried, the pain of hurting yet another woman too hard for him to handle. But instead, she pulled herself tall and spat silently on the tilted floor near her feet. He flinched, but it felt right, somehow, that for once, a woman would spit at him, rather than the other way around. Then she was gone. A month later, she accepted another job. He never saw her again.

That had been a year ago. He had spent the time since the breakup with Philomena cultivating his only hobby—alcohol. Once again, Adi's neighbors in Wadia Baug got used to his sad, drunken steps going up the stairs late at night. Children sensed something unbalanced about him and often burst into tears at the sight of him; women swore that there was something fishy about him; teenagers snickered at him behind his back; their fathers felt a blend of pity and disgust for him. "Some *jadoogar* has cast a spell on that Adi, I swear," Dosamai said to anyone who would listen. "What *naatak-tamaasha* that boy does. Should've been a movie star, with all his drama. Imagine, a Parsi acting like a common drunk."

Still, in their own way, the members of Wadia Baug kept an eye out for their resident drunk. When his uncle and aunt went to spend a week in Kerala, Adi went home each evening, to find a plate of mutton cutlets or *biryani* left at his door. Rusi Bilimoria and Soli Contractor once treated him to a meal at a restaurant and spent the evening counseling him against drinking. And if any of the non-Parsi thugs who loitered around the neighborhood made fun of Adi as he staggered home, his neighbors were quick to see it as an insult against the entire Parsi *com.* Then they would alternate their fury against Adi for conducting himself in a manner that allowed these illiterate *gaatis* to make fun of him and against the *gaatis* who dared harass a Parsi.

As if he had conjured him up, Adi saw Soli Contractor approaching him. "How goes it, *bossie?* You ready to go home soon?" Soli asked.

"Fine, fine," Adi lied. "Everything's okay. I was just needing some air. I was wondering, Soli Uncle, are you leaving soon? If so, can I get a lift home?"

"Jimmy's made special arrangements for the Wadia Baug people to go home together. He's chartered a minibus or something," Soli informed him. "But he's wanting some of us oldies and baldies to wait until the other guests leave. Says he has a surprise for us. So if you don't mind waiting . . ."

Despite his earlier desire for privacy, Adi suddenly knew he could not face the thought of riding home alone in a cab. "I'll wait," he said. "That is, as long as Jimmy Uncle doesn't mind me tagging along."

Soli Contractor peered closely at the bloated, once-handsome face of the youth before him. He felt a wave of pity run through him. What a waste, he thought to himself. What a bleddy waste of a young man. "I'm sure Jimmy won't mind, *deekra,*" he said mildly. "After all, you're part of the Wadia Baug family."

Adi looked away. "Thanks," he mumbled, wishing that Soli would stop staring at him.

There was a sudden barrage of whistles and catcalls. "C'mon, Soli," a voice called. "We're all here waiting for you to open our surprise."

"I swear, *yaar,* he's worse than a blushing bride," another voice said.

Adi rose unsteadily and began walking toward the group. Soli gripped the younger man's arm in an effort to steady his drunken gait. "Adi, if you're ever needing a friend to talk . . ." Soli began.

They had been down this path before. "Soli Uncle," Adi said, his voice sounding harsh even to his ears, "I told you, everything's okay. Please."

Soli stiffened. "*Achha,* okay."

When they reached the group, Soli caught a flicker of annoyance on Jimmy Kanga's face as he looked at Adi. Jimmy did not have much time or patience for Adi, Soli knew. But the next moment, the smile that had been etched on Jimmy's face all evening long was back.

Jimmy gave Soli a quick hug and presented him with a box covered in pink satin. He noticed that every couple had a similar box perched on their laps. "Soli, in commemoration of my son's wedding, Zarin and I would like you to have this. It is nothing much, simply a token of our love and appreciation for all of you and the role you have played in all three of our lives."

Pulling Adi along, Soli found an empty chair and began opening his gift.

Nine

It was a photo album.

They sat in a half circle, this group of middle-aged men and women, hunched over the albums resting on their laps. Sheroo and Bomi Mistry stared at the cover, which said, *Memories of Wadia Baug.* Tehmi was a few chairs away from them, holding her copy of the album primly in her lap. Mehernosh and Sharon sat holding hands, their dark hair standing out like a lighthouse in this sea of gray. They, too, had an album in their laps. In their midst sat Jimmy and Zarin Kanga, looking as pleased and excited as children. "Some of these pictures we hadn't looked at in over thirty years," Jimmy was saying. "Most of the credit for assembling them should go to Zarin. This was her idea, actually. I'm just pleased the copies turned out so well."

Out of force of habit, Rusi Bilimoria wiped his hands on his pants before touching the book and turning to the first page. He let out a guffaw, which was immediately echoed by the others. The first picture was of a very young and very dirty Jimmy sleeping next to a very young and very dirty pig. "Let me see," Coomi murmured, and pulled the album closer, so that it now rested on both their laps. For once, Rusi did not mind this enforced closeness with his wife. It felt good actually, this warmth from Coomi's arm as it brushed against his. "Oh, those were the days," Soli chortled as he looked from the picture to Jimmy. "We should have sold this picture to the opposing lawyers when our *bara sahib* was arguing before the Supreme Court."

"So this is the pig that almost prevented my being born. Interesting little fellow—I mean the pig," Mehernosh said, grinning at his father.

Coomi turned another page. Two photographs here. Both of them group pictures of the time they'd all gone to Poona for the weekend. How absurdly, perilously young we all looked, Rusi thought. How confidently we were looking at the eye of the camera, as if we felt capable and strong enough to face down life itself. He cast a swift glance around and found it hard to reconcile this gray-haired gathering of hunched men and women with the handsome, upright people in the photograph. For a minute, his heart cried out at the injustice of it all, the unfairness of growing old. What a waste it seemed, if all the hard work, the economic successes, the sexual conquests, the pursuit of dreams, the nights spent seared by desire or ambition ended in a sad soup of double chins and weak bones and feeble flesh. And as if the outer, superficial changes—the shriveling up of the flesh, the bending of the back, the frailty of the limbs—weren't painful enough, there were the inner changes—the wretched shrinking of courage, the dimming of the eyes, the pessimism of the heart, the failure to dream, the terrifying fear of tomorrow. That is the true growing old, Rusi thought, and the outer changes are simply a manifestation of hearts that have turned yellow and fibrous with age.

He could sense Coomi's impatience as she sat beside him. "Ready?" she asked, and without waiting for a reply, she turned another page. And a few more memories tumbled out. There was a picture of Soli standing on his hands at Bombay Gymkhana and grinning hideously at the camera. Rusi looked at the squat, muscular youth with thick dark hair and searched in vain for a glimpse of the bald old man who was sitting across from him. The only thing they had in common was that big smile and a spirit that remained irrepressible. Rusi felt a surge of affection for Soli. That Mariam treated him so shabbily, he thought. Soli had known betrayal at such a young age. The few other relationships he had been involved in since Mariam had also ended badly, Rusi knew. And yet, miraculously, some part of Soli had remained alive to the promise of the world. Once, Rusi had accompanied Soli to a Beethoven concert at Homi Bhaba auditorium and saw a side to Soli he had never seen before. Soli, whom Rusi thought of as a good-hearted buffoon, sat still and transposed, a look on his face that suggested that he had just seen the face of God. Looking at Soli now, the top of his bald head gleaming under the lights, Rusi resolved to ensure that Soli responded to Mariam's letter. Like a monster under a child's bed, the past had to be faced up to, Rusi decided. He himself was a good example of the consequences of not dealing with the past. For a moment, he felt the silence that stretched long and thin between him and Coomi snap like a rubber band against his heart.

More pictures. Of Jimmy sweating under the hot Bombay sun, improbably dressed in a leather jacket and scowling like Brando. ("What was that, Jimmy? A costume for a play?") Of Bomi and Sheroo—the first of their gang to get married—at their wedding reception, Bomi winking at the camera and holding two fingers like a gun to his forehead. ("You *gadhera,* Bomi. How come I never saw this picture before? Acting like I chased you, instead of the other way around. Even at your own wedding, you had to be a joker?") Of Coomi, slender and beautiful in her black graduation robe. ("I tell you, *yaar,* Coomi was always the brainy one in the group. *Ae,* Coomi, remember how that Professor Sinha was all *lattoo-fattoo* over you in college? Used to forget his lectures when you'd walk in.") Of a grinning Rusi in a white shirt and khaki shorts, dangling upside down from a tree at Victoria Gardens, while Sheroo stood next to him, holding her head in a gesture of exaggerated horror. ("There's Rusi and his sugarcane legs. Look, the twigs on the tree are fatter than his legs.")

Then, as if someone had pulled a switch, the joking stopped. The turning of a page had revealed two other pictures, ones that many of them had spent years trying to forget. Cyrus Engineer stood in the middle of the group of adoring boys, squinting at the camera and leaning on his cricket bat, looking for all the world like a young prince. The midday sun lit up the brown hair that fell on his forehead and his grin was as wide as a continent. Even seen through the prism of time, it was clear that Cyrus was beautiful. Below that was a picture of Cyrus and Tehmi sitting under a tree at the cricket *maidan* where Cyrus used to coach the Wadia Baug team. His white cricket clothes stained with the red-brown dust of the field, Cyrus sat with his head on Tehmi's shoulder, his eyes intense and bright as they faced the camera. Even to a casual observer, it was clear that Cyrus was very much in love with the woman in the picture. "Wow. Who's that dreamboat with that girl?" Sharon Kanga asked, failing to recognize the fresh-faced woman in the picture. Several sets of eyes turned cautiously toward Tehmi, who sat looking at the picture with a sad, mysterious smile on her face. Just when they thought she would let Jimmy answer the question, Tehmi spoke up. "That's my Cyrus," she said. "He was—is—my husband. He died. A long, long time ago."

There was a short, awkward silence. Nudged by Zarin, Jimmy finally broke it. "Tehmi, I'm sorry if this was a mistake. I meant this to be a tribute. Cyrus was such an influence in my—"

"Oh, no. No. No mistake." A pause. "In fact, I'm proud of Cyrus being included in a group of such fine people." And Tehmi smiled, a quick, shy smile that made the others gasp with surprised pleasure.

Rusi saw that smile and felt a pang of regret. Tehmi had always been the quiet sort, but he and the others had been genuinely fond of her in the days when Cyrus was alive. How could they have abandoned her so after his death? Wadia Baug was populated with so many lost souls, and here was another. He thought back to his own complicity in Tehmi's becoming a recluse. Could he and the others have made a difference? Had they given up too easily, been too put off by Tehmi's bad breath and bad temper? After that encounter in the street, when he had first gotten a whiff of Tehmi's problem, Rusi had made several more attempts to get in touch with Tehmi. But each time he rang Tehmi's doorbell, Dinabai answered the door and made excuses for why her daughter could not receive him. The old woman seemed grateful for Rusi's efforts, but something in her eyes also told him that it was futile to try to reach Tehmi. And tell the truth, Rusi now said to himself. Weren't you also relieved when Tehmi refused to talk to you? Weren't you afraid that the stench of her breath would make you turn your head away and thereby hurt her again? Thinking back, Rusi also remembered another thing. After a few weeks, Khorshed Bilimoria had pulled her son aside and told him to stop going over to Dinabai's house so often. "I know your intentions are good, Rusi," she said. "And I know you are just a boy. But you know how our neighbors are. I don't want any tongues wagging about you and the young widow."

Rusi looked up at the starless sky and took another sip of his scotch. I have been unable to help too many people in my life, he thought. Unlike Jimmy, whose Midas touch rubbed off on those he came in contact with. From the poor Parsi families in Udwada that he took care of to his wife, Zarin, Jimmy made people happy. That was exactly what Rusi had wanted from his own life. The ambitions of his youth—the desire for a successful business, his hopes for a large family—had all sprung from a central desire to create happiness in his tiny corner of the world. What others had seen as personal ambition was not personal at all. But none of it had worked out the way he had planned. He had not been able to help Tehmi. Coomi, he was sure, believed that he had destroyed her life. And by marrying Coomi, he'd brought disharmony and grief into his mother's life. In fact, the only person he'd been able to help was Binny. She was his one true success story. In order to help Binny, he had to kill himself, but never mind. He had stuck a knife into his own heart, but that same knife had also cut Binny's from the misery of Bombay. He had set her free. Free to fly, free to climb. Free to have the life fate did not decree for him.

As if he had conjured her up, Binny was peering at him from the pages of the album. He let out a splutter of delight. "Look, it's my Binny," he said, his finger circling the outline of her sweet face. Beside him, he felt Coomi smile at the image of their seven-year-old daughter. It was a picture of Binny dressed as a cowboy for a costume party at Jimmy's home. Binny stood scowling at the camera, her hands on her hips, ready to draw a gun. The expression on her face made Rusi smile, and he looked up, to see a similar look on all his friends' faces. "That Binny. Always was a ham," Sheroo said. Then, as if to make sure her words were not misunderstood, she added, "God, I miss her. *Chal ne,* Rusi. Call that daughter of yours and tell her to hurry up and give us a little baby. About time Wadia Baug had some new blood. If not for the Lakdawalas and the Vajifdars, we'd have no children in the building." Taking a quick look around to make sure both families had left the reception, Sheroo continued, "And they are newcomers, after all. Bit stuck-up, if you ask me. Not like the old days, when Binny and Mehernosh used to run in and out of our flats. I tell you, it's no fun being surrounded by all you *boodhas.*" Despite her years, Sheroo always prided herself on fitting in with the younger generation.

Bomi took the bait. "Pardon my wife's ignorance," he said happily. "She is not knowing that England, where Binny lives, is not located within Wadia Baug. Even if Binny has a baby—which I pray to God she does soon—how will it infuse Wadia Baug with new blood, my dear?" Bomi turned his drunken gaze on Mehernosh. "No, we have to rely on our young stallion here to help us out. It is up to him and Sharon now to come to our rescue. Even though they will be living in Cuffe Parade, their child will be our newest resident. They can drop the baby off with his grandparents on weekends. Though mark my words, Mehernosh and Sharon will be moving back to Wadia Baug before we can say one, two, three. After all, who can resist Wadia Baug's lovely sights—such as Dosamai peering through her curtains and spying on us all—and its delicious aromas—like those street people using the wall of our building as a urinal? I'm sure Cuffe Parade doesn't have half the piss that our beloved neighborhood has collected over the years."

"Chup re, besharam," his wife chided. "Why do you drink so much, if it gives you diarrhea of the mouth?" The others chuckled at the familiar bantering between Bomi and Sheroo.

Coomi spoke up now. "Say what you will, Sheroo's central point is valid. It would be nice to hear the pitter-patter of young feet in the building. It's been too long since I was running around behind Binny. Mehernosh, I just hope you and Sharon don't make us wait as long as our Binny has."

Mehernosh smiled. "We'll try not to disappoint all of you, Coomi Auntie," he said lightly as he squeezed Sharon's hand. "After all, we aim to please."

"Sukhi re, sukhi re," Sheroo murmured. "Long live both of you."

Rusi drained the last of his scotch, and, ever the attentive host,

Jimmy immediately signaled to his driver. "*Ae,* Hari, go in and bring another bottle of scotch and some more soda, will you? Come on, go *fatta-faat.* Bring out some cold drinks for the ladies also." Hari walked around the small circle, refilling everyone's glasses. Rusi lifted his glass to take another sip, but Coomi had turned another page of the album, and his hand remained frozen halfway up to his lips. He stared at the picture of Coomi and him.

He remembered that windswept day at the beach. He and Coomi had walked the length of the beach that day, planning their wedding, laughing and hugging each other at the thought of what happiness awaited them. We had really believed our own words, our own prophesies, he now realized with wonder. That much was obvious just looking at the photograph. He looked at himself dispassionately, as if looking at the picture of a stranger. He noticed the proud angle of his head, the arrogance of his gaze, the clear, unlined brow, the starch in his back. How could he have stood so tall? As if he'd had two extra vertebrae in those days. Above all, he noticed his eyes, which burned like coal in the cavern of his face. They were the eyes of a man who was not afraid of what lay around the bend. These eyes did not dart nervously; they did not wish they could look around corners or gaze into a crystal ball. These eyes were rooted in the present and they looked life in the face. These eyes, he now thought, which had not known what lay in store for them, what disappointments and trials they would witness. They were the eyes of a child. And for a second, he felt both envy and irritation at the boy he had been.

But there was another person in the photograph: Coomi. Despite himself, he noticed how beautiful Coomi had been, took in the arched eyebrows, the sharp features, the strong white teeth, the long, dark hair that framed her face. But what took his breath away was the love and tenderness on Coomi's face. She was gazing up at him, her face shiny with love and passion. Her right arm was at his waist, drawing him close to her as they stood with their upper bodies fused together. Rusi felt the sting of tears at the back of his eyes. He had not seen that look on Coomi's face in so long. He felt a sudden urge to see that look just one more time, to feel loved and cared for one more time.

He knew it was dangerous to think this way, but for a moment he gave in to that urge, permitted himself to think of what it would take for them ever to be that gentle with each other again. But nothing came to mind. Instead, he thought of the woman he had been chatting with earlier this evening. What was her name? Sharmila, that was it. Rusi had reservations about talking to an attractive woman at Mehernosh's wedding, had known that he was donating his head on a silver platter to Dosamai's gossip factory, but he didn't care. He liked the way Sharmila paid attention to what he said, liked the assessing, curious look in her eyes. He had a feeling that if he told her he would like to see her again, she would say yes. This, despite the fact that he had told her that he was married. But he knew he would never see her again. He was too old and too tired to start an affair, had nothing to offer a woman except a laundry list of failures.

"It's not fair," he heard Coomi say, and for a guilty moment, he felt that she had read his thoughts. But Coomi was addressing the crowd. "It's not fair that we were once so young and now all we have to deal with are heart problems, and hernia operations and arthritis. I tell you, I've visited three people at Parsi General in the last month alone. No, it's not fair that we were once so young. I mean, look at us—we were actually beautiful once. Now it's hard even to imagine that."

"But we're still beautiful," Soli replied, so softly that the others were not sure if he'd spoken. "We're just beautiful in a different way. It's like . . . Beethoven was composing music even after he went deaf, you know? And some of his later work is so magnificent. . . . Abe Uncle used to say that the sorrow of his disease and old age just made his music even richer. . . . And so it is with us."

"Who's Abe Uncle?" Jimmy asked, ready to pounce on Soli for his uncharacteristic profundity. It was hard for Jimmy to take Soli seriously. "What are you blabbering about, old man?"

But Soli stayed serious, his gray eyes blurry.

And Rusi felt as if he understood both Coomi and Soli—understood the outrage of the one, the lashing out against time with the fury of the cheated; and understood the wisdom of the other, the acceptance of limitation, the transcendence of time. Both Coomi and Soli had said something true and from the heart, and he was grateful. All evening long, ever since he had heard that disturbing story about Kashmira, Rusi had felt restless, slashed by conflicting, contradictory emotions. The scotch had done its job and left him feeling expansive but desperate, as if the planet were a giant alarm clock and only Rusi could hear its relentless ticking. He wanted to save all of them, this entire collection of broken hearts and arthritic fingers and sagging skin that surrounded him, these men and women whom he loved and feared at the same time. And some of them old enough that every gathering like this was charged with poignancy, with menace. Nobody knew how many of them would be around the next time they met for a happy occasion. Nobody knew whether the next time they met would be for a happy occasion.

He caught himself. That's morbid thinking, he told himself sternly. Everyone in this group is healthy and strong. This is what Binny always accuses you of doing, thinking negative thoughts. Stop it. Stop it now. But out of his swirling sentimentality, there arose one clear goal: He wanted to distill some of his thoughts until they were as pure as the scotch he was drinking and then present this gleaned truth like a bouquet of roses to Mehernosh. All the lessons he had learned, all the things he could not say to Binny on the phone, he now wanted to say to Mehernosh. Mehernosh was just a few months younger than his Binny, after all. Although Jimmy Kanga was younger than Rusi, Jimmy had wasted no time in marrying Zarin or in having their first and only child. Naturally, Rusi thought to himself with a sad smile. Men like Jimmy don't ever wait for anything. They don't need to. And now they were all here at Mehernosh's wedding. Binny had married Jack in England, a small secular wedding, which he and Coomi had attended. He had wanted to throw a lavish reception for his daughter when she and Jack had visited Bombay the following year, but Binny wouldn't hear of it. "You know how I am, Dad. I'd die if I had to play queen for a day. Never mind, that's just an expression. Anyway, Jack's mom would kill us if she heard we allowed you to throw us a party after we'd refused her pleas. No, if you like, the four of us can go someplace quiet and celebrate." But Rusi knew that Binny's refusal was at least in part because of his financial situation. She simply did not want him to spend his money on her. Faced with joint opposition from Binny and Jack, Rusi had given in. There would be no wedding reception in Bombay for his only child. He would fold up yet another dream.

And yet, the lingering feeling of shame and disappointment remained, like a fish bone in the throat. Every time he attended a wedding, there was a moment when he saw Binny and Jack in the place of the bride and groom. Rusi knew that Parsi custom would not permit Binny to have a religious ceremony with a non-Parsi, but he would have liked to have had a reception. Binny and Jack could have sat up on a stage decked with flowers and Rusi could have strutted around like a proud peacock, slapping backs and shaking hands.

But none of this came to pass. Instead, there was this hollow feeling at Mehernosh's wedding, the shame of envying a decent man like Jimmy and resenting him for his good fortune. But there was also an avuncular pride in Mehernosh, an excitement at the promise of his future. Mehernosh was a sweet, intelligent boy and, like many Wadia Baug residents, Rusi was delighted when Mehernosh returned from America. It felt like a victory of sorts, a body snatched from the jaws of the monster that had swallowed up so many Parsi children. Mehernosh had been inside the belly of the beast but had remained unmoved by its glitter and promise. That alone was cause for celebration and wonderment. Suddenly, Rusi felt like celebrating.

He was not a man used to speaking in public; therefore, Rusi was surprised to hear his voice say Mehernosh's name. "Mehernosh," he said. "There's something that I want to say to you and to your new bride. Some words of wisdom from an old man, if you will." He ignored the good-natured groans and exaggerated cries of "Oh no" and "Cut off his drinking quota, right this minute." He felt Coomi stiffen by his side, as if she was afraid that what he was about to say would implicate her in some way. Jimmy, too, had a guarded expression on his face and looked ready to pounce if Rusi said anything that would cast a shadow over the evening he had so carefully sculpted. But Rusi ignored them all and stared resolutely at Mehernosh.

"I am not an educated man, Mehernosh," he began. "You already know more and have traveled farther and risen higher than I ever will. But I have one advantage over you. I'm older. Yes, looking at me with my loose skin and ugly face, it may be hard to believe that I'm calling old age an advantage. But although time takes away a lot, it also leaves you with something. I would not be bold enough to call that something wisdom. But the truth is, you can't live as long as I have and not learn a few things." Beside him, he felt Coomi relax. As he took a short sip of his scotch, his hand brushed up against hers and he felt a shot of warmth run through his body.

"Mehernosh, what I've learned is simple—that life moves faster than we do. During all the time that we while away by telling jokes, standing at street corners, going to dances, sleeping eight hours at night, life is still moving, like a river we cannot keep up with. That river does not wait for us to build a bridge across it; it just keeps doing what it must. That is the nature of rivers—to flow. So, it is important not to waste time, not to waste a day or a minute of a day. Important to put all the time we've been given to good use. That's what I believed as a young man and what I still believe today."

He paused for a minute, forcing his drunken brain to move down the labyrinth he had built for himself. "But here's the paradox," he continued. "If we don't do any of the things that seem wasteful, that seem like we are squandering time, then life itself becomes meaningless. Telling jokes, walking the beach, falling in love—these are the things a man remembers at the end of his life. If he's done enough of these, then he dies a rich man. If he hasn't, he dies empty-handed, even though his bank account may be full. And this, Mehernosh, it took me a long time to learn. In some ways, I'm still learning this lesson."

There was an embarrassed silence, born out of an unspoken consensus that Rusi had been too naked, had infused an occasion of gaiety with an ill-fitting solemnity. Sheroo spoke up to rescue Rusi. "*Wah,*

wah. All these years I was thinking Rusi was a businessman, and actually he's our philosopher-king. I'm calling you Mr. Aristotle from now on, Rusi."

The others laughed. "Come, let's finish looking at the rest of the album. Only two more pages left," Jimmy said hurriedly.

Rusi knew he was on the verge of losing his audience. He had a feeling of great letdown, knowing that his words had revealed neither the expansiveness of his thoughts nor the pounding of his blood. He wanted to say so much more, wanted to describe to all of them this wonderful feeling of connection that was sweeping over him. How, as he sat here, he felt hooked up to the universe, how his blood felt as if it could flow directly into the Arabian Sea and his heart felt like a continent waiting to be discovered. He wanted to describe to them the seamless blending of his mind with the outside world—how sometimes he felt as if there were no boundaries between what happened on the outside and what went on inside his head. Some days, he felt as if his head were a globe. Every war ever fought and every peace waged; every heart broken and every flesh made whole; every child ever born, every man who ever died—all of history distilled into his own life. But how to say all this without it sounding absurd? Mehernosh was already looking at him with an expression of grave concern. Soli had opened and shut his mouth several times, as if he were trying to rescue his friend from a burning building but didn't know how. Zarin had a tight, embarrassed smile on her face, while Bomi was searching to catch someone's eye so that he could let out a loud guffaw. Rusi looked at Coomi out of the corner of his eye, but her face was expressionless.

Suddenly, it came to him, what he wanted to say to Mehernosh, as clearly as if the words were typed on a sheet of paper. "Mehernosh," he said. "I have already made enough of a fool of myself for one evening. But because you are like my son, I will try once again. What I want to say is very simple: Be happy. In many places, that is easy to do. In America, they tell me, they even have those words written in their Constitution. But not in India. Not in our Parsi *com.* Here, people are always telling you not to laugh too loudly, not to dream too big, not to fly too high. Pride comes before a fall, they tell us from the time we are children. But Mehernosh, a man who dives for fish catches fish. One who aims for the stars catches a star. So a man who owns fish can only share fish with others, not stars. Nobody can share what they don't possess, you see? All these old folks—all our lives, they told us God does not like proud people, that God clips the wings of those who fly too high. But I say, nobody has seen the yardstick of God. Too many people in this community of ours who will try to pull you down, who will tell you you have no right to your own laughter. They will point out all the misery of the world to you, to make their point. But listen carefully to me: You have not only a right but a *responsibility* to be happy. What I'm saying to you, I would say to my own Binny. All of us gathered here are like your own family. Most of us saw you the day you were born. We need you to be happy, *beta.* For us. For all of us. It's the only way to make sense of all this—this city that's hell on earth, this life where we've all sacrificed so much, the losses and disappointments we've all suffered. Our chance has come and gone. Some of us fared better than others. But young ones, like you and Sharon and my Binny, you are our hope and promise. We wish all success and happiness to you. More important, we need this for you. And *from* you. Do you understand what I'm saying?"

He stopped abruptly, exhausted and suddenly mortified. A thick shyness descended on him, forcing his gaze to the ground. He prayed for someone to shatter the unbearable silence that gathered like smoke around him. He felt Coomi's eyes on him but was afraid to look up, for fear of what he'd see on her face.

"I do." The words rang out like a shot into the embarrassed silence. "I know what you mean, exactly. *Exactly.*"

It was Coomi. He turned around to face her, slowly, like a sleepwalker waking up. Coomi's face was shiny and there was a fierce, protective expression on her face that challenged the others not to destroy her fragile, sentimental husband with their words or laughter. Rusi dimly remembered that expression from years past. It was a look that used to make him feel omnipotent, that shielded him from his own weaknesses and made him feel capable of laying the world's riches at Coomi's feet. He did not know what he had said or done to resurrect that look, but he was grateful. Suddenly, he remembered how she had tried making up with him in the days after his mother's death and how he had rebuffed her. Now he wondered if that had been a mistake, and he felt a piercing pain at the thought of the wasted, barren years that lay behind and ahead of them.

Then he heard the sound. They were cheering him. Strangely, inexplicably, they were cheering him. Clapping, slowly at first and then vigorously, as if they were at a concert. "Hear, hear," one of them said. "Well said, laddie, well said," another voice responded.

Mehernosh had risen from his chair and was now pulling Rusi up from his. The younger man embraced Rusi in a bear hug. "Wow, Rusi Uncle. If I'd known you were so good at speechifying, Dad and I would've made you a law partner years ago."

Everybody laughed. Rusi's words had suddenly made them see Mehernosh in a different way. Whereas Mehernosh had always been part of their past, they suddenly saw him as their future, and this cheered them up.

"Rusi's right. You must always keep our collar up, Mehernosh. I say, someday you will be attorney general of India," Sheroo said.

Jimmy laughed. "It's not that easy, my dear Sheroo," he said lightly.

They turned on him like angry bees because he was interfering with their new dream of Mehernosh. Rusi's words had anointed Mehernosh as the custodian of their future and they swarmed to that vision.

"If anybody can do it, our Mehernosh can."

"Our Parsi boys need to rise again. It's not like the old days, when we ran this city. Now even those *paan*-chewing Maharashtrians are better educated than we are."

"*Arre,* in a few years, even the Central Bank won't have a single Parsi department head."

"Yah, the Bank of America now probably has more Parsis than Central Bank."

"Don't talk to me of America. Remember that story of the old woman with the gunny sack filled with cockroaches, the one our parents used to frighten us with? These days, I'm thinking of America as that woman, kidnapping all our children."

"*Arre, baba,* it's hard for anybody to resist the riches of America. Not for nothing they call it 'the land of opportunity.' "

"All except our Mehernosh. He came back to us."

"Those Americans must've been dumbfounded. Imagine, an Indian turning down America?"

"And why not, indeed? After all, his daddy has built an empire for him here."

"Three cheers for Mehernosh and Sharon," Bomi said. "Hip hip . . ."

"Hooray."

"Hip hip . . ."

"Hooray!"

They were being watched. Thirty pairs of eyes followed their every move—every flash of a jeweled hand, every rustle of an expensive embroidered sari, every turn of a gold-clad neck. Thirty pairs of ears heard their tinsel laughter, the deep baritone of the male voices, the glassy tinkle of female giggles. Thirty pairs of nostrils breathed in the lingering scent of their imported perfumes as it commingled with the glorious smell of the leftover dinners being packed for distribution.

They were being watched. The rumblings of thirty stomachs grew louder and louder, until this ragtag group of street people who stood outside the iron gates dissolved into one giant stomach, until it became hunger itself, a vacuous ache, a heavy groan. With increasing restlessness, they watched a tall man in a brown suit distributing individual boxes to the small group of old men and women sitting in a circle. They watched them pull books out of those boxes. They gritted their teeth as they noticed how the old men and women settled back into their chairs before they started flipping through the books. As if they had all the time in the world. With sinking hearts, they watched the tall man signal to someone to bring out another bottle of alcohol, watched as the man poured fresh drinks into their glasses.

Old as they were, it seemed as if this band of revelers was in no hurry to go home. Silently, they watched the glassy look that many of the guests got in their eyes, cursed the fair-skinned man who suddenly started to speak and looked like he never would stop.

Still, they were patient. They had not come this far without learning patience. Like a dog who must wait for scraps from his master's table, they had mastered the art of patience. Sooner or later, these well-dressed old men and women must rise and go home. Sooner or later, they will get bogged down from the weight of their heavy jewelry, will get drowsy from the weight of their filled stomachs, will get burdened by the weight of their guilt. Sooner or later, something will happen that will send them home. Won't it? Won't it? Or is it possible that they will stay so long that the caterer may get tired and irritable, may decide to call it a day without going through the nightly ritual of distributing the leftovers to them, they who had waited so patiently, so silently? They had walked several kilometers, some of them, for their daily bread. They had come, with infants on their hips and holding their other children by the hand. They had come, leaving grandmothers at home, promising them a full meal when they returned. When they returned to the strip of pavement that they called home.

"How much longer, Baba?" Bhima asked, tugging at her father's shirtsleeve. He had just wiped his nose on that shirtsleeve a minute ago. He had woken up this morning with a sore throat and a fever that left him so tired, he had even thought about skipping dinner tonight. Only the crushed look on his seven-year-old daughter's face had made him change his mind.

"Should be soon," he replied. "See that? That's the bus that's going to take them home. Can't be much longer."

But he was wrong. A minute later, the tall man in the brown suit rose to his feet and signaled his driver. Now there were new glasses. And a different kind of bottle. The driver poured small quantities of a creamy light brown liquid into each glass. "Thank you all for being here for the happiest day of my life," the tall man said. "Cheers."

"Cheers, cheers," the rest of them replied.

He hated them then. Hated their stupidity and their silly indulgences. Hated their indifference to him, their oblivion. His body ached with fever and hatred. He wanted to smash their glasses over each of their heads, wanted to tear their happy smiles from their fat, light-skinned faces. Without thinking, he ran his fingers over his own face, a canvas of taut skin under a foundation of bone. He thought of Bhima's thin, weary face, caked with dirt and sadness, and the thought of her lighted a fire under his simmering anger. Since Bhima's mother died of pneumonia two years ago, she was all he had. The village that he had left as a teenager now seemed as remote as a dream. Fueled by the rags-to-riches fantasies of Hindi movies, he had come to Bombay with great hopes. "City of dreams," they called Bombay in his village, and indeed, some of the men who had left had returned with enough money to buy their own land and build their own homes. But somehow, things had not worked out for him that way. In the beginning, he used to return to the village at least once a year, regardless of whether he had money for a train ticket. But once, they caught him. Unable to pay the fine, he served three months in jail. The experience broke his confidence and the visits home became less frequent. Also, he could not face the bewildered disillusionment in his old mother's face. It was impossible to convince the old woman that money did not grow on trees in Bombay. After Bhima was born, he stopped going home altogether. Now he was one of the millions of ghosts who walked Bombay, a man without a past or a future. He lived everywhere and nowhere, just like air.

But he was a father, nevertheless. He reached over to pat his daughter's head and draw her closer to his side, but his hand touched space where she had been a second ago. He turned around to look for her. But she was gone.

When he saw her again, he recognized her by her small hand. Unable to wait any longer, losing faith in his empty promises of deliverance, Bhima had crossed the street to where a large city Dumpster lay. Yesterday, her *baba* had come home and told her that they would eat well tonight, had made her mouth water with descriptions of fish baked in green chutney and yellowed rice with big pieces of chicken in it. But pangs of hunger had driven that vision out of Bhima's head. She could not wait any longer. She climbed the tall Dumpster with practiced ease and then foraged around. The Dumpster didn't look too picked over. Maybe if she was lucky she would find a half-eaten banana or a piece of chicken with some meat still left on the bone.

It was her lucky day. She emerged from the Dumpster triumphant, with half of an overripe orange in her hand. Her father saw her little hand as she gripped the inside of the Dumpster and lifted herself over to the other side of it. "Baba, look," she said excitedly. But he could not look, blinded as he was by guilt, shame, and rage. He knew she would eat the orange slowly, savoring the sharp trickle of the juice down the back of her throat. He knew she would then chew on the peel, unable to throw any part of her precious treasure away. Most days, he shared her excitement at the discovery of edible food. But tonight, it made him sick. Tonight was to have been different. He had found out yesterday that there was a big Parsi wedding on the next day. He had promised Bhima that they would dine well, eat the same food that the *bara sahibs* did. He had ignored the whimpers of his aching, fevered body to keep his promise to his girl. And now a bunch of bastards who did not know when it was time to exit had wrecked his plans. And the worst part of it was, they did so thoughtlessly, oblivious to his and Bhima's existence. As if all of them who stood hunched and crowded outside these tall iron gates were simply an extension of the black night. Invisible. As if his daughter, his beautiful, serious, hungry daughter did not exist.

Well, he would show them she existed. That he existed. If they refused to acknowledge his presence, he would acknowledge theirs. He would send them a present, a gift from the shadows. After all, it was a wedding. He was sure that the van that waited to take them away from here was already loaded down with fancy gifts. He would give them one more gift, unlike any that they already had. A slow grin formed on his lips. He shivered with fever and excitement.

"Go to the number five bus stop and wait for me," he said to Bhima.

She looked at him uncomprehendingly. "But, Baba, the food. I'm still hungry."

"Forget the food," he hissed. "Do what I say. Go now."

"But you promised," she said. But already she was obeying him, whimpering as she walked away from the crowd. He waited until she turned the corner and then crossed the one-way street. Close to the Dumpster, there lay a pile of cut bricks and rocks. He ran his hand through the debris until his fingers closed around a rock that felt heavy and substantial in his hand. He looked quickly to his left and right. A man rode by on his bicycle, and he waited until he was gone. He looked again. Nobody was paying him any attention. Weak with hunger and anticipation, the huddled crowd at the entrance was transfixed by the antics on the other side of the gate. They did not wish to look away for a minute, for fear that they might miss some vital signal. For an instant, he felt contempt for them, for their naked hunger and their willingness to go to any lengths to appease that hunger. He felt free, as if he had severed the ties that bound him to their cowering servility.

He stood on his toes and his right hand formed a perfect arc against the black Bombay sky. As the stone left his arm and sailed over the iron gates, he felt a minute's pride, as if he had created a work of art. He heard the stone land with a satisfying thud, followed by a woman's scream. The satisfaction that he got from hearing those two sounds, close enough together so as to be in unison, made him forget his hunger and the disappointment in his daughter's eyes. Laughing out loud, he ran into the waiting arms of the warm Bombay night. For a moment, he felt strong and beautiful.

Ten

Jimmy Kanga saw it first, the black danger sailing toward them from the other side of the gate. He opened his mouth to warn his friends, but no words emerged. But Sharon saw the look of horror on Jimmy's face, followed the line of his pointed finger, and deftly stepped out of the path of the descending object. She tried to pull Sheroo out of its way, but Sheroo was a large woman and moved slowly. There was a thud as the rock hit Sheroo on her upper arm and then fell to the ground.

Sheroo screamed in fright and in pain. An ugly purple stain formed against her lemony skin almost immediately. Bomi, who was standing a couple of feet away from his wife, ran up to her. "Sheroo, my God. What happened? Oh God, look at her arm. Ice, somebody get some ice quickly."

They all spoke at once:

"Here, Sheroo, sit down. Anybody have some eau de cologne? Sprinkle some on her forehead. She looks ready to faint. . . ."

"Thank God it missed her shoulder by a few inches. Would've shattered the bone like glass. . . ."

"Here, Sheroo, swallow this. Just some homeopathy pills I'm always carrying. Just Arnica. Good for shock and bruises. . . ."

"Try moving your arm. . . ."

"No, better not to move it yet. . . ."

"I'm okay, really. Just the shock of it is worse than anything. . . ."

"*Baap re,* look at the size of this rock. It's a miracle she's not dead. . . ."

"Outside. It came from the outside. . . ."

"Unbelievable. Someone threw a rock in here. . . ."

"Barbarians. Uncivilized barbarians. What did we ever do to them? . . ."

"Here we are, minding our own business. . . ."

"Bombay has become unlivable, I tell you. We've been run over by slums and violence. Where will it all end? . . ."

"It was probably one of these people at the gate. Have been staring at us like vultures all evening long. . . ."

"A few more minutes and we would've been gone. But they couldn't wait. . . ."

"Look at them, even now. Staring at us like we're bleddy animals in a zoo. . . ."

"Where the hell was the *chowkidar*?" Jimmy roared. "Why the hell did I spend money getting a security guard if he can't offer us basic protection?" He strode purposefully toward where the sentry stood at the gate. A thin, dark-skinned man of medium build, the *chowkidar* seemed transfixed by the events of the last few minutes. A resident of a nearby slum, he had landed this job five months back. At that time, the job had seemed like a gift from the gods. Now it seemed as if the gods were ready to snatch their gift back. Jimmy was signaling for him to leave his post by the gate and come to where Jimmy stood, but the *chowkidar* seemed paralyzed with fright. "Come here, you *madaarchot,*" Jimmy screamed, and finally the sentry managed to walk a few feet on his shaky legs.

"I'm sorry, sir, so sorry. Hope madam is not badly hurt. What to do, hard to know what mischief someone is doing from the outside. . . ."

"You bastard, you're not nearly as sorry as you're going to be tomorrow. You better not show your face here again. First thing in the morning, I'm going to call the hall people and make sure they fire you. Your incompetence has caused one of my guests to be seriously injured and has ruined our evening. I know your type—probably were drinking on the job. Now, go make yourself useful and see that everything is under control while we board the minibus."

"Oh *seth, maaf karo.* Please to forgive, *sahib.* Just one more chance, sir. I'm a poor man, with wife and children to support. Nothing I could've done to prevent this, sir."

Jimmy spoke as if addressing a courtroom. "That's the trouble with this country. Nobody wants to accept responsibility for their actions." And ignoring the *chowkidar*'s pleas, he strode away.

The *chowkidar* pulled nervously at his mustache as he walked back to the gate. He could scarcely believe what had just happened. For the past five months, he had been able to feed his family on a regular basis. His salary was meager, but often he carried a couple of leftover dinners home to his eager children. He had worked so hard to land this job, ingratiating himself with the Parsi gentlemen who ran the reception hall. He had run last-minute errands for them, helped them decorate the hall before the guests arrived, helped the band unload its instruments. And all this for naught. A rock thrown by an anonymous hand had landed in the middle of the reception and destroyed his life. Just like that. He thought of his two years of unemployment before he got this job and his heart froze at the thought of returning to the desultory laziness of those years. He had spent his days looking for odd jobs or sitting at home playing cards with the other unemployed slum dwellers. Day had followed day. He had felt his limbs get weak and lazy with lack of exercise. He took to beating his wife for entertainment, to break the monotony of his days. His children began to avoid him. But all that had changed in the last few months. Every evening, he dressed in his khaki security guard's uniform, slipped his baton into his leather holster, and left the slum with a swagger in his step. Some nights, he returned home with enough leftovers to feed not only his own family but also some of the neighborhood children. How good that made him feel! But now, those days were over. The Parsi *seth* did not look as if he would change his mind. He wondered if they would ask him to return his uniform when they told him he was fired.

He had been back at his post for a second, when he heard it. A giggle. Someone was giggling at what had transpired between the *chowkidar* and the Parsi *seth.* Someone was laughing at his misfortune. He looked at the ragged crowd standing behind the iron gates, but their faces were impassive and serious. Still, he had heard it, distinctly. One of these bastards had taunted him with his heartless laughter. Probably the same bastard who had thrown the rock. He was in this crowd, then, the culprit. If he could just nab him and teach him a lesson, perhaps he could redeem himself in the eyes of the Parsi *sahib.* Perhaps they would even allow him to keep his job if he caught the stone thrower.

But who? He ran his eyes over the crowd and they stared back at him. His eyes narrowed as they focused on the face of a youth of about nineteen. The youth was holding on to the bar of the iron gate and staring at him. He imagined that he saw a look of insolence on the youth's face, a certain smirk on his lips. Look at you, the youth's expression seemed to say. You're no better than any of us suckers waiting out here. Even your khaki uniform couldn't save you from being stripped naked by the Parsi *bawa*'s tongue-lashing. We all heard his threats and we all saw you, even our women and children, standing naked, with your dingdong hanging helplessly in front of you.

He let out a low, guttural sound and rushed to his feet. Swinging open the iron gate, he thrust his hand into the surprised crowd and plucked the smirking youth from it. He pulled the youth inside, slammed the gate shut, and slapped his stunned face, all in the same swift motion. *"Chalo jao,"* he screamed at the crowd, wielding his baton in a menacing way. "*Sahib* has already called the police. Disperse immediately or there will be hell to pay. Each one of you will pay for that hurled rock, ten times over. Now, get lost." He made a movement toward opening the gates again, and that was all it took. The authority in his voice, the crazed look in his eyes told them that he meant business. The crowd melted into the night that it had earlier sprung from.

The youth was still cradling his face, a bewildered look in his eyes. This only infuriated the *chowkidar* more. "*Madaarchot,* let's hear you giggle now," he said softly. The youth opened his mouth to protest, but before a word could escape his lips, the *chowkidar* had brought his knee into the youth's stomach. As the boy fell, the sentry brought the savage baton down on him over and over again. "Come on, let's see your balls now. Come on, you coward, no words left in you now, eh?" The youth was down, trying to protect his head with his hands. The *chowkidar*'s heart sang with each satisfying thud of the baton. He had found his rhythm. The first sight of drawn blood only excited him more. As the youth writhed on the dusty ground, the *chowkidar* felt as if he were stomping on a snake, like he used to do in the village of his youth. "I'll kill you," he said in a low voice, as if speaking to himself. "Giggling like that. Think my children starving is funny, do you? Well, here's something to laugh about. And this. And this." His hands and feet flew, happy each time they found their target.

"Put that baton away! Stop it right this minute. My God, man, have you gone mad?" Rusi came as close to the *chowkidar* as he could without getting caught in the centrifugal force caused by the baton. Jimmy stood a few paces behind him. At a distance, Soli sat down heavily on a chair next to the injured Sheroo, his face covered with perspiration.

The *chowkidar* flew out of the nest of his fury as suddenly as he had entered it. The baton hung limply by his side as the madness slowly drained out of his body. He stared at the torn, broken body at his feet as if he had just come upon it. The servile look came back on his face. "That's the culprit, *sahibs,*" he said as he gasped for breath. "I found him myself and gave him such a pasting, he'll never pick up another rock again. So sorry about all this, *sahibs.*"

Rusi turned to look at Jimmy for direction and thought he was staring at a ghost. All color had drained from Jimmy's face and, for a second, Jimmy looked as lost as the nine-year-old orphan who had attended Rusi's birthday party decades ago. Jimmy was transfixed, unable to take his eyes off the youth's bloody body. "The bastard has bashed his head in," Jimmy murmured to no one in particular. "Blood spilled, and on such an auspicious occasion. A bad omen. My poor Mehernosh. What on earth happened here? And what do we do now?"

The youth was fluttering on the ground, like a dying fish washed to the shore. Rusi saw his bloody face, his bruised, blackened fingers, his hideously swollen feet and he felt sick to his stomach. The savagery of the attack took his breath away. What the *chowkidar* had done was ten times worse than what had been inflicted on poor Sheroo. The youth was saying something, and Rusi rested on his haunches to hear him. He was amazed the boy could still speak. *"Janne do, sahib, janne do.* Let me go. Please, *maaf karo,"* the youth said. Rusi stood up in disbelief. The fellow actually thought Rusi and Jimmy were going to beat him some more. Pity welled up in Rusi. "Nobody's going to hurt you anymore," he said. "Understand?"

He turned to confer with Jimmy about whether to call the police, but one look at Jimmy's horrified face told him it was useless. Jimmy seemed broken, a look on his face that tore at Rusi's heart. Glancing back, Rusi saw Mehernosh standing at a distance, holding Sharon's sobbing face to his chest. The rest of the group looked like sleepwalkers, dazed and confused. He searched for Coomi and found her sitting next to Sheroo, holding a bag of ice on Sheroo's arm. She looked at him inquiringly and he shrugged his shoulders. He was glad that Coomi had not come here, had not seen the youth's beaten, swollen face or heard his low moans.

A slight movement outside the gates caught his eye. Something moved out there, he thought. The hair on the nape of his neck stood up in anticipation. Suddenly, he had a vision of the invisible outsiders tearing open the iron gates and pouring into the reception hall, seeking to avenge what had been wrought upon the man on the ground. We would be mincemeat in half a minute, he thought. They could destroy us in the blink of an eye. The precariousness of their situation dawned on him then and this helped focus his mind on the problem at hand. They had to leave the reception hall immediately. There was no time to call the police. No point even. What the *chowkidar* had done, however despicable, was justice, Bombay-style. Involving the police would just muddy the waters. What was done was done.

He turned his back on the *chowkidar* and hoped that the man did not see him pull out a hundred-rupee note from his wallet. Bending down, he pushed the note into the front pocket of the youth's torn shirt. He knew that the note would be stained red within moments, but he couldn't help that. "We're letting you go," he whispered to the youth. "We don't want to make this a police *ka mamala.* As soon as I say the word, just try to get up and go. Understand?" Straightening up, he yelled at the *chowkidar.* "Open these gates. Now. Come on, move." And to the youth, he said, "*Chalo,* try to pull yourself out of here. Walk, crawl, fly—do whatever you need to do, but leave. No telling what will happen if you don't leave."

Fear attached itself like wings to the youth. Half-crawling, half-sliding, one foot hanging limply behind him, he pulled himself out of the iron gates and into the anonymous night. Rusi could hear him as he moved his body painfully across the street. He waited until the youth melted into the night, until he could no longer hear the hissing and heaving of his broken body. Then, with a heavy heart, Rusi walked back into the hall.

The dusty ground near the entrance of the hall still bore the imprint of the youth's body. There was blood smeared into the dust where he had lain broken and from where he had crawled away into the waiting night.

They were mostly quiet during the bus ride home. They had boarded the bus tired and subdued as schoolchildren after a field trip. Rusi had hurried them onto the bus. "There may be more trouble tonight," he mumbled as he gathered them in. "Best if we get out of here, *jaldi-jaldi.*" While the others were boarding the bus, Jimmy Kanga turned to Rusi. Jimmy's usually dignified, wise face had been rearranged, so that now he looked confused and lost. "Rusi," he said, his eyes flickering uncertainly. "What just happened here?"

Rusi gazed at the frightened face in front of him and wondered why he had ever been jealous of Jimmy. Why, he is nothing but a little boy, he thought. For all his wisdom and all his degrees, he is scared. Years of wealth and comfort have softened Jimmy. He may argue cases before the Supreme Court, but he knows nothing about the city he lives in. He just sees it from the inside of his car window.

Then Rusi's basic sense of fair play took over. And who understands this time bomb of a city? You certainly don't, he scolded himself. "I don't know," he replied. "I really don't know. It all happened so fast. . . . But we'd better make a move, *bossie.* There will be time to talk later." He felt embarrassed as he climbed onto the bus.

There was an awful moment when they were all aboard and Sheroo remembered that she had left behind her photo album. Bomi hesitated for a split second before volunteering to go get it, but it was long enough for the others to realize they were afraid to linger. They felt a burning shame at their fearful retreat and hurried departure. How relaxed, how expansive they had felt only an hour ago. And now they were fleeing like common criminals, fleeing from the imaginary and nonimaginary demons of the night. Rusi suddenly remembered those photographs of helicopters hovering nervously over the American embassy in Saigon in 1975 and the tight, shameful expressions on the faces of the evacuees. The fall of Saigon. Now he felt as if he had traded places with those evacuees. At least the Americans had been at war with another country. But he and his friends were fleeing their own people. There was no safety even in the city they had all been born in. This city, which their forefathers had helped build with their industry and their capital, was being stolen from them, large parts of it cut out from under them by knives that gleamed and flashed in the still of the night. He remembered the story about Kashmira that Bomi had told earlier in the evening and felt as though that ominous story had foreshadowed what had happened later. A strange feeling had gripped him earlier and he wondered now whether it had been a premonition. All evening long, he had been achingly aware of his own mortality, had felt a fraternity with his Wadia Baug neighbors that he rarely felt. He wondered about the compulsion he had felt to share his life lessons with Mehernosh, to pass on to the younger generation all that he knew. Had that been a premonition of the violence to follow? Had the rock been meant for him and had he somehow twisted out of fate's grasp one more time? If so, what did that mean? Should he feel relief or guilt at the thought?

He glanced at Mehernosh, who was sitting a few seats ahead of them, saw the back of the boy's big proud head, and for a second, he questioned Mehernosh's wisdom in returning to Bombay. Binny made the better choice, he told himself, even though she made it for the wrong reasons. Binny, he knew, had not fled Bombay because of the menace lurking in its streets, but because of the grief that dripped like candle wax from the walls of Wadia Baug. Binny's demons lived in the Bilimoria flat and not the streets around it. But whatever the reason, Binny had fled this graveyard of a city, where women got struck with rocks and young men lay writhing in their own blood. And he was glad for her escape.

Rusi turned to where Sheroo was sitting behind him. Even in the dark of the bus, he could see Sheroo's face, which looked tired and unimaginably old. She was looking out the window, watching the deserted city streets flit by. "How is the arm?" he whispered, but she only nodded noncommittally. Now he could see that Sheroo was crying softly to herself, and he felt a sharp stab of anger on her behalf. Sheroo was legendary for her generosity, for buying ice candy for the street children who played outside Wadia Baug, for donating her used bedsheets to their parents each winter. The bastard who had hurled the rock had no idea whom he was hurting. It was the random savagery of the attack that angered Rusi. Just earlier that evening, he had thought about how all of them were sitting precariously on top of a bomb that could go off at any moment. And it had. Not as explosively as it was capable of, but enough to tell him that he was right. The purple bruise on Sheroo's ample upper arm was proof, an apocalyptic warning, the writing on the wall written by an anonymous graffiti artist.

But then he remembered the bloated head of the youth as he lay tossing on the dirt. He, too, had been a victim of random violence. Despite the *chowkidar*'s protestations, Rusi was sure the man had no way of telling whether the youth had hurled the stone or not. And they had all stood quietly watching as the *chowkidar* had yanked the youth in, pulled the baton from his holster, and yelled at the crowd to disperse. It was true that none of them had foreseen the savagery of his attack. It was true that the brutality of his attack had paralyzed them, so that Rusi had not intervened until it was much too late. But was it also not true that they had expected the *chowkidar* to rough up the youth a bit, to slap him a few times, to make an example of him? Had they not felt better at the fact that the *chowkidar* was acting as their emissary, that he was evening the score on their behalf? And if that was true, did they not all have blood on their hands? At least the man who had thrown the stone had done the foul deed himself, had risked getting caught and punished. What had they risked? They had simply hired somebody else to do their dirty work for them.

Victim upon victim. Hadn't the *chowkidar* himself been a victim of Jimmy's unreasonable wrath? How had they expected that one poor man to protect them from the jealousy and hatred their sheer presence aroused among those waiting outside the gates? Why had he, Rusi, not intervened when he heard Jimmy threatening to fire the sentry? Why had he not pulled Jimmy aside and appealed to his sense of fair play? Admit it, Rusi said to himself. As far as we're concerned, these people are interchangeable and replaceable. So we hire and fire them at our will. Already, he could not remember what the *chowkidar* looked like. The next time he and Coomi attended a function at the same reception hall, there would be another man at the gate, perhaps wearing the same frayed khaki uniform. And once again, he would look through him, barely glancing in his direction as they walked in.

Beside him, Coomi stirred. "I keep thinking, What will happen to that *chowkidar*?" she said to him in a low voice. "We got on the bus and left, but he's got to stay behind to face the music."

She had done it again. She had read his mind, tapped into his thoughts, and said something that made him realize how well she understood him. She was reading him like an X ray. Was this some new trick she had developed? And if so, when? He had never noticed this uncanny ability before. Had she always been like this? Or was this sudden compatibility part of the strangeness of this entire evening? After all, he had felt his usual distance from her when they had walked into the reception hours earlier. He tried now to call up that protective distance, but the memory of her sticking up for him earlier in the evening made that difficult. What had Coomi said? "I know what you mean, exactly. *Exactly.*" How warm, how safe he had felt in the glow of those words. And now she was doing it again. Rusi knew without a shadow of a doubt that none of their fellow passengers were worried about their culpability in what had happened. Jimmy would most likely make good on his threat to have the security guard fired. Mehernosh and Sharon would busy themselves with preparations for their honeymoon. Sheroo and Bomi would occupy themselves with Sheroo's injured arm. Tehmi and Adi would crawl back into the cocoon of solitude they each occupied. And Soli, poor Soli would spend the next few days agonizing over Mariam's letter. Coomi, he knew, would probably stay up half the night worrying about the *chowkidar*'s fate.

He touched her arm ever so lightly. "I'll talk to Jimmy tomorrow morning," he said to her. "I'll see if I can calm him down. No sense in you worrying about this. Try to forget it."

When she spoke again, her voice was so low, he barely heard it over the rattle of the bus. "Tonight, for the first time in my life, I'm glad Binny's away. This city is getting too unpredictable. Maybe you were right after all to send her away." Then Coomi turned her face to look out the window, and he knew for sure that she was blinking her tears away. He knew what it had cost her to say those words, and his heart ached for her so badly that it frightened him. He did not want to resurrect his feelings for Coomi. It was much too dangerous. Sympathy, pity, any of these feelings could pierce the glass shield that he had built around his heart. And yet . . . And yet, who could understand better than he how much Coomi missed her daughter? He had thought that the longer Binny stayed away, the easier the heartache would get. But exactly the opposite was true. As he got older, the thought of spending old age without Binny, of someday dying alone, without his daughter by his side, haunted him. He wondered whether Coomi battled the same thoughts.

Despite his better judgment, he felt compelled to respond to Coomi's half apology. "Thank you for saying that," he said, and heard the tremor in his own voice. "I know how much you miss her. I miss her a lot, too. I console myself by thinking we sacrificed our happiness for our daughter's sake."

Coomi was silent for a moment. Then Rusi heard her say, "Whatever happened between us, we'll at least always have Binny in common.

Nothing can change that." Rusi's eyes welled up with tears and he did not trust himself to speak. Before he could respond, he felt Coomi's hand reaching for his. He stiffened from force of habit, but she did not draw her hand away. Instead, she shyly pulled his hand on her lap as words poured incoherently from her, fast as water from a tap. "What you said to Mehernosh tonight—it reminded me so much of the people we used to be. Nobody there understood what you were saying—not at first anyway—but me. But *me.* And it made me proud that I understood you, like in the old days. And Jimmy's thoughtful gift. Watching ourselves in that photo album. Unleashing memories, like a monster that had been tied to a tree. So young we were, so happy. I'm tired of this loneliness, Rusi. I have been much too lonely. And you have, too. Something has to be done about this. Something must be done."

He searched desperately for the plaster cast that he normally sealed his heart in, but he couldn't find it. He told himself not to fall for Coomi's theatrics, that she would hurt him again as soon as he let his guard down. But Coomi had never before spoken to him with such desperation and sincerity. Or maybe he had just forgotten. In any case, he let his hand relax on her warm lap. As soon as he did that, he was aware of how tense his muscles had been and how god-awfully tired he was. He closed his eyes, trying to keep at bay the thoughts that were trying to flood his brain. There would be plenty of time to deal with them later.

Suddenly, all he wanted was to be at home. Rusi wanted the bus to speed past these unfriendly streets and deliver him to the relative safety and security of Wadia Baug. His heart lifted at the thought of the old apartment building's solid presence. For 120 years, it had stood on the same spot, indifferent to the vagaries of life. Rusi wished he could feel that rooted, instead of this wretched, teary feeling he was experiencing. He tried to call up that large and lazy feeling the scotch had conferred upon him earlier in the evening, but the rock that hit Sheroo had shattered his glassy drunkenness. He felt tired and irritable. He wished he was already in his pajamas and asleep in his own bed. He wanted to cover his face with his sheets and shut his eyes, to block out this confusing city, this bewildering life. The more he thought about either one, the less he understood. He was tired of thinking.

Soli Contractor was saying something in the back of the bus, and his voice shook Rusi out of his reverie. Now, as he looked, Soli was walking to the front of the bus. In his right arm, he was holding the photo album. As Soli walked by Sheroo and Bomi, he nudged Bomi. "How is she?" he asked quietly, and Bomi replied with a halfhearted thumbs-up.

Soli stood facing them and rocked to the motion of the lurching bus. "Ladies and laddas, there's something I'm wanting to say before we get home. In the midst of all the commotion, I have forgotten my manners. We all have, I think. Because none of us remembered to thank Jimmy and Zarin for their thoughtful gift." Soli held up the photo album.

"No mention, no mention," Jimmy said from his place across the aisle from Rusi. He could tell that Jimmy was trying hard to capture the lightheartedness he had felt earlier in the evening.

"But no, something else that I want to say," Soli continued. "Jimmy, what you have given us is more than a few pictures. You have reminded us of who we are and what we are to one another. You've given us ourselves back, our youth and our promise. Our real selves back, minus a few double chins and bald heads, you could say." From behind the bus, they could hear Adi giggling. Soli smiled, a sudden guileless smile that dislodged some of the sadness from the bus. "You know, wounds heal—and I hope our Sheroo's injury heals *fatta-faat.* Yes, wounds heal and scars fade. But memories live forever. And tonight, we carry many happy memories in our hearts, despite what happened. After all, it's not every day that one of our own gets married. And Zarin and Jimmy, with their magnanimous gesture, have bound us all together even closer. This is what we will remember—this happy, close feeling—when the other, bad memory fades."

God bless Soli, Rusi thought. Always trying to make others feel better. Perhaps it took a broken heart to prevent other hearts from breaking. As Soli walked shakily back to his seat, Rusi grabbed his arm. "Well said, *bossie,*" he murmured. "Let's talk about the other *mamala* soon, okay?"

Bomi, who could not bear to be overshadowed by Soli, cleared his throat. "You know, in some African cultures, it is said that if a female guest is hit by a stone at a wedding, it is a sign of fertility—for the young couple who just got married, of course," he added. "So at this rate, the stork should be visiting the Kanga residence within nine months."

Rusi listened in amazement as Sheroo's familiar voice penetrated the dark. "God, what a *dhaap*-master my husband is. Mehernosh, can't you arrange for Harvard to give him a bachelor's in bullshit? He'd stand first in his class, my Bomi would."

What a people we are, Rusi thought with bemusement. Nothing keeps us down for too long. No wonder our ancestors survived the perilous journey from Persia, no wonder we thrived and prospered in a land to which we came as refugees. The rush of affection that he felt for his fellow passengers temporarily banished the chill he had experienced since boarding the bus. And yet, he knew that something important had happened today and that it was vital to hold on to its memory. And that it would be up to him to be the custodian of that memory, because, left to themselves, the others would be only too happy to forget. But I must not forget, Rusi thought. Somehow, he had to learn to navigate between contentment and complacency, between caution and fear, between the known safety of Wadia Baug and the unknowable world outside its walls. Just as his ancestors had occupied the safe small strip of space between Hindu and Muslim, between Indian and English, between East and West, he had to live in the no-man's-land between the rage of the stone thrower and the terror of the stoned. But where to begin, he didn't have a clue.

And then suddenly, they were home. A murmur went through the bus when Wadia Baug finally loomed in front of them. A gush of relief ran through Rusi. He felt as if he were the survivor of a shipwreck and the building were a large, majestic ship that would rescue him. Obviously, the others felt the same way. "Oh, thank God," Bomi whispered. "Home sweet home."

Yes, home. Once again, the whiff of urine from the outside wall as the minibus enters the building compound; once again, the tall outline of the six coconut trees inside the compound. And then the short walk through the foyer to their individual flats, the murmured chorus of "Good night" and "See you in the morning." The turning of keys and the turning on of lights. For those on the top floors, the long climb up the wooden steps, the steps that usually made their arthritic knees grind in protest. But tonight, no one is complaining. They are just so glad to be home. They are already imagining how good their beds will feel tonight, how wonderful they will feel when sleep finally comes, *if* sleep finally comes. They are determined to wake up tomorrow having put all this badness out of their minds. Arguing with the butcher and fighting with the milkman will drive all other thoughts out of their heads. In the days to come, they will check in on Sheroo a few times, but other than that, they will concentrate on how wonderful the reception was, how good the food was, how much fun they had had before . . . before—but they are already beginning to forget. They will hold on to their dreams of Mehernosh just as they will hold on to their photo albums. Yes, they will remember Wadia Baug and they will do their best to forget the city that it is housed in. They will choose memory over imagination. It is less dangerous that way.

Glossary

Abroo-ijjat: Shame; reputation.

Achha: Okay, all right.

Ayah: Nanny.

Bas: Enough.

Besharam: Shameless.

Biryani: Rice dish made with spicy meat and potatos.

Boodha: Old man.

Dava: Medicine.

Deekra: Literally means "son" but often is used as a term of endearment by an older person to address someone younger.

Dhansak: Quintessential Parsi dish consisting of spicy lentils eaten with caramelized rice.

Fatta-faat: Immediately; quickly.

Gadhera: Donkey, fool.

Guss-puss: Conspiratorial whispering.

Hijra: Eunuch.

Inshallah: God willing.

Jadoogar: Magician.

Jaldi-jaldi: Hurriedly.

Kanjoos: Cheapskate.

Khoollam-khoolla: Openly, with nothing to hide.

Lattoo-fattoo: Head over heels in love.

Maaf karo: Forgive me.

Mamala: Affair; business.

Paagal: Crazy.

Samosa: Deep-fried triangular pastry stuffed with mutton or vegetables.

Su che: What is it?

Tingal-tangal: Tricks; mischief-making.

Yaar: Buddy.